About Darry Fraser

Darry Fraser's first novel, *Daughter of the Murray*, is set on her beloved River Murray where she spent part of her childhood. *Where The Murray River Runs*, her second novel, is set in Bendigo in the 1890s, and her third novel, *The Widow of Ballarat*, takes place on the Ballarat goldfields in the 1850s. Darry currently lives, works and writes on Kangaroo Island, an awe-inspiring place off the coast of South Australia.

Also by Darry Fraser

Daughter of the Murray
Where The Murray River Runs
The Widow of Ballarat
Elsa Goody, Bushranger
The Last Truehart

THE GOOD WOMAN OF *Renmark*

DARRY FRASER

First Published 2019
Second Australian Paperback Edition 2020
ISBN 9781867208051

Published by
Mira
An imprint of Harlequin Enterprises (Australia) Pty Limited (ABN 47 001 180 918), a subsidiary of
HarperCollins Publishers Australia Pty Limited (ABN 36 009 913 517)
Level 19, 201 Elizabeth St
SYDNEY NSW 2000
AUSTRALIA

A catalogue record for this book is available from the National Library of Australia
www.librariesaustralia.nla.gov.au

Printed and bound in Australia by McPherson's Printing Group

To my mum, Gilda, and to my grandmothers,
Lena, always in my heart, and Doris, never forgotten.

One

Renmark, 1895

Maggie O'Rourke's heart pounded. Standing over the body, the iron rod still clutched in her shaking hands, she was ready to swing it again if she had to.

The rutting had ceased abruptly when the *thwack* copped the side of his head. A last grunt had escaped him, and a soundless Robert Boyd collapsed over Nara, the woman he'd snatched. His breeches were taut over thick thighs but in his frenzy, the back seam had given way and his buttocks gleamed white.

Nara kicked and wrested her way out from under him, shoving his head off her. Her dress had hoicked up to her waist, and her heels skidded as she rolled to get away. The cheeks of her backside scraped on the gravelly dirt.

'Get up and run. Did he—did he get you?' Maggie waved the iron rod, her gaze never leaving the big body.

Nara scrambled to her feet, pushing at her dress as she tried to dust off. She pressed her hand between her legs. 'He nearly stuck it in, but you got 'im before—'

'Oh God, oh God. I'm so sorry. Are you hurt?'

Rubbing herself, Nara squeezed her eyes shut a moment. 'Maybe.'

'Oh God. Bad, Nara? Are you hurt bad?' Maggie felt sick for her friend, sick for herself. But she wasn't the one that monster had defiled.

Nara rubbed again, considering. 'He didn't get me. Just fell down on me.'

Maggie, blinking hard, peered at the body. 'Is he dead?'

'I reckon.' Nara straightened her dark dress under the dirtied pinafore. 'You got 'im good.'

Pointing the rod at Boyd, ready in case he leapt to his feet, Maggie seethed. 'He is an evil man.'

'Just a dead one now.'

She stared at Nara 'Why did you do it? Why did you get in his way?'

Nara and her husband, known only as Wadgie, had been friends with Maggie almost from the day she'd arrived to work at Olivewood a few years ago. The Wadges had been in trouble before, defending themselves. They were rabbit trappers, poor people making a meagre living from what they could scrounge off the land. They were often vulnerable to unscrupulous rogues, some said even more so than the blacks.

'He bashed Wadgie. Accused him of stealin', and that was a lie. This time he were after you. But the troopers will kill me if I kill him, so better he chases *me*, and *you* bash him.'

Maggie squeezed her eyes shut a moment. 'I know, I know. But he got you. I'm sorry he got you.'

Nara waited a beat. 'Me. You. He don't care.'

Maggie could hang for this, especially if no one believed they'd both been in danger. Robert Boyd had begun pestering Maggie a month ago and, despite her rejection, had kept it up. Earlier today when he'd arrived unannounced at Olivewood, he'd become more than a nuisance. He'd tried to touch her, had made a grab for her arm.

Maggie had snatched herself away. Hands on hips, she'd faced him at the foot of the verandah steps. 'Mr Boyd, I have said before today, and very politely, that I am not interested in your attention or your company.' She squared her shoulders. 'Even if you were not married. Yet still, you have persisted, unwelcome, uninvited, and now you dare lay your hand on my person. Go away.'

He had mimicked her hand on hips. 'Ain't you the feisty one? Nice and built well, too, takin' a man's eye.' His gaze settled on her chest a moment before he grinned at her. 'All that mussy black hair tied up tight, and them big blue, invitin' eyes. Can always tell the ones what've already lifted their skirt. Got a certain look about 'em.'

Maggie's mouth had dropped open. *How could he possibly know any such a thing, and how dare he say so, anyway?* No one knew what had happened between her and Sam, her old beau from back home, no one.

Sam. Lately, he'd popped into her head at the most inopportune moments, and she'd just wanted to reach over and ruffle his thatch of blond hair and see the mischievous grin once more.

Boyd hadn't known about *anything* to do with Sam, of course not—he was just being his vile self.

'See? I was right. That look on yer face gives you away.' He gave a derisive snort. 'A tart, all right. I'll get what I've come for. All your fancy blatherin' about rights an' such mean nothin' to me.' He looked around with an exaggerated swivel of his head. 'And looks like there's no one here to stop me.'

'I'll stop you,' she cried, the blaze of anger streaking her cheeks. Maggie was strong, but she knew she'd be no match for him. Her heart thumped hard. *It's broad daylight for God's sake, how could he even think he'd get—*

'I don't think you'll be able to stop me.' He'd taken a step towards her. 'Now, I've been nice, and you shouldn't keep knocking me back, playing me. So, I'm just gonna take what I want.'

'Get away from me,' she ordered at the top of her voice, and backed up the steps, scuttling to the front door.

'You're a neat little piece, ain't ye? Little thing like you won't be too much trouble.' He was on the verandah in two strides.

'I'm no little thing,' she shouted. 'I'll defend myself.' Behind her back, her hand had found the door latch. She well knew there was no one around to help. The Chaffeys had gone to visit another family across the river.

Boyd barked out a laugh. 'Defend yourself, will ya? Now that is funny. Might be nice inside this big house. What do you say?'

Nara, one of the housemaids, had appeared in a rush from the side of the house, her feet thudding loudly. She'd stopped, her eyes wide, a forge tool—an iron pick-up rod—in her hand.

Boyd flicked his hand at her. 'And there's another little thing. Get, before I bash you like I did your bloody kin,' he snarled.

Ignoring that, Nara crept forwards, her glare fixed on him.

'Nara, get away,' Maggie rasped. 'Run!'

But Nara came closer still, risking capture, *daring* capture. She got within his easy reach then sent the rod slithering across the boards to Maggie, before she turned to run off the verandah. Boyd grabbed Nara, threw her over his shoulder, and loped across the dusty concourse towards the rows of older trees near the stable. Nara yelled and kicked and writhed, and then he'd tossed her to the dirt.

Maggie had snatched up the heavy rod and darted from the verandah.

Boyd had already dropped his weight on Nara and she pounded him with her fists, then gouged at his eyes. He brushed her off with one hand, fumbled with his flies and shoved his pants open.

As he pushed Nara's dress up and thrusted, Maggie let out an enraged cry and, still running, had taken a wide swing.

Thwack! And he'd dropped like a stone.

Now, she shook the rod at the body. Her heart thudded, her pulse pounded. 'But he hurt you, Nara. I'm so sorry.'

'He's sorry,' Nara said and lifted her chin at the inert body. 'Good for you and that iron.' She pointed at the pick-up then. Taking a deep breath, she winced but stood tall.

'But he—'

'We're not gonna stand here and talk like ladies,' Nara flashed. 'We're gonna run away. No one will believe that he attacked me.'

Maggie still wielded the rod. A dog barked somewhere off in the distance. It would be Bucky. *Bucky, Bucky, Bucky, don't come, my friend, don't come.* 'Yes, get going, Nara. Get far away from here.'

Nara waved her hand between the two of them. 'Let's go.'

'I can't. I need my money. I need my job.'

Nara rolled her eyes. 'You made a funny, Maggie. The job with Missus Ella is finished for us.'

Maggie knew it as soon as she'd said it. *Of course it was ridiculous.* There'd be no job with Mrs Chaffey after this—she'd just killed a man. She'd go to prison and then be hanged. Dear God, having no job was the least of her worries. She felt her mouth dry. *Is he really dead?*

'We 'ave to go, now,' Nara insisted. She backed away, brushing at her clothes.

Maggie tossed the rod aside as if it was aflame. She'd just killed this self-proclaimed pillar of society—this *family* man. He lay dead at her feet. Not liked by many, if at all, but she'd killed him. A blow to the back of the head. Who would believe that it was in defence of another? She would run. She'd have to.

A chill cooled the sweat on her back. She spun about and eyed the young olive trees at the front of the house. Too open, no hiding places. She swung around to stare into the scrub at the back of the house, past the olive crushing plant and beyond the packing sheds.

That way was down to the creek. She'd have nowhere to go once she got there, no way to escape. The river. She'd go the other way and get to the river. It was a bit of a run, but if she got a move on … If she could just pull herself together.

Nara had run some paces when they both heard a bellow, 'Oi, you two!'

Maggie sucked in hard breaths, rooted to the spot. Robert Boyd's brother Angus, that strange postal clerk, was pedalling fast on his bicycle towards them, waving an arm in fury.

Nara turned. 'Hurry, this way.' She beckoned urgently.

Maggie shook her head, stuck fast.

Angus Boyd bore down on her. 'No, no, *no,*' he yelled.

'Maggie.' Nara began to go back for her when a tall sun-browned man appeared from the scrub, his hair a black frothy mess and a smoke clamped between his lips. Wadgie, Nara's husband. She squawked as one of his sinewy arms hooked around her chest. He lifted her off the ground and charged behind the shed, out of sight.

Snapping out of her stupor, Maggie hitched her skirt and bolted in the other direction. She charged through the young olive orchard, her booted feet thudding the earth.

Angus howled behind her. 'What have you done?'

She heard the pushbike slide on the gravel and, with a quick look over her shoulder, she saw Angus fall to his knees at his brother's body, his hat flying off and his stringy blond hair falling over his face. Now, her eyes glued on the track ahead, she ran fast, not even daring to look sideways.

Is he dead? Is he really dead?

Where to go … Where to go? Police? *No, the constable is twenty miles away.* Mrs Chaffey? *No.*

Pounding feet. Breath hitching. A stitch in her side. Dirt on her face, in her eyes …

Dog barking, far away.

Ma. Pa. I need help. I need help.

Sam. Sam, I'm not so brave. I need help.

Two

Angus grabbed his brother's arm and tugged. 'Get up, Robert.'

On the floor of the shed, Robert Boyd tried to focus on his brother hovering over him. 'Where am I?'

'Packing shed. We grabbed you up from out there thinking you were dead.' Angus dropped his voice and goaded, 'Bein' dead would be no good, would it?'

'You followin' me?'

'I told you. I'll always follow you, see what you get up to. I know there's no cure for your type of madness, I just try and keep you out of trouble. Not very well, by all accounts.'

'You wouldn't know madness if it poked you in the bloody eye.'

Gruff though he sounded, Robert felt fear in his guts, and not because of his brother. He could easily have been killed by what she'd clobbered him with. It must only have glanced off him but laid him out just the same.

'Who else helped grab me up?' He struggled to sit.

'Watson from the farm over the way. He came to get some olive oil for his missus. He didn't see nothin', just them two running away.'

Robert grunted. 'Jesus. What did she hit me with?'

'This smithy's rod.' Angus pointed to a single-bit, long-handled pick-up at his feet. He leaned back on a bench and folded his arms, a smirk on his face. 'Good thing you weren't finished off.'

Sarcasm wasn't lost on Robert, but he ignored it. Grunting, he rolled over to his other side, sat up and began to button his trousers.

Angus pointed at his brother's flies. 'Your missus won't want to know you been at it again. You know what she's like about all that.' He shook his head. 'What in God's name were you thinking, trying that on, trying to roll her out there?'

'Didn't do no such bloody thing.'

'Well, that's what I mean about your madness, Robert. It bloody looked like you were trying to roll one of 'em to me until that high-and-mighty Miss O'Rourke drubbed you,' Angus said, his face thrust close to his older brother.

'So you saw it?'

'You were out in the open, bare arse in the air.'

'Not that. *Her* beltin' me.' Robert grabbed Angus's shirt. 'It don't look like anything to you, not now, not ever, except that uppity piece bashing me.'

'You never learn, do you? There's summat wrong with you, summat deep in your mind.' Angus pried off his brother's large hands.

Robert felt his blood boil up. 'Don't start that shite again. And what do you care, anyway?'

'I don't care except I can't have that Miss O'Rourke beat me to it and take your guts for garters.'

Robert stood up. 'Jesus Christ.' He braced his head between his hands, stumbling as his balance skewed. 'She won't have my guts for garters any more than you. Where'd the other woman end up, anyways?'

Angus swiped a forearm under his nose and let his glare slide away. 'Her husband came out of the scrub yonder, carried her off.'

Robert grunted. He shoulda bashed her old man harder when he'd had the chance. And that bitch, Maggie O'Rourke, she was the one whacked him with that iron rod. He'd heard her yell a moment before the clang landed. The pain had exploded between his ears and down he went. It's all he remembered. He glanced over at the discarded tool. Christ, his head hurt. His teeth hurt in his gums. He ran his tongue over them, sucking. No blood. No loose bits. *Bitch.* He sniffed, hawked and spat. She'd done it now. She was dead meat. She was going to pay for this, and a hefty price.

Fire flamed in his belly and prickles of heat stung the backs of his hands. He clenched his jaw. No one showed him up. No one. And if he ever caught that other woman, she was going to pay, just like he'd made her husband pay. He stopped himself then. He'd got away with it only because he knew they hadn't gone to the troopers. Well, they didn't frighten him with their long stares. 'Cept they did. A bit. He should go to the troopers himself, have them moved along, especially if he made sure it was known the woman had helped try to kill him. Dirt-poor nuisances.

He snorted, and a clot of blood shot out of his nose. He wiped the remaining dribble on the back of his hand.

But Maggie O'Rourke, you upstart Irisher baggage, I'm going to hunt you down.

'What you going to do now?' Angus asked. He pulled his bicycle from where it leaned on the shed wall and straddled it.

Robert roughly swept dirt and debris off his clothes and straightened up. 'I'm going to go about my business. There's wool and timber waiting to get loaded at the wharf, and maybe my stock to off-load.' His ears rang. His head pounded. Suddenly he bent double, vomited, and sagged to his knees.

Angus didn't move to help. 'Hurry up, then. I can see old Harold's just got to the crusher and is staring over this way. Must be wonderin' what we're doin' here. And the bloke with that new camera thing was skulking about the place, too. I passed him when I was coming in.'

'What bloke? Who're you talkin' about?' Robert got to his feet, leaning an arm on the wall to steady himself. He took a couple of deep breaths, and his head stopped spinning.

'He takes photographs.'

'So?'

Angus shook his head, slowly. 'What if he took one of you at it?' He looked over his shoulder, across to the olive trees, and then over to the house and the shed beyond. 'Could be anyone saw you this time.'

'Ballocks,' Robert growled. 'Nothin' happened, no one saw, and no one took a photograph. I've heard you can't take 'em quick, anyway. And even if they did, no one would want to say anything, just like before,' he said. He straightened up. 'What's his name, this photographer?'

Angus shrugged. 'Dunno. Heard he wants to set up business in the town. Takes pictures of anything.'

'Bah. No money for that in a town like this one.' Robert stalked off, mindful of feeling a little shaky.

'Comin' from you, waitin' to be the big rich merchant here. Where are you going?' Angus called.

Robert didn't bother turning. 'I'm going to see if the boat's brought in my stock,' he yelled over his shoulder. *Going to see if I can find her quick …*

'Well, you might want to wear your coat then, hot as it is,' Angus called out. 'Your fat arse will get sunburned otherwise. And keep your hat on low. I have a feelin' you'll have two beautiful shiners tomorrow that you might not be able to see out of.'

At the gate, Robert wrenched his own bicycle upright and climbed on, shoving his coat under him. He set off over the dusty road, his legs pumping the pedals. This mode of transport was no longer fit for purpose.

If I'm going hunting, I need a horse.

Three

Dragging in great gulps of air, Maggie slumped against a tree, its bark rough under her hand as she steadied herself. She wiped sweat from her forehead and squinted into the tangle of scrub behind her. No one was coming.

She recognised her surroundings. She usually came this way to visit the banks of the much-loved river. She was a long way from the road, she knew that, so going north, the river was ahead of her. It wouldn't be far that way.

She pressed a hand over her heart and firmly tried talking it down from its rapid hammering. Her jaw ached where the pulse banged under her ears, and her throat was dry. Squeezing her eyes shut, she listened with all her might to the sounds of the bush around her. Except for a few birds and buzzing flies, she couldn't hear a thing—but the voice in her head that kept shouting she'd killed a man.

Why doesn't it feel like I've killed a man? Stupid. How would she know what that would feel like?

It wasn't as if it had been done by someone else. But it felt as if she'd been standing outside her own shoes and some angry, terrified, righteous *other* woman had slammed that rod down on

Boyd's head. No. She'd done it, all right, and there was no time to stop for any ladylike trembles. Not that she'd ever been ladylike, but she had improved since being at Mrs Chaffey's. To get ahead in the world, Maggie knew she had to be a little more refined than the tomboy she'd been in the past. All the same, it was not her intention to have weak-kneed wobbles or to stop and grizzle, as her mother would admonish in her quiet, lilting voice.

Deep breaths, Maggie-girl. Be brave. When were you ever not brave?

Her mother. *Ma.* Maggie crept a hand under her pinafore and felt for the tiny drawstring purse she always wore. It had her savings in it. On her mother's advice, she'd always kept it on her person, ensuring that she would never be without money in any situation. Rubbish to the thinking that a woman shouldn't mind her own money. How was a person to get by if she didn't have any money? Couldn't trust the banks, that much was clear to anyone these days, and had been clear for a while. And, because she was a woman, she wasn't allowed a bank account of her own; her father or, if she had one, her husband would take care of it for her. *Bah to that.* So it made perfect sense to carry her own money, and to hide it.

Maggie closed her fingers over the sturdy, soft leather purse. Its contents would be her salvation now. There might only be four pounds, six shillings and sixpence in it, but she knew it was her fortune, every penny hard won.

Yes, yes, you have money. But where are you going to go? You just killed *a man.*

Her side pinched where the stitch still hurt. One thing she'd yet to learn was how to run without killing herself. Breathing deep into her abdomen, the stitch eased. Still she waited, alert, her eyes darting towards every flit of a bird and every rustle of leaf litter. Then she heard the faint whistle of a paddle-steamer.

Ears straining, she heard it again. The river wasn't too far away now. If she kept going …

And then do what? Stroll out to the riverbank and wave? Would the news of her having murdered a man reached the townsfolk already? Would it be racing along the river as fast as a bushfire?

She leaned back on the rough tree trunk. Dear God. What to do? What to *do?*

Home. Go home to your parents, to Echuca. No, no. They'd catch her there. They'd take her away to gaol and hang her not long after … What a terrible thing that would do to her parents.

But would she be a criminal in the colony of Victoria? She didn't know. And who would she ask? *Oh, excuse me, protecting myself and my friend, I've killed a man in Renmark, South Australia. Does that make me a criminal in Victoria too?*

She had defended herself and always would. She was a strong woman and no man was going to inflict a denigration on her, or on anyone near her, and get away with it. Maggie was the one who didn't allow stray hands and fingers of others to linger when they'd tried touching her as she'd stood in a packed crowd somewhere. If they believed it was their right to handle her and other women like they were possessions, why do it so furtively? No, she'd concluded, they knew they were wrong, and she would say so every time.

Apart from her father and her brother, there was only one man she'd ever wanted near her, and it was Sam. Down to earth, happy, laughing Sam, with his broad chest and his kind brown eyes. *Oh, stop bringing Sam into this.* For goodness sake, she'd given him marching orders too.

But now what? *Think, Maggie.* A sob escaped, tearless and scratchy, and she swallowed down the next one. *Think, Maggie O'Rourke. Dammit, dammit, dammit.*

That was a very good mimic of Sam's mildest cursing, his voice now in her head. Oh, and now tears might come—*Sam, I only wish … all right, I know I've opinions that are just as strong as yours but no less valid because they're mine.*

She'd sent Sam packing after their last little tryst, and he was not a happy man. But sending Sam away had been the best thing to do. For Sam. Well, for her, really.

She'd always tried to do the right thing in her life … like helping sick people, or defending those weaker than herself, especially in the play yard at the Camp Hill school in Bendigo, where the family had lived before relocating to Echuca. Or like picking up that iron rod and cracking it over the head of the monster attacking poor Nara. Surely the law would see why Maggie had done it? Surely any policeman would understand the need to—

Her stomach plummeted. The police would ask what the woman had done to attract the ire of the man who attacked her. The law would ask why a so-called decent man like Robert Boyd would lower himself to such a thing. With no witnesses in their favour, it would be the servant women's word against that of a *so-called* pillar of society—so-called by himself, that is. Maggie had seen and heard enough about how working-class women fared under the law, let alone the poorest of women like Nara. She and her husband eked out an existence however they could. This terrible economic depression had displaced so many for years.

Oh yes, there were some decent magistrates, but they were moved along in the country circuit too quickly for Maggie's liking. She had often been asked to assist with transcribing at the makeshift courts when the male clerk could not attend. That drew raised eyebrows, and on occasion, objections. How ridiculous that was, and she'd said so—she was merely using the skills her mother had taught her. Besides, the loutish, lazy clerk hadn't shown up, so who would have recorded proceedings? There wasn't even a reporter for the newspapers for miles around.

This was how the law worked. Women had some rights under the law, but they were not upheld as much as the rights of men. Maggie had been vocal in her views about it, a firm believer in her rights, *human* rights—that was how some of the suffrage ladies described it in their articles and letters.

Mrs Chaffey had quietly warned her that perhaps the local people weren't so keen on the things she believed in. After that, Maggie had tried to temper voicing her own opinions, but she couldn't help it. She'd let anyone know that she was all for the vote for women, and she'd scoured the newspapers for any word of it.

What would her rights be in gaol? She'd have none.

Bah! The law would ask why she had taken it upon herself to inflict grievous harm upon a person. Was it because she was in some nefarious scheme with her accomplice to steal from the man, or worse? Maggie squeezed her eyes shut. Didn't matter a boot that the man was a ruffian, a low scoundrel masquerading as someone with morals. His poor family … although she doubted anyone would have alerted his wife that he was a dangerous brute.

Maggie wasn't the violent person, *he* was. She wasn't someone who hurt people. She was a woman who stood up for herself and her friends, for people who had befriended her, like Nara and Wadgie.

She opened her eyes but all she saw was how quickly he'd sunk into death. How quickly the light went out of his eyes. Maggie had never seen a dead man, only dying or dead animals, but the light snuffing out when life departed had looked the same. *He was dead.*

She drew in short shallow breaths. Staring at the dusty ground at her feet, at ants scurrying by, at crackling-dry fallen leaves, Maggie suddenly knew with alarming clarity that life as she knew it was gone. In its place was a strange unknown, with no safety, no shelter. No haven into which she could crawl.

Hearing another faint blast of a paddle-steamer whistle, she pushed off the tree and grabbed at the strings on her apron to tug it open. She needed to get rid of it—it was white, and therefore a flag, waving that she was likely a servant, a maid. She pulled it off over her head and was about to fling it into the bush when she stopped—it could be useful. She lifted her skirt, and retied the pinafore underneath, hiding it from view. Besides, she shouldn't leave anything behind for someone to find, to track.

She looked down. Her dress was presentable, a classic check in a dull brown with a bodice of box pleats nipped at the waist. It wouldn't attract too much attention, if any at all. She brushed quickly at the full skirt, smoothing its creases and ensuring the pinafore wasn't showing. Feeling it tied there, it seemed as if it had a role in a greater plan that she hadn't fully thought out yet. It felt mildly ridiculous to be thinking such an odd thing. Is this how a murderer thinks and acts, as if outside of oneself looking in? As if the crime committed had been carried out by someone else?

A waft of breeze found the loose tendrils of her hair. She must look a mess—she'd been running like a mad woman and would have hair to match. She deftly picked out the hairpins and poked them onto her bodice, dropped her long hair and finger combed it. Knots and snarls nearly defeated her, but it was becoming manageable. She plaited it swiftly, wound the finished braid to the back of her head and stabbed in the pins once more. It felt tight, but it would have to do.

Now, move quickly. The quicker, the better. She could beat any news of her terrible felony reaching the local people near the river if she acted fast. But oh, for a plan. She had to have a plan. She had money. She looked respectable. No, she didn't, not yet—she needed her hat, and a bag of some sort. A lady always carried a bag when she was travelling.

Her own hold-all—something she had fashioned from an old dress of her mother's—was still back at the house. She had to have it. Apart from anything else, it held her latest letter to Sam, yet to be mailed.

'What is wrong with me?' she whispered, aghast. She'd hit a man over the head, she'd run from the crime, was hiding in the scrub and now worried about needing her bag and her hat. *Dear God, my mind is skewed.*

Finally, impatient with herself, she took a couple of steps away from the tree. Nothing happened. No smite from high above. No voice suddenly calling her out from behind. No thundering of policemen's boots crashing through the bush. There was nothing except a whisper of leaves on the breeze, perhaps a wallaby skittering away. Again, she put one foot in front of the other until she was heading towards the river, her pace swift, her steps light.

Out of breath after what seemed like ages, Maggie stopped, resting by a fallen log, hidden by a copse of straggly mallee near where the bank dropped away to the river. To her left and a little distance away, paddle-steamers and their barges were tied up with ropes thrown to the low water mark and secured to posts sunk deep.

It wasn't a robust-looking river in this area these days. Drought had decimated the flow, but the water level was still high enough. The single wharf of sturdy beams and cross-trusses rose above the water. Men were unloading what looked to be household furniture from one barge, and others were stacking bales of merchandise—wool perhaps—ready to be loaded.

Further along, there was a group of people milling about, out of the way of the workmen but keen on their industry. Perhaps someone would recognise her. Maggie took a deep breath. Hopefully no one would take too much notice unless she got in the way of the workmen. She would go down quietly and identify for herself which boats were which, and which way they were headed, and when. If boats were going upriver to Mildura and onto Swan Hill, and even to Echuca, she wouldn't go that way. The police might think she'd run to the closest border and might even be waiting for her there.

And she couldn't take passage on the coach—it didn't depart for days and she couldn't wait. She was sure to be known as a criminal by then. She'd have to go by boat the long way, downriver, perhaps all the way to Tailem Bend and somehow, by some stroke of luck and good fortune, find a way into the colony of Victoria. Then go to Melbourne, and write to her parents from there. Have her father come for her. Maybe Sam would come.

Was it the best idea—going downriver? Well, it would have to be for today.

It was a *foolhardy* idea, that's what it was. Her mind was still skewed but working fast. She pinched her nose and shook her head. *Just do something, anything!* Trying to calm the terror mounting in her belly, she stood tall then froze as a low voice spoke almost in her ear.

Four

Warm fingers closed over her arm. 'It's me—Nara. You move fast.'

Maggie didn't turn. 'Nara,' she said, and caught her breath. 'What are you doing here? You should hide for a while.'

Nara pointed to Wadgie standing just behind a tree beyond. 'We will, but I couldn't have my friend going anywhere without being prepared, could I?'

A bag was slapped to Maggie's chest. Astonished, she said, 'I was only just thinking of this.'

'You don't go anywhere without it. And you need your hat. I just went into your room and got it. Look, I got mine too.' Nara's own cotton bag was slung over her neck and shoulder. 'Then we followed you.' Her face creased in a smile. 'You were runnin' so loud you sounded like a big old kangaroo jumpin' in the scrub.'

Maggie heard the crinkle of paper buried deep inside her bag. It was the letter to Sam. She hadn't yet had the opportunity to finish it, never mind post it—she kept adding things. *Sam*. Goodness, if only to see him just around the next tree, laughing at her, his broad shoulders leaning against the trunk, his hat tipped back …

She clutched at the bag and relegated the letter to another part of her mind. 'What happened after I ran off?'

'That man's kin and another man carried the body off to the shed. That's when I went into the house. Then Wadgie said we'd be able to find you easy enough.'

Wadgie, a big smile flashing at Maggie, called over softly, 'Very loud kangaroo.'

'Thank you,' Maggie said. Nara and Wadgie had taken a risk bringing the bag to her. 'But you better go. There could be trouble if we're seen together now.'

Nara's mouth downturned. 'Come hide with us. We know some good places.' She and Wadgie were friendly with the blacks who lived further along the creek behind Olivewood, and they knew their way around the district just as well.

Maggie shook her head. 'I'll get on a boat. I hope. I have to get out of here before they know what I've done.' She clutched the bag, her nerves taut. 'You go on, go where you need to go.'

'But come—'

'Nara.' Wadgie beckoned his wife over. He took her shoulders and murmured, nodding in Maggie's direction. He spoke urgently but softly, and Maggie couldn't make out the words.

Whatever he'd said, Nara finally appeared to agree. She walked back and squeezed Maggie's hand. 'All right. You get on a boat, go back to your family,' she said with a firm nod. 'We'll hide for a little bit, further down the river, see what happens.' She smiled brightly. 'We'll see you again.'

'But what will you do?'

'No time to chat, Maggie. Off you go.' Nara caught her in a quick hug. 'No goodbyes, now. Friends don't do that.'

Then, giving Maggie a wave and a nod, her mouth clamped shut, she followed Wadgie. They headed for the scrub that lined the banks of the river, just two people out for a stroll, it seemed. They didn't look back.

Maggie was on her own. She swallowed, took a moment to smooth her hair, shoulder the bag, straighten up and calm her frayed nerves. Then with a deep breath, she took a step out from the shade of the copse.

The autumn sun was still warm. Drawing her hat from the bag, Maggie shook it out and sat it on her head. As she tramped down the slope, the fine spongy dirt of the riverbank gave way under her tread and her shoes sank, grit sneaking in and niggling her stockinged feet. As she neared the first boat, she could see there were passenger cabins aboard, and her heart tripped in grateful anticipation. Its name, the *Lady Goodnight*, hung over the wheelhouse, an elegant painted carving of script letters. Something rang a bell about it, but her thoughts were too crowded to concentrate.

A couple of men swept past her on their way down to the boat. Maggie stepped aside, bumping another, who growled until he recognised her and grinned, tipping his hat.

'Uh, sorry, Miss O'R—'

'It's all right,' she said, cutting him off.

She turned her head, pretending to brush off her skirt. She knew him. Bert was a fellow who occasionally delivered goods from the store to Olivewood where she worked—the home of Charles and Ella Chaffey. He was stepping out with Lucy, one of the girls she'd befriended who worked there. Maggie's cheeks burned and she stood aside, gazing away, hoping he'd forget he ever saw her here. When he passed, she looked back and could see men unloading great sacks of flour and sugar from the *Goodnight*, and others loading boxes of fruit in their place. An older gentleman stood on the shore, checking the stock against the inventory as it came off the boat. More men trudged up the slope to carts waiting to transport goods to the merchandise store.

As she approached, Maggie felt her heart thud anew. The older man looked up, watched her a moment, tugged his hat in deference, then returned to his record sheet. She cleared her throat. 'Good afternoon, sir. Are you in charge of this boat?'

'I am, miss.' Once again, he only looked briefly at her. He tugged his weathered hat again to shade his eyes from the sun. Bushy salt-and-pepper eyebrows frowned as he stared over his numbers. His short scraggly beard was streaked with tinges of carroty red. He called over his shoulder, 'By my reckoning, Bill, we should have another six sacks of flour to come off.'

'Right you are, Mr Finn.'

He sidestepped her and began to head for the boat, his stride broken by a slight limp.

Maggie followed. 'I wonder if you would have passage downriver?' she asked.

Mr Finn turned at the water's edge and started to answer her. Then he looked at her anew, faded brown eyes under a squint. 'Have we met before, miss?'

Taken aback, Maggie shook her head. 'I don't believe so.'

He seemed to peer at her. 'Well, I'll be blowed if you don't have the look of someone I know. Hmm.' He nodded. 'Indeed, you do.'

Panic was rising. 'Really? I don't—'

'Are you kin of the MacHenrys out of Swan Hill?'

Ah. That was it. Her mother had written that her father's twin Liam had a son near Swan Hill by the name of MacHenry. He was a new-found relative, and apparently the family resemblance was strong. 'Um.'

'At least, kin of Mr Dane MacHenry. You could be his sister.' Mr Finn straightened up. 'But then that's impossible. Miss Elspeth is his only sister.'

Maggie barely remembered if she'd known of an Elspeth. Not important right this minute. 'Very odd, Mr Finn. But passage downriver, perhaps?'

'Matter of fact, we're about on our way to deliver this lot downriver to Morgan, got to get it to market in Adelaide. Testing the water, so to speak, for the new Raisin Trust here. We'll go on from there.'

Maggie had heard of the trust. Word had it that the government had put up a loan to save the Renmark area because the irrigation scheme had failed. The Mildura market was failing too, so fruit growers were drying their crops and finding markets elsewhere, or that was the hope.

'In that case, might I buy passage?' At his slight frown, she went on, hoping to forestall a question about why she was travelling on her own. 'My job has ended and I'm looking to find work further on.' Well, that was true, her job had abruptly ended. Now, haste was paramount.

'You could, miss, certainly. Let me check the last of the stock off my boat here and I'll attend directly.' He tipped his hat once more and stepped onto the gangway.

'Might I also come on board to sit in the shade?' Maggie wasn't bothered by the sun; she'd revelled in it as a child, much to the consternation of her parents—her mother in particular. Irish heritage meant their pale skin was not any defence against the fierce Australian climate, but Maggie had been born in the dirt, literally, and the open air and the blazing sunshine had never bothered her. Right now, she just wanted to be out of sight.

'Of course, you might, but I don't want you in the way.'

'I wouldn't want to impose,' she said sweetly. He seemed kindly enough, and today was not a day to kick up a fuss.

'Just one minute—Bill, is that the last of it?'

One of the three men who trudged up the hill under a couple of sacks turned as he neared the cart at the top of the bank. 'That's it, Mr Finn,' Bill shouted back.

Mr Finn held out his hand for her. 'All right, then. Careful of your footing, it can be a mite slippery sometimes.'

On board, Maggie looked around for somewhere to sit out of sight. But Mr Finn directed her under the shade at the stern, out of the sun, but not hidden from view.

'Now, your name, miss,' he said and flipped a page of his record sheet, ready to take her particulars. The pencil hovered, its graphite tip rounded with use.

'Miss … Lorcan. Ellie Lorcan,' Maggie said, and the blush burned her cheeks at the lie. Eleanor and Lorcan were her parents' names.

'Lorkin,' Mr Finn said. 'L-O-R-K-I-N, Miss Ellie,' he recorded, and she didn't correct him. 'And you're going to?'

'I'll pay for passage to Morgan.'

Mr Finn's brows rose. 'Morgan, will ye? Who do you know there?'

'There must be work there. It's a busy rail town on the river.'

He tilted his head. 'It was, but there's no policeman there now, and I've heard it said that bushrangers roam through the place, in and out of houses and the pub and the like on horseback. A wild town. Not the place for a young lady on her own.'

Don't make a fuss about that now. Maggie glanced around. There was no one on the banks besides the workers loading and unloading stock. A couple of men had stopped for a smoke, and Bert was nowhere to be seen. She wrung her hands over the handle of her bag. *Dammit, dammit.*

'Ye're not going to family?' he said, squinting at her.

'Family's in … Melbourne.' Again, the blush scorched over her face and neck. She was not afraid of speaking up, but of lying, she was mortified.

Mr Finn appeared not to notice. 'Melbourne, I see. Betwixt and between here, then. Ye could go upriver to Echuca, then take the rail to Melbourne.'

Maggie frowned, but stayed silent.

At her resistance, he said, 'Or ye could go to, oh, let's see … Murray Bridge. Perhaps a coach, or train from there. You'd have to go to Bendigo or Ballarat first.'

Relieved, she tried not to sag against the wheelhouse at her back. 'Murray Bridge it is, then.'

'Right you are. There's any number of good folk there, and plenty of work for an enterprising girl, I'm sure. Now, the fare.' He glanced at her and back to his papers. 'Let me see …'

Maggie would have to excuse herself to retrieve the purse hidden under her clothing, but that wouldn't be a problem in the next few minutes. Certainly it would help get her off the deck and out of the way of curious or searching eyes. She flicked a glance along the bank and saw nothing to alarm her, but it didn't calm the rapid pounding of her heart. When she glanced back at Mr Finn, he was watching her.

'How about one pound six shillings?'

How much? She hadn't given a thought to the cost of the fare. Well, it wasn't as if she didn't have it with her. And it was there to make her escape.

Something of her consternation must have shown on her face for Mr Finn was looking at her like her father often did. A little concerned, a little thoughtful.

'It's been a while since we carried paying passengers downriver, miss.' Mr Finn's brows rose. 'We don't any longer, so I haven't charged you full price. Trade has taken a downturn, you see, so we're mostly just carrying freight off the boss's place. But we can clear out a cabin, make it ready for you. Find some clean linens in the trunks.'

Swallowing her worry, she said, 'Yes, thank you. That would be fine.'

'You just wait right here, and when the boys are finished we'll get underway, get that cabin cleared out.' He started to leave.

Maggie sat upright. 'Would you direct me to the cabin, Mr Finn?' If she was in a cabin, especially if the door was on the other side of the boat, she could rest out of sight.

'Well, the one I had in mind has all manner of boxes and beasties in it. If you can wait—'

'I don't mind starting to clear it. Helping.' She stood up. 'I am quite used to hard work, and I am a proficient cook, and housekeeper.' Maggie heard herself rattling on as if her words were just going to keep tumbling out of her. At least she had those skills. She'd always intended to sustain herself using them.

There was that kindly look again from Mr Finn. 'Let me get the boys back on board. We have to get crackin', have to pick up downriver. We're a bit behind the schedule but they can lift out the heavy stuff for you after we head off. But certainly, go around the other side—'

Maggie breathed gratitude.

'—and you'll see a door with a "D" on it. That's the one.'

She thanked him, crossed the small deck and turned down the side of the boat that faced the bank across the river. Safe from prying eyes, and thankful, she leaned against the wall, clutching her bag. Deep, steadying breaths filled her, and she waited. Slowly, the shivery chills that ran down her arms and tingled on her hands dissipated.

A sudden cry welled in her throat and she slapped her hands over her mouth, holding on to the aching sob of it, leaving it stuck in her throat. For the moment, she was safe. The relief was bittersweet.

She was a murderer, and on the run from the law.

Captain Finn watched as she found her way to the cabin. He called across to his remaining crewman, Bentley. 'Here, lad. Take this paper to old Barney Cutler, the fella who thinks he's the wharf master.' He scrawled on it: *Miss Ellie Lorkin, passenger on* Lady Goodnight, *Cap R Finn*. He dated it. 'Ask him to record on his day sheet that this is who I took on board just now. He'll take his ledgers up to the postmaster for proper recording.'

It was just a precaution in case the forlorn young woman had family looking for her. He'd do his best to see her safe. Then he remembered fondly that he'd given refuge to another young woman a few years back, his boss's wife Georgina, Mrs Dane MacHenry. Ah, the *Lady Goodnight* had her uses.

Five

Angus Boyd watched as his brother stomped towards his bicycle, pulled it away from the fence and rode off. Straddling his own bicycle, Angus stepped to the doorway of the shed. His brother's lumbering great arse rolled on the undeserving seat, the small pedals just bearing up under the powerful push of his feet. *Ludicrous bloody sight.*

The great dolt should just get back to the store and put in a good day's work instead of trying to make out he was a rich man at leisure. The store represented what slight legacy their father had left to them when he died in Adelaide years ago, but it hadn't come to much. It was a shop carrying small stock stuff, clothing and implements, a few swags, and tents. It had been especially hard to make a living lately, when business was dying all along the river, and his brother's affliction becoming worse.

Although Robert was the older brother, their father had entrusted Angus to keep a look out for him. The old man must have known that his first-born was not quite right in the head. When Robert married—great surprise—Angus hoped he'd have smartened himself up. Not so. Now, Angus had a debt-ridden store, a brother descending further into madness, and a family of leeches that was a millstone around his neck.

Angus also suspected Robert was a murderer.

He let go of the handlebars and gripped his elbows, arms across his chest. Ducking his head, in his mind's eye he saw Maggie O'Rourke rush to help the woman under attack. Saw her flounder, then he'd watched in disbelief as she'd swung the pick-up rod at his brother's head.

Now he gnawed his lip. In that one moment, he thought he'd seen all his plans evaporate in the blue sunshine of the autumn morning. *No, no, nooo,* he'd yelled.

Adeline, Adeline. Desolation as sharp and cold as a knife had slashed through him. He had to find out what happened to her, and if his brother had been killed, Angus would never know the truth. All these years waiting for a woman who would stay, and not run from the endless sneering derision of his sister-in-law, and he'd found Adeline. She'd stood up to her, and Myra had backed down with only that thin smile of hers and a gaze that slid away.

He felt the guilt again now, remembering when Adeline had come to him. She'd blamed Robert, and Myra's open contempt … So yes, at the moment when it looked like the O'Rourke woman had wrenched his vengeance from him, he'd wanted to punch her to the ground.

At one time, Angus had thought she might have stepped out with him. He'd asked, but no, Maggie O'Rourke had been too good for the likes of him. Well, he'd fixed her. Nothing like a little mail-tampering from him, the postal clerk. After she'd returned the first two letters from her beau in Echuca, and refused Angus a second time, he'd easily stopped any more letters reaching her—he'd recognised the broad scrawl. When she'd started writing to this fella again, Angus had stopped them, too. Nicely burned in his fireplace. The bloke had finally stopped sending mail. Guess he'd figured, after receiving numerous *Return to Sender Sam Taylor* letters, he had better give up. Angus had let other letters from Echuca come through to her—that would have been suspicious otherwise.

With Robert lying there earlier today, it looked as if she'd killed him. Angus hadn't been able to grab any one of those feelings galloping through him. All he'd thought at the time was that Robert had been killed, and that his quest to find Adeline, to seek revenge for whatever Robert had done to her, was lost to him.

He'd roared his anger, his furious frustration. But when both the women had fled, and Watson was yelling to him that his fallen brother was still alive, Angus had snapped back into himself. Now, sapped and stupefied, he looked out towards the main road and saw Robert still barrelling along on his bicycle, a man on a mission.

But where was Adeline, his beautiful Adeline? Angus had met her in the post office, not long ago—she'd been a customer, such a sweet girl. They'd only been courting for a short time but he was keen to make her his wife. There weren't so many single women—suitable ones, that is—in the town, and any good one was snapped up. Adeline didn't have such a good job in the boarding house where she lived, but Angus would soon have had her out of that.

She'd come to him one morning, only two months ago, to tell him. He'd been on a break from work in the middle of the day. With a tremor in her voice, she'd said, 'Your own brother has approached me, and has improperly touched my person.' Adeline had hidden her face in her handkerchief, a square of fine cotton, and on it, a blue flower—the result of her embroidered stiches. 'I was fearful to resist him, but I did, and ran for my life as soon as I could. He has threatened me, followed me. I've told no one but you. I am so ashamed to speak it aloud. He is a monster, Angus.' She'd stood there, wiping her eyes and waiting for his response.

He'd stared wide-eyed, not comprehending at first, but then he'd recoiled. She wasn't complaining about Myra. 'My brother?'

He'd been shocked—his brother had tried to harm even Adeline. He knew Robert was afflicted, but this was truly terrible. Angus had only stood there, dumbfounded, while Adeline, aghast to think she hadn't been believed, had fled in tears.

He'd had to return to work, promising himself he would visit her immediately after his shift, but he'd never seen the woman he loved again. She'd already gone. Her employers too had been mystified, along with the rest of the townsfolk.

He spent days and days with worry, with disbelief that she'd just run off—like Robert had insinuated. Then Angus insisted on searching the river, the scrub, and the creek behind Olivewood. During the search, he'd needed a spare pair of boots. The ones he wore were falling apart, and the shoe-smith from Mildura was weeks away. Robert had a second pair that would fit if Angus wore his new, thicker socks. When his scornful sister-in-law had gone to the stores, Angus had crawled under their bed to grab the boots. He'd found a woman's handkerchief, folded neatly, a little dusty, caught in the springs. He reached for it. *Not Adeline's.* Lying on his side to stare at it, he felt a loosened floorboard. Intrigued, he'd pried it open and found a small box. Inside, trinkets—a broach, a pair of earrings, not Adeline's. To whom did they belong? What did that mean? Perhaps they belonged to Myra, but he couldn't imagine it. She was a strong, brawny woman, intelligent and sharp-tongued when it pleased her. He'd never known her to have baubles and the like, but even so, why would she hide them? He'd returned the box and the floorboard. And when he thought more carefully, he put the handkerchief back where he'd found it.

All he knew, as he stumbled out with the spare pair of boots, was that his brother had something to hide.

Robert had scoffed when confronted. 'Myra must have found the bits and bobs in the house when we took up the lease, and hidden them from the children. No need now, of course, they've grown up a bit. She's probably forgotten the trinkets are there.' He shook his head sadly. 'It seems this Adeline business has sent you mad, Angus. You're seeing evil things in the most innocent. Remember, I searched the river and the scrub with you. Would I have done that if I'd committed a crime? Your chit has run off, probably with that lackey Donaldson. No wonder we found nothing of hers. You knew he was skulking around, and he's gone too.'

That was true. But Donaldson was never a worry to Angus, or to Adeline. Angus had protested the insinuation that Adeline had stooped to a man like Donaldson, someone who camped by the river. At his stuttering indignation, Robert waved him off, condescending. 'Of course, of course, she would *never* have done that. But they *are* both missing from Renmark now, aren't they, hmm?'

Chewing through Robert's explanation, Angus had nothing. What terrible things had happened that she couldn't come back to him? He would wait. He would wait and not despair that he hadn't yet got a confession from his brother. He would wait for the right time, for the very moment after he'd gleaned the information he needed, to exact a revenge. He had to, he owed it to Adeline.

For days after the confrontation, the brothers had kept their distance from each other, and their tempers. More and more, Angus was convinced that his brother had committed a heinous crime. He had seen Robert's vile tendencies for himself.

Angus would find Adeline, or her body, and he would send his brother to hell for it.

Six

The men Maggie had seen lugging sacks of flour and sugar off the boat earlier had cleared the small cabin. There were no more 'boxes and beasties' that Mr Finn had mentioned, and it had taken hardly any time at all.

She eyed the bunk and its striped mattress but couldn't see anything crawling on it. Nevertheless, she would drag it off the timber frame and shake it out. She'd asked for a brush and pan, a broom, a pail of hot water and some rags. Once they'd been delivered to the cabin, she removed her pinafore from under her dress, retied it where it was meant to be and had set about cleaning while she waited for Mr Finn to locate some linens.

The boat rocked gently as other craft steamed up and down river, whistles blasting in the still air as they chugged by.

After pulling the mattress, a light and lumpy thing, off the bunk, Maggie ventured a look outside. She saw that the huge paddle-steamer, *Gem,* had rested her bulk not much farther along, pointing upriver, and was tied to the dock by long thick ropes. There was a rowboat being guided to it, a man on either side, wading deeper into the river as they got close. Amid much yelling and hand-waving, a prone man was carried on board from the smaller craft.

Hissing in a breath and ducking back out of sight, she wondered if it was the body of Robert Boyd. Yells reached her ears as crew directed one another, but it was the silence immediately after that set her on edge. It felt as if all had fallen quiet to make way for the announcement that a policeman was about to board the *Lady Goodnight*. Nothing happened. Then there was another yell, this time from the bank—a harried male voice calling for Mr Finn.

Stepping outside again, Maggie willed her breathing to calm so she could hear what was being shouted to the captain. In a mad moment, she glared into the water lapping at the boat, wondering if she should just jump in and swim to the other side. *How stupid*. If she did, with boats gliding along this way and that, she'd be seen, or mowed under, or—or worse, have her dress catch a sunken log and be drowned before she got ten feet across. *Ridiculous idea*.

'Cap'n Finn,' the voice shouted again. 'It's Priddo. He's been snake-bit. He won't make it back on board your boat for downriver.'

Maggie could hear the voice more loudly. Clearly the man was approaching, charging down the bank to where the *Goodnight* was docked.

'We were only waiting for him. Where is he?' Mr Finn bellowed.

The voice from the man on the bank dropped from a shout to a worried out-of-breath level. 'Miz Carter brung 'im in. We laid 'im out flat in a rowboat and her boys got him on the *Gem*, and they'll take 'im to Mildura. Quickest way for help. They just let the ropes go and she's underway.'

In the silence, Maggie imagined Mr Finn was weighing up options. Finally, she heard the captain's voice, subdued and resigned. 'Right y'are, lad. Tell Mrs Carter I'll square up with her on my way back. I know she'll have looked after him.'

'Proper, Mr Finn. I'll tell 'er.'

More silence on deck was a worry, and then she heard the sombre tones of the conversation between Captain Finn and his crewman.

'… Snake-bit. He's not comin' back from Mildura …'

'… Mrs Carter would've done her best …'

'… All we got is prayers.'

Then, a moment after their voices fell silent, Maggie heard the low, rumbling hum and hiss of the *Gem's* steam engine as she picked up pace, reversing away from the wharf.

Footfalls thudded to the back of the *Goodnight*, and one of the men yelled, 'Look after our lad, Mr King.'

Any answer from the *Gem* was lost in the piercing steam whistle and the slap and whoosh of the massive side wheels on the water as the passenger boat headed upriver.

Maggie pressed back into the cabin and grabbed up the mattress. As she was trying to flap it in the doorway, footsteps clomped on the deck and the crewman took it out of her hands. 'I'm Bentley, miss,' he said. He gave it a good shake for a minute or so, then excused himself as he took it back into her cabin and tossed it on the bunk.

He tipped his hat. As he ducked out the doorway, Mr Finn filled it. 'We'll be on our way, Miss Lorkin. Unfortunately, one of our number needs medical help and has gone back to Mildura. That means we're short-handed with only two of us, and because the boss won't have any rabble working on his boats, we'll get underway sooner than later. I don't have time to find another decent fellow.'

'I did hear someone had been bitten by a snake.'

Mr Finn nodded, his face sombre. 'Never good, lass.'

'I'm sorry for it.'

He sniffed and wiped a hand over his mouth. 'So, we might take longer than normal to get where we're going. Loading and unloading with a man down will take a while wherever we stop. Will that be an inconvenience for you, miss?'

'No, Mr Finn.' *Just let's hurry up and get going.* That inner voice sounded a trifle ungracious considering the circumstances, but she felt in need of a hurry-up.

'Right. Well, we have tea available most of the time in the galley, but as for meals now that our man has taken a snakebite—' He stopped. 'If you've a mind to, Miss Lorkin, perhaps we can counter your fare to Murray Bridge if you would cook for us on the way there?'

Maggie felt the boat chug underfoot and heard the *Goodnight's* engine power up. Another chug and she knew they were leaving the wharf. For the first time since her run from Olivewood, she felt a glimmer of hope and a tingle of relief. 'Of course, Mr Finn. I would be very happy to do that.'

'Thank you. If one of us doesn't have to cook as well, we might save some time. When you're ready, I'll show you what we have. And the linens for your bed will be brought directly.'

A moment after he left, Maggie stepped outside and looked upriver, watching the lumbering grace of the *Gem* as it glided away on the clear water. She wondered again if she was going in the right direction. Shrugging a little at that, she thought any direction right now was better than staying where she was.

She would have to talk again to Mr Finn about her fare, and the counter payment of wages for cooking. She would much prefer to pay him and take a receipt for the fare of one pound and six shillings, and then issue him a bill for her services, in the name of Ellie Lorkin.

It would fit her plan—the plan she'd had before the altercation with Robert Boyd. Once she'd left the Chaffey's employ, she was to have found herself decent lodgings where she chose to live, and find work on a contract, like the shearers did. Some women had scoffed at her idea: *They'll never allow you to do it.* Others had looked a little wistful, but each still longed for a man to make her his wife—where she would work for free. Aghast at that thought, though it was the norm, Maggie wondered if perhaps that was the price a woman paid to be safe and looked after. Her own mother certainly did her fair share of work, had toiled alongside her husband, and then cooked and cleaned and laundered as well. Eleanor hadn't scoffed at Maggie's view, but she did ponder aloud her daughter's decision to remain a single woman. 'No one enjoys being a spinster, and a woman's role is to bring children into the world.'

Maggie hadn't broached the subject again. How could she possibly say to her mother—or any woman—that she was terrified of having children? They die. They can die before they're born. Their mothers die. Oh, too awful. She knew so many. Maggie shied away from those thoughts and back to safer ground.

Only a couple of women in Renmark had applauded her entrepreneurial notion but no one had a clue how she would survive. 'Will people want to employ a woman who demands payment under contract?' they'd asked.

Now she had nothing to lose by trying to put her plan into place. Maggie O'Rourke might have just clobbered a man to his death—she shuddered and felt sick—but Ellie Lorkin was about to launch a career as an enterprising businesswoman.

Just how she would do it after she left this boat, she had no idea.

Seven

The piercing whistle jolted her out of a daze. Maggie had taken the offer of a chair for her cabin, and she'd put it in the shaded doorway where she could sit with fresh air on her face. At the calming rate of six miles per hour, with the opposite bank seeming to glide by as if it were moving and not her, she'd drifted, exhausted.

Late afternoon sun approached dusk, and the boat's speed began to drop away. She sat forwards, bracing an arm on the doorjamb. Perhaps another boat was about to pass them—there had been a whistle, maybe a river signal, and they'd slowed down. Peering towards the front of the boat, Maggie saw nothing but the expanse of river, barely a ripple on it except for the draw of the *Goodnight* as she glided along.

She knew it would have been the best part of six or seven hours since leaving Renmark. Rested, though not calm, she didn't feel inclined to head for the wheelhouse to enquire where they might be. She would stay put and as she sat, her pulse pounded again. Seemed her heart remembered what had happened earlier today even if she'd tried to forget.

Her hollow stomach gurgled but the thought of food did not appeal. Still, she should head for the galley to check if she was expected to cook this evening, or at least prepare something. It was, after all, the start of her new life.

Sam. Would she ever be able to face him now? She'd managed to swallow her pride and write the letter she still had in her bag. But now, any fleeting, tiny hope she'd had of seeing him again was dashed. Would her world be so contracted that her only refuge was a cabin on a freight boat?

Wringing her hands, Maggie decided that would *not* be so, that she needed to appear as any normal person—interested, engaged and social. Sam, and his place in her life, would have to remain where it had been these last couple of years—in the past. So be it.

Drawing in a ragged breath, she straightened and stepped onto the deck outside her cabin. As she stood there, Mr Bentley appeared with a large drawstring bag in his sinewy arms.

'Came by earlier, miss, but you were snoozin'. Didn't want to wake ye. This is for your bunk,' he said, and slung the bag past her into the cabin. 'Cap'n says they might need a good airin' out, but that you'd know what to do.' He tipped his cap and gave a nod. 'If you need anythin', let me know.'

'Thank you, Mr Bentley.' He nodded again, a gummy smile revealing only a few teeth. As he turned to go, she said, 'I'm to cook, I believe. Would you let Mr Finn know I'm going to the galley?'

'Aye, I will do, miss. I'll tell 'im directly but we might not need dinner on the boat tonight. He'll be goin' up to the settlement once we're tied up at the landin'.'

On cue, the engine cut, and the boat's now silent glide drifted to a halt. Maggie heard voices calling about throwing ropes and tying up, and Mr Bentley began to head in that direction.

'Which settlement is this?' she asked.

'Lyrup's Hut, miss. Or it's just called Lyrup, now.' Mr Bentley disappeared into the open deck area in front of the wheelhouse.

Maggie knew of Lyrup. It was one of several settlements, villages they were called, set up along the river by the South Australian government. The idea was to create a communal land system to combat unemployment after the banking crash of 1893, and to give families a chance on the land. However, it was well known they were not without discord.

Lyrup was too close to Renmark, she thought, and the settlers here numbered less than four hundred. Not enough people to get lost in—even if she could find work. In Renmark she'd heard that the people who resided in the settlements downriver were barely eking out a living.

Nervous now that the boat had stopped, she edged after Mr Bentley, sliding along the walls of the cabins. Just before the wheelhouse a door was open, revealing the galley. At a glance, it was neat and tidy. A low lamp glowed on a bench. Pannikins were on a narrow shelf, tins labelled tea and sugar were behind the flue of the small cooker, the heat of which curled around her. A few dinner plates were stacked on a bench beneath and cutlery rested on the plates.

Through a door jammed open on the other side of the galley, Maggie had a good view of the timber landing to which Mr Bentley was tying the vessel. Crossing the room to peer outside, she saw a number of folk greeted the captain. Lanterns lined where they stood. Further along the dirt bank, a group of children gathered to stare at the boat. A couple of young girls carried toddlers, and three young barefoot boys wore ragged short pants and oversized shirts.

Four men padded over the landing onto the boat. Amid the greetings, back slaps and handshakes, boxes of dried fruit and some sacks of flour and sugar were unloaded as well as a small bag of mail. Two women appeared and gathered most of the children out of the way, but failed to secure the attention of the young boys, who raced onto the landing. They dodged the workmen shouldering the freight and scurried aboard the boat, shouting war cries as they sped around.

Maggie darted out of sight, wincing as the wild yells and wilder boys charged past her, the noise bouncing in the confined space. Gangly arms waved about ears too big for their heads, and dirty feet thudded over the floor. In an instant, they were gone, heading towards the back of the boat.

Ignoring the shouts of the men, they were back for another run through. Maggie kept herself out of their way, pressed against the small bench holding the lamp. Still yelling, the first boy came to a dead stop as he spied Maggie, and the other two following crashed into him, shoving him sideways. He went down on his hands and knees and yelled. The others lumbered over him, tripped and fell. Blood spurted from someone. A howl erupted.

Oh, dear God.

The yowling reached a new crescendo as a bloodied hand was raised above the writhing tangle of knobbly limbs. 'I'm shot, I'm shot, damn you, Ned Kelly,' the hurt boy raged at one of the boys.

The motley tangle unwound itself, split apart, and three gangly boys bounced upright.

'You ain't shot, idiot, and *I'm* Ned Kelly, not Ronnie,' one of the boys grated.

'*I am* Ned Kelly, Michael,' Ronnie insisted. 'You just fell over and got a scratch, yer big sook.'

Michael waved his bleeding hand. He yelled, 'Someone's shot me in the hand.'

In the dim light, it looked to Maggie as if a nail might have pierced the fleshy part of his palm.

'No one were shot in the hand,' Ronnie yelled back.

Maggie held up both hands. 'Boys. *Boys!*'

Their yells stopped abruptly, eyes widened and mouths dropped open.

She beckoned the boy who was bleeding. 'Michael, I think you fell on a nail.' She turned to Ronnie. 'Are you hurt?'

A quick shake of the head.

'And what's your name?' she asked of the third boy.

'John. *I'm* Ned Kelly.'

And the argument started again.

For heaven's sake, I'm trying to be invisible here and all this noise …

Michael thrust forwards but clutched his bleeding hand with the other. 'Hurts.'

Desperate to keep attention away from her presence in the galley, Maggie beckoned again. She used a rag to lift the kettle from the stove and tested the water's heat on her hand. Then with a firm grasp, she took Michael's wrist and poured some over his wound. He cried aloud but let her wrap his hand in the rag. 'You must go and find your mother and tell her to use carbolic soap on it.' She leaned over, tightened the rag and tucked an end in. 'Don't forget. Carbolic soap. Now, off you go.' Michael slouched out, head hung.

'He's one o' them troopers what got Ned Kelly,' Ronnie said to her.

'Yes, of course, he is.' She glanced about, pulling back to the bench as she heard a woman calling the boys' names. 'Go on, both of you. I won't say a word if you don't.'

'No, miss. Sorry, miss.' Then they were gone to the shouts of men roaring at them to get out of the way, and the admonishing, worried female voices.

For a moment, Maggie waited to see if anyone would poke their head inside. When no one did, she dropped to the floor to feel about for the nail. If she was to work in the galley, she didn't want it to pierce her foot and risk a horrible illness. She hoped the boy would not develop the tetanus. The nail had worked itself loose. She found a fry pan and with a couple of solid taps, the nail slipped back into its hole.

Mr Finn was back on board. 'Miss Lorkin, we'll take our dinner with Mr Ross and his family. There's a short walk to the village proper, but would you care to join us? I'm sure the womenfolk of the village would be happy to entertain ye.'

Maggie couldn't risk being recognised, but at the same time, refusing to undertake hospitality would arouse suspicion. After a brief internal struggle, good manners prevailed. With a shaky smile, she said, 'Certainly, Mr Finn. How long will we be there?'

'Perhaps an hour or so, to be neighbourly. Then we'll overnight here.'

'In that case,' she said after a moment's hesitation, undoing the pinafore, 'I should get my hat.'

Eight

Maggie hoped by now that Michael's mother, Betsy, an anxious sort with dark brows in a constant frown and her hands clasping and unclasping the whole time, wouldn't remember too much about her visit. Michael had pointed at Maggie and said that she was the one who'd saved his hand after the troopers had shot him. The boy's mother had been grateful—yes, she had used carbolic soap on his hand—but her wan pallor and her trembly smile seemed to indicate that she'd been likely to burst into tears more than anything else. Surely not just over her boy's sore hand?

It seemed to be a very hard life for the women here. The few who had prepared tea and then a light meal had not remained in the company of the men. They'd asked Maggie to join them on a tour by lantern light of their small town. It looked almost make-shift to her. Some dwellings were small stone buildings but mostly they were huts, each with a crudely thatched roof, or a canvas tent with a roof over it, all sat in the dirt as if an afterthought for the dwellers. There were sturdy shops, though—a butcher, a baker and a general store.

She found she'd had to impart all sorts of news about Renmark, about any up-to-date fashions that might have arrived there, or more work, or … Maggie had tried to extricate herself from any conversation that might implicate her if the police widened their search for Robert Boyd's killer. That thought made her feel sick.

The women had sat at a small cooking fire, and damper and jam had been offered. Maggie had a tin cup with black tea from the billy, too hot for her to hold in her hands, so it balanced on her knees. She'd lowered her head to blow into it to help cool it down.

The damper was fresh, and the dark jam lacked the sugar of her Ma's recipe that she was used to, but it was flavoursome, and seemed to have a spice in it. Maggie tested another bite to try and discern what fruit it might have been.

Leaning towards her, a woman said, 'It's muntry jam, Miss Lorkin. Bush fruit.'

She'd been introduced as Mrs Wilson. She had bony fingers, stained the colour of Maggie's tea, and her wiry dark hair, streaked with grey, fell around her face. Her eyes were sunken, and deep wrinkles creased as she smiled. She appeared happy enough.

'The land holds plenty, you just have to know how to grab its secrets,' she almost whispered. 'We have to grow our own vegetables on our allotments. Good thing, I suppose. I can't afford to buy out of Renmark.' She sighed. 'It's the old problem. Markets are so good for the produce out of the communal garden that there's none left for us—is why I forage in the bush. We grow apricots and peaches. Lemons too, and of course there are the vines.'

Maggie nodded, then took up her cup to sip. A good garden here, Mrs Wilson had said. *If I were staying, I might have explored it.* Nara and Wadgie had often shown her edible berries and tubers when they'd ventured near the boundary of Olivewood.

'Is there talk in Renmark, Miss Lorkin, about us women getting the vote?'

Startled out of her thoughts, Maggie looked up, at a loss for a moment. She met the eyes of the woman, stocky, white-haired, but perhaps only as old as Maggie's own mother would be. Her heart skipped as that thought crept in.

'Yes, plenty of talk for and against,' Maggie said. 'The election is scheduled for the colony within a year or so.'

Another woman laughed aloud, her thin frame shaking, her brittle voice derisive. 'Bah. Vera, why would we bother to vote? I do what I like anyhow.'

'We know you do, Mrs Graham, but I'm speaking of a much wider franchise.'

'Well, I'm only talkin' of our own village, here. I don't care one way or t'other about a vote for me. What changes would it make? I'd still have straw on me roof, and fleas in me bed.'

'I'm sure the men are intent on getting you your roof. You and your husband are not far down on the list.'

'It don't do anybody any good. Best to give up on all this communalistic notion rubbish,' Mrs Graham went on. 'Share and share alike, it's supposed to be. Half the men don't work a good day, anyhow, and still get paid the same coupons as the men who put in three times as much work.' Her voice got louder. 'Why, my Stanley works that steam engine at the sawmill, day in, day out, keeping it going, where others sit around watchin' him.'

'Yes, we know all about it, Mrs Graham. You take great pains to let us know,' Vera said. Other ladies cleared their throats and shuffled themselves on their cut timber seats. 'But back to our discussion about—'

'And besides,' Mrs Graham cut in, 'the men don't want us to vote. So, it won't happen,' she'd finished.

Glancing at Vera, Maggie deduced that the conversation was not a new one.

Vera—earlier introduced as Mrs Olson—inclined her head. 'There is to be a polling booth here for the big election, you know, and for that we are very grateful.'

Maggie brightened. 'Here, at Lyrup?' How wonderful. A polling booth here in this little, out-of-the-way place.

'We are in the Albert electorate, a designated station for voting, apparently. To vote from our settlement here is such a grand thing, and more so, to have our collective women's voices heard in parliament, well,' Vera said, as if it were her lifeline, 'it will change our lives.' She held up her hand to stop Mrs Graham from interrupting and looked across at Maggie. 'What do you think, Miss Lorkin?'

No point trying to hide from anything now, Maggie-girl. Evasion would only have drawn more attention. 'I think if we had greater control of our lives financially, and with more education, it would suit us well. We would not be subject to as much poverty and—' She stopped in surprise. A crack had opened in her belief that she would always have of her own place in the world. Would her vote really ensure she could better herself? Looking at these women, she wondered what, if anything, would change their fortunes.

Mrs Graham snorted. 'Another high-and-mighty born, are ye? Our lot won't never be educated.'

'Precisely why we need a voice in government,' Vera said quickly.

'Not high-and-mighty born, at all, Mrs Graham,' Maggie said, swallowing down a retort. 'My parents were fruiterers in Bendigo, in competition with the Chinese people there, and things were very hard. Then not long ago, the orchard burned to the ground and they had to find work elsewhere. When I was a child, it was my mother, taught by her mother, who gave me my reading and writing before she made sure I went to school.'

'Fat lot of good it got ye. And Vera, have ye had a look around? Ye still live in a hovel like me, an' the rest of us. Bah to this idea of communism.'

'You know that if we had a vote in the matter, here on the settlement,' Vera said, raising her voice, 'we might very well revert to individualism, and have blocks in our own names, not the communal ones. I've heard talk it is being proposed to the Lyrup Board.'

'A vote. It'll never 'appen. These men can't make up their mind one way or t'other. Fightin' among themselves, they are. Some are drunks, some are blow-hards. Can't even plant trees at the right time of year.'

There was a collective murmur agreeing that some of the decisions made had been folly, and that the consequences were disastrous.

Vera straightened, and Maggie could see her bristle in the low light. 'We women should be standing up and making noise.'

Mrs Graham kept grumbling.

Vera only smiled benignly. She seemed to be trying to let Mrs Graham's comments slide by her. 'And you are going where, Miss Lorkin? Back to family in Bendigo?'

'They are now in Echuca—' Maggie caught herself but it was too late, '—and I had thought to find work in Murray Bridge, downriver, before heading home.' In the taut silence, a crack, a fissure that had allowed a glimpse of her future, teased out her plans. 'I am an accomplished cook and will look for a contract. And perhaps if not successful there, I'll go on to Melbourne, to … cousins.'

The hush was eerie as the women stared at her. What she'd uttered must have seemed a very foreign concept. Maggie waited for someone to say something. Perhaps she'd somehow spoken another language.

A younger woman sat forwards. 'Like some men do—ask their own price? Not wages?' Dusty boots, the toe of one loose from its stitching, showed from under her ragged skirt hem. Her dark blonde hair was scraped back into a bun held by combs, and her grey eyes were intense under dark brown brows. She looked to be about Maggie's age, in her mid-twenties, perhaps.

The attention she'd hoped to avoid was now fully upon her. Maggie nodded. 'And to spend and to save as I wish in order to keep myself.'

'Oh,' the young woman said, her eyes wide on Maggie. 'And you'd ask your own price for cooking and the like?'

'Yes. A contract price.'

'*If* someone were willin' to pay ye, Jane,' Mrs Graham started, 'otherwise yer—'

'Because we don't get paid for it, now, do we? We just do it,' Jane interrupted, still wide-eyed at the notion.

'Ye used to get yer keep,' Mrs Graham snapped. 'That's ye pay, right there. That's all ye get. Now ye got nothin', have ye?'

A couple of other ladies gasped at that, and the young woman frowned. 'If I got paid for the work, I wouldn't be this poor, would I?'

Mrs Graham snorted a laugh. 'And who'd pay ye? Yer husband?' She stood up, slapped her thighs and marched off, muttering, 'No idea. No idea.'

Jane watched her go. 'Don't mind her, Miss Lorkin. She's a very hard person. Has chided me for my weakness. She'd tried to warn me, and of course I didn't take her advice. Told me I should pay more mind to … Well, my husband has left, you see. Teddy Thompson. Gone downriver, but hopefully he'll send me something for my living until—'

'No need to burden Miss Lorkin with all that, Jane.' Vera smiled again.

Jane seemed to warm to her subject. 'But in the meantime, I'm looking for ways to keep myself. I might yet have to leave the village and I'm very interested in what you have to say.'

Maggie had not wanted any attention. She sighed inwardly.

'In your plan, who'd keep you when you get old, when you can't work? Would you marry and have children, so they would keep you when you got old?'

If Maggie did indeed live to an old age, how would she keep herself unless she had married and had a stipend from her husband's estate? But then marriage would inevitably bring children … Her plan seemed not so tight now. How did a woman survive if she was too old or infirm to work? *Oh dear.*

Mr Finn found her and tipped his hat. He held a lantern, and his pipe was clamped firmly between weathered lips.

'Excuse me, good ladies.' He nodded at Maggie. 'Miss, it's time for us to be leaving.'

Once on board the paddle-steamer, her crowded thoughts vied for attention. There was still much to achieve, but was her plan to achieve it on her own a good one? Too many thoughts, too many thoughts. Her mind was intent on keeping her awake, and she'd tossed on her bunk. Finally, a little sleep had taken her.

They were underway early the next morning, just as the yellow tinge of dawn crept through the treetops. Maggie took a glimpse back as they sailed away and was surprised to see how much she'd missed the evening before. Sunlight revealed a hive of industry on the riverbank. There seemed to be some sort of timber mill, alive with men stacking hewn logs and planks, and those operating the saws. All at barely past five in the morning. Though she hadn't seen it, she remembered reading newspaper reports of a busy brick-making industry too.

The rhythmic whoosh of the paddlewheels was comforting, but the night had been unsettled and too warm for sleep. Her thoughts had raced.

Now, with the morning light stronger by the minute, she grabbed her bag, and felt the crinkle of the letter inside it. Her heart gave a thump. *Life with Sam.* Should she think that over again? No, no, not to save her from being lonely and destitute, but to be his companion in life? But how could she have a man in her life and not give him the thing he most wanted? Perhaps there were ways a woman would not get with child.

Where had that thought come from? She sank back on her bunk. Would Sam even want her after all this time? She hadn't seen any letters from him for many months, perhaps almost a year. Oh, she'd sent back his first two, still so angry with his thick-headed expectations. After that, there'd been no more anyway, according to Mr Boyd. He'd told her so without looking at her—he'd probably been embarrassed for her. Well, how dare he?

At first, Maggie had been glad there'd been no more letters. At the time, she'd felt more than a little justified—and only a little miffed—that Sam had seemed to give up too easily. Then she'd chided herself well and truly. *She* had told *him* to grow up and work out what he wanted. Perhaps that's exactly what he'd done, and it had meant life without her.

But she'd sent him a few more letters over the next months, sort of hoping to coax a response—just general newsy type letters about what she was doing and how happy she was. He'd never answered.

Served herself right. All of this with Sam was her own fault. Now she tapped a foot in frustration. The niggle of doubt about her feelings, her fears, gnawed at her.

Thoughts of Sam often found their way in. That boyish smile, the soft tunes sung in his glorious tenor voice—when he wasn't roused up on rum with her brother and making a terrible ruction. His kind eyes. Sam had kind eyes that crinkled when he looked at her. And he'd made her laugh. He loved his family, his horse. He loved her brother as mates do.

Sam had wanted to marry her. There'd have been no other life than the drudgery of a housewife, and never following her own dream. But drudgery wasn't the *only* reason she'd made sure he hadn't followed her to Renmark. She was afraid of becoming a mother, and bearing child after child. If she was near Sam, she knew she wouldn't resist taking for herself what felt so good—fearing a conception didn't stop her wanting Sam in *that* way, and afterwards she was so exasperated with herself. They'd been lucky—only lucky, she was sure—that she hadn't become with child. But if they married, she just knew it would happen time and again. She was scared. Wasn't ready.

And the last she'd seen of him, well, they had got carried away—only for the second time—and had gone way past just a furtive kiss or two behind the haystack where they'd gone to be together. Way past a couple of long needy sighs. She'd clutched his big shoulders, greedy for the hot, hard weight of him. She'd held him tight, hooked her strong legs around his, her skirt rucked high. Captive, and fallen to his knees, he'd laid her on her back and the fresh, clean hay whispered under their clothes. They'd gone past caring for anything but themselves and the burning need for each other; past the deep, warning rumble in the back of his throat when she'd flicked open his flies, reached into his pants and closed her hand around his warm erection.

He'd gone past worrying then. His big hand slipped under her chemise and over her nipples, so taut she'd cried out at the exquisite, breathless sensations that followed. The coarse, scratchy whiskers of his cheeks and chin nestled in the nape of her neck had sent cascading shivers over her, inside and out, and she hadn't waited for him to take her. She'd taken him. Wanted him, had drawn him inside her, warm and wet, and slippery with need, and he thrusted, eager, straining. Clutching his back, she'd felt his muscles bunch and move under her hands, then urgent tingles rushed to her belly. Her knees gripped, and his hips drove down hard, and then that powerful, wonderful last thrust buried deep inside her.

And when he'd rested, heavy on her and languid, she'd taken his hand and shown him what she needed, and she'd rocked against him, his fingers teasing between her legs until she couldn't hold on to it any longer. She rushed towards that sweet peak, and waves of intense bliss had rolled through her.

Now, with her arms over her belly, she closed her eyes and had the sudden craving for more. She thought back to how she'd taken more for herself than she'd ever taken before, more than she'd ever thought possible.

Then Sam had to go and spoil it with a proposal of marriage right after.

'But Sam, I just told you I wasn't interested in that. Not the drudgery, and the laundry tubs and fifty children.'

He'd seemed a bit sleepy. 'But we should marry,' he said, ruffling his scruffy thatch of hair. 'I should propose.'

'I don't want you to feel as if you should propose,' she stormed. 'I've just said I'm independent.'

He'd looked bewildered but determined. 'I know I've said something wrong, but I don't know what. You make me crazy sometimes, Maggie O'Rourke. I want to marry you. And if something does come of this, I *will* marry you.' He stood up, pulled on his pants, shrugged into his shirt covering up that smooth hard body she so desperately wanted more of. 'I'm going to the pub.'

Typical.

In the light of Sam's love of a drink, his carousing to his horses with Ard—*Maggie, he did have a heart-rending voice when he sang for you*—his lack of ambition to get ahead *and* that he'd put his foot down, she'd pushed him away. Snapped at him, 'Go ahead. Oh, grow *up*, Sam Taylor. Why would I want to marry *you*?' Maggie muttered something more and left him to figure that out for himself. She'd brushed herself down, retied her chemise and taken off in the opposite direction. In her heart she knew she'd been selfish.

So after that, the future of a job in Renmark, with the support of her parents close by—they'd just moved there—made it too easy for her to flee. If she wasn't near Sam, she wouldn't get 'in trouble', she'd manage to live the life she wanted. But her heart had ached. She knew now that she could've done with some growing up, too.

Her pride was strong, but now, right now, even after she'd left Renmark in such a hurry under such awful circumstances, would it be the right thing to ask for his help? What would Sam think of a woman who'd killed? Oh, he would understand her defending another from attack. But what if she was to hang? Would he be better off never knowing that she'd committed such a crime?

Her heart skipped a beat. She had killed someone. All thoughts of making a life with Sam were now stupid. Useless. It could never be so, especially if she was caught. Even if not, her conscience would make her confess to him that she had murdered a man—*in defence of another, all right all right, but killed a man just the same*—and she knew, she just knew that no good man would ever want her after that.

She was doomed to a life as Ellie Lorkin. How would she ever see her parents and her brother again? That brought a rising gorge from her stomach that twisted her mouth. She took a couple of deep breaths to steady herself.

At the settlement, Jane's words had echoed the deep thoughts Maggie had barely recognised until that moment. Fear of a lonely old age was not enough of a reason to marry. She had to truly want to marry, and only if she could forge her own way. *If only Ellie Lorkin could forge her own way.*

Now, setting the bag aside, she washed her face and neck and emerged, only a little refreshed, from her cabin.

Nine

Angus Boyd wiped his hands on an oil-streaked rag. 'I've ridden all over the place. It's been three days, there's no sign of her. She's gone.' The O'Rourke woman was gone, all right, but not the same way his Adeline had gone, he was sure.

He couldn't stop the tic flicker under his left eye, but his breathing remained calm. Everywhere he'd looked for Maggie O'Rourke, he'd also scoured the place for evidence of Adeline. Nothing.

His brother rinsed the face flannel in the bowl of water and pressed it against his head once more. The ugly bruise was still coming out, and streaks of yellow had appeared only to be followed by more black smudging. 'You check with Olivewood again?'

'Not there. Gone.' Angus picked up the bicycle and laid it on the bench. He bent closer and peered at the tyres.

'Can't have gone far.'

The store had been closed for the last three days. There always had been plenty of work to be done—repairs, inventory, sales and the like. Aside from his brother wanting to hide out since the attack, lately Angus had noticed the store was being neglected. Not much stock had come in from the freight boat, so he knew Robert wasn't ordering much. Money would be tight again, and that always made Robert twitchy. Angus was glad he had his own wages from the post office, but his brother, the man who thought he was a big deal about town, was as poor as any other bugger. Angus had no sympathy for Robert; he was clearly lazy, and deluded.

'Could be anywhere,' Angus said. 'Forget about her, she's gone. Just another woman disappeared, isn't that right?' He kept his features bland as he looked across at the frown on his brother's face. 'And if you did nothing wrong this time—'

'It was me who got attacked with that iron bar,' Robert exploded. He threw the flannel to the wall and shoved the bowl off the bench. The china burst on the floor, scattering shards and splinters, water flying in the air.

'Then go to the police.' When met with stony silence and a furtive glance, Angus added mildly, 'So maybe you should remember who attacked who.' He concentrated on his task testing the chain. He watched it pull the pedals and wheels and nodded, satisfied.

Robert wrenched it from Angus's hands and flung it off the bench. 'You need to remember who calls the shots around here.'

Angus stood for a moment, holding on to his own temper. He'd learned to wait until the bright white-hot flare of it had fizzled before he let the cold rationale ice his veins.

'I do, and it's not you. I manage the money, remember that too,' he said, and heard the soft threat in his tone. He wiped his hands slowly, watching his huffing and puffing, touched-by-madness older brother sidle away. 'That was my bicycle you just damaged,' he said quietly, knowing Robert would one day realise the menace in him. One day.

'Bloody bicycles. I need a bloody *horse.* Why the hell you sold the horses I'll never know.'

So you couldn't run. Angus said, 'Because we needed the money. I told you.'

'I need a horse.'

'Hold on for a bit longer. Winter's coming and we'll all have to get through that first. Think of your wife and kids.' *If you ever do.*

Robert grunted. 'I'm going to get a drink.'

Angus looked up. Renmark was a dry town, but sly grog was everywhere. 'Just watch that those flies of yours don't bust open again while you're out.'

Sometime, Robert was going to break the jaw of that stupid smart-mouth brother of his.

He didn't bother with his bicycle. He headed back towards the wharf on foot, certain that he looked more dignified that way. When he got there, he stood atop the bank and watched the boats unloading. Wool was coming off in great bales. There were boxes of fruit, and some furniture off a bigger boat whose name he couldn't see.

Bugger it, someone would know if she got on a boat. Plenty of people would have known Maggie O'Rourke. About time he asked about her. He could pretend to be all worried about her disappearance, of course, her being an attempted murderess. He'd just be protecting himself and his family. Just making sure she was no longer around, and dangerous.

His neck hurt like a bastard and his wife Myra's ministrations weren't helping. He rubbed a sore spot. Seemed aches and pains were travelling into other areas of his body, not only where Maggie O'Rourke had clanged him on the head. The bruising was all colours, and still creeping out from under his hair. His wife had remained tight-lipped as he'd explained the attack. Clearly, she was so distracted hearing of the terrible thing that had happened to him, that her hand, dabbing with the cold flannel, was not gentle.

'And just who was this nasty young woman, Robert?' Myra had been close to his ear, her voice sibilant. It sounded like she'd been talking between her teeth.

'Don't you worry yourself over me, Myra, my love,' he answered.

She dabbed harder for some reason. 'Oh, I'm not.'

'It's only a little knock. The poor thing probably thought I was attacking her, rather than saving her from that common woman.'

'Is that so, Robert?' Myra's dabbing hand got even stronger. 'Where was this again?'

He winced and pulled away. 'Olivewood, my dear. But no need to worry. No need to make a fuss—wouldn't look good if I called in the troopers to deal with a little lady half my size over a mistake, now, would it?'

Myra had glared at him. He'd cleared his throat and shifted in his seat.

Now, he gazed down at the river. Lots of boats were tied up. Seemed to be many more than usual, and some were over on the opposite bank, and still more barges moored further back. It almost looked like a backlog of boats, as if the unloading was slow or something. Yet workmen were everywhere. Robert hadn't seen it this busy for a few years.

Men shouldered loads, or stacked carts harnessed to horses ready to pull them up the hill. He headed down the slope, picking his way carefully to be clear of men who laboured under the weight of their cargo.

'Nasty lookin' bruises you got there, Mr Boyd,' someone said as they passed.

'Yeah. Won't be back on a bicycle for a while,' he said, and chortled, making out the joke was on him. Maybe best to let people think he'd taken a fall. All very well to put it out there that he'd been attacked, but it was working against him. It was embarrassing—he'd let a woman get away with it. One eye still felt a bit off. Myra said it was all bloodshot. He could still see out of it, so it couldn't be too bad. He was just bloody lucky he was alive to tell the tale.

'Aye, heard ye got clobbered good by a little lady.'

Robert spun back, looking to see who'd spoken, but was met only by the broad backs of those who strode up the hill. 'I was attacked,' he insisted gruffly.

'Doin' what?' the voice drifted back amid snorts of derision.

Robert grunted and turned to resume his descent to the water, careful where he put his feet. He bumped hard against a man coming up. 'Watch yerself,' he snarled, then recognised the big redhead who carried a sack on his shoulder. He pointed. 'You. Bert. You deliver for me sometimes to Olivewood.'

Bert's placid face creased in a frown. 'I do. An' now I got a job unloading from all these boats. Good day.' He started to pass Robert.

'Wait a minute. There's a lot of boats, what's going on?'

Bert stopped, stepping out of the way of those following him. He juggled the sack on his shoulder. 'Fire comin' upriver from down Pyap way so boats have turned back to here, waitin' for it to burn itself out. The boats already comin' down from Mildura and such have had to wait here. River's full of boats all vyin' for space.'

'So, no boats gone downriver the last few days then?'

Bert looked away a moment, as if thinking, as if deciding on an answer. He shifted the sack. When he looked back at Robert he said, 'Can't go downriver yet, riskin' lives an' all if there's live embers. Boats'd catch alight. Only upriver since three days ago.' The big young fella eyed him square on.

Upriver. And three days since she attacked him, so if she went by boat it would have been the only way she could go. He knew no coaches had departed, and it was unlikely she'd be on foot, or still hiding in the town—someone would have said something by now. Robert looked at the line of boats tied up. 'I could get passage,' he mused to himself.

'Don't reckon. River will take a while to clear, so no passengers until stock and stores get away first. Maybe folk will have to cart freight back to the railway if it's a big burn. Now, I gotta get on.'

'Wait. Wait. If you're busy doing all this unloading and such, I'd like to buy or hire your horse—'

'I don't own a horse.' Bert shrugged the sack again and went on his way, taking his place on the track uphill.

Maggie O'Rourke couldn't have gone downriver, according to Bert. She had to be somewhere upriver. Robert stood aside from the trailing men and stared down the river. At least he'd be able to track her easily enough. Wouldn't be too many young women taking a solo passage. Then a thought struck him, and he looked up the hill at the back of the hefty lad he'd spoken to.

If Bert was telling the truth. You couldn't trust anyone these days.

Ten

Echuca

Sam Taylor was singing his lungs out as the sun went down. Trouble was, he was sitting on the dirt road outside the hotel and the publican had had enough.

'Lad. *Lad!* Get on with yer, stop that caterwaulin' about yer black-haired woman, yer silly bastard,' he shouted. 'Get on yer way and find somewhere to sleep it off.' And a door slammed.

Sam started another. *'Twas early one morning a fair maid arose …'* He wasn't that drunk, and he had an audience.

A fella shouted back to the publican, 'He's not half bad, Jimmy. We was enjoyin' that.'

Someone slapped his shoulder. 'Brings me to tears, lad, that song. Reminds me of the old country. Yer got the sound of a true Irish, that's for sure. Keep goin'.'

Another man stood by. 'I can hear them pipes of home in your voice, laddie.'

Sam had needed to blow off steam tonight. The O'Rourkes, Ard and his ma and pa, had got another letter from Maggie earlier today, but once again, he'd received nothing from her.

He had hopes that he'd have heard by now, but they were fading fast.

So late in the day he rode into Echuca to collect some stores for Mrs O. They were stacked at the wharf waiting for him to load up on the steamer first thing tomorrow. He'd made for the pub as soon as he could to drown his sorrows. The *last* of me sorrows, he swore to himself.

Now the wind had gone out of his sails. If he was to get Mrs O's groceries onto Ned Strike's boat at dawn, and hitch a lift back to the Run—every opportunity he got, he'd ride the boats—he had to be sober and tidy. Not be heard all night wailin' the high notes and annoying the good citizens of Echuca.

Besides, he and Ard had to help Lorcan, Ard's pa, cut down the last of those gums when he got back. He didn't want a bloody hangover doing that.

Sam wandered back to where he'd tied Pie. 'Come on, horse. We have to find a place to kip for the night.' He didn't bother mounting; he'd walk Pie down by the river, tie him up, roll himself in his blanket and wait to be woken by dawn's early light. 'Thank God you're a good sort yourself, Pie, me old lovely.' Pie nodded.

When Sam found a place to lay down his weary head, the colour of his true love's hair, her wide blue eyes, twinkling and merry, her shout of laughter, and her ready smile meant only for him were all he could think about.

It wasn't doing him any good. He knew it. He tossed, lay on his back and stared at the stars, turned, only to toss some more.

Maggie, I reckon I've got to let you go. Then he shut his eyes and slept.

He'd presented himself, respectable, at the wharf for a steamer ride back to the Run. Sam offloaded the stores at O'Rourke's landing, grabbed the cart and took the stores to Mrs O's cookhouse. Nice lady, Eleanor O'Rourke. She'd warmed to him a bit of late, probably used to having him around. Now he stood with Ard at the base of a gnarly, aged eucalypt in the searing heat of midmorning.

'Not bad for a bloke his age,' Sam said. He nodded at Lorcan O'Rourke, who muscled his way further up, already twenty yards above in the old gum tree. The rope tied around his waist also spanned the tree trunk. 'He'd have to be as old as my pa, heading for his sixties.'

Ard peered up the tree. 'Pa's done it a thousand times,' he muttered. 'But why does he have to do it today? It's still too stinkin' hot.' He pointed at the stack of sawn limbs over near the cart. 'That lot will be right for fence posts once we get them neatened up, and the rubbish wood will be right for the fireplaces. We don't need to do this now.'

Sam swiped at flies. 'The limbs are dropping in this drought. It's gotta come down, it's too close to the houses. Your pa said he wants to make a big dinner table for Linley outta the trunk, like that beauty he made for your ma.'

Ard wasn't distracted. He watched Lorc edge his way higher, the saw strapped to his back. He said, 'Yeah, but Pa won't be making the table for my wife, I will. He doesn't have to prove himself by getting up there. He'd be better leaving that to us, and then helping to saw off the trunk. It's massive.'

Sam gazed at the broad base of the tree. 'It's the last of the big old dead 'uns. Thing must have been a hundred years old. Can't stop him. Hey, Mr O,' Sam shouted. 'Steer clear of that branch on the right. I reckon it's rotten.'

Lorcan lifted a hand for a quick wave. He changed direction, his hands working the rope as he tugged around the trunk. Ard followed at the base of the tree. When his father stopped and grinned down at them, Ard barked a laugh. 'Hurry up,' he yelled. 'We left those three little ones for you.'

'Run rings around you two scrawny lads,' Lorc shouted back. Sweat gleamed on his bare arms. His thigh muscles bunched, his thin trousers bearing the strain. His booted feet gripped the trunk, his knees pinned tight. Readying to reach for the saw, he steadied as he lined up the first limb.

The end of the rope flipped out of its knot. Sam called up. 'Mr O, get yeself tucked in, the rope's gonna fray.'

Lorc waved again, shuffled again, and straddled a sturdy branch where it attached the trunk. He kept the rope about his waist as he dragged the knot around. 'Thanks, lad,' he said. Thick fingers deftly plied open the knot to retie it. 'Nearly done, good as new—Shit,' he barked and slapped hard at his right knee. He yowled and reefed up his pants leg. Leaned too far. The rope let go and he toppled over and, still yowling, bit the dust with a thud.

'Pa!' Ard yelled and slid to his side.

'*Christ almighty*,' Lorc breathed, writhing. Shaking his head, growling, he fought Ard off as he tried to sit up, tried to reach his leg. Sweat popped, his face blanched and he dropped on his back in a dead faint.

'Shit. He's broken it.' Sam had heard the sickening crack, and the shin was bent at an ominous angle. He pulled off his shirt and began ripping at the sleeves. 'We need to splint the leg, mate, while he's out to it.'

Ard thrashed around in the dirt and found sticks sturdy enough to strap the shin. 'Gotta straighten the bastard first.'

'Do the best we can.' Sam had one sleeve free of the shirt. He wrenched the other off and knelt by Lorc's leg. 'I only know me pa did this for me when I was a lad. Hold his knee.'

White-faced, Ard wrapped his hands around his father's knee.

'Hold it steady.' Sam gripped Lorc's heel, held his calf muscle and moved the shin until it looked straight, aligned. He hoped they'd only have to do this once for Lorc, hoped he'd done it right.

'Seemed too easy,' he said. 'Come on, let's strap it quick.'

He tossed Ard the torn-off sleeves and held the sticks in place for the splint. Ard wrapped fast, firm, and tied a knot at his father's knee and ankle.

Sam said to him, 'I'll get the cart, mate. If we're lucky he'll stay knocked out 'til we've got him in bed.'

Eleanor O'Rourke sat by her husband's bed, a hand on his arm, the other clutching Mrs Chaffey's letter, the words of which swum before her.

Dear Mr and Mrs O'Rourke,

It is my sad duty to inform you that your daughter, Miss Mairead O'Rourke, employed at Olivewood and known to us as Maggie, has fled our home for parts unknown, two days ago at the time of writing. It is the consequence of a terrible act of assault in which bodily harm was perpetrated on a citizen of our small community here.

Our personal sense of your daughter's integrity is not one of a criminal, nor would her apparent accomplice, another woman sometimes in our service, Nara Wadge be so attainted, but it would seem that they were both involved in the altercation in which Mr Robert Boyd, the alleged victim, was most terribly harmed. His brother, Mr Angus Boyd, came late to the scene of the crime and can attest to their presence and their flight.

I am so sorry to be the harbinger of this awful news. And worse, to advise that your daughter, and the other woman, have not been sighted anywhere in our district.

Should you need further information from this household, please contact the writer.

Yours most sincerely from one mother to another,
Ella Chaffey, (Mrs. Charles Chaffey).
May Twelfth, 1895, Renmark, South Australia.

Eleanor had only read the thing one hundred times since it arrived this morning, delivered by her son who'd ridden off before she could open it. Her fingers on Lorcan's arm tapped by rote, a comfort more for her than for him. He was sleeping, and teetered between consciousness and unconsciousness.

Thank God that Ard and Sam had been with him. Then Sam had ridden hard into Echuca for Dr Eakins just as Lorc had come around, roaring in pain before he fainted again.

How ironic that only three days back when Lorc had fallen, Eleanor had thought of Maggie then, wanting her close, wanting to wrap her arms around her. She'd thought to send a telegram to Olivewood, but hadn't—no point worrying her daughter. Maggie was living her own life, being the independent woman she wanted to be. Eleanor had decided to wait. She knew that if Lorc got worse, she wouldn't hesitate sending that telegram and Maggie would drop everything to come.

The lines on her face had deepened today. She could almost feel the drag on her sun-baked skin, the days working in the hot sun on the river property taking their toll. But it was more the thought that Lorcan could have died out there, and still could die because of the break. It was clean, they'd said, hadn't broken the skin, but the threat was always there.

Eleanor stared at her husband's face, grey now as he fought not only the likelihood of some infection, but a nasty concussion about which the doctor had warned her. Three days of waiting, and this letter arrives. Her neck felt hot as the worry swirled in her gut.

Clearly, Lorcan couldn't rise and take off for Renmark to go and find his daughter. Ard couldn't go either. He was waiting for a baby to come, and any time now.

Eleanor would run onto a paddle-steamer and fire the damn thing downriver herself if she thought she could leave Lorcan. Boats often tied up here at their landing on the Murray. Established for the last couple of years, O'Rourke's Run was a popular stop for captains and passengers visiting the family. There was always traffic between Lorc's property here, and his nephew's property just out of Swan Hill. No mistake—Eleanor was capable enough of charging downriver with passage on a steamer to search for her daughter but who would care for her husband? She'd not leave that to just anybody, and tough as he was, it would worry her more to leave him. It would not do, either, to leave Ard with that added burden right now.

As if to encourage her, she heard the faint draughty whistle of a paddle-steamer as it chugged past the landing. She briefly wondered which boat it was, then wondered why she was dallying. The letter in her hand had told her that Maggie had fled Renmark over a week ago, under dire circumstances, and here she was, as if paralysed.

Someone would have to go look for Maggie and find her. Someone would have to bring her daughter home, safe. Heat fired over her neck again and she put a hand to it. Worry always brought on these surges of heat and the sweats.

Lorcan stirred. 'Ah, my girl,' he croaked, a twitch of his mouth the only smile he seemed to be able to muster.

'Lorcan O'Rourke. You made me an *old* girl overnight.' She leaned over and pressed her lips to his forehead.

'Me leg's right sore.'

Patting his hand, she smiled. 'So it should be, it's broken clean, but not through the skin. The lads had to straighten it out before they strapped it tight.'

'I'll not lose it?'

Eleanor felt the cold slide of fear burrow deep inside her. 'Dr Eakins doesn't think so,' she said, cheerily. 'Your head should be sore, too, but there's no straightening that out.'

He gave a nod, but his eyes had closed. He'd drifted off again. Eleanor knew she was to wake him every couple of hours for another day or two, to satisfy the doctor. She leaned over him again and let her cheek brush his whiskery one. 'And when you wake up, my handsome, I'll have some of your favourite apricot jam on hot damper for you.'

There wasn't a smile from him. She knew he hadn't heard her, but it made her feel better to say it.

Pushing off the chair, and with Mrs Chaffey's letter still clutched in her hand, Eleanor took a lingering look at her husband, who appeared as comfortable as he could be, and left their bedroom. In the short hallway, she closed the door and leaned against the timbered wall, blinking back tears, and with her pinafore hem wiped away the ones that had already spilled. When Ard returned, she would talk over a strategy with him. Though to what end, she didn't know. All she knew was that Maggie had run from something, something which must have frightened her deeply.

Her daughter was not a timid young woman. Lorcan would tease her, call her his 'little tempest'. There was nothing Maggie shied away from: no challenge, no dare, and she met all with a sensible head on her shoulders. But to run off so sudden-like, with no word to anyone. And to cause someone harm. That wasn't her Maggie. Something had gone badly wrong.

Eleanor's heart thudded, a dull pound as if it echoed her thoughts of dread. She rubbed her hands over and over …

Wait. She did know someone who would search for her missing daughter as soon as it was asked of him. And she knew in her heart, that loving Maggie as he'd done all these years, he'd be exactly the right man to find her.

Eleven

Sam was in his hut, a temporary dwelling while he finished building his own place on O'Rourke's Run. He sat on the edge of his bed, a narrow cot, the base woven with rawhide strips and a thin mattress atop. It served well enough. The day's work was done, and sundown was changing day into night. His heavy boots lay where he'd kicked them off outside the door. He stared at his holey socks that would have to be washed; they'd been a week on his feet already. Maybe he'd have to wait for laundry being done this week, what with Lorcan on his sickbed and his missus having to tend him.

It didn't matter. Mrs O'Rourke usually made sure he had two clean pairs of socks at the ready. Mrs Eleanor, that is. Mrs Linley was a bit otherwise preoccupied, a baby due out real soon, and all. Ard, proud as punch, was gonna be a pa again.

No such luck for him. A twist sharpened in his gut. He snaked a glance at the rough timber table he'd built to serve for his letter-writing, and to the small bundle of envelopes, unopened, and returned to him by a scratchy pen boldly stating *Return to Sender.* Why he hadn't already burned them, he didn't know.

Write a letter, Ard had said. Tell her how you feel, he'd said.

What did Ard know about his own bloody sister? *Write a letter* is all well and good, *if* she'd only accept them, read them and reply. But oh no, Maggie O'Rourke, stubborn as hell—still—had to return them unopened.

Well, what was a fella to do?

He peeled off one sock and threw it into the basket Mrs O had supplied for his dirty laundry. There'd be no new letter going to Maggie, and hadn't been for a while. No sir. He'd written his last over three months ago. He tugged off the other sock, dangled it from his hand and eyed the hole in it. What else was a bloke *supposed* to do? He'd already said he'd marry her. And that had not gone so well.

He couldn't talk it over with Ard. Maggie was his sister, and Ard had said time and again that he was keeping out of it. And Sam couldn't bawl on Mrs O's shoulder—she'd only just thawed out towards him, especially since helping poor Lorc after he fell out of the tree. She believed that something bad had happened between him and Maggie, and after that, her daughter had gone to live in Renmark with them. Old man O'Rourke had taken a job working for the Chaffey brothers on the new irrigation scheme.

The scheme had failed so Maggie stayed in her job there, and the older O'Rourkes had come back to Bendigo. They'd sold their plot of land after their orchard had been torched, and bought a block on the Murray here, at Echuca. Ard had followed his parents, and Sam had followed Ard. Why not? His own family was fine in Bendigo. His pa ran a successful shop blacksmithing and doing building work. Even in a depression, he'd done all right. Work was thin on the ground in Bendigo—so Sam told himself—and here on O'Rourke's Run he had a chance to start a fine business working with Ard's family.

At first, the stumbling block had been the old man, Lorcan O'Rourke. He didn't like that Sam might have made his little girl unhappy—what did he call her? His little tempest. Sam had won the old man over. He'd worked hard on the new plot, helping Ard rebuild the two old and abandoned original houses back to a decent living standard. He'd helped construct fences and the landing at the river for the paddle-steamers—even that new-found cousin of Ard's, Dane MacHenry from Swan Hill, stopped by in his fine boat from time to time.

The extra positive benefit on O'Rourke's Run was that he'd have been close to Maggie if she ever cooled off from wanting to bash him on the head. He wondered what she'd think of the new house he'd nearly finished building, the third one on the property. Ard and his parents had offered him a square of dirt for just such a purpose. Quarters for the homestead's manager, they'd said. *Manager.* He'd come up in the world. He laughed at himself. Having a title didn't mean much, but it was good of the family to offer. It would surely have impressed Maggie, had she known about it. The closer he got to finishing the house—a two-room dwelling with a verandah, a cookhouse and laundry room out the back, and its own privy—the more he wondered if he'd ever live there at all; it didn't appear as if it would ever be with Maggie. Maybe it wouldn't matter if he took up Dane MacHenry's offer of a job.

Dane was paring back his riverboat trade, he'd said. The railways had been operating a while now and it was killing the river merchants, beating them on freight. Dane had come up with a new business idea while he'd tried to keep his crops and sheep alive through the drought. He'd had been thinking of breeding horses, starting up a stud. His own horse, MacNamara, was a fine sleek and strong stallion, and clearly had good bloodlines.

Dane had approached Sam about Pie, running his hand down the horse's flank. 'If you ever want to make some money, Sam,

I'll make you a good offer to buy your horse. These Walers are sturdy stock. Much in demand back in New South Wales so they will be here, too,' he'd said.

Sam recalled his answer. 'If I ever leave O'Rourke's Run, I might take you up on it. Thing is, wherever Pie's goin', that's where I'll be goin', too. I'm sturdy enough, but not sure I'd be much good at stud.'

MacHenry had barked a laugh. 'If that's the way I get Pie—you and your horse coming as a team—then there's room at my place for you, too.'

Maybe Sam would take up that offer. He dropped the sock, ignoring an odorous waft that reached his nostrils. He rubbed both hands over his head, messing up the already thatched mop that fell into his eyes. He pushed it back. A thought drifted through that maybe it was time for a bath, to wash the dirt off him, and out of his hair that used to be the colour of straw but was now the colour of riverbank dirt. He studied his hands, gritty with the dust that had come off his head.

The reason for staying here—mostly—was to be close to Maggie. Sam loved her, loved everything about her. He loved the glossy black hair with that wavy kink in it when she had it out of the bun-thing. He loved her wide blue eyes, the firm breasts she'd let him hold, heavy in his hands as his thumbs brushed taut nipples. He loved the creamy skin of her thighs close to her …

Dammit, dammit, dammit. He took a deep breath to stem the tightening in his groin, but he couldn't hold back his memories. He loved the flashes of her gleeful laughter, and her banter, quick and clever. He loved that she loved being on the land, and literally in the dirt, working hard, looking after her animals, her garden. Her family.

He loved that she wasn't afraid. She'd explore and take what she wanted. She had a strong curiosity and he hadn't resisted for long before taking her to the place she was most curious about. For her first time, she revelled in it, encouraged him, had been delighted by it. She'd matched him for fervour. She'd even taken his hand and placed his fingers between her legs to show him where she found most pleasure. She hadn't been furtive nor looked guilty like other girls when they'd gone too far. Instead, she'd wanted all the mystery of it, all the wonder. He loved that she trusted him enough to share herself with him.

He would look after her, he'd said, if anything happened. Boy, somehow that was the *wrong* thing to say. But why?

He didn't love that she hadn't want to marry or have kids, not at all. He wanted her to love him and marry him and be the mother of his kids. He wanted her. And just when he thought he'd won her over, just when they'd gotten close again late one afternoon, and had gone beyond temptation—breathless and hungry, and with their blood humming—into that *wondrous place of mystery*, Maggie had called it, just when he swore his undying love afterwards, she'd looked astounded at him, and had backed off.

What? He'd yelled, bewildered.

Grow up, Sam Taylor, *why would I want to marry you?* she'd hurled at him. I don't want those chains on me. Nothing will happen to make us have to marry, she'd said. Then she'd run a million miles and more, all the way to Renmark with her parents and stayed there.

Nothing must have happened from their *wondrous* thing, because he hadn't heard. He would have heard if Maggie had been in the family way—either Ard would have knocked his block off, or old man Lorc would have flung Sam's guts all over the paddock before holding a rifle to his head and marching him up to the altar.

He wouldn't be gutless—he wasn't—because he'd wanted to marry her anyhow, family way or not.

He hissed out a loud breath, forcing it through taut lips. He picked up the sock and hurled it into the basket, a faint nasty aroma of sweat and bad boots following it.

A man should wash his own stinking socks and not expect a woman to suffer it. He laughed to himself then. He'd heard his mother's voice as clear as if she was sitting here with him. It was the sort of thing Maggie might say, too. In his life he had strong women with strong opinions and he had no bloody clue how to get around 'em. Hah! Maybe you didn't get around 'em, maybe you just gave in and let them go their own way.

It was the sobering thought he'd had more than once these last few months. He glanced at the last returned letter again. Time to get on with it. God knows, there were plenty of girls here in Echuca coming up from Melbourne all the time, looking for a husband.

The thought made his lip curl. Yeah, well, a man was no hermit.

He had let Maggie go. Not that she *wasn't* going her own way. Not that he'd had any say in it, in any case, but in his mind, he had moved on. He turned thoughts of her aside. Buried them. He was too old to pine over a sweetheart who didn't want him.

Grow up, Sam Taylor, she'd said.

He picked up the bundle of letters. Well, he'd done just that, Miss Maggie O'Rourke. He was going to burn—

The door crashed open and bounced on the wall. Ard's muscly arm slammed against the door, keeping it still. His frown looked painful-deep, those blue O'Rourke eyes flashing.

'Sam, quick, come to the house. Ma's worried.'

Oh Christ, no. His old man—he must be more poorly after all.

'She's had a letter from Maggie's boss down Renmark way. Says Maggie's in bad trouble, gone off and nowhere to be found.'

Out of breath, Ard wiped a hand over his nose. 'Someone's gotta go look for her. Christ knows, it can't be me—I can't leave the place while Pa is lying on his sick bed. Come on.'

Maggie. Sam sat stock still. 'Right,' he croaked. Then he shot to his feet, dumped the letters back on the table. He stared blankly after Ard who'd run out of the hut, not waiting.

Sam tugged boots on his bare feet, and crossed the yard to the main house. Though the sun hadn't yet lost all its light, he could see that candles twinkled in Mrs O'Rourke's front room. She'd be poring over that letter, nothing surer. He stopped at the verandah. They'd want him to search for her.

He loved Maggie O'Rourke, no question. And no question, he'd look for her till his dying day, and right to the ends of the earth, or whichever came first. But sure as hell, when he found her, and when he brought her back safe and sound to her family, he would let her go.

Twelve

Sam had followed Ard into Mrs Eleanor's house and she'd read him Mrs Chaffey's letter. He'd been right assuming he'd been summoned to go find her. 'I will,' he'd said, not hesitating.

Eleanor had frowned. 'We are grateful, but you should feel no obligation, Sam.'

'Mrs O'Rourke, there is no obligation. I've no expectation that all will be well between Maggie and me. But I will find her.'

Mrs Eleanor seemed glad of it and had held Sam's hands tight in her own.

Now, only just daylight and inside the stable, Sam tightened the girth on Pie, then he patted his glossy flank. 'Good boy. We're going on an adventure, young Pie. We're going to find Miss Maggie.' He checked the saddlebags and his new swag strapped behind before stroking the horse's muzzle. 'Now, you gotta keep up, Pie. We're heading into unknown territory in that South Australia colony, so no skiving off looking for tasty green shoots or fair maidens when there's work to be done.'

'Same could be said for you, Sam.' Ard leaned on the stable door. 'I wish I was going with you.'

'This adventure is all mine, laddie. You got a new baby coming, your pa to worry about, and your ma, as well as this place. We'll be fine, Pie and me. We'll find that sister of yours.'

Ard wiped his hands down his trousers. He blew a low whistle. 'I know you and my sister, well, I know there's been … I mean to say, she's tetchy, she's not an easy one to—'

'It's all right, mate. Maggie and me are over and done in that way, have been for a long while.' Sam swung into the saddle, the leather creaking, his boots scraping as they slipped into the stirrups. 'But your ma knows I'd do anything for Maggie.' He stared down at his lifelong friend. 'I have to go. The boat's at the landing already.'

'I know.' Ard looked at his feet. 'Got the jerky Ma packed up?'

'Yeah. Don't forget to post my letter to Ma and Pa.'

'I won't. Look after Pie.' Ard patted the horse's neck, and he responded with a nod.

Sam snorted. 'Be the other way 'round.'

'I know that, too. And no singing when you get drunk. You're still terrible.'

'Reckon those days are long gone.' Sam held out his hand.

Ard gripped it hard. 'Never say never, boyo.'

'Might be a while between drinks, then,' Sam said catching the blue flash of Ard's bleak stare, the flash that mirrored Maggie's. 'I'll do my damnedest to find her, mate. I hope your pa gets back on his feet real soon so he's good when I bring her back.' He nodded at Ard. 'And I hope to Christ your new little 'un looks more like your missus and not you,' he said, and Pie answered the nudge to leave the stables. 'I'll see you.'

Out of the yards, Sam turned the horse's head and set off for the landing at the river a quarter mile away. His chest was heavy with the weight of leaving, and on his task for the days ahead.

The *Lady Mitchell*, once a fine passenger boat now converted to carrying mainly freight, glided away from the O'Rourke's landing. Still regal, she was headed downriver, first to Swan Hill to upload more freight then on to Mildura, Wentworth and Renmark.

Pie had wandered onto the boat, stepping daintily on the gangway as he'd done many times before. Not a lot bothered this sturdy horse of his. Sam tied the reins to a post at the stern of the boat and patted Pie's sleek neck. 'I'll be back directly, old fella. Got to go talk to the cap'n.'

In the wheelhouse, the captain, Ned Strike—a short, weather-beaten wiry man with what looked like a permanent squint in his left eye—cast Sam a glance. An unlit pipe wobbled between thin lips as he spoke. 'Horse tied up good?'

Sam nudged his hat back a little farther and rolled his shoulders as he stopped beside the wheel. 'He is. You know he won't make havoc.' He eyed the panel forward of the wheel where navigation instruments sat in their housings, some with needles that wavered or ticked. He looked over the spread of charts on a fixed lectern attached to the wall of the wheelhouse, one of which showed a tight curling channel. It didn't look anything like here that he could tell, but if this boat was going to get him to Renmark, that was all he needed to know.

The pipe wobbled again as the captain spoke. 'Good. Carried all manner of things in me time and a problem horse was one of the worst. Now,' the squint blinked open once or twice, 'just so ye know, I don't sail the river after dark. Agin regulations, but some do it. I don't.'

'Right.' Sam had only travelled between Echuca and O'Rourke's Run with Captain Strike, no further until now.

The story was that Ned Strike had lost good mates when the *River's Best* sank years ago, snagged at night by a huge gum that had recently fallen into the water. He was a highly skilled captain but refused to navigate the river once the sun had gone down.

'No matter to me,' Sam said. 'Paddle-steamer by day is still the quickest way for me to get to Renmark without killing my horse.'

'Watched him wander on board these last few times. Fine lookin' animal.'

'Maybe breed off him later. He's got a calm temperament, got some brains in his head.'

Captain Strike switched the pipe to the other side of his mouth where it bobbed to get settled between his nut-brown lips. 'Heard nothing much fazes them Waler horses. Looks like he'd outlast all of us on a long trek. They say they can go for days without too much to eat or drink. Can carry a load, too.'

'True, but I want him well rested. We'll be on a long trek leaving Renmark, I reckon.'

'Yeah, heard you was going off somewhere downriver. Good thing you didn't start out last week.' He sucked in a breath around the pipe, winced a little as if something had hurt him. He shook his head a little sadly. He said, 'There was a big fire down way past Renmark. Meant boats clogged the river there. Just gettin' all the back traffic through now. Yer might not have got much further south on horseback either.'

Sam didn't comment. *Jesus, a fire.* His job might have now become a whole lot harder.

The easy chug of the steam engine and the soft paddle of the side wheels filled the silence. Sam couldn't detect a breeze on the banks. The scrub on either side was still; nothing moved at ground level or at the tops of the gum trees. Their mighty stunted branches were thick with faded green leaves, some dead waiting to drop when the life was finally seared out of them by an unrelenting sun. Lining the river, outreaching tree roots hung over the grey sandy banks as if trying to coax the water to a higher level. Fallen boughs, rotting and crumbling, lay like sentinels, waiting for the river to rise. Drought was gliding in again—if it had ever left. Those trees would be reaching for water a while yet.

Ned Strike coaxed the wheel a quarter turn and the steamer obeyed, taking a long gentle bend in the river. 'Whole place was opened up all along that way, to help folk who was doing it hard, but now the rail's gone through here and there, river trade is down. It don't look so good for the little settlements now.'

Interested, Sam folded his arms and stood alongside. 'Many settlements?'

'There's a few of 'em. They call 'em villages. Folk share what they grow, what they find, what they have. Dunno how it works, all that sharin'. Communism, communal, communist or some such thing they call it. Don't ken to a man not owning his own holdin', if he can afford it. All that sharin' business, I dunno.' Captain Strike shrugged. 'But it means you'll have plenty of places to kip if you had a mind to. Could pick up a bit of work in exchange for vittles and whatnot.'

Plenty of places to search too, that meant. Sam's gut warmed suddenly, and a dribble of sweat trickled down his back. He hoped he *could* find Maggie. The sheer size of the country … a man could travel for weeks and not even be out of that South Australian colony. But it had a sparse population, so maybe with luck …

If she was alive.

He'd been shoving that thought aside since Ard had told him Maggie was missing. Now, on the river, with Pie packed to the hilt with swag, saddlebags, and his rifle, leaving one colony for another, the reality of his task was taking hold.

He shoved the thought away again. Removing his hat, he rubbed the side of his head hard, digging into his scalp and creating more knots in his already matted thatch. He jammed his hat back on. Knowing Maggie as he did, having a haircut might be a wise move. Not that it mattered to him, a haircut, but he could do with more wise moves. He hadn't had many to date.

Before he'd left Echuca, the family had wondered if Maggie would try at first to go to Dane MacHenry in Swan Hill. Along the way it was clear to Sam that no one had sighted a young woman named Maggie O'Rourke. At Swan Hill, Ned Strike said they weren't scheduled to stop at the boss's place, so Sam would have to make his visit a quick one. He leapt off the *Lady Mitchell* at the MacHenry's Jacaranda landing and ran to the house.

'Nah, mate,' said a workman, a smoke dangling on his bottom lip. 'No one home. There's been bad trouble with one o' their boats downriver, and the boss has gone there. The missus has taken the kids with her up to Swan Hill. I ain't seen no one back yet and had no visitors.' He tipped his hat back, and a line of grime separated his tanned forehead from the pale skin at his hairline. 'See if you can catch the boss down a-ways. Might have word of your friend.'

Sam thanked him, and bolted back to the steamer. 'Dane's not there. They've gone on to sort trouble with a boat downriver, the bloke said.'

Ned grunted. 'I heard. Good mate o' mine gone, Ranald Finn, and one of his men, Johnny Bentley.' His face closed under a deep frown. 'Blowed an engine, they reckon, on the *Lady Goodnight*. Bad business.'

Sam snatched off his hat. 'Sorry to hear that, Mr Strike. I knew Mr Finn.'

There was a terse nod. 'Bad business,' the captain muttered again and turned away. They got underway; the stop had barely slowed them up.

Thirteen

Three days later, just after dawn, the *Lady Mitchell* pulled into Renmark after mooring for the night not far upriver.

Ned Strike wasn't about to dally here; his crew would take a hasty bite, perhaps find a billy tea brew with workers on the wharf before heading downriver. He didn't want the men to head off in search of a drink. There'd be no grog or drunks on a boat under Cap'n Strike's command.

Pie didn't need to be coaxed off the boat. He led Sam as he headed for the dusty incline to the top of the bank. Sam tied him away from the carts and the haulage equipment and returned to the *Lady M* to help unload the freight, putting his back into it alongside others.

They'd carried wool bales destined downriver for rail transport from Morgan to Adelaide. He'd do his bit before leaving them, then find this Olivewood farm and visit the lady of the house there. Mrs O'Rourke had given him a letter to deliver to Mrs Chaffey. It was the quickest way to get it to her.

The size and scope of operations on the river had amazed Sam. Here at Renmark, things looked the same as they did at Echuca, where the wharf was always busy. It still bustled with traffic up- and downriver, despite everyone saying trade was slowing. Freight was varied, from wool and grain in bales on barges, to stock, and people and their belongings being transported to resettle in newly opened areas of the country. Hard to believe it was slowing down.

A bloke was running his hands down Pie's flank. The horse was throwing his head in the air, his eyes wide. Sam knew Pie wouldn't do anything stupid, but he was a stallion, and could be as pernickety as the best of them. Shouldering a couple of sacks of flour, Sam headed back up the bank towards an already heavily laden cart.

He tossed off the sacks, and they thudded onto others in the cart. He dusted himself down and strode for his horse. 'Help you, mate?' he asked, taking Pie's bridle. The horse, shying and stamping his feet, settled a little.

'G'day to you. Was just thinking what a fine beast this is.' He patted Pie's rump again with a meaty hand. 'I was looking to buy a horse, and this one here is just the sort I'm after. What say you—'

'He's not for sale.' Sam let the horse throw his head a bit more, then he pressed a soothing hand on Pie's neck.

The stranger seemed to consider the flat reply. 'Pity. Horses are in short supply here. Only so much riding around the countryside a man of my size can do on a bicycle.' He gave a roll of his eyes, winced, and thumbed over his shoulder to the bicycle that leaned on the spindly trunk of a young eucalypt. He had a deep bruise on his neck that seemed to spread from under his hairline. His eyes were swollen and the skin discoloured, not so much like black eyes, but damaged all the same. The man's chest was like a barrel, his guts solid, and he had thighs like they were bursting out of his trousers. *Squash a man flat if he sat on you.*

Sam glanced at the bicycle contraption where it rested. It sure as hell didn't look sturdy enough to carry this bloke around. 'Wouldn't be ideal,' Sam agreed. How'd a body expect to get around? Not on that thing, anyhow. He couldn't begin to think what life would be like without a horse.

'Where'd you get him?' The big man thrust his hat back, revealing a thick mop of dark hair.

Sam rubbed Pie's neck some more. 'Down Bendigo way.'

'Ah. Over the border. Goldrush country, eh?'

'Used to be,' Sam said.

The man inclined his head. 'True,' he said. 'So.' He nodded at the *Lady Mitchell*. 'Just in town for a while? That your freight on board the boat? Looks to me like Mr Strike is still the captain.'

Sam glanced over his shoulder and saw Ned Strike at the dock. The captain looked up, noticed the man Sam was talking to, and immediately started up the hill.

'Mornin',' Captain Strike called, terse again.

The big man called back as Strike approached. 'Mr Strike. Good to see the *Lady Mitchell* still hauling freight and the like. We're a lucky township to have such fine boats dock here and servicing our community.'

Ned Strike made it level with Sam and looked at the man. 'There's nothin' on my manifest for you today, sir.' He didn't wait for a reply and turned to speak directly to Sam. 'The house you're lookin' for is not a mile that way,' he said and pointed beyond the buildings on the flat above the riverbank. 'You can't miss it. It's built with logs, has olive trees in front and anyone could direct ye.' He stared pointedly at Sam. 'We'll be heading downriver directly. If you want to come, there's maybe a couple of hours in it.' Then he nodded his goodbye, glanced at the other man and headed back down the riverbank.

The man gave a small grunt. 'Still got enough of the Scot in him to be nice and gruff.' He turned to Sam, his booming voice too friendly. 'Sounds like you're looking for a place called Olive-wood. I can take you if you have a mind to go there.'

Sam, trusting Mr Strike's reaction, shook his head. 'I'll be right.'

The man ignored him and reached out again to stroke the horse's neck. 'Looks like I don't have to wait around for any freight to come off the boat. We can go now, if you're ready.'

'Thanks all the same, I'll be right,' Sam repeated, keeping his voice even. His temper didn't feel even. 'No need to waste your time.'

'No waste of time. Still, speaking of that, there's a grog shop not far along. Young fella like you could do with a drink.'

Sam started to lead Pie away. 'Thought grog was illegal here.'

'Sure is, for the next little while. The place is trying to get a community hotel up and running,' the man said jovially. 'But I can get you into a place or two, on the quiet.' He had to hurry to keep up with Sam. 'Know what I mean? I'm well known in town, my name's—'

'No need for it right now.' Sam held up a hand. No one liked a drink more'n he did, but always with fun company, and not in some place where the law was gonna come down on top of a man. This fella didn't seem like fun company. 'I'll press on. Good day.' At the top of the bank, Sam swung into the saddle.

The man looked up, huffing to catch his breath. He patted Pie's flank and the horse flinched. 'Well, I'll come find you again if you're in the area long, check that you're ready to let go of your horse. Name your price. I'll be ready.'

The idiot couldn't be much of a horseman the way he kept slapping a stallion from behind. Good thing Pie was not so nervous these days. As a youngster he might've stomped the man to the ground, and Sam was still careful about who he let get close. Only Ard had the other free rein, and he was an experienced horseman. Pie liked him. Ard loved Pie. Sam turned Pie's head and they started in the direction Ned Strike had sent them.

The man called out. ''Course, you'll be able to find me easy enough. I'm—'

Sam acknowledged him with a wave over his back. The man said something else, his name maybe, but Sam had already tuned him out. He headed towards Olivewood, the last place anyone had seen Maggie O'Rourke.

Mrs Chaffey was on the front verandah, reading the letter from Eleanor O'Rourke that Sam had handed to her. Holding Pie's reins, Sam stood silently with his hat in hand. His heart beat a dull thud, and every so often he glanced about, hoping he'd see Maggie emerge from somewhere and hurtle towards him.

All he saw and heard were the five children who raced around, excited to see a stranger and no doubt waiting for their lunch and a cup of tea with sugar. The oldest looked to be about nine; George, Mrs Chaffey had called him. He watched as a dark-haired maid hovered, fluttering a hand over the plate of shortbread to shoo flies. She hesitated, nodded briefly at Sam before she turned and walked into the house.

Mrs Chaffey sighed, looked at him and indicated that he take up a chair alongside hers. 'I think, Mr Taylor,' she started, her Canadian accent cultured on a soft voice, 'that you might have a big job ahead of you. Maggie has been gone a couple of weeks now, along with the other woman, Nara, and her husband, and no sightings of any of them whatsoever.'

Sam felt his gut squeeze, and his lungs fill. He pulled out a chair on the opposite side of the little table and sat, dropping his hat under him. 'Mrs Chaffey, I must start somewhere.'

'Have you spoken to Constable Tate yet? He's stationed at Overland Corner but should be hereabouts again.'

Sam shook his head. 'I wanted to see you first.'

She sighed. 'I tried to report a missing person, but because Maggie has taken her bag with her …'

In that case, Mrs Eleanor could have her home by now.

'… he thought she'd just run off, left of her own accord, and because Mr Boyd has not laid a complaint, you see. But there have been other women gone missing lately, in slightly different circumstances, I admit, though it does make me anxious.'

Sam's gut plummeted. 'Then I would be pleased if you'd tell me everything you know about the day she left.'

Mrs Chaffey referred to Eleanor's letter once again, pressing her palm over the paper. 'Her mother, the poor woman,' she said almost to herself and poured two cups of tea. She pushed the plate of biscuits towards him. 'She says in her letter that you are a friend of the family.'

Sam was happily surprised that Mrs Eleanor had made a fair introduction of him.

'You must feel a great affection for Maggie to have offered your services to come and find her,' she continued, glancing to check the letter, then fully turning her attention on him.

Sam tried to concentrate on Mrs Chaffey's words but by now the lads, Master George and his brother Charles, were having a fine rowdy old time. *This is what it would be like with a houseful of kids.* They sped around the corner of the house and onto the flat, heading for the olive grove. War cries sallied forth as they wove around the lithe saplings and dodged the older trees. At the end of the verandah, another of the children, Margaret, looked after two stripling younger siblings. Sam couldn't remember their names.

'Yes, Mrs Chaffey, a great affection for Maggie. Her brother is my mate, and he would have come too if he could have. It is an unhappy time for the family, for all of us. So, if you can help?'

Sam shifted in his seat. He needed to ask her a question. All very well to be here for clues and a starting point. He wasn't that comfortable with a real lady sitting right beside him, eyeing him off about his feelings for Maggie. He needed to know. He studied his pants for any dirt he could surreptitiously flick off and took a breath. 'Do you know if she had—did Maggie have a beau?' There. He'd said it. He still held his breath.

Mrs Chaffey gave him a small smile. 'No, Mr Taylor, I don't believe there was anyone here who interested Maggie.'

He nodded his thanks and let go of the breath. *All right.*

She sat back and stared towards the olive grove. 'On the day, we'd been visiting friends, and had taken our other house girl with us. Maggie was here alone, so we had Nara Wadge—the other missing woman—come do a few chores with her. They were good friends, you see. They got along well, and I knew things would get done properly. By the time we got back, it had already happened. It seemed that Maggie took it upon herself to attack this Robert Boyd—who believes he's a very fine citizen—with an iron rod from the smithy's forge.'

Sam's brows shot up. *An iron rod? Jesus, Maggie-mine.*

'Consequently, now he has somewhat the look of a raccoon,' she continued. 'It's not as if it hasn't ...'

Raccoon. Whatever that was. Mrs Chaffey's soft burr ran on. What he'd already heard wasn't sounding like the Maggie he knew. Sure as anything she was opinionated, had hold of her convictions, knew her own mind and made it known to all and sundry, but to pick up an iron rod and clobber a bloke?

Well, wait a minute, Sammy-boy. If the bloke was being an ar—

'... Then, by all accounts, after that, she ran off. That way,' Mrs Chaffey said, pointing at the olive grove where young trees stood proudly in rows.

Sam sat up. 'By all accounts?' he asked. 'Does that mean someone saw her?'

'Mr Watson, from a farm just out of town.'

Sam's gut churned. 'And he was sure she just up and bashed this fine citizen?'

Mrs Chaffey cleared her throat. 'It seemed there was something indelicate being perpetrated on Nara Wadge.'

Sam glanced at her, and the faint pink blush on her cheeks confounded him. *Not exactly something you ask a lady for more details about.* 'Right.' He felt his own face burn, and the roots of his hair itched. No wonder Maggie bashed the fella. He took a gulp of tea. 'So Maggie was helping her friend, and trying to defend herself.'

'Exactly, Mr Taylor. But the man she hit—Mr Boyd—is a very brash person whose belief in himself is exaggerated. He likes to think he has the ear of important people and so he has already ensured that Maggie's character has been well tarnished. He has suggested apparently that she tried to murder him.'

Sam was staggered. 'And what has this Watson fella said?'

'Nothing. A case of not wanting to upset Mr Boyd, who is known to be a very vindictive individual.'

Sam's blood simmered.

George and Charles thundered along the verandah in a flash of tumbling limbs, roaring young voices and the swish of long sticks brandished as swords. Mrs Chaffey gave Sam a look then called sharply, 'Boys.'

Her two sons stopped for a moment, staring at her, before they dashed off in silence, waving the sticks.

She lifted the plate of shortbread. 'Please, you haven't had one yet, and they are excellent.'

He nodded his thanks, took a biscuit and bit. Smooth and buttery, he thought he'd crave shortbread forever. He devoured the rest of it, took another and put it on the small china plate she had set in front of him. Mrs Eleanor back in Echuca had taught him some manners; his own mother had tried.

'And so, the other woman is also gone?' he asked.

'Yes. She and her husband have an abode down by the creek,' Mrs Chaffey said and lifted a hand indicating somewhere at the back of the house. 'But they're not there now.' She set down her cup. 'I'm sorry I'm not able to help further. Maggie was quite well liked here, and we miss her.'

Sam took his cue that it was time to leave. Then one of the youngsters appeared at the end of the verandah behind Mrs Chaffey. His crumpled red face, the angry eyes and the tears pouring meant that an eruption was close. He let out a bawl and Mrs Chaffey spun in her seat. 'Oh dear. What is it, Francis?'

Francis let her know what was troubling him, but for the life of him, Sam could not decipher the garbled protest, full of wails, pouts, and rage.

Clearly, his mother could. 'Well, I'll speak to Harriet about that,' she said to the boy. 'Now wait just a moment.'

Sam ears were ringing as the boy continued to wail his grievances.

'Mr Taylor,' Mrs Chaffey said, a little louder, and stood up. Sam stood as well and pocketed the last shortbread. 'I'll have to attend to this, I'm afraid.' She turned. 'Francis,' she admonished the boy abruptly. He took a few gulps and quietened, remembering his manners. Addressing Sam, she said, 'However, I would like to pack you a hamper to take on your journey. I expect you won't stay too long in Renmark if Miss O'Rourke is gone.'

Sam hadn't planned that far ahead, but he would be grateful of a meal to take with him. 'Thank you, Mrs Chaffey.' He remembered his hat was under the seat and bent to grab it.

'Lucy,' Mrs Chaffey called, and the maid who'd appeared earlier came to the door and stepped out. 'I'll deal with Francis—' who'd begun to yell again about the injustices done to him '—if you would please attend to a packed lunch for Mr Taylor.' She took the boy's hand firmly and said to Sam, 'Follow Lucy around to the kitchen. Good day, Mr Taylor. I wish you luck. Do let me know when you have found her.'

'I will. Thank you, Mrs Chaffey,' he repeated as she led away the aggrieved boy.

Lucy's glance darted at Sam. 'This way.'

They headed in the opposite direction to Mrs Chaffey, around the side of the house and along to the kitchen room. Lucy pointed to a seat outside the open back door. 'I won't be a moment.' She ducked inside.

Sam sat again and stared across at the two great stone wheels on a circular slab. A slight man, fair to red hair, wearing a singlet and loose trousers was cleaning the set up. 'What's over there?' he asked of Lucy, poking his head into the kitchen and thumbing over his shoulder.

Lucy looked past him, her dark eyes frowning a little as she focused into the light. 'The olive press. It's resting now. Mr Mead is waiting for another crop.'

'Olive press?'

'We extract oil for cooking here, bottle and sell it.'

Sam had never heard of olive oil, but then he wasn't a cook either. That was Maggie's department, and the last time she'd cooked anything when he was nearby was—

'I have information.' Lucy was wrapping damper in a brown paper bag. Then she packed dried fruit and jerky and boiled eggs.

Sam stood in the doorway. 'Yes?'

Lucy kept her voice low. 'After it happened, Nara snuck back and told me how Maggie got that iron pick-up, run over and crashed it on his head.' Nervous, darting a glance here and there but not at Sam, she kept packing his hamper. So far, she had three packages for him to take and she was still reaching for more. 'Then Nara left.'

Sam took a deep breath in. 'Did you speak to Maggie after?'

She shook her head. 'She'd long gone, Nara said. I haven't seen her. But my Bert—he delivers goods here—he says he saw her at the wharf that day. He thought she got on a paddle-steamer. I'm not sure which one.' Lucy ducked around him to peer out the door. 'I haven't told anyone about this, and neither has Bert. Mr Boyd is right nasty. Nothing proved, mind, just people gossiping. There's horrible things said about him.'

'What horrible things?' His heart felt like it rolled for a moment as he faced the last thing he wanted to hear. 'Do you think she's alive?'

Lucy's eyes widened. 'Oh, I've worried you unduly. I'm sure she is. Nara said that she and her husband would keep an eye out for her, and they've gone too. They were friends with Maggie. She made us all friends, even real poor people like them, like Nara.' She stopped a moment and took a breath. 'Besides, if she did get on a boat, Mr Boyd might not even know about it. We certainly haven't said a thing, not even to Mrs Chaffey.' She chewed her lip. 'We'd get into such trouble if she found out we hadn't said anything. It's been two weeks now.'

Sam rubbed his chin hard. Two weeks. He needed to hurry up, be on his way, back to the wharf, at least. Mr Strike said he'd be there a couple of hours more if Sam needed to go further and time was passing. 'Did Bert say which way she went?'

'He thinks downriver. There was a few boats in, he told me, and he was helping unload.' She shoved a thick slice of some sort of cake into the last of the three bags and dumped all of them in front of him. She swiped the back of her hand over her forehead. She frowned again, thinking then finally looked at him. 'I forget which boats.'

'Right.' Sam peered at the bundles of food in his arms as aromas of pastry and fruit reached his nose. His stomach growled, and he looked up. 'Your Bert, how do I find him?'

'He's a big fella. Bright orange hair, lots of freckles. Always smiling. If he's at the wharf, you won't miss him. Here,' she said and wrapped a piece of paper around a small biscuit with a dollop of jam poked into it. She handed it to him. 'Give him this. He'll know it's from me.'

'Thank you, Miss Lucy.' He tucked the treat into his pocket. If he didn't find Bert at least he'd have this sweet to enjoy.

'Mr Taylor,' Lucy said as he turned to go. 'If any of us could have a crack at Mr Boyd, we'd go at him the same way he uses his fists and give him a taste of his own medicine.' She demonstrated double-handed thumps on a lump of dough on the table. She stopped. 'Not me, personally. My Bert would, and others, and not half for his wandering hands and all, on us women.' Her frown appeared. 'Don't tell anyone I told you about where she went.'

He stared at her pinched face, the flour-dusty hands clasped over her apron. 'I won't. Good day.'

Sam left her and went back to the hitching rail at the front of the house. He stowed the packets of food in the saddlebags and gave Pie a couple of soothing rubs. 'Back to the wharf, old boy,' he said, and Pie's ears pricked. 'We've got a trail to follow.' He'd just put a foot into the stirrup when Pie snorted, skittered a little. 'Whoa, Pie.' Thinking it might have been a snake spooking the horse, he stepped out of the stirrup and looked around.

Nearby and sitting patiently, was a liver-brown, curly coated dog, stocky-built, deep-chested, and with large floppy ears. Golden-yellow eyes stared solemnly up at him. The dog's glance shifted quickly to Pie but settled back on Sam.

Holding Pie's reins, and making more soothing sounds, Sam squatted close to the dog. 'Mate, my old Pie doesn't know too much about dogs. Who're you?'

'Bucky,' a voice piped up.

At his name, the dog's tail swished in the dirt. Sam looked across and young Margaret stood on the verandah. 'Bucky, is it?' he asked of her as he looked down.

Another swish.

'He's come off a boat,' she said. 'His master died, and Bucky hasn't taken to another boat. He come up here to us and the men don't mind him around. He gets rats and things. He's good at getting the ducks when they fall in the water after being shot.'

'Fine-looking dog.' Sam lifted his foot to the stirrup again and the dog jiggled his body expectantly.

'I heard you talking to Lucy about Miss Maggie. She right took to Bucky.' Margaret's soft burr seemed urgent.

Sam swung into the saddle. He looked at her, then at the dog. 'Did she, now?'

'You going to find Miss Maggie?'

Sam doffed his hat at her. 'I intend to do just that, miss.'

'And Bucky right took to Miss Maggie, they're friends,' she blurted. 'He's not really ours. You could take him with you.' She seemed on the verge of tears.

'I don't know much about dogs.'

'Don't need to.' Margaret stood solemnly on the verandah, one hand by her side, fingers fiddling with the edge of her pinafore, the other hand in a pocket. Her stare was intense. 'If you're going to get on a boat, he's a boat dog. They're called river dogs.'

'You said he hasn't taken to another boat.'

'He will with you, if you're looking for Maggie.'

Margaret seemed intent on Sam taking Bucky. The dog still sat expectantly, looking up at Sam, his tail swiping a hollow in the dirt. Seemed Bucky was intent on Sam taking him as well.

'Nara said he could track things too, like she and Wadgie can. They learned some from the blacks,' the girl said.

'Where is Nara?'

'Don't know. Bucky sometimes lives with her, but she's now gone, too.' Margaret's chin puckered as she withdrew her hand from her pocket. In it was a clean and folded handkerchief. 'This is Maggie's. I went in her room. Don't tell Mama.'

Sam's heart thundered.

Margaret took the steps down to where Pie stood and held the handkerchief to Bucky, who was still watching Sam. The dog took a sniff, eyes on Sam, and his tail thumped.

Sam reached down for the handkerchief. He also put it to his nose and breathed in, not sure he could pick up Maggie's scent, but at least it was something of hers.

The dog's tail thumped hard and he got to his feet. 'All right, dog,' Sam said. There was an elated full-body waggle from Bucky.

Margaret burst into tears. 'Goodbye, Bucky.'

'I'll look after him, Margaret,' Sam said.

'He'll look after you,' she answered, her bottom lip quivering.

As he turned Pie, the dog following a safe distance from Pie's hooves, Sam muttered, 'He probably will at that.'

Fourteen

Eleanor held her husband's hand. The doctor from Echuca had just been to see him, and had left without being able to give her much more information.

The big warm hand in hers was still callused, even though he had been in his bed for days now. The pads of her fingers traced them, and she stared at the scars across his knuckles. Her thumb brushed them, resting on his wedding finger that was bent at the big joint. Each injury, big or small had a story. Lorcan's story.

She looked up as her son spoke.

'The doctor told me that Pa is in a deep sleep.'

Eleanor nodded. 'He said not a coma, but alike to one. That perhaps there is a deep infection somewhere and his body is fighting it.' Even as she said the words, the heaviness in her chest deepened.

Ard folded his arms across his chest. 'So we have to wait until the infection breaks. I will sit with him, Ma. You need to sleep.'

'Perhaps later. I'll call you in.' She smiled at him. 'No movement from my new grandchild? No expectation of an arrival?'

Ard pushed off the doorway, shook his head. 'Linley is still waddling about and has now decided to clean windows.' He shrugged. 'I wouldn't have thought windows would be on her mind right now.'

'Ah,' said Eleanor. 'Windows. Well, lad, let her go. It occupies her, but you keep an eye out when you can.' She didn't say that a burst of energy in the mother sometimes augured the baby's readiness to come into the world.

'I'll be at the stables,' Ard said. 'The two new stalls are nearly done. I can hear your shout from there, if it comes to that.' He came across and planted a kiss on her head. Reaching over to brush away a lock fallen onto his father's forehead, he said, 'He's not too hot now.'

'We have to take him off the laudanum, slowly. Perhaps the persistence of pain will wake him.'

Ard squeezed her shoulder. 'I'll just be over behind my house, Ma.'

She watched as he left the bedroom. Her son was almost a mirror image of his father. Strong, built solidly but with height to balance. Black wavy hair. Piercing blue eyes, twinkling most of the time, but when stormy, they would darken. As she gazed at her husband's face, she wondered when the deeper lines on his cheeks had appeared. Eleanor knew almost the exact month the silver streaks had appeared in his hair, though they'd arrived in his beard long before—bristly tufts at his chin when he'd not shaved for days.

She sighed aloud. Maggie's colouring was just as dark as her brother's, but her temperament was very different. Where Ard was slow to anger, Maggie was quick, and her blue eyes would flash like her father's ... Where was she now?

Eleanor squeezed Lorc's hand again. He didn't know she was missing. Couldn't bring herself to say so. It had only been days since Sam had left. No point waiting for any news yet.

She wouldn't tell him; it would be a fright to him. The doctor had assured her it was most likely Lorcan couldn't hear her, but Eleanor knew her husband. He'd hear *everything*. She smiled a little at that. So, she decided she would talk to him of other things while she sat. Even if he wasn't interested, she had a captive audience.

She placed her other hand on his as well and her fingers found his pulse, the solid pump of it. It heartened her, and she lifted his wrist to her lips, pressing a kiss there.

'Our son tells me the two new stalls in the stable are nearly done, and that Linley is waiting for baby by cleaning windows. That reminds me, so long ago now—of course, we didn't have windows then, but do you remember when ...'

Fifteen

The previous day's steaming out of Lyrup had been an uneventful short few hours, and Maggie had hoped the calming sail would allow a good night's sleep. By the time they'd tied up somewhere yesterday, if anything, she felt more agitated and her night was restless once again. How long would it take to settle down? Four days had already passed.

It hadn't been the first time today that she'd smelled smoke on the breeze, thinking nothing of it until she realised it persisted. It wasn't coming from the tiny galley stove; she'd checked. Only big enough for two cooking hobs on the top and for a small damper inside, it was easily managed. She supposed that sometimes the men cooked outdoors on open campfires so a big oven inside wasn't required. Besides, she had tamped it down to glowing coals after they'd had tea. Her mutton stew was sitting in the pot waiting to be reheated later for the evening meal, so no new wood was burning in the galley.

She went to the door and looked out across the river. She wondered about Nara and Wadgie, and about the folk at Olivewood—Mr and Mrs Chaffey and the children, Lucy who worked at the house with her. About Bucky, the happy-go-lucky dog who rarely left her side. Would she ever see any of them again? Sorrow sneaked into her heart, but there was nothing to do about it.

Glancing up and down river, nothing seemed amiss, yet the smell of wood smoke hung in the air. Just as she was about to search for some flour and dried fruit, she heard the steam engine drop, and the paddle-wheeler slowed in response.

Where were they? Maggie couldn't see a landing on either side of the river. Perhaps they were pulling in for the night, but it seemed too early for that. Pressing a hand to her thumping heart, she took a deep breath. She's been hoping they'd be a lot further downriver before stopping. She would go to Captain Finn right now and find out what was happening. If they were stopping here, she guessed it would be safe enough. No point worrying needlessly. She was sure no one from Renmark would be following her but it was still too close for her liking.

At the wheelhouse, only a step or two from the galley, she looked out over the silent river. 'Are we stopping for the night, Mr Finn?' she asked when she got to the wheel. Mr Bentley was there with him.

'We are, miss. Heard a grumble or such from the engine, and our old *Lady G* doesn't usually have grumbles. We'll shut her down here in this neat little tie-up and see what's what.' He adjusted his hat, glanced at Mr Bentley, who nodded. ''Course, the other thing is, I reckon the smoke we can smell might be a bushfire ahead. Won't do us any good trying to go past that.'

He unrolled a chart, and he and Bentley gazed at it. 'We're here, Johnny,' he said and tapped a tight curve. 'Good a place as any. Let's get to that engine.' He looked back at Maggie. 'Now, Miss Lorkin, not to alarm you, but it's best you get onto land while we work out what to do.'

Maggie was about to object when the sombre look on the captain's face stopped her.

'Nothing to worry about,' he went on. 'We've tied up to a strong tree, so we can pull her in a bit closer, get you off quick smart. You might get your feet a little wet but in this weather you should dry out soon enough.' His tone brooked no resistance. 'So gather your bag, miss, and Bentley will get you organised.'

Her heart sank. *More waiting, more worrying.*

Captain Finn shrugged, not mistaking her dismay. 'I hope it's nothing and we can get on our way as soon as we know it's safe. But it's best you're off the boat.' He turned away and let his hands rest on the great steering wheel.

Bentley said, 'Once I get Miss Lorkin on land, Cap'n, I can scout up ahead on foot a few mile if you want, check to see which way the fire's goin'.'

Captain Finn was grim. 'I don't like the sound of that. We'll have to set up a watch for the night, is all. If we can fix the engine, we'll turn back to Renmark tomorrow.'

Dear God in heaven—what are the chances? 'Mr Finn, do we have to turn back if there's a bushfire?' she asked.

He nodded. 'If it's a bad 'un and it's whipped up the wind, it'll likely jump the river to the other side. Sparks and embers land on the boat, and we go up in smoke too. No hope getting out alive.'

'But—if you can't fix the boat?'

'We'd need to be towed back to Renmark, and no one likes doin' that on this river. Even if another boat is following us and capable of it, we've no way of knowing. *If* there's a bushfire comin' this way, *if* we can't fix the engine, we must abandon the boat and walk back fast, at least to Lyrup.'

'I don't understand.'

He turned back to her. 'Otherwise we would be trapped here,' he all but snapped. His eyes were red-rimmed, and the frown deepened. 'My life's been on this old *Lady Goodnight*,' he said finally, the snap gone.

'Miss Lorkin,' Bentley said softly. 'If we try to run the boat with a bad part, the boiler will blow and we'll all be killed. So it's best we do like the cap'n says and get you off the boat. Then we'll look at the engine. Might be nothin'. We might be back under way in no time. But if a bushfire is headin' this way, we won't be goin' downriver.'

Horrified now, Maggie looked from the captain to Mr Bentley, but their faces were closed. 'Of course. I'm sorry to sound so dense. I'll get my bag.'

She knew that if she was off the boat on the bank and there was an explosion, she would be safe. Her heartbeat sped up again. Had it slowed at all since fleeing Olivewood the other day?

'Hurry along now, miss,' the captain said, his usual calm having returned.

Maggie fled to her cabin. She rushed to stuff her few things back into her bag: her little sewing kit, the now crumpled letter to Sam, her handkerchief, her hat, and the pinafore. She knew her savings were safe, snug against her chest. Back on deck, she felt the boat move as the captain and Mr Bentley drew on the mooring rope.

She studied the bank. Spindly saplings were scattered here and there between sturdier trees, which at least would offer shade. Bark and leaf litter, tinder-dry, carpeted the dusty bank, bare of any green. The early afternoon sun had lost none of its bite, so she would find a comfortable place to sit and wait.

Bentley beckoned her to the side of the boat closest to the land. 'Right you are, now miss. Let's get you—'

A voice from the bank cut across him. 'Oi there, aboard the boat. Have ye got room for a passenger?'

Bentley turned, and Mr Finn straightened to stare. Slipping and sliding down the bank, cut away by falling tides and erosion, a slender man holding his hat got to the edge of the water.

'Tried walkin' my way down along the river,' he called, 'but I reckon there's a nasty fire gallopin' this way. Can ye smell it? I didn't want to go too much further in case I couldn't get 'round it. If you've a mind, you need to turn about and get back to Renmark. Be grateful for a lift.' At their blank stares, he said, 'Y'are turning back, ain't ye?'

Mr Finn sighed. 'Damn and blast,' he said under his breath. 'Stay where y'are, lad,' he called. 'Boat's disabled.'

The man clambered into the shallows. 'I can work for me passage. Ah, you're Cap'n Finn. I met you—'

'Stay on the bank,' Mr Finn said sharply.

'Maybe I can help. Name's Thompson. Um, been an engineer.'

'So's Mr Bentley, here. Won't do any good if we don't have parts for repairs.'

'Shit, Cap'n. Not good.' Thompson spotted Maggie. 'Beg pardon, missus.'

The captain nodded in Maggie's direction. 'Miss Lorkin is our passenger.'

Thompson snatched off his hat, and gave Maggie a nod and a smile, his eyes lighting up. 'Miss Lorkin.'

Maggie nodded back, her hackles up at that smile. Something rang a bell at his name but she couldn't grasp the thought.

Bentley eyed the man standing in the water. 'No swag or nothin'?' he asked gruffly. 'Leave that behind for the missus, didja?'

'Best I did, Mr Bentley. I dint need it, used to sleepin' rough. Me back's still good, and I don't drink. Can work up a storm.'

'Cap'n,' Bentley said, not seeming to share the man's enthusiasm. 'What say we ask Thompson here to get to Lyrup on foot and send word back upriver for help.'

Thompson blanched. 'We fix the boat and we can sail right past Lyrup, straight on to Renmark.'

Captain Finn looked him over. 'You get us some help and send riders back with horses. We'd pay you once you get back.'

'Ye not taking me on board?'

'No one but me and Mr Bentley will be on board. We're going to set Miss Lorkin here on the bank, under a nice shady tree, while we work. But before we do that, we'll bag up some vittles for you to take. Then you can be on your way.' Captain Finn glanced at Maggie.

She dropped her bag and ran to the galley, grabbing beef jerky, a hunk of day-old damper, and a handful of sweet biscuits she'd made and stashed in a tin. She wrapped it all in the first clean rag she found. Raised voices reached her but she didn't take too much notice. Surely Mr Thompson would help them by going on, on foot. Rushing back on deck, Maggie handed the parcel to Mr Bentley. He threw it to Thompson, who was still at water's edge. Scooping up her own bag, she went to the rail of the boat.

'You'll be doing us a service, lad,' Captain Finn said, not unkindly. 'Now, on your way so we can get Miss Lorkin settled and we can get on with it.'

Smoke wafted on the breeze. Thompson clutched the bundle and backed away from the water. He stumbled, righted himself. 'I'll get help.' He stood a moment as if wondering what had just happened. Then he turned and stomped back up the bank and disappeared into the scrub.

'He weren't no engineer's boot,' Bentley said quietly. 'He'll follow the river for water, so he won't die o' thirst. No point relyin' on him. He's a few days walk out of Lyrup. But he won't go there.'

'Why won't he?' Maggie demanded. 'You've given him food—'

'We seen him a time or two before when we've dropped off goods,' he said. 'Teddy Thompson. Always lookin' for a free ride. He abandoned his missus at Lyrup. He'll go on to Renmark before he gets us help, and that's half a day's walk further on if he dodges the settlement.'

Teddy Thompson. Maggie remembered it was Jane's husband's name. 'But he'd put that aside to get help, wouldn't he?'

'I don't have much faith. But he'll survive if he's as smart as he thinks he is. Maybe then he'll figure he can raise the alarm.'

Maggie wondered if Mr Finn thought it might be too late. Bewildered, she stared at him. 'What do—'

'He could be three and a half days or more walk out of Renmark in this weather,' Captain Finn said, as if she hadn't spoken. He looked skywards. 'We'll take four-hour watches tonight after we check the boat. Fixed or not, if the smoke gets worse, we head off on foot to go back.'

Maggie held her breath. Go back? *Oh, dear God, please not*. Either to walk or to sail back to Lyrup meant she was too close to Renmark. When she breathed out, a great fatigue hit and her shoulders slumped and her head dizzied for a moment. Her bag was heavy in her arms and she sagged against the rail.

Mr Bentley was speaking with the captain, but she could barely hear what they were saying.

'Could be a leaking pin …'

'… Steam pressure. But I wouldn't …'

'… Safety valve? Looked all right when …'

'… Gettin' on, now, the old girl …'

A breeze tickled, and once again the smell of smoke drifted by her. Now it seemed a menace, but Maggie was too tired for its threat. Sliding to the floor of the deck, she let another great sigh escape. Resting her head, she closed her eyes, gathering some strength, she hoped. Seemed for only a minute …

'Come on, miss. On your feet. I'll take you up the bank a-ways and leave you with this,' Bentley said, her mattress draped over one shoulder. He held out his free hand. 'We might have to sleep out in the open, but the cap'n and me have to work while we can still see before dark.'

As she gripped his hand to get up, the rough callused palm enfolded hers and the confident grip heartened her. Oh, but she was tired. As soon as she was on firm ground, she'd have a sleep. Just a little one.

Mr Bentley guided her to the very top of the bank, threw her thin mattress down and waited until she'd sat. 'Now,' he said. 'You pick up any thicker smell of smoke, yell out, miss.'

'I will.' She watched him return to the boat, and without being careful of how she landed, she fell on her back and was soundly asleep before she knew it.

'Get out,' a voice roared. *'Juuump!'*

Then the loudest sound in the world ripped Maggie's eardrums and ricocheted inside her head so hard she thought it would burst. She bolted upright. Her hands flew to cover her ears, but it was too late—the thunderous boom banged through her head and chest and shook her down to her feet.

The earth shuddered. Another explosion rent the air. Ducking then, her forearm shielding her face, she squinted in stunned disbelief as bits and pieces of the *Lady Goodnight* flung high into the air and then dropped to the water. Debris and shrapnel sliced thin saplings. Chunks of rotting gum flew into the air. Jagged shards rained down, clunked nearby or thudded painfully into her. She screamed, clamoured to get out of the way. She dashed for the mattress, pulling it over her head, and took cover behind a big gum tree. She dropped to her backside, curled into the mattress and waited, wincing as bolts and chunks of metal hurtled to the ground around her. Then it seemed to fall silent and she dared breathe again.

She looked out, unfurled the mattress and sat up. The hull and the wheelhouse were sinking fast. The deck, all that was left of it, poked up out of the water, spun weakly in a circle in the middle of the river. Embers died around it.

The captain and Mr Bentley must have floated the boat out—

Maggie blinked, clearing her eyes. A man clung to the deck then he staggered up, blackened, seared and bleeding. He clawed at his throat, seeming to gasp for breath. He spun once, blindly. Then he steadied and deliberately plunged into the water. The deck followed him, and both slipped silently beneath the surface.

She sucked in her breath as the horror descended. *Burned so badly he preferred to drown … Which man was it? Which man? Where's the other man? Dead? Must be dead. Dear God.* Maggie couldn't shout. No voice.

Bubbles rose up from the deep. Then the denuded body floated up, face down, and drifted away.

Shaking, she tried to stand, but her legs came out from under her. A yelp as she hit the ground. But she didn't hear a sound. Didn't hear her own voice … Nothing but the ringing in her ears. *Deaf.*

In a panic, she patted her ears, willing them to wake up, to hear again. She tried to speak, tried to make a noise she might hear. Clapped her hands. Nothing.

Scurrying on the mattress, she groped for her bag, slung it across her shoulder and clutched it. Waited. Shook. Looked about her and saw nothing other than the silent bush, a wide, serene river and the expanse of bright blue sky. *Heard* nothing. *Infuriating!*

A wisp of smoke curled close to the edge of the mattress. She slithered down on her backside and, with her heel, stomped on its source. Spun around on the mattress. Other sparks? *Oh God, in this crackling drought, the place is set to ignite. Sparks there. And there. Heaven help me.*

Maggie clambered upright, wobbly, but at least on her feet. Holding her dress out of the way, she stomped on embers she found close by. Stomped on yet more, and more.

There's too many.

Breathless, she held her bag tight against her chest. Standing for a moment in her silent world, she cast around. Too many sparks. Too many wisps of smoke.

Run.

The ringing in her ears had come down a notch. All Maggie could hear now was her thudding heartbeat inside her head as her feet pounded over the hard earth. She couldn't hear herself huffing and puffing as she ran. She stumbled and fell, her hands flung out, scraping the dirt. Scrambling to her feet, she ran on again. Nothing mattered as long as she could see the river. If she decided to stop, she would drink. She'd be able to follow it to safety. Perhaps if there was time, she'd wash off the sweat and the dust. Clean the scratches on her face that had stung as she'd ploughed through the scrub.

Oh God, what if I'm following some offshoot stream and get lost good and proper?

No. No. No. Veering closer to the bank, she stopped a minute, doubling over as she caught her breath. She stared at the vast expanse of slow-moving water winding its way peacefully away from her. Moody, calm, and barely a ripple, she knew she was on the Murray. It was home. It was her *way* home. It would *take* her home. Perhaps the long way around, but it would. It would set her down at Murray Bridge and then she'd find a way to get to Echuca from there.

Home. Then she snivelled. *Mairead O'Rourke, don't you* dare *snivel.*

Her eyes squeezed shut and her face scrunched. Her throat hurt because tears wouldn't come. She thought of good, kind Captain Finn. And Mr Bentley …

Don't you dare *snivel. You get on and make sure you stay alive. No time for snivelling.*

Letting her sobs go, and gulping in air, she set off again. *Oh, if only Bucky was here.*

The smell of smoke was still strong, and it had freshened since she'd run from the explosion. Its stench was in her nostrils, tickled her throat, but it goaded her to run on. God, how far could she go before she'd fall to her knees, exhausted? Could she even outrun a fire? And sleep—how would that even be possible with a fire on her heels? She thought she'd been tired earlier—no time for *tired* now.

Stumbled. Would her boots hold out? Her bag thumped as she ran. Clamping it against her body, she felt her savings cache rub her chest. If she got out of the bush, she'd be safe with the little money she had. Finding her stride, she ran on.

Her dress caught on a stiff branch jutting out from a fallen log and, yanked to a sudden halt, she crashed backwards. A great rent had entangled itself and she struggled, trying to wrench it free. No good. Tried coaxing it free instead. Fumbled. *No good. No good*. Enraged, she jerked, and it tore away completely. She threw the shredded fabric aside, disgusted. *Damn and bother. Now I need a new dress.*

She staggered on again. Thin twigs and spindly branches whipped her face, her cheeks, until she raised her forearm to fend them off.

No idea how far she'd come … Her feet slowed. Her legs felt like Lucy's jellies had looked: wobbly and not set properly. *Oh dear, why am I thinking of Lucy's jellies?* Get to the water's edge, girl. A boat might come. Sit and wait. *In the dark?* Just get to the water's edge.

Her knees were weak and her feet were sluggish but she forced herself to turn back towards the bank. She found a clear place, a gentle slope, and dropping to her backside she slid down a way. In the fading light she found a little knoll with a slight hollow. She crawled into it, and slumping, she eased her clenched fist open and the shoulder strap fell to her chest.

The ringing in her ears still clanged with her heartbeat but it was slowing up. Her head was heavy, her neck sore, and it seemed her body just wanted to lay itself down. So she gave in, and down she went, rolling onto her side. In the dirt, she gathered her bag close with both arms, and closed her eyes.

The dog had been barking. Goodness, Bucky was loud today. 'Shoosh, Bucky,' she said, raising her voice over the top of him. 'Shoosh, you'll wake everybody.' Her mouth felt funny as if her tongue wasn't working.

Shaking. Someone was shaking her. A murmur of words. She could *hear* a murmur of words. Her eyes popped open. There was no Bucky. Smoke was close.

The sun glowed dusky pink through the trees. A fire crackled nearby, throwing its low light. Maggie nearly cried out when she saw it a little distance away, merrily burning without a care for all its menace.

Then she focused on the person who was shaking her arm as he beamed at her.

'*Very* loud kangaroo.'

Maggie's head hurt as if she was parched. On her hands and knees at the river's edge, she scooped handfuls of water but couldn't get enough into her to make the thirst go away. The scrapes on her hands stung, and the scratches on her face pulled when she moved. Her legs still wobbled, and it seemed every ache she could have had in her body was paining now.

Nara studied Maggie's face and hands and declared, 'Not too bad. There's really nothing to treat.'

'How did you get here?' Maggie blurted through thick lips.

'We decided that if we had to hide for a bit,' Nara said, 'we might as well follow you.' She pointed to where their canoe was wedged between the trees up on the bank.

Only big enough for two people, it was nevertheless a fine, sturdy craft. They used it for fishing back home. The first time Maggie had gone out on the river with Nara, she'd fallen overboard and Nara, laughing, had quickly hauled her back into the canoe. Though Maggie could swim, the river wasn't safe. The day had ended with Wadgie chuckling at her sodden clothes as she tramped, unhappy with herself, back to Olivewood. There'd been more successful days fishing since, without any unintended dunkings.

Maggie's hearing was woolly, but she understood Nara and nodded. 'I'm glad you did. Thank you,' she said. 'I'm very happy to see that little craft again.'

Alarmed, Nara held out both hands. 'You're loud. Speak soft.'

'Sorry,' Maggie whispered, not realising her voice had risen.

Nara spoke softly into her ear. 'We seen you get on board that boat. Followed for two, three days, kept out of sight, just in case of trouble. We reckoned you'd be all right 'til we smelled the smoke. We knew that old cap'n wouldn't keep going downriver, that he'd turn back. But then, *boom*. By the time we got there, the fire had burned back. Wadgie picked up your tracks easy.'

'I had no idea where I was going, was just hoping it was away from the fire.' Maggie pressed Nara's hand. 'We seem to get into some scrapes, you and me.'

'Nothin' like this. Always just fun stuff, but now …' Nara shrugged and shook her head. 'We'll stay with you, at least 'til we know what's going on.'

'What will you two do?'

Tucking her dress between her knees, Nara sat back on her haunches. 'We didn't hear nothin' about no murder before we left, so we gonna sneak back and see what we can find out.' She lifted a shoulder. 'Maybe Lucy in the kitchen has heard something by now.'

'Should you risk going back there?'

'We're good people, we should be able to keep our jobs. We been there a long time, Maggie, you and me. Boyd was the evil one, and he's gone—good riddance.' Her voice drifted off. 'Mrs Chaffey is good too. Don't worry. We'll find out.'

Maggie didn't feel happy about staying close to Renmark. 'I'll still move on.'

Nara nodded, agreeing. 'You have family, go to them. They'll be waitin' for you. I remember your ma. She's a good person too. And your pa. Kind people. We need more kind people.'

Maggie blinked hard, felt her dry skin stretch. 'You should come with me, you and Wadgie.'

'We like it here. Maybe you'll come back one day.'

'When I'm old and grey, and no one recognises me.'

Nara squeezed Maggie's hand. 'And we'll be friends even then, gettin' up to mischief.' She turned suddenly as something caught her eye.

Maggie gasped until she saw it was Wadgie. He'd disappeared earlier, and returning now with his reed net, he happily waved a decent-sized fish. He poked a couple of long sticks into it and set it over the campfire. Freshening up the coals with his breath, a little flame leapt and soon his skewered catch was grilling. A few minutes later, he said something to Nara. She reached over and took a piece of cooked fish from him, offering it to Maggie.

'Perhaps after,' Maggie said, her tongue thick again, her headache thumping now. 'I have to sleep some more.'

Not trusting herself enough to stand and walk, she crawled to a tree with branches still thick with leaves, found a comfortable spot and slipped to her side.

Nara followed her, and after tucking Maggie's bag into her arms, she leaned down and patted her shoulder. 'Sleep. We're here.'

'You sure the big fire's finished?' Maggie asked.

'It's finished, don't worry.' Another couple of pats on her shoulder. 'Sleep.'

'Wait. What about Bucky?'

'With the missus.'

Oh good.

Nara squatted beside her. 'In the morning, after food,' she said, 'we'll go back to that village and let them people help you.' She indicated the direction upriver with a thumb over her shoulder. 'Wadgie and me, we'll return to Renmark, keep out of sight, but if the troopers do come lookin', we'll move a bit upriver.'

Maggie wanted to protest about going back to Lyrup but it was the only sensible thing for her to do, and for Nara and Wadgie, who shouldn't have to keep an eye on her. Besides, weariness was upon her and her head was heavy. No point being silly about it. She knew she'd have some chance buying passage on another boat going downriver from Lyrup without having to go back to Renmark.

She hugged her bag. Maggie's last thought was how happy she felt to hear the crinkle of her letter to Sam.

Sixteen

She couldn't tell what noise she'd heard, her ears were ringing so loudly. A bird? A magpie, perhaps. Waiting a moment to adjust, Maggie steadied herself on the fallen log she'd slept beside before tottering to her feet. Blinking into the sunshine, she guessed it was about midmorning. A tentative step towards the river tested her balance; the muscles in her legs remained tight and sore, but they'd ease with movement. Dusty, thirsty, knowing she needed to bathe, she crept closer to the water.

No sign of Nara and Wadgie. A chance look around, and nothing seemed amiss. The little cooking fire wasn't smoking, but it was aglow, ready to be teased into flame. The canoe was still on the bank, so her two companions would not be far away.

Plopping on her backside, she stared at her boots. Oh dear. They would have to come off. Roughly scuffed and dirty, the pliant leather was still holding together at the seams. She pulled at the laces, which she'd tied sturdily so many days ago, and eased them open, tugging them from her feet. *Oh, heaven.* Her toes wiggled. Dismayed, she found her stockings had not held up as well as the boots. No matter. A hole here and there was certainly nothing to cry over now. The toes of her hose were intact, but ladders ran all the way down to them. This pair wouldn't last much longer, but that didn't matter either. She could sew …

Her bag. Craning her neck, she could just see it tucked under the log where she'd slept. Relieved by the sight of it, she edged towards the water and sunk her feet. *More heaven.*

While her toes squiggled deep into the mud, she cupped her ears and listened to the hum in them. Lord, was she to be deaf forever? It brought a little thud to her belly. How would a deaf woman manage to survive—a deaf woman running for her life, after bashing a man and killing him? A sob escaped but no tears, thank goodness. She had only a little sound getting through her stubborn ears. Perhaps they just required more time to heal after the blast.

The blast. She squeezed her eyes shut. She had hearing loss, but she still had her life. Not like those two poor men on the *Lady Goodnight.*

Smarten up, Maggie O'Rourke. It was her mother's voice again. How she wished her mother was here now. Well, Eleanor was sort of here—in her head she could hear her mother's lilting voice. So, smarten up she would. She had things to do—if she ever found her way out of the bush.

Of course she would find her way out. Nara and Wadgie would make sure of it. But what was taking them so long?

She looked around again. All alone, she was, in this great expanse of bush. Deaf, or mostly. A little trill of alarm beat in her chest. Hurriedly, she pulled her feet from the water, shook off the muddy sand and wiped them on the hem of her dress. Pushing away from the edge, she drew on her ragged stockings and thrust her feet into the boots. She scrambled back to the log where she'd left her bag, and dropped alongside, hoping she was out of sight. Her hands shook as she retied her bootlaces and settled back.

Why is my heartbeat racing again?

She reached out and grabbed her bag. Cradling it against her chest, she made herself as small as possible and waited.

It was late afternoon and hours had passed, it seemed, before Nara and Wadgie finally came back. Maggie had kept snug against the log and had only moved to ease her cramped limbs, or to scoot away from a line of ants determined to track over her.

Maggie watched as Nara knelt in the sand and blew on the coals, laying some fine leaves and twigs over the top and waiting until the lick of flame appeared.

'Where have you been?'

'Just checking around,' Nara said, giving Maggie a quick look as she moved to sit beside her. 'You been scared?

'A little bit. Don't know why.'

Leaning closer to Maggie's ear, Nara said, 'Nothin' to be scared of.'

'True. Or at least, nothing to be scared of right now.'

Nara sat back, a look of mild surprise on her face. 'Since when you ever been scared? Never once, not even when your parents left and you was here by yourself.'

'But you and Wadgie and I were already friends by then.'

'We were. I remember that first time you came down to the hut. I was so surprised to see a lady from the big house, I nearly fell over.'

Maggie laughed. 'You did not, and I'm no lady. Your cooking pot smelled so delicious, I couldn't resist coming, even though Mrs Chaffey was worried I'd disappear, never to return.'

'Hah, not the missus. She's a game one, too. And there you were, large as life, askin' me where to find berries and the like.'

'I knew you'd know. I knew it would be good for our kitchen to have some bush food. And don't forget that Lucy was at Olivewood by then. So I wasn't all by myself.'

Nara wagged a finger. 'Don't change things around. You weren't scared when the creek come up that time,' she said. 'And all dressed in Sunday best you went in to grab them two silly kids out of the water.'

'Someone had to, and I was closest by far. Wadgie was off rabbiting, and you were up at the house in the laundry.'

Not to be put off, Nara said, 'What about when that horse bolted pulling the cart while young Miss Margaret was tryin' to drive?'

Maggie rolled her eyes. 'Young Miss Margaret would have been in bad trouble except for you and me, and not just from the horse bolting. From her mother, too.'

Nara gave a short laugh. 'But you, Miss Maggie, could have got yourself killed running in after it.'

'And you, Miss Nara, were there as well, remember?' Maggie smiled recalling Nara's gleeful shout and poor Margaret's terrified squeals. 'You jumped on the cart to haul on the reins.' Maggie rubbed her stiffened fingers, letting go of the bag. 'I'm not scared of things outside of myself, not when I think of those adventures. I'm more scared of things inside.'

'I dunno what that means.'

Maggie agreed. 'You wouldn't, I know. You've never been scared of anything.'

'Scared of that Boyd when he bashed Wadgie for no damn reason.' She folded her arms over her belly and rocked a little.

'Nara, you swore.'

'Not scared of doin' that, neither,' Nara said, and snorted. 'Or bashing him back. But you did that, not me. You're not scared, Maggie, you're just unsure of all this.' Nara waved her hand around, and Maggie knew she didn't mean just of the bush.

'I seem to be unsure of everything. How do you get sure?'

Nara patted her shoulder. 'Do like always. We make up our minds and get the job done,' she said. 'You are sure about leavin' here, though, so you just have to find the best way to do it. Then you won't think about being afraid.'

'You're helping me to leave. I'm not doing it all by myself.'

'What else would we do? You'd help us. You already have anyway, just by being a friend. People look at me, at us, different because of you.' Nara gripped Maggie's hand. 'I mighta been living near Olivewood when you arrived, but I wouldn't have got the job if you hadn't been there. And when Mr Chaffey is home, you know that he likes Wadgie to come work every so often in the packin' shed. That wouldna happened before we were friends.'

'And now look. No job for any of us.'

Nara tut-tutted. 'We dunno that. When we go to Olivewood, we'll see. No need to worry about me and Wadgie.' She looked over at him at the campfire and back again. 'You have been a good friend when a lot of others haven't.' Nara patted Maggie's hands in loose slaps then stood up, cupping her belly and smiling wide, her small form in profile. 'You are the first besides Wadgie to hear the news.'

Maggie hadn't noticed the roundness there before. She gazed, speechless.

Nara, whose eyes widened in delight, tapped her stomach. 'A Wadge is coming. Maybe a strong girl who'll make her way in the world.'

'Like you will,' Maggie said. 'You both will.'

'And you,' Nara insisted.

She couldn't stop herself. 'But … aren't you afraid, Nara?'

'Of what?'

Maggie thought then of what she was really afraid of, and the stories she'd heard. The little lives lost before they were born, the cruel births, mothers dead leaving tiny babies with no one to feed them, babies dying after they were born. 'Of birthing, and all the things that can go wrong …' She began to feel breathless.

Nara shook Maggie's shoulder a little. 'I'm afraid of nothin'.' She looked across at her husband once more, then back to Maggie. 'And neither are you, remember?'

Wadgie, skewering a good-sized Murray cod over the low flames, must have said something and Nara responded. She turned to Maggie and, leaning close to her ear again, said, 'After food, we'll sleep. Just before sun up, we'll head for Lyrup.'

Nara looked at Wadgie when he waved for attention. As he spoke, he held up two fingers and waved them at the canoe, and kept speaking. All Maggie could hear was a low cadence.

Nara said, 'You an' me, Maggie, we'll take the canoe, and Wadgie will run. Two more sleeps to the village.'

Perhaps they were now keen to get her back, not wanting the responsibility after all that had happened, and rightly so, too. Apart from Maggie being a burden, with a baby on the way they would need to look after themselves, as it should be.

A baby. Now that was true bravery.

But going back to Lyrup. No point feeling any trepidation about it; Maggie wouldn't have survived at all out here without these two. Crashing about in the bush for much longer by herself in any direction wouldn't have done her much good. She'd likely have been a dead *very loud kangaroo* before the week was out.

The only thing that she could do now was survive, get her hearing back—*of course it will return*—and make a life for herself. Somewhere. She would secure passage downriver and all would be well—for Ellie Lorkin. She need not be afraid about that.

She pressed a hand to her chest and felt for the soft leather purse. All would be well.

At dawn's light, Nara and Wadgie already had the canoe at the water's edge. Wadgie flashed his great grin when Maggie attempted to get in it. He was saying something to her but his voice was too soft.

She'd taken off her boots and stockings and had stood in the water, trying to take the best opportunity to launch herself on board without ending up on the other side. At home, she'd done it plenty of times before—it shouldn't have been difficult, but Nara had always stood on the other side as she'd climbed in. Not here, though. The river here was much deeper compared to the creek at home. Laughter erupted from Wadgie as the canoe wobbled and threatened to tip until she sort of slid in. She heard another shout of laughter, then he said something, smiling broadly.

'He says he can't help it. You make him laugh,' Nara said up close, and smiled just as broadly as her husband.

'Wonderful,' Maggie replied, and then let a laugh go, too.

Wadgie steadied the craft with his gnarly lean hands and, finally settled, Maggie gathered her possessions and took the crude paddle from him. He showed her what to do by crouching as if he were in the canoe.

The canoe rocked as Nara climbed in. Maggie sucked in a breath and Wadgie laughed again. 'You'll be fine,' she heard him say in his gravelly voice. She was sure he was still chuckling as he made his way over to check the fire was completely out. He kicked more dirt over it, then he waved them off.

Nara turned. 'Come on.' She indicated she was ready. 'We have at least two full days of this. You keep up with that paddle.'

Maggie nodded. She'd keep up.

Seventeen

As Nara swivelled in the canoe, checking for her husband's whereabouts on the bank, Maggie's hands, shoulders and arms ached for reprieve. This was now the third morning they'd paddled. But Nara was the one with child, and who'd done much of the work all the way, so Maggie couldn't complain. At least she'd slept well each of the past two nights, exhaustion taking over almost as soon as dusk arrived.

They spotted Wadgie in the distance by a huge river gum, its roots exposed above the water line. He beckoned and Nara steered the canoe towards him. After picking his way down to the water's edge, he waded in a few feet, reached over and gripped the nose of the canoe as Nara climbed out. Together, they pulled it to the bank.

Maggie angled a leg over the edge of the vessel, and Nara grabbed her arm, steadying her in the cool water. The squishy mud under her feet was a welcome relief, and not bothered at all that her skirt was already wet, she leaned back in and picked up her bag and boots. Despite having her hat—it had saved her head and face from the still fierce heat of autumn—a tinge of sunburn stung her neck. Her forearms and her feet had taken on a golden hue and she feared freckles would abound.

Stretching, and with her feet still in the river, she wondered what a sight she would look to the Lyrup villagers. *Oh, who would care, anyway?*

Wadgie said something. Nara nodded. He flicked a hand towards the east and kept talking. Nara nodded again and replied.

Maggie's hearing had improved, but they kept their voices low, had explained that sounds carried easily in the silent bush. It was still difficult for her to follow conversations, and she had no hope of understanding any of their hand signals. Succinct and rapid. They'd learned a little from the blacks near the creek at home.

Maggie sat on a fallen log, dried off her feet with her raggedy hose that she'd tucked deep in her bag, and pulled on her boots. She looked up when Nara approached.

'That way is the village,' she said, crouching by Maggie and pointing in the same direction Wadgie had. 'Not a long walk. You go and we'll follow. No one needs to see us.'

Maggie stared a moment. This was it. *Where to start?* 'Um, Nara, thank you for everything.' She peered over Nara's shoulder to the man standing at the canoe. 'Thank you, Wadgie.'

'All right, miss,' she thought he said and he lifted a hand in farewell. He turned to face the river, rolling a smoke.

'Nara,' Maggie started and took her hands.

Nara squeezed them quickly and let them drop, then standing, pulled Maggie into a fierce hug. She stood back, her hands on Maggie's shoulders, a deep scowl on her face. 'Now, you best be off,' she ordered. 'No goodbyes, Maggie. Friends don't do that.'

'No, they don't.' Maggie looked towards the slope, and slung her bag over her shoulder, fighting off the lump swelling in her throat. When she looked back, Nara was standing with her husband, pointing her in the direction she needed to go.

''Til next time,' was all Maggie said, and set off gamely. Nara, her chin puckering, had nodded.

Nara was right, Maggie didn't see them as she trudged along. Perhaps she might have heard a bird-like call once, then a return call, but she couldn't trust her hearing enough to believe it was them and not wildlife.

It dawned on her slowly that she was approaching the landing near where the Lyrup village had sprung up. She could see that it was deserted. There were no boats moored, no one nearby. No way out.

Ma. Pa. For a moment, a memory of sitting at her mother's prized kitchen table hit her squarely as though she'd had a blow to her chest. Maggie had been watching her stir the apricot jam, and the aroma of bubbling fruit was so strong that her mouth watered. She swallowed it down, wondered if she were finally going mad.

A sick wave overcame her. Finding a sturdy tree, she leaned against it while she caught her breath. The memory of apricots faded, and the nausea subsided. Adjusting her bag over her shoulder, she walked resolutely from the water's edge up the slight incline to take the short walk to the village.

As the timber mill came into view, her ears hummed with the sounds of sawyers hard at their task. The steam engine used to drive the saw bench was idle, so the sibilant, whispering *zuzz-zuss* noise of the manual saws was like a music to her ears. Maggie stopped and listened—she could hear even better today—and heard the shouts of men, and the crashing of planks as they were thrown into the stack. One by one the sounds died. Men stood at their stations and stared at her. A tumble of boys raced in her direction and they too stopped in their tracks, agape.

Maggie glanced beyond the boys towards where the huts would be and took a few more steps. Level with the youngsters, she recognised one. 'How is your hand, Michael?'

Struck dumb, he held up his bandaged palm for her to inspect. Then he snatched it back, spun about, and yelled at the top of his lungs, 'Maaaaa!' and raced back the way he'd come with the other boys following.

Maggie took a deep breath. The men still stared. She tried not to brush down her clothes but there seemed not a lot else to do with her hands. She couldn't hide the large rent in her dress and the missing piece showing her chemise, so she fiddled with the handle of her bag. She walked on, nodding at the men as if she was out for a midmorning stroll.

Someone shouted, not at her, it seemed, and so she kept going. Another shout, and then someone fell in alongside her. 'Miss, where have you come from, walkin' in out of the scrub like that?'

The man was wiry, dirt-streaked and grimy with sweat. His plain shirt was open over a singlet and patched trousers. He tipped his hat, more so to get a good look at her face than just a polite greeting. 'Do you need help, miss?'

Now to have to tell someone, no words came. She kept walking.

'Is there folk out there that need help?' he insisted and waved a hand towards someone else. Another man joined them.

Maggie shook her head. 'Dead.'

Another wave from the man, and Maggie looked up to see a woman running towards them, the boys flying at her heels. It was Michael's mother, Betsy, the nervous woman. Jane was running along behind her, skirts high, boots pounding.

'Dead, did you say?' he asked.

Maggie stopped. Thought of that burned man who took a deliberate step into the river off the scorched deck. 'The boat blew up while I was on the bank. The *Lady Goodnight*,' she said. 'They'd told me I should sit on the bank, so I was saved when it exploded.'

Betsy and Jane pushed their way in around her, and Maggie was herded towards their homes.

Eighteen

Robert Boyd slammed a fist onto the counter in the Renmark post office.

Angus leaned over and hissed at him. 'This is my place of work. Don't come in here with your whinges and your bellows about what you can and can't have.' He looked over Robert's shoulder and thankfully saw no customers about to enter. 'I told you, there's no money to buy a horse.'

'I know a bloke who's got this good lookin' animal. But I'll need money to go buy him. I know you've got—'

'I've got what I need to keep me, and you—and your wife and kids—alive if it comes to that,' Angus said, his voice low and firm. 'So, no money for no horse.' He flattened his hands on the countertop. 'I know you've been up and down the wharf carryin' on about that woman, askin' everyone where she might be, makin' a damn fool of yourself.' He watched as Robert's face mottled. 'She's gone. Took off for God knows where. Leave it be.'

Robert stabbed a forefinger at the bruising on his face and neck. His blackened eyes had not begun to fade. 'I still got this, the brand she left me.'

'You never went to the doctor—'

'Someone's got to *pay* for this,' Robert snarled, still shaking a finger at his head.

Angus snatched Robert's shirt front with both hands, pulling him over the timber counter. 'You still wanna murder her, Robert?'

Stunned at his brother's vehemence, Robert blinked. 'I don't murder. I just get mad.' He shoved off Angus's hands. 'I'm still mad.'

Angus pointed his own finger. 'You're lucky no bastard has gone to the troopers about you and your shenanigans. They get a whiff of what you get up to with those poor women—'

'Bah. No one cares, is why.' Robert adjusted his clothes.

Angus squinted at him. *I care, but I want to get you first before they get you.* 'Get out,' he said. 'Go and open the damn store. You reckon you're such a big man about town—why don't you show us, then, hey? See if you can trade for at least half a day.'

Still settling his clothes back into shape, Robert sniffed and wiped his eye. 'Don't like folk seein' me like this. Since I was attacked, my nose leaks, my eyes leak, I got bruises still coming out all over my face and neck. Some said I got my skull cracked. The pain's nearly gone, but there's still all this nuisance comin' out of my head.'

Angus scoffed at him. 'Folk don't care about you 'cept to keep out of your way. Go on, get. I've got wages to earn.' He looked up as the door opened. 'Morning, Mrs Beaton,' he said cheerily.

An older woman, a letter in her hand ready for a stamp, shifted her basket to the other arm. 'Morning, Mr Boyd.' She hesitated, then nodded at Robert.

'And what bit o' news do you have for me, today?' Angus asked, the welcoming smile stuck on his face. The old biddy loved a gossip. Good thing he did too. A man in the post office got to hear all manner of interesting things.

'Well, I don't like to spread news unduly,' she said and swished past Robert, her head down to avoid looking at him again as she stepped up to the counter. 'But it is welcome news in a way, and sad in another.' She pushed her letter across to him and her free hand swept loose tendrils of greying brown hair back from her face.

The smile was still plastered on Angus's face. 'And what is that?' He rolled a stamp on his sponge, poked it onto the envelope and hammered it with the postal endorsement. He accepted the penny she slid across the counter. 'Go on, do tell, Mrs Beaton.'

'Well,' she said, and checked Robert's whereabouts before she bristled. 'A boat blew up, just down from Lyrup, last week.'

'I heard that news only this morning,' Angus said congenially. 'Captain Wallace off the *Bourke* came in and said it mighta got caught in the fire down that way.'

'Yes. And on it was a young woman.' She leaned further over the counter. 'Travelling on her own, it seemed,' she said, and sniffed, imparting such scurrilous news.

'No,' Angus breathed and looked aghast at her. 'Captain Wallace never mentioned that. Well, you know some of these modern young women, taking it upon themselves to get around the countryside.' He glanced at Robert, who'd paused at the door and turned. He looked interested suddenly. *Damn.*

'Oh, I know. And with the vote coming, they think they can do all manner of things. The boat has sunk and there's no sign of any of them. All gone.'

'Awful. And how do we know this, Mrs Beaton?'

'Just now, I've come from Mrs Jenkins and she said that her husband had found a man wandering on the outskirts of town. Almost starving, he said he was, and that he was the last man to see them all alive. The poor man—though he thinks himself lucky now—was ordered by the captain of the steamer to walk for help.'

'My goodness gracious,' Angus said. 'That is some news. Good about the survivor coming out of the bush, not so good for the boat crew and passenger. Paddle-steamers do blow up, we know. Those are the risks, but the loss of lives is terrible.' He stared pointedly at his brother. 'Terrible, too, that the young woman has perished as well, isn't it, Robert?'

Robert seemed to relax. He rubbed his forehead as if sorting the new information. 'Terrible.'

Mrs Beaton cleared her throat a little. 'Well, terrible, yes, for the crew. But not so for the young woman apparently.'

'What?' Robert snapped.

Mrs Beaton kept her gaze steadfastly on Angus. 'There's the mystery, Mr Boyd. The man who brought the news has said that she was already on the bank at the time he left. She wasn't allowed on the boat until they'd fixed it.' Her eyes lit up. 'So, where is the poor girl?'

Nineteen

Sam took a good look around from the saddle, his hand gripping Pie's reins. Bucky sat at his feet, surveying. All seemed right.

The Renmark wharf was humming. More so than when he'd landed hours before. Boats end to end, and a couple of steamers had cruised across to the other bank. Looks like they'd tie up there if they could get a spot. Men yelled, boats and barges bumped, men swore, arms were waved, and hats were jammed on under the glaring sun. He glanced around. Where the hell would Miss Lucy's Bert be? Could be any number of blokes, by the looks of what was in front of him.

Damn me, there's a big bloke right there over by the dray. Red hair. Got his hat off and roughing up his carrot-top.

He urged Pie along a little, dismounted and tied him to a makeshift rail where other horses had been tethered. Pawing and shying a little, Pie settled in. The dog waited.

Sam, his eye on the redhead fella, made his way over to where the carts were being loaded. Bucky was at his heels, distracted by the water, but seemed happy enough by Sam's side.

Someone shouted, 'Last of the backed-up freight, lads.' Half-hearted cheers went up.

'Beg pardon. Are you Bert?' Sam said as he approached the young redhead, solidly built, with a mass of freckles on his sparsely bearded face. The man nodded, and Sam pulled the paper-wrapped biscuit from his pocket and held it out. 'From Miss Lucy.'

Bucky immediately sat at his feet and looked up.

The fella's face split into a gap-toothed grin. Taking the biscuit, he said, 'Bet it's one of her jam drops. And that's Bucky, I reckon.' He slapped a pat on the dog's head. 'How can I help ye?'

'She said you might have information about Miss Maggie O'Rourke.' At the man's hesitation, Sam said, 'I'm Sam Taylor. Her family in Echuca sent me to look for her.'

The redhead nodded and stuck out his hand. 'Bert Hicks.' He looked around. He lifted a hand to catch the eye of another man, who waved him off. 'Reckon that means I'm done here anyway. We can go sit over yonder.'

Sam followed and Bucky tagged along. The men sat on a fallen log where others had taken their smoko. Rusty pannikins lay around a small fire still glowing with coals. The dog investigated discarded bully beef tins, and finding nothing, settled close to Sam.

'Some say river trade is slowing down,' Sam said. 'If this looks like it's slowing down, I have to buy myself a boat.'

Bert grimaced. 'Nah. It's slowin' down all right. We just had lots of boats stuck here waitin' for the bushfire to burn out. No boats could go downriver for a bit.' He picked up a stick and poked the coals, glanced at Sam and chewed his lip. 'Might not have good news for ye.'

The heat of the day seemed to burn through Sam's hat. 'Why's that?'

'I seen Miss Maggie talkin' to a cap'n that day.' He checked Sam was listening. 'That day when she was supposed to have clobbered Mr Boyd. She looked rattled, all right. Dodged right past me to get to his boat. I didn't think nothin' about it, not right then.'

'She got on his boat?'

'Well, I reckon she mighta. I didn't see her after that.'

'Anyone else see her?'

'Dunno anyone else woulda took any notice. Folk are moving up and down the river now like freight used to, plenty o' people about. I noticed 'cause I knew her from Olivewood.' Bert rubbed his big hands together. 'But sorry, Mr Taylor, the boat I thought she got on, it were the *Lady Goodnight*, what blew up down past Lyrup not long back.'

Sam's breath shot out of him as Ned Strike's sombre voice came back to him. *Good mate o' mine gone, Ranald Finn and one of his men, Johnny Bentley. Blowed an engine, they reckon. Bad business.*

He swallowed down the shock. Snatched off his hat and jammed it back on again, his hands shaking. He tried to hold onto the sounds that came up his throat, but the noises grunted out of him. Bucky sidled across and pressed against his leg.

'Sorry, mate,' Bert said again, and sat hunched over his hands.

His mind reeling, grasping for something to hold on to, Sam said, 'Are you sure it was the *Goodnight* she got on?'

Bert brushed flies away and wiped a hand under his nose. 'There was a fella, a settler done a runner from Lyrup days before, tried to get to Pyap and beyond but had to turn around. The fire was comin' up along the river.' He poked at the coals some more, glancing at Sam. 'He come back through here nearly a week ago, half dead from living in the scrub. Weren't darin' to go to Lyrup, folk said, the silly bugger. Anyhow, when he seen Mr Finn moored—because no boat woulda gone downriver with fire on the banks—he asked him for a lift back here to Renmark. Said that Mr Finn warned him off, sent 'im on his way with a parcel of food that a young miss had packed.' Bert looked at his hands. 'And since the *Lady Goodnight* never got to Pyap, and never come back here, it has to be that one she got on, don't it?'

Sam squeezed his eyes shut. Shook his head. *Maggie was dead?* No—he'd *feel* it, he'd *know* she was dead, wouldn't he? He tried to slow his racing heart. 'Anyone found?' Sam knew that some bodies—if they were still intact—might float, but some might be snagged under the surface, never to be found.

Bert spread his hands. 'No bodies. There's a bit o' boat poking outta the water there, some have said, but nothin' much else. Owners reckoned there was nothin' to salvage.'

Sam's voice careened around in his head. *Not goin' back to Mrs Eleanor with news like this. Not when I don't know for sure—and how do I find out?* Some place over his heart hurt. *Jesus. Maggie.* He looked at Bert, but the young fella was staring at the coals. 'How do I—*who* do I see to find out for sure?'

Bert shrugged. 'Wharf master here, he and Mr Finn were sorta mates, said Mr Finn always let him know what he was doin', where he was goin'. Maybe he left word.'

Sam held his head in both hands a moment. 'Wharf master. Right.'

'Somethin' else.' Bert shifted on the log. 'The bushfire never come up past where the boat went down. From the skippers steamin' through afterwards, they reckon it looks like the explosion set off a fire that burned back on the big one on that side of the river. Killed it. Other side burned itself out. Everything back to normal.' He caught Sam's eye. 'Almost.'

Back to normal. Sam hands curled on his knees. 'Wharf master is where?'

Thumbing over his shoulder, Bert said, 'It's late in the day for someone mannin' it, but it's that hut up there.'

Sam stood, adjusted his hat. 'Thanks. I'll head that way.'

Bert got to his feet. 'Lucy liked Miss Maggie. I didn't know her much but—I dunno—if you need anythin' else …'

Sam only nodded; the lump in his throat was too big for words to get around. Bucky bumped his leg as Sam left Bert at the smoko fire. Heading for the hut, one leaden foot after the other and the dog by his side, Sam's heart was heavy with things he couldn't grasp, couldn't comprehend.

Twenty

Sam tied Pie outside the wharf master's hut. When he opened the door, the dog followed him in, and he saw no reason to stop him. The way Bucky loped around the place made him seem at home with everybody.

The man bending over the desk looked up briefly. 'Afternoon. Do for ye?' Bushy eyebrows rose over a pair of wire-rimmed spectacles and pale brown eyes blinked as if focusing. The line where the man's hat had been still creased his thin hair, and a kerchief was tied at his neck. One of his hands held open a big ledger book.

Sam snatched off his own hat and ruffled his hair hard. 'Afternoon. I, ah, am looking for someone who's gone missing. Heard she might've got on board a steamer for downriver.'

The man stared at him, his hand still resting on the open page of his ledger. 'And you are?'

'Sam Taylor. My friend's family is worried for her. O'Rourke, they are, from up Echuca way.' The man gave no indication he'd heard of that name. 'Though they were livin' here at Renmark till a year and a half back, maybe more,' Sam added. 'Irrigation with Mr Chaffey.'

'Was all irrigation here, till it went belly up. Hope they got their wages. Many didn't.'

Distracted from his main task, Sam said, 'From Mr Chaffey? Looks like they're doing all right at that Olivewood place.'

'Different brother. George with his brother William went bankrupt. On Olivewood, that's their younger brother Mr Charles Chaffey, and his wife, Mrs Ella.' The man still leaned on his ledger.

'Right.' That was the Chaffey family tree then. No help to Sam at present. Bucky shuffled at his feet, which reminded him to stay on track. 'So, would you know if a passenger took a fare downriver?'

The man straightened up and patted the open page. 'You know we lost a boat not long back?'

Sam nodded. 'The *Lady Goodnight*. That's the boat some say my friend might have boarded.'

The man sniffed, wiping a hand over his nose and mouth. 'Aye. Mate o' mine skippered the boat. He's gone.'

'I knew him. Mr. Finn.'

'That's him, lad.' He looked resigned to having to speak the truth.

Sam already knew there was a possibility Maggie might be dead, but he still needed to know for sure that she had got on that boat.

Mr Cutler went on. 'Sure enough, a young lady did get on board.' He flicked back the pages of his ledger until he found what he was looking for. Looking at Sam, he asked, 'What name?'

'Maggie O'Rourke.' As he said it, Sam's breath stopped, his heart thudded. He steeled himself with fists at his side, one clutching his hat.

A pause hung in the air as the man blinked at the note stuck in his book. Sam couldn't breathe. The bushy eyebrows rose. 'That's not the name of the young miss I have here.'

Sam was rigid. 'Not O'Rourke?' Bucky nudged him, leaned against his leg.

'No, lad.'

Sam's shoulders dropped. Not O'Rourke. *Jesus. Jesus.* It wasn't her. *Jesus.* The breath he'd been holding shot out. If he'd been a crying man, he would have blubbered on the floor. *It wasn't her.* He reached down to scratch Bucky's ears. Could have hugged the dog instead, but that would look strange. His relief was so great he wanted to sing. Have a drink and sing.

The man slumped to his chair. 'Sad business, all the same. The captain, his engineer. This lassie.' He tapped her name in his book.

Sam glanced over, read the name, *Miss Ellie Lorkin*. Wasn't Maggie, that's all that mattered. He looked up and noticed the red rims of the wharf master's eyes and the firmly set line of his mouth. 'Yes, bad business,' he said and turned to go. 'Thank you.'

'Funny thing, though,' the man said. 'Few days back, maybe a week, a young fella walked into town from out the scrub, bit worse for wear. Said he'd seen the boat just other side of Lyrup. Reckoned the girl was on the riverbank, not on the boat. Chances are …' He shrugged. 'But out here, even close to the towns and the like, if she got herself lost she might not have survived a walk. And the fire might have got her, too. Was a big 'un down that way.'

Sam nodded, keen to be gone. If Maggie hadn't been on that boat, where the hell was he gonna start to look for her? Bucky shuffled again and stared up at Sam but hadn't moved from the desk.

The wharf master laced his hands over the ledger and seemed to want to talk. 'Me ol' mate Captain Finn didn't have no relatives. I had to telegram his boss, Mr MacHenry, who's up Swan Hill way. He come here and he and his crew waited to get word of the bushfire before they could go downriver, find where it blew up. That was bad enough. Then I writ a letter to the engineer's folk somewhere down Victoria to let them know. But I dunno who to write to for the lassie.' He shook his head. 'Got kids meself. Wouldna like to lose one, and never hear they were lost.'

'Aye.' Sam, a weight in his chest, felt the last of the day's heat trapped inside the hut. 'I'm sorry for your friends, and for the girl.' He opened the door. 'Maybe she's alive.' He stood in the doorway and the late afternoon air breezed by him. He looked out over the river to the scrub on the other side. *Not likely.*

'No way of knowin' unless she walks in somewhere.' The man took in a deep breath. 'Poor soul.'

Sam hung his head. How to find out what he needed to know? 'So how far is this Lyrup place?'

'You'll see a signpost. About nine mile by road. But the river's up a bit and ye'd have to flag down a steamer to take ye across. One took off for there yest'dy, ye'll catch that one. Or 'nother one due to leave later today. Why you wanna know about Lyrup?'

'I might get on down to where the boat blew up. Pay my respects, for me and for the O'Rourke family in Echuca. We all knew Mr Finn. Might just get on and camp somewhere down that way.'

'Nice country if you like scrub. Nice views of the river on the way if you like peace and quiet.'

Sam figured that would suit him well. 'I do.'

He hadn't been thinking anything. He hadn't intended to find any rotgut. But he had, and found it easy. He handed over two shillings for a mottled brown bottle with a cork in it. Swore to himself the rum would just take the edge off his worry as soon as he found a quiet site to camp, away from the town. For sure as hell, when it came upon him, he'd sing at the top of his lungs. Some folk back home in Bendigo, and then in Echuca, hadn't been overjoyed by his strong tenor—not in the middle of the night on the way home from the pub, that was for sure.

Riding out of town, with Bucky running alongside, Sam wasn't real sure where he was going. The ride would give him a chance to think. Or not. How could a man think on what to do when he had no information?

Night was descending, and the sun had sunk low. Clouds on the horizon glowed yellow then a deep vermillion, and soon the moon would begin its rise over a clear sky. He estimated he was a few miles out of Renmark, maybe seven, eight. He'd followed the road around cliffs on the river for some time before deciding he should stop and check for that steamer he'd need to flag down. He had no idea where he was, but that didn't matter. He needed time to let his head sort itself.

He dismounted and, when he looked around in the fading light, he figured others had thought the same about stopping here. A log had been dragged into a small clearing and the coals of a small campfire were heaped nearby. He bent and hovered a hand over it. No warmth in the coals; long dead.

Pie headed for a few tufts of greenery and Sam followed to tie the reins over a nearby tree. He undid the girth, removed the saddle and rifle and took them to the log. He threw his thin swag down nearby, and Bucky hunkered down with his front paws on it.

Yep. Seemed to be the place to camp. He grabbed the bottle of rum and set it by the log. He foraged through the saddlebags for Miss Lucy's packets and found the damper and the jerky. He shared them both with Bucky. Found a jam drop but kept that for himself. He slid to his backside and rested against the log. Bucky shuffled over to be close.

He closed his eyes.

Maggie. Where the hell are you?

Twenty-one

It was stuffy. Maggie lay there a moment, trying to think where she was. A small brick and daub dwelling. Jane's hut. She sat up on the cot and realised she was wearing someone else's chemise.

Yesterday, Betsy and Jane each had an arm around her as they'd guided her towards Jane's house. She'd felt all right, a little disoriented, and relieved, but otherwise fine.

It wasn't until Jane said to her, 'My goodness, Miss Lorkin, you do look a sight. Let's get you out of the sun at my house' that Maggie understood perhaps she didn't look as good as she'd hoped.

Betsy had yelled across to Michael. 'Bring another water jug to Mrs Thompson's, boy.' He'd shot off somewhere.

Inside Jane's house, she'd been directed to one of two chairs by a small table. Betsy, who seemed to have lost her anxiety, removed Maggie's hat, and tried to loosen her fingers around the handle of her bag. Met with resistance, she knelt by Maggie's knee. 'We'll look after it, Miss Lorkin. You must let us look after you, too.'

Jane had poured water into a bowl and wet a flannel, wrung it out and pressed it over Maggie's face and neck. 'Oh dear, it's not just dirt. I'm afraid you've coloured up under the sun.'

'What did you say?' Maggie asked. 'My hearing was damaged with the blast.'

Jane bent to her ear. 'No matter. Now for a cool bath and a change of clothes for you.'

Then poor Michael had been dispatched to get a wash tub and lug water for a bath. He'd enlisted the help of the Kelly gang and then all the boys had been shooed away by his mother. Betsy had then gone to get Vera Olsen.

Jane had helped peel off Maggie's dress and chemise. When she attempted to take the purse on its string from around her neck, Maggie stopped her.

'I keep it on me all the time.' Then wrapped in a thin towel, Maggie stepped into the shallow bath. A sigh escaped her.

'You do look quite done in.' Jane handed her a thin bar of soap. 'Your fingernails are torn, you have lots of scrapes on your arms and legs. There's sunburn, and your clothes are ruined, and covered in twigs and dirt and such. I can wash your hair for you too.' She looked at Maggie's pained face. 'I mean, you are reasonably well despite it all, but what about food? How did you manage? Are you hungry?'

Maggie had slipped lower in the tub. It was cramped, but she was cool and scrubbing with the soap had started to melt away the dirt. 'Um, some people who live in the bush found me,' she said, not wanting to elaborate in case it would cause trouble for Nara and Wadgie.

'Goodness me, really? Black people?'

'White people.'

'In the bush? Though not surprising; this day and age I suppose there are a lot of folk in the scrub scraping out a living. It's why the government set up these villages,' Jane said. 'Doesn't appeal to everyone, though, I know. Mrs Wilson hates it here. Reckons she'd rather live in the bush. She nearly does, anyway.'

Maggie remembered the woman and her muntry jam. 'We had plenty of food. We ate fish, and berries.' She wondered where Nara might be now. Knowing her, she would be watching to see that Maggie wasn't about to be thrown into the scrub again.

Maggie finished in the bath. She dried off and Jane handed her a chemise, then a simple day dress. By the time Vera had arrived, Maggie was sitting on a chair, sipping tea, and Jane was leaning in the open doorway.

Vera sat opposite Maggie. 'What a delight to see you again. What you must have been through.' The older woman squeezed Maggie's hand. 'What say we look after you here for a bit then get you back to—'

'You have to get up a bit closer, Vera. Miss Lorkin seems to be deaf from the blast.' Jane had tapped both her ears.

'Oh dear, that's awful.' Then Vera had repeated herself loudly.

'That would be wonderful,' said Maggie. 'But I'll continue my journey downriver—if I can bear to step foot on another boat.'

'Of course. Such an ordeal. Those poor men.' Vera pressed her lips together a moment, then leaning closer said, 'As soon as we heard word of the explosion, some of the men searched but only found the remains of the boat. No bodies.' She had then looked as if she shouldn't continue, but she did. 'That was one reason why no one searched for you. Everyone assumed you were dead, too.'

'Oh, I see.' Maggie hadn't been sure if she was disappointed or not. Her brain had whirred. *No one looked for you.* But as soon as word got back to Renmark that she was alive, Maggie was certain someone would come looking for her—that awful man, or the police. In that case she'd better get on with things; no time to dilly-dally. 'I would be glad to buy a dress, and some under-clothes. My boots should still be good. I'd get on the first steamer to offer me passage. I only ask that if anyone from Renmark comes here after me, that you don't tell them I'm here, or when I go, my whereabouts.'

Vera had frowned. 'But my dear, if you have left loved ones worrying—'

'No one. There was an unsavoury character who'd made unwanted advances. I wanted to get away quickly.' Had she told a lie? Not really. Just omitted the 'I killed him' part.

Jane nodded. 'I'm sorry to hear that,' she'd said firmly. 'And you are quite right to ask our protection.'

Vera had looked stern. 'Now, listen to me, both of you. I think we should let someone know that Miss Lorkin is in fact alive and well.'

Jane had pushed off the doorjamb. 'Unless someone rides or walks to Renmark, we can't get word to anyone. The *Pearl* has just left for upriver, and I don't know what boats might be steaming back this way.'

Vera capitulated. 'You're right for the moment.' She looked at Maggie. 'If you would stay with Jane, as we have no quarters for single women here, you'll be quite safe until you can be on your way.'

Now Maggie remembered that Vera had enunciated her last few words quite clearly. Lying on the cot, she determined to do just that—be on her way. She fumbled to get her feet on the floor, then reached for the dress Jane had given her.

She was shrugging into it as the door opened and Jane looked in. 'You're awake, good. You've slept most of the day again, and I was beginning to get worried. I have tea when you're ready, and I'll help you to the privy.' She plonked two steaming cups on the table and went to help button Maggie's dress. 'Do you feel well enough to get out and about?' she asked, her voice raised.

'Of course. I think.'

'Get that into you, then,' she nodded at the tea, 'and I've found some lanolin to help with the sunburn. Your clothes are drying off out the back and won't take a jiffy. But you're welcome to that dress. You might need it for your new ventures.'

Maggie reached for her boots, and although without her hose at present, she slipped her feet in and began to lace. 'Thank you, but won't you need it?'

'I'm very good with my sewing needle. I make a lot of things for the children out of the flour sacks and such. Sometimes, there's enough left over to save and I should have a dress soon enough. Nothing fancy, mind. I'll find more fabric to make a better one when I can.' She gave a little laugh then sighed. 'With Teddy gone, I don't have money to buy new when the trading boats come.'

Maggie remembered the Teddy Thompson that Mr Bentley had not been so happy about. She stared at Jane. 'The settlement houses are for married men with families, and single men only, aren't they? How will you manage?'

Jane's cheeks coloured. 'I'm allowed to stay for a little while. But soon I will have to go to a women's refuge home somewhere. I will have to apply for a divorce.' Her voice cracked but she remained steadfast.

Maggie's mouth dropped open. 'Divorce? Can you even hope for such a thing? I thought only a man could do so.'

'That is why I was so interested in your plan.' Jane looked over her shoulder as if checking that no one else could hear and then, close to Maggie's ear, said, 'It seems that soon it will be law that I can apply to a magistrate if I have been deserted. Rather, if I can *prove* I have been deserted.' She shook a little. 'But until the law is passed, I have to prove he's been an adulterer *and* that I've been viciously beaten numerous times *and then* deserted. Except for the last bit, nothing of the sort has happened. Seems a lot for me to try to prove, when all he would have to do to divorce me is to cite my adultery. *Not* that I have been an adulterer,' she was quick to add. 'It seems unfair that I would've had to suffer all of that to obtain a divorce, when he needed only to suffer a blow to his ego. At least I can be spared all those horrible things when this new law takes effect.'

Maggie shook her head, frowning. 'I had no idea.' It was bewildering. Once the world had looked a safe place, but now it was likely never to feel that way for her again. *Once* it had looked a safe place ... when she'd been living with her family.

'And why would you have any idea? I've had to look at what is available to me now and not scurry about in terror for myself like poor Betsy has had to do, her husband gone as well.'

'Betsy?' Maggie had never known any abandoned women, and now she knew two.

'Yes. Her husband went to Renmark on a steamer and never came back. Left her with the children. I suppose I should be grateful now that I wasn't lucky enough to have had a family. How does anyone cope? So I hope it becomes law soon. I want to be able to fend for myself, and not be frightened every day for my life, or for my future. I might try and go downriver like you.'

'But why not stay here, where it seems safe?' Maggie asked. 'Where there are people who know you, and a number of single men, one of whom might one day—'

'Oh,' Jane said dismissively. 'There are plenty of single men, and some lining up, I might add. But I am freshly abandoned, so say the ladies, and it would be unseemly to attract attention as I'm still married. So I'm untouchable. Thankfully, if you know what I mean. I will never earn my keep on my back, though I know some poor women must.' She dusted down her dress, missing the bloom of colour on Maggie's cheeks. 'You see, I can't earn wages here, only earn like for like. For example, labour in exchange for food, and for lodgings in this house for a little while longer. This is a communalistic village, which means we're supposed to share everything we produce. We have a committee and a chairman to run the place but almost everyone believes the scheme has failed. So I must go.'

What sort of life would Jane have? What sort of life would Maggie, herself, have?

Jane gave a laugh. 'Don't look so worried. My family would say, "we told you so", and if I can't find refuge or a job, I'm sure they would take me back. Embarrassing for them—and for me, I suppose—but I know I'd have at least that. I have known of some women whose families did not want them back.'

Maggie thought of her own family. Would they even know she'd left Renmark? And once they found out what had happened …

Jane took a chair at the table. 'You got me thinking the other day. If I can be strong, and work and keep myself, I will be all right.' She frowned. 'It's just, I haven't worked out the old-age part of the plan, yet.'

Maggie's ears rang, but she'd heard that. 'Neither have I,' she said, and a short laugh followed. 'Perhaps a plan will come when the journey begins.'

'So,' Jane asked tentatively. 'You don't have a story like mine?'

Finding words hard to garner, Maggie shook her head.

'No beau, no courting man anywhere?'

'There was someone ages ago, but I thought he wanted too much from me.'

What had Sam wanted again? Just the normal things. Had he ever said he didn't want her to work, or to do the things she wanted to do? She shook her head more at herself than anything. Where had her thinking got so muddled up, believing he would tie her to the kitchen and to the cradle?

He didn't have to say anything, anyway. It was very much frowned upon for a married woman to take a job outside the home. And that brought her back to not wanting to be married.

Well, not yet.

Where had that come from?

But her brother wasn't like that—insisting that his new wife not keep her job. Admittedly, Linley didn't have to go outside the home to carry on her refuge work, as well as look after the house. So Sam probably wasn't like that either; he and Ard had been friends for all these years and were very like-minded.

Her father always said that there had to be a lot of talking, negotiating, and that whatever worked between two people was what made things run smoothly.

She squeezed her eyes shut. Too late to worry about it now, *Maggie O'Rourke. Ellie Lorkin.*

Jane mistook her frown and patted her hand. 'Then we should hope that our new vote releases us from the shackles of drudgery.'

'We should.' Maggie got to her feet. 'I need some fresh air, and a walk.' She reached around and grabbed the back of the chair to steady herself. 'Oh dear.'

Jane shook her head. 'I think you still have a touch of the sun. I'll walk with you in case you're a bit wobbly.' She looped her arm with Maggie's.

Out on the dusty paddock that seemed to be the town centre, a few people going about their chores had stopped to stare. The Kelly gang was once again roaming and they hooted and waved as they flew past Maggie and Jane. Betsy came out of a house shooing them away, and lifted her hand in greeting, only to retreat once again. Mrs Graham stood at the door of another hut and glared. Maggie wondered if it was her one and only expression. She could see Mrs Wilson foraging in the garden.

Once they'd returned to Jane's house, Vera was waiting for them at the back door. She followed them inside, appeared to be uneasy. 'I've been told that we're to have a meeting about you, Miss Lorkin,' she said, matter-of-fact.

'About me?' Maggie sat heavily on a sturdy seat. She had been dizzy for a time walking back to the hut. Jane had given her a bunch of gum leaves and, to avoid fainting, she flapped them in front of her face to cool off.

'You're a lone woman, a survivor come in from the bush after a boat disaster. The fact that you don't want to notify anyone of your whereabouts has sent an alarm signal through the committee members.'

'I see.' Maggie kept fanning.

Jane gaped at Vera. 'You've already met with committee members?'

'It's all over Lyrup that Miss Lorkin is here, and how she just wandered in from the scrub.'

Jane let out an exasperated breath. 'What on earth are they worried about, exactly?'

Vera sighed, and kept her eyes on Maggie. 'If there's to be any trouble, we—they don't want to be blamed for any wrongdoing.'

'How could they possibly think that?'

Maggie kept fanning. 'It's all right, really.' She looked at Vera. 'All I ask is that I can stay until the next steamer arrives and I can buy a passage.' Thank goodness for her little money purse, still safely about her neck. 'Will you let them know that? I'll be gone as soon as I can. But I would so appreciate no mention of me to others outside of the village.'

Vera tried again. 'That is the part that worries the men, Miss Lorkin. Is there something more we should know? Perhaps we could help.'

Maggie shook her head.

Vera looked at Jane, who also shook her head and shrugged. Then Vera said, 'It's going to be very difficult preventing the children from mentioning a stranger in their midst if someone was to—'

'I'm sure they'll forget me soon enough. I'll do my best to be gone as soon as possible.' And then Maggie had that sinking feeling, knowing things could really go badly wrong.

Vera pressed on. 'They've told me they're expecting a couple of freight boats sailing upriver tomorrow to take our produce to Renmark now the water has risen a little. Another one is due downriver day after, as well.'

'Perfect,' Maggie said, her heart in her throat. 'I'm sure I'll secure passage downriver.'

Jane, open-mouthed, looked from Maggie to Vera. 'And I just might try for passage as well,' she said and huffed loudly. 'After all, two single ladies travelling together would be much more appropriate, wouldn't you say, Ellie?'

Oh dear. Maggie wasn't sure she needed a companion. Then again, when she looked at the determined lift of Jane's chin, she agreed that two ladies travelling together were a lot less conspicuous than one. 'I agree.'

At least Jane could be her ears until they had properly healed, as she certainly hoped they would. Her stomach fluttered.

Twenty-two

Robert Boyd turned and stared into the late afternoon sun. He'd caught sight of that fella with the horse, and he'd been coming out of the wharf master's hut. One of them curly dogs had followed. Then the man mounted up and rode away, as if some sort of fury was chasin' him, the dog galloping on his heels.

He'd visit Barnaby Cutler, who thought himself some sort of wharf master. Cutler had set up in a hut and made ledger records of boats coming and going, so the old codger would know a thing or two.

Man has to have a horse. None of this flamin' bicycle rubbish anymore. He lumbered up the hill, careful to keep his back and neck rigid. If he forgot, the headaches returned with a vengeance.

He opened the door to see Cutler wiping his spectacles on his shirt tails.

'Was just closin' up, Robert. What can I do fer ye?'

'Young fella just in here—I asked him earlier today about wanting to buy his horse. You know where he was off to?'

Cutler slammed shut the big ledger. 'No idea.'

'What was he doin' in here? Picking up some freight, or wanting to buy a ticket somewhere?'

'His business, I reckon.' Cutler tucked the ledger under the desk.

Robert lowered his tone. 'Just that he said he'd have an answer for me by now. So, I'm lookin' to catch up with him, is all.'

Cutler eyed him from under eyebrows that were thick and wiry as if shot with steel. 'He was gone lookin' for a place to camp the night, and he said he'd go downriver. Other than that …' He let his voice drift.

Robert sniffed. 'Nothin' else?'

Cutler scratched his beard stubble and seemed annoyed. 'I dunno where he was goin'. We talked about me mate's steamer blowing up, about the passenger who mighta been on board. That's it.' He waved a hand at the door. 'Now, if you don't mind.'

Cogs and wheels turned in Robert's mind. The young fella had been headed to Olivewood when he'd seen him earlier in the day. Now he was asking about a passenger on the *Lady Goodnight*. Chances are that meant he could be looking for the O'Rourke girl. Maybe he was on the road to Lyrup. He might've heard the same thing about her being alive like that woman in the post office had gossiped to Angus. So maybe, just maybe, Robert should follow and find out for sure. He'd have to cross the river, but no big deal. There was always a steamer to take him one side to t'other. If the girl was alive, he'd finish her off. Maybe the young fella as well. He'd have himself a new horse at the same time. All for no expense.

Cutler was ushering him out the door.

Robert stalled. 'Barney, you got a horse, haven't you?'

Robert was on the back stoop stuffing a leather satchel. He'd grabbed a paper bag and filled it with a fresh lump of damper and a piece of last night's corned beef from the cookhouse. His wife would've served it again tonight, with white sauce, thickly sliced onion, and sprinkled with parsley, fresh from the garden tub. His mouth watered thinking of the meal, but he had other things to concentrate on.

'What are you doing?' Myra asked. 'It's barely gone dawn.' She wrapped her shawl over her nightdress and stood in the doorway, her thick ankles showing and her feet jutted into slippers.

'I know where I can get a horse. Is why I borrowed this nag of Cutler's yesterday.' He strapped the bag closed and headed for the gelding tied to Myra's clothesline. 'I have to leave now so I can still catch the man, bring the horse back with me and be back to open the store.'

'We don't need a horse,' Myra said. 'Angus says we can't afford a horse. The money all has to go back into the store.'

Robert slipped the bags over and attached them to the saddle. 'Angus gets paid wages. We don't. A horse makes us look like we're making a good living. It's all about the right image,' he said, grunting as he checked the girth was tight enough. The effort pained his neck and a throb hammered in his head. Damn. He thought he'd be past the pain of it by now.

'Is it, now?' Myra said, folding her arms. Her hair was capped but the mousy-brown tight curls had fallen out.

'It's an investment,' he said, and hauled himself into the saddle. 'And it's good to have a horse for the children. Teaches them respect for things—never too late, is it?' Everything was for Marcia, their daughter who acted like she couldn't tie her own bootlaces, and for Gregory, who was so gangly and awkward that his knees knocked. His children. So if he mentioned he'd be giving them something, he had his way. Being spoiled by their mother had been the ruin of them. When he looked at Myra, he wondered how he'd even begat his two children.

'Bit late for that now they're in their teen years,' she said. 'And who's to teach them this respect?' She raised an eyebrow.

Not now. Not now, Myra. He swung the horse's head. 'I'll be back before lunch.'

'You might want to go by the wharf today. Your last order from Mildura should be coming in for the store,' she called.

Robert forced out a breath between his teeth. How in hell would she know that? Snooping on his order book again, no doubt. But her nagging wouldn't stop until he gave in. 'All right. I'll make a quick detour and check.'

Myra watched him ride off. At least the hasty check of stock coming off the boat would slow him down. Just where was he going this time? She hadn't caught a hint of his usual behaviour when he was chasing down a woman—the furtive glances anywhere but at her. As if by looking at her she'd be able to tell that he was up to no good. The moody visage, the gazing into the fireplace until all hours, and the late-night jaunts. This time it seemed it was something different.

And a horse was required. *Well.* Although not a new whine of his, it appeared that the horse he'd found this time was a special one. Why else would he be on a borrowed mount and charging off at dawn? She could hardly take a clandestine ride after him—no transport.

Myra went back inside and shut the door. Leaning against it, she searched her mind for any hints over the last few days of what he might have been up to, something that she might have missed. There was nothing at all she could put her finger on. Since her visit to Olivewood had assured her that Miss Maggie O'Rourke had indeed disappeared, there'd been nothing to suspect he was plotting anything.

Pushing off the door, she headed for the room they used as a parlour. Inside, she withdrew her sewing box from under a chair and rummaged around. Her new trinket, a large hatpin, was still there. She would put it with the others under the bed, out of the way. Setting it aside, she pulled out a flask. A couple of sips of sherry before breakfast would see her right for the day, would take the edge off the demands of two lazy children, and a disappearing husband. Yesterday she'd gone a bit strong on the sipping, and most of the flask had been drunk before she realised. It'd been a very good thing no one had been home to see her wobble back and forth until the effects of the liquor had subsided. She wouldn't do *that* again but took another couple of sips for fortification. That done, she slipped the flask back under some mending and tucked the box under her chair.

In her room, she tossed the hatpin onto the unmade bed. She shrugged into her day dress, pulled it down over her chemise and studied her face in the little mirror on her dressing table. She didn't look so bad—not too many wrinkles, a sprinkle of grey in her hair. And she was only a little plump, really. Why did he have to stray?

It was his own fault they had no money, not hers. If he was any kind of man, he'd work hard to keep his family. Instead, he blamed her for tying him down, and so he womanised, getting back at her, she deduced. She'd always managed to find whichever woman held his interest at the time. As the aggrieved wife, she could be very damaging, and gossip could be cruel, so in exchange for her silence she'd demanded payment from the women. If that hadn't worked, she'd had another solution. Silly Adeline hadn't been as smart as she'd thought she was. Myra had fixed her.

Grabbing the hatpin, she bent to check under the bed for her house shoes. She also checked that the last woman's clean handkerchief was where she'd left it, tucked neatly into the springs. It hadn't been disturbed. She gave a certain piece of floorboard a tap, and when the hollow noise satisfied her, she pried it open and dropped in the hatpin. Good thing it was the size of a small knife. Very handy.

One day, when she really needed to, she might venture to sell more of the other baubles hidden there.

Twenty-three

A wet nose was nudging his elbow, and a whine followed. Bucky.

Sam cranked open an eye. Shit, was it the dead of night? But for a haunting glow of the moon just rising beneath the stars, it could have been any time. He'd dozed off at the tree stump. Groaning, he straightened up, his back protesting, stiff and sore, and now he was hungry. He figured that might have been the dog's problem, too.

Dogs fed themselves, didn't they? Bucky nudged him again. *Maybe not this one.*

Pie was standing close by, his silhouette clear. Sam groaned again and stretched his legs, heard the horse's nicker.

Right. All present and accounted for, but God only knew where he was—somewhere on the road to that settlement Lyrup, to pay his respects to Mr Finn, to the engineer whose name he forgot to ask, and to the unfortunate woman who'd been the passenger. He'd read the name of the poor girl—what was it again … Ellie? He couldn't remember. It wasn't Maggie, and that was all that mattered. After that, he didn't need to be around here. Didn't need to be in a place if Maggie wasn't in it.

As he got to his feet, he felt the kinks in his back and neck loosen. His stomach growled. Food. He'd still have plenty of what Miss Lucy had given him. Fumbling for the saddlebags, and Bucky bumping his hand, he pulled out a packet of something. Sniffed it. Cake.

'Not for you, dog,' he said. He reefed into the bags again and found some more jerky. 'There you go, boy.' Bucky snatched the dried beef and took off. Sam gulped the cake, bent and felt for the rum bottle.

He took a swig or two to wash it down. *Christ, awful bloody stuff.* His eyes watered. His throat burned. His gut warmed. A man would be singing well off-key if he swallowed any more of this, which was exactly what he did. He slumped back to the ground, bottle in hand. It might be better next go at it so he swigged, and nearly spat. It wasn't.

The songs didn't come. What point in singing if he couldn't find the girl he was looking for? Where to start looking? No one had sighted her. Which way would she have gone? He was sure she hadn't gone upriver into Victoria, and back to Echuca. Someone on the way would have reported seeing her—he'd asked many river people.

What point in singing if the girl he was looking for was never going to be found, was never coming back? He swigged some more, then pulled a face. *Lord above, the stuff didn't get any better.* But his gut had stopped growling and a soothing warmth crept through him.

Jesus, Maggie.

He stared up at the sky. It covered a big space and he was not even a dot on the landscape beneath it. How to find the one person he searched for, *longed for* in this vast country when any which way he turned could be the wrong way?

Find her and let her go—remember that, Sam Taylor. He swigged some more, but that was it. *Christ, laddie, pour the bloody stuff out.* He let the bottle rest in the dirt close by.

Bucky crept alongside him, and snuffled under his hand, crawled over to put his dusty woolly head in Sam's lap. His paws and belly were wet; seemed he'd been to the river for a drink. 'Good boy.' Sam absently patted the dog's head.

He'd search for Maggie, all right—he'd promised himself: *till his dying day, and right to the ends of the earth. Or whichever came first.* But yeah, he would let her go.

He lifted the bottle and peered at it in the low light of the moon. *Real rotgut, worst I've ever had. Hope my teeth don't fall out. My pa's rum is a top drop compared to this.*

'We got things to do, Bucky,' he said. The dog moved his head and settled again. 'We can't sit around all maudlin and cryin' in our rum. First, we need sleep, we got to be up at first light, got to get going to Lyrup and put that sad place behind us.' He stared at the sky. 'Then God only knows where to after that.'

One last swig before he tipped the remaining contents onto the dirt. *The stuff would burn a hole clear through to China.* He tossed the bottle and leaned back on the log. The dog shuffled and nudged for more pats. 'We'll find her, won't we, boy?' Bucky nodded on Sam's lap. 'Right answer, dog,' he said, and sat for a moment, letting his thoughts drift. Closing his eyes, he shuffled into a comfortable position. Bucky stayed with him, his wet paws across Sam's thighs.

Just don't think. Morning would come soon enough, and he had to be ready, even though his heart felt like a boulder that he'd have to lug with him for the rest of his life.

Maggie, Maggie.

Sleep, when it arrived, had come by stealth.

Twenty-four

Eleanor squeezed Lorcan's hand. He was restless again, and the frown on his face had deepened. Perhaps his pain had worsened after the laudanum had worn off. She thought he might have woken because of it but he hadn't yet, hadn't given any indication that he even knew she was there. Touching her fingertips to his forehead and his cheek for the hundredth time, she found no cause for alarm; no fever raged in him that she could tell.

Two weeks now. She couldn't make sense of this. If it wasn't a coma, what was it?

Sighing, she wiped her face and smoothed a flyaway tendril of hair back into the pins that held her bun. She reached across and took a sip of tea from the cup she'd brought with her earlier. Tea seemed to settle her, so much so that her reminiscences to Lorc were smooth-voiced and not troubled by the shakes with worry for Maggie.

No letter or telegram from Sam didn't mean anything. Eleanor just had to trust that he would find her, and that he'd bring her home. She suspected that he might have his hands full when he did. He'd looked so saddened to learn that she had disappeared.

Clearly, as Eleanor had long suspected, Sam still carried a torch for their Maggie.

Scooting her chair a little closer and settling by the bed, she lifted the covers to check that the splint on his leg was secure. Nothing looked out of place, no swelling or discolouration in his ankle or his foot. Satisfied, she leaned in further.

'I'm here again, my beloved,' she whispered. 'I've no doubt you'll be sick of me well enough and wake up soon to tell me so.' Taking one of his hands in both of hers, she realised the thick calluses on his palms were softening. How Lorc would hate that. She traced her fingers over them. She'd never known a day when those hands, roughened and stained with the dirt of the land, hadn't kept her safe, kept her children safe.

She looked at his face, and then watched the low rise and fall of his chest. Remembered when he'd first touched her. How the thrill of that moment hadn't dimmed after all these years. He'd slid a hand down her cheek and rested it on the nape of her neck. It was as if everything he had been offering her was in that touch.

She lifted his hand to her cheek and held it there, closed her eyes to summon the memories of those early, heady days in Bendigo.

'Do you remember the first dance you took me to?' she murmured into his hand. 'Well, you called it a dance, didn't ye? A mere jig with your brother and his mates and their girls, in the paddock behind old Mr Ah Lim's cabbages.' Eleanor smiled and pressed her lips to the warm skin. 'It was a night of magic for me, Lorcan O'Rourke, watching you step-dance. Watching the proud Irish ye are on show for all the world to see and listenin' to Billy Byrne piping on his flute.' She breathed in the scent of his soap, fragranced with citrus and cinnamon, that Maggie had sent from Renmark. She'd used it to bathe him.

Maggie. She squeezed her eyes closed.

'Well, enough our Ard was born not a year after that night, but you canna forget when our little Mairead popped into our world.' Eleanor heard her whispered Gaelic pronunciation, *Mawr-aid*—tentative, rusty, but alive with the soft burr of the old country. They'd been on the orchard and planting seedlings when Eleanor's labour had descended. Ard was a toddler of three years, asleep in the cart.

'Lorc, I think there's enough time to get to the house.' A contraction had crushed deep inside. Her back was turned to him, her foot already on the step of the cart as she tried to climb up, her dress high. She felt the head crown and she went down to the dirt on her knees. 'Maybe not. Help get me into the back—'

'Jesus, Mary and Joseph,' Lorc had shouted from behind her. 'It's too late for that, Ellie. This bairn is comin' out quicker than it got in.'

Even now, Eleanor laughed at that. Lorc was *never* quick when there was lovin' to do. There was nothing fast about that. Never had been, and these days it was still a slow dance to pleasure that ever made her heart sing.

'It's not funny, Lorcan O'Rourke,' she'd squeezed out, barely able to breathe. Bearing down with one almighty push, her daughter arrived in a slippery rush, right into Lorc's big hands.

'Born on the earth, Ellie. Will ye look at this beauty?' He'd crawled to her with the wet baby in his arms and the tears streaming down his face.

Now she whispered into his hand. 'You remember the mop of her black hair, and the squall she let out the moment you caught her? And she's never been any different, our Maggie, has she? Always loud, always right, always quick and determined. But with a heart as big as this country.' She swallowed down her fear, which was a great lump in her throat and a mountain in her chest.

'Always of the land, born in the dirt. So she knows where her home is, that she does.'

She will come back. Eleanor saw a tear drop on his hand and she smartly wiped it off, angry at herself. Hadn't realised she was weeping.

Sniffing quietly, she rubbed his hand between hers. 'Remember when you first taught her to ride? She took to it better than Ard, and on that old mare we had, old Mossy. And didn't she look grand, our little bairn, could barely reach the stirrups but proud as punch, until she realised she couldn't get down.' Eleanor smiled. 'She just sat there and yelled until poor Mossy took her to the rails and our little girl climbed off, all dignified.'

There were many memories of Maggie. Her heart pounded. *I want my daughter back.*

'And the time we found her down by the creek, when she was seven, teaching herself to swim. D'you remember that, Lorc? Of course, you do. Terrified both of us. In you waded.' She gave a laugh. 'But she yelled and yelled until you taught her how to float, then taught her how to swim.'

Taking in a deep breath to stem the tears, Eleanor went on. ''Course, now she's up by the Murray, she won't attempt swimmin' in that. Fiery and stubborn, she is, but she's not silly, is she, Lorc, our daughter?' She stared at his face. He looked calm except for that small frown again.

Where was he? Was he thinking, or dreaming?

She sat back. She knew he'd wake sometime. And she wanted to be able to tell him that his daughter had come home to them.

Twenty-five

Maggie had managed to avoid the stares of most of the ladies, and the pointing fingers of the children. With Jane's help, they'd let it be known that she was still poorly but that today, she would meet the boat due to sail downriver and buy passage. If she could. She crossed her fingers.

She thought that her hearing was a little better but wondered if it was just her imagination. When Jane burst back into her hut and crooked her finger, shouting, 'There's a boat coming,' Maggie had not been hard of hearing.

She clapped her hands together—Jane's excitement was catching. Then she slipped the handle of her bag over her head and shoulder. 'I'm as ready as I can be, Jane.'

Jane went to Maggie and clasped her hands in hers. 'I will come too. I will pay my passage as far downriver as I can and hope that perhaps we can find work together, so I can earn more money to keep travelling.' She pulled Maggie to her feet. 'Come on. Let's go outside and down to the wharf. We'll show all these folk that we're leaving and not staying to entice their poor men with our wiles being single females.'

Maggie would have found that funny in weeks past.

Outside, strong daylight watered her eyes. She tugged her bonnet a little lower and followed Jane to the banks of the river. Sure enough, there was a steamer and they went to investigate further.

'It's the *Jolly Miller*, and a little beauty,' Jane said when she came back to Maggie, who was sitting nearby under the shade of a tree. 'Not sure it looks big enough to take us on any overnight fare; it's not a passenger boat by the look of it, but I'll enquire of the captain when they finish unloading. They're usually accommodating if needs arise. He's busy now, arguing with a man on board with a horse trying to disembark first.' Jane turned back to the boat and shaded her eyes as she watched the men unloading. 'You think the captain would want the horse off first. Oh, I don't know about these things. In any case, if there's room for man and horse, there should be room for us, don't you think? Even if we only get down as far as Pyap.' She turned to look at Maggie. 'Ellie, did you hear me?'

Maggie was on her feet staring in horror at the man on the boat, the one holding the reins of his horse. He stared back.

Without a sound, and shrinking against the tree, she rounded its trunk, clutching her bag. Two thoughts clanged in her head. The first was that he was alive—*alive!* How could that be? She'd clobbered him so hard and he'd gone down like a sack of potatoes. Nara had declared him dead. How could it be him? But there he was, the great lumbering toad, complete with blackened eyes—and how could that still be the case after all this time?

That meant she wasn't a murderer. Thank God. The second thing was that he'd seen her. Dear God. *Maggie, run …*

Alarmed, Jane followed. 'What is it?'

Maggie just shook her head, stuck fast.

'You're worrying me.' Jane reached out and touched Maggie's arm.

'I have to run for the privy,' Maggie said, breathless, as she gathered her skirt with one hand, clutched her bag with the other and took off at full speed up the slight incline towards the houses. She didn't look back to see if Jane had run after her, and ran straight past the closest privy into the scrub far over beyond the vegetable garden. *Dear God, dear God, it was him. It was* Boyd. *He's found me.*

Think, girl. Think. Get far away from here. She ran on, crashing through the low scrub. *No. Wait, wait.* She slowed a moment. *Well, don't stop, stupid girl, keep running just don't go too far away. Stay close to the water.* She veered back towards the river, reckoning she was perhaps a little north of the village.

Was Nara still close by? No, no, she and Wadgie would have gone home by now, believing her to be safe.

Maggie didn't have the strength to keep running this time and felt the sun sap her energy. Oh God—but what had she done by running? Why had she not just quietly led Jane away, kept low and out of sight until he'd gone? That mightn't have been any good either. He could have found out from anyone that there was a lone female in town, the survivor of the boat blast. It would have been easy to find her.

Dammit, dammit, dammit. Oh, there was Sam in her head again. *Dammit.*

Oh dear—was that Jane behind her, calling? She wasn't sure, wasn't sure—her blasted ears still betrayed her.

She slowed her run and tried to breathe deeply as best she could. One hand clutched her bag. As she ran, her bonnet slipped from her head, luckily still tied under her chin. In the distance, she caught a fleeting glimpse of a man on a horse, and thought she heard more noises, short and sharp …

Oh no, no. Maybe Boyd had followed her from the wharf after all, was on her heels and bellowing at her. She bent low and scampered to a line of straggly bushes, ducking and weaving her way around them, and headed for a stand of gums that likely would be at the water's edge.

That's odd, she thought. It struck her that this rider was coming from the other way. Had Boyd cut in front of her somehow? That other noise she'd heard—could that have been a dog barking? *Dear Lord*. She couldn't trust her ears. It could have been anything.

Perhaps there was another track he'd taken if someone from the village had seen her running and pointed her out to him. She should look for that track when the danger passed. Maybe it would lead her away from here as well, and to safety elsewhere.

Poor dear Jane. Whatever would she think?

Maggie O'Rourke, get to the river. And for God's sake, stay low, and keep your eyes peeled—your ears are still next to useless. Then think about your next move.

Twenty-six

Well, well, well. Robert Boyd hefted himself into the saddle once he and the horse were on dry land. He'd seen her, all right. He'd know her anywhere. There she was, running up the hill and into the town. Another woman had followed.

The O'Rourke woman had seen him and recognised him, that's for sure. *Fancy that. A man comes looking for a decent horse to go hunting and finds the chit who's assaulted him right here. No need to go hunting much further now.*

He kicked the horse into a gallop, ignoring the curses and the yells aimed at him to 'slow up' as he charged up past great stacks of hewn timber. Kids—brats—leapt out of his way and women waved their fists at him. No matter to him; he'd even had to shout at the boat captain to hurry up and let him off. He'd waste no time on pleasantries now that he'd seen her scurrying up the riverbank.

'Don't think ye'll be gettin' back on board, mate,' the captain had yelled after him as Robert had finally coaxed his spooked horse off the gangway. 'Don't want the likes o' you, ye rude bastard.'

No matter to that, either. After he'd done what he'd set out to do, Robert would just amble on home to Renmark, feeling pretty good with himself.

Despite his impatient yells at the captain at the Lyrup landing, by the time he'd been able to get off the boat, the O'Rourke tart had disappeared. He headed into the village as fast as the sorry horse could take him, only to be slowed up by another group of brats who were running zig-zag across his path.

Boyd slewed to a halt. 'Boy,' he barked at one of the them. 'Did you see a woman running this way?' He wheeled the horse about as the boys stopped.

Five faces stared up at him. A kid with his hand bandaged brandished a stick. 'Kelly gang don't dob on no one,' he shouted fiercely.

'I'll give you bloody Kelly gang, you mongrel kid.' Boyd reached down and whacked the stick out of the boy's hand. All at once, three of them squawked and pointed in separate directions. The other two boys pointed back to the boat. Growling, Boyd swiped at thin air as the boys split up and darted off full pelt, each going their own way, and yelling like there was no tomorrow.

Bloody kids. He sat up straight and looked ahead. Looked around. There was no sign of her. He kicked the horse and belted into the open paddock. After galloping past the few timber houses and a few tents on its boundaries, he spotted a track leading off and hurtled onto it and into the scrub beyond.

Twenty-seven

On Barney Cutler's advice to flag a steamer, Sam had picked his way down to the river's edge before first light, figuring he wasn't far from where he needed to be, and waited. Just after dawn, he heard the low chug of a steamer coming downriver. He waved, and Bucky barked for attention. Sam saw a crewman wave back and the boat edged over. After a small exchange, Sam led Pie on board, and the dog followed. The captain said they'd pre-arranged to take cut timber on board a little further down on the other side just shy of Lyrup, and that's where Sam decided he'd disembark. He'd wanted time to plan what he was going to do, and landing directly at the village wharf did not sit well on him. His sense of foreboding had surprised him and he didn't like it. He'd tried to shrug it off, wondered why he couldn't.

Now he'd been in the saddle long enough and Sam reckoned he must have been close to this Lyrup village place. He'd kept Pie at an easy pace since crossing the river, and the track had been reasonable most of the way.

Bucky had kept up, darting off here and there, only to belt back alongside when he felt like it. Sam liked the dog; he always seemed to be grinning, and when he wasn't, his big gold eyes looked all doleful. He was a thinker, was Bucky. He had to be—he'd taken to Sam. Still, the dog hadn't heard him sing yet. Now that would be the test of a good dog.

His ma had said that he'd had an Irishman's folk tenor. His pa just thought he was a carousing bloody git who got all maudlin with a few grogs. Then he'd always ruffled Sam's hair with affection. Maggie … well, Maggie seemed to be enthralled by the one tune he'd sung her, time and again. 'Black Is The Colour Of My True Love's Hair'—he'd changed the lyrics around to suit a man singing it to a woman. She hadn't cared if the song was from Scotland, England, Ireland or America, she'd said, just that he sang it for her. She said he had a lilting, poignant voice. When she reached over and placed her hands either side of his face to kiss him full on the mouth, he figured that lilting and poignant were good things.

Bucky flew into doing his round-and-rounds and barked. Pie threw his head a couple of times shying and snorting, and stepped quickly, unsettled. Maybe they were near the town, after all.

Sam heard a voice, a female voice calling, 'Ellie … *Ellie*.'

Bucky went wild, barking and charging off through the scrub. Sam waited, murmuring in Pie's ear, staring into the scrub, trying to locate the owner of the voice.

Then he heard a shrill, 'Get away from me, dog. Get away,' and Bucky's excited yips.

Sam called for the dog, gave a sharp whistle and all went quiet. He sat high in the saddle, twisted to see behind him, but nothing appeared. Bucky was silent. Now, what would that mean? He hardly knew the dog. He swung back, surveying the terrain as Pie danced beneath him.

'Whoa, boy,' he said, soothing the horse with a couple of solid pats. 'It's just a lassie callin' in the bush, and our dog is off lookin' for her.' He whistled once more, and this time Bucky came hurtling towards him, looking happy as a lark. He skidded around Pie and took off again, dust and twigs churning in his wake.

Baffled by the dog's behaviour, Sam stretched in the saddle but still couldn't see anyone. He called out, 'Are you lost, miss? My dog won't hurt you.'

'I'm not lost,' he heard behind him.

He twisted again and saw a young, slim woman walking swiftly towards him from a line of scrub. She was slapping at Bucky who looked as if he was trying to make friends.

'Lyrup village is only over there,' she said, pointing, and seemed out of breath. She brushed a hand over her face and tucked loose tendrils of hair under her hat. Again, she shooed Bucky away. He immediately sat, and stared up at Sam.

'Morning, miss.' Sam tipped his hat. Perhaps, being local, she could save him some time. 'Lyrup's where I'm headed. Or, I'm headed through there, to find where that boat blew up and pay my respects. If you know, how far it is from here?'

The woman stared at him, still catching her breath. She glanced over her shoulder and then back to him. She almost looked blank, or maybe she was thinking hard. How the hell would he know?

'Miss?' he prompted.

'Go straight into the village—' she pointed again, her voice firm, '—and go down to the landing. Someone there will tell you where the boat blew up. It's not too far riding, perhaps half a day.' She checked over her shoulder again, her dark brows wrinkled with worry. Other than that, she stood rigid, not moving.

A little puzzled by her, Sam asked, 'You were calling out. If you're not lost, is someone else lost, maybe a child? Can I help you?'

'No. Was a game, only,' she said, dismissing it with a wave of her hand. 'Ridiculous in this midday heat,' she said and pointed again. 'The village is that way.'

Bucky began whining and stamping his front feet as he sat, still staring up at Sam. Nudging Pie forwards, Sam touched his hat again. 'Thank you, Miss—'

'Mrs Thompson.'

He nodded at her as he passed, and Bucky followed.

'And your name, sir?' she asked.

'Sam Taylor, ma'am, from up Echuca.' Sam stopped Pie and leaned towards her a little. Might as well ask everyone he came across. 'A friend of mine is lost. There was a chance she could have got on a boat at Renmark, to go downriver. Heard anything of that?'

Mrs Thompson's eyes darted back and forth before she answered. 'I'm sure we would have heard something. We sometimes have the passengers stop for tea if a steamer ties up for the night here.' She held a wide-eyed grey gaze on his. 'What's your friend's name?'

'Maggie,' he said, and Bucky did a sudden whirl and stopped. 'Maggie O'Rourke.'

Mrs Thompson gave a hint of a smile. 'No one by that name.'

'Well,' Sam said, disappointed, though he knew it was too far a stretch to expect that finding Maggie would be so simple. 'If it wasn't my friend on that boat, then I'm grateful for it. Sad story for the lost crew, though, and I knew the captain, met him a few times. Sad for the passenger, for her poor family.' He thought of Eleanor and Lorcan.

Mrs Thompson nodded. 'It is.'

She kept looking around and Sam straightened, figuring she wanted to get on. The sweat dripped from under his hat, and the blaring sun was getting to him. It would have been bothering her, too. 'I'd better get going, Mrs Thompson. Can I walk you back to the village?'

'Thank you, no. I know my way around. I'm sure I won't be long.'

'Good day.' Sam nudged Pie into a slow walk, leaving her to play her game in the bush.

Across the expanse of scrub, he saw another rider in the distance, heading away. Maybe that fella was on the track Sam would have to take to find the destroyed boat. He was so close now to where it had exploded. Suddenly he wondered why he still had to go there. He shrugged. He was so close, he might as well. Maybe something would come to him there in the silence on the riverbank, and he'd take a new direction to try and find Maggie. Who knows? Or maybe on his way through the village, he'd speak to someone who'd say something, and his brain would click and whir … Or maybe, after finding the boat site, and putting it to rest in his mind, he'd retrace his steps and head back upriver and search for Maggie on more familiar territory. Wouldn't she stay close to places she knew?

He made up his mind. He'd go to the site of the explosion first. From there, anyone's guess. He took one last quick look at Mrs Thompson as she trudged back into the line of scrub. She was heading for the river. No matter; it seemed she knew what she was doing. He stayed on the track, and Bucky kept up beside the horse, his tongue lolling.

As the houses in the village came into view ahead, Sam heard Mrs Thompson's voice as she called for her friend again. 'Ellie. Miss Lorkin … Ellie.' Her voice drifted.

This Ellie Lorkin must be well and truly hiding …

Sam hauled on the reins. *Am I such a flamin' idiot?* He remembered the wharf master's log entry: *Miss Ellie Lorkin, passenger on the* Lady Goodnight. He turned so fast in the saddle trying to catch a glimpse of Mrs Thompson that the horse faltered. Sam squinted hard but couldn't see her.

Ellie. Miss Lorkin. Ellie Lorkin. Eleanor. Lorcan.

Maggie.

Twenty-eight

Eleanor had just put her tea cup down on the bedside table. She sat and rested a moment before attempting a sip. It needed to cool before she could try to get some into Lorc.

Her glance flicked to his face and she noticed the same slight frown. Then his mouth twitched, and the frown deepened. She watched a moment more, and leaned towards him, trying to catch anything that would give her an inkling as to what might be happening with him.

Nothing. The twitch settled, and so did Eleanor, letting a sigh escape. She picked up her cup and blew into it, then tested it against her lip. Still too hot. She set it down again, straightened the bedcovers a little and caught the sound of his swift intake of breath.

Startled, she stared at him, but she saw nothing anew on his face. The frown hadn't deepened any more. Dear Lord, was she starting to imagine things? Taking his hand in hers, its warmth heartening, she closed her eyes to think of some other memory to bring to him. These last days with Maggie on her mind, relating something to her husband of their daughter soothed her.

She hoped her beloved Lorcan could hear her, and be soothed by it, too.

'Remember that time, Lorc, when Maggie and her little Chinese friend Mee Ling were down in the orchard. Maggie always managed to find friends that were different folk. A Bendigo winter, it was. Do you remember?'

She didn't expect an answer and kept talking. 'We went looking for them, they'd missed coming in for lunch—ten, or eleven years old, they were. We'd had a hard enough time convincing Mr Ling that his daughter would be safe with us, and we thought we'd gone and lost her, lost both of them. But no, there they were playing happy as anything down by the water channel, fresh dug. Just a boggy hole it was, down one side of the paddock. It had been raining for days, hadn't it?' Eleanor pressed his hand to her face, cupping her cheek. 'Little mites. They both looked like they'd been rolling in the mud.'

She smiled into his palm, kissed it. 'Then into the mud you go, bellowing like a big old bull, and grab up your daughter.' A laugh escaped. 'Only it wasn't our Maggie you grabbed, was it? It was poor Mee Ling. Frightened the life out of her. They'd changed their jackets and their hats, and we couldn't tell one from the other, both black-haired little girls with plaits.' She gave his hand a little shake. No response. 'Then we had to cajole Mee Ling inside to get her washed up and dry before sending her back to her father. That was a job, Lorc.'

She stared at his face as his mouth twitched again. Could he hear her, after all?

She went on. 'I wonder whatever happened to Mee Ling, my love? I used to see her brothers—they were all grown lads by the time we'd left—but not her. Perhaps her family sent her back to China. 'Twas a shame if so, but Maggie said naught about it.'

Lorc's hand was hot and damp now. Eleanor took it away from her face and looked at it. Then with a glance at his face, she saw that sweat had popped on his forehead in tiny bubbles. Lorcan moved, grunted, and now the frown was deep on his face. His mouth opened, and his breathing had become rapid. Her heart gave a thud. Resting his hand on the bed, she drew back, shoved the chair away and stood.

'Oh, God,' she cried softly and pulled back the light cover over his leg. It looked hot, and the bandages over his shin now looked too tight. Gingerly, Eleanor peeled back an edge, and saw his skin was red. Streaks of colour were shooting up into his knee. Dear God, no.

She'd have to find Ard. *Hurry.* He'd have ride into town to bring the doctor. She turned …

Ard burst inside, his face creased with worry. 'Ma, quick. It's Linley. She's on the floor of our house. I can't move her, she's screamin' with it, says the baby's coming.' Then he glanced from her face and stared at his father's bandaged leg. 'Oh, Jesus.'

Twenty-nine

Maggie sat tight—hidden, she hoped—from that horrible man, Boyd. Her ears couldn't be trusted, so it was best that she stayed quiet, and low down and out of the way, but in a place where she could still see clearly. That didn't seem to be working out; she was by the river and couldn't see on top of the bank. She hoped that he wouldn't think to come over this way and find her.

He was alive and had come after her. Why after all this time? Two weeks, wasn't it? Had someone seen her leaving and told him which way she'd travelled? Surely, being alive, he wouldn't be bothered looking for her, but there he was, large as life. And here she was in little old Lyrup, not half a day's journey by road from Renmark, the place where she'd thought she'd killed him. All the running, all the trouble she'd been through, and he was alive … Then she spared a thought for Mr Finn and Mr Bentley and bit her lip. She was grateful. Those two men had helped her. Mr Finn had put her ashore and had saved her life by doing so.

A noise … a voice. Female. Was it Jane? It must be, but Maggie dared not leave her hiding place to check. Damn her hearing. She strained and heard the faint melodious call. Felt sure it was Ellie being called. With her hands on the trunk of the tree ready to make a dash for it if she needed to, eyes wide, she saw Jane pop into her line of sight.

'Ellie? Where are you?'

Peeking out from behind the tree, Maggie couldn't see anyone else nearby. Furtive, she blew a low whistle, and waved an arm.

Jane came slipping and sliding down the bank, trying to keep her balance. Maggie stepped out from the tree to grab her and when their hands clamped on each other's forearms, they steadied.

'Jane, Jane. That man. He tried to do me and my friend grave harm, back in Renmark, and I cannot be anywhere near him.'

'The man—off the boat?'

'Yes, the man off the boat.' *How odd she should ask that.* Maggie still had hold of Jane's arms. 'How do we get away from here now? Should we go on foot somewhere, or try to get back to the boat and hide on board?'

'Hide?' Jane looked blank, then worried. 'Um … back this way,' she said and pointed along the river's edge. 'We will come up on the landing from behind the boat, but the riverbank is flat and wide open, nowhere to hide. Perhaps we'll be lucky and no one will stop—'

'Maggie O'Rourke!'

Maggie heard a man's voice yell her name, but her hearing was still woolly, her ears ringing. She glanced at Jane. 'It must be him,' she rasped and stumbled over the soft sand of the bank as she ran in the direction Jane had pointed.

'Ellie, wait,' Jane called, lagging behind her. 'That man …'

Maggie wasn't waiting. She just had to get away from Robert Boyd.

Sam wheeled Pie around, but Mrs Thompson was nowhere to be seen. Which way had she gone? There was only one place to stay out of sight and that was to get to low ground, on the river's edge. He nudged Pie along the way they'd just come, then veered towards a line of straggly trees.

Bucky started to bark as he ran alongside the horse. *No sneaking up on Mrs Thompson now, that's for sure.*

He called out, 'Mrs Thompson, I need to talk to you again. It's urgent.' He could barely hear his own voice over the thundering boom of his heartbeat, over Pie's slow canter and Bucky's excited woofing as he searched the scrub.

Before the land dropped away to the edge of the water, Sam hauled up his horse, but Bucky leapt down the gently sloping sand and charged into the water, barking and carrying on, well pleased with himself. He splashed out of the river again and gave a huge shake, spraying water in a wide arc. Then he stopped and put his nose in the air. He stared a moment at Sam, made half barking, half crying noises, as if he were hankering after something before he took off along the river, hot on a scent, back in the direction of the village.

Maggie could see the boat up ahead and slowed, glancing around.

Jane was coming along behind and waved her hand when she noticed Maggie looking.

'Thank goodness. Will you stop a moment? I'm so out of breath,' she said when she caught up. 'I don't know that trying to get on this boat is the right thing to do after all. We won't be hidden from sight really—just look at it, it's not very big. And we'll have to beg and plead with the men now we're in such a rush. I'm sure that'll make them suspicious.' She put her hands on her knees and leaned over, breathing deeply. 'I understand you fear this man, but couldn't the authorities do something about him? We don't have much in the way of law enforcement in the village, but we could alert the chairman, Mr Wainwright.'

Maggie had been staring at the *Jolly Miller.* A medium-sized side wheeler, it had a top deck through which the chimney stack poked and where the open-air wheel was attached. It looked to have a wide walk-through under that. There were closed-off areas she could see, rooms of some sort, only narrow, so not a lot of space. When she'd first seen the boat, a stack of cut timber was on the foredeck and Boyd's horse had been close to that. Where on earth could she and Jane hide on it?

A noise distracted her, something from behind, coming from where they'd just been—a dog, barking. She turned to look and there was a sturdy liver-coloured bundle of grinning energy hurtling towards her.

Jane turned as well. 'Oh, good Lord—there's that dog.' She took a few steps back. 'He's with a man riding in from Renmark, who says the dog's harmless but … Ellie? Are you all right? Ellie?'

Bucky. Maggie's heart missed a beat. It looked like Bucky tearing towards her, with his big dog-grin and his tongue hanging out. It looked just like Bucky. How could that be? And then he launched at her.

Jane shrieked.

Maggie went down on the dirt, her backside hit hard and her head bounced a little in the sand. The dog sat on her, snuffling and licking her, leapt off and went into round-and-rounds and back again. He charged off and grabbed a stick and brought it back, standing over her as she counted stars in front of her eyes.

Jane dropped to her knees out of the dog's way. 'Are you all right, Ellie?'

Maggie nodded at her, couldn't speak just yet. She was sort of laughing. Sobbing too, but happily. 'Bucky,' she gasped, and scratched his neck. 'My dear friend, how did you find me?'

She felt tears close. Would Nara and Wadgie have had time to come back from Renmark to check on her? She held Bucky off with one hand and wiped dirt and sand and twigs from her face with the other.

The dog dropped the stick on her chest, very pleased with himself. He nudged her a couple of times, shuffled back and forth and nudged her again. Then he spun around and, standing stiff and alert, gave two robust barks in the direction he'd come. He began to back up over her, barking again.

Maggie's ears rang with it as she struggled to get up onto her elbows. Pushing Bucky out of her way, Jane helped with an arm under her shoulders. Then the bony knees and the deep chest of a horse appeared in front of them.

Jane squeaked. The dog stopped barking and got onto his belly beside her. Looking up, Maggie's breath caught at the sight of the man who leaned over the saddle, staring down at her.

Bucky growled low, a rumbling sound from his chest.

'Look who I found. If it isn't Miss Maggie O'Rourke,' the man drawled.

The dog launched at Maggie, and down she went. If Sam hadn't been searching for her, if he hadn't been tearing out his own heart at letting her slip by him, he would have laughed aloud.

There she was, large as life, sprawled on the dirt. *Alive.* And well, by the looks of things—apart from a dog sitting on her. She wasn't burned or singed. Jesus, his heart was singing at that. Her face was a little browned from the sun, more than he remembered, and she looked thinner, like she needed a good feed. He liked her better with curves.

Stop thinkin' of that, Sammy-boy.

So there she was, flattened on the riverbank, with the stocky dog going all stupid over her, bringing her a stick and beating the dirt around her with his big nimble paws. Sam knew exactly how Bucky felt, the dog had just beaten him to it.

He stayed mounted on Pie, breathing deep and low and leaning over the saddle, watching her. The fire building in his belly wasn't going to crackle him to cinders, nor was he going to let the welling emotion deep in his chest rise to choke him. He had the strangest notion to jump down off Pie, pick her up and … and he didn't know what. What would he do? Grab her? Hug her? Kiss her? Hold her close and rock her hard against him, saying prayers of gratitude he'd forgotten to a god he didn't remember, thankful that she was safe?

He set his mouth and didn't let a muscle move on his face for fear it would splinter into shards and he'd never be able to pull himself together.

So he stared down at her and said, 'Look who I found. If it isn't Miss Maggie O'Rourke.'

She stared back, those blue eyes wide. 'Sam.'

He never thought he'd hear her say his name again, and all breathy like that—as if maybe she was pleased to see him. It was all he could do not to grin like an idiot.

Bucky growled again, his keen yellow stare on Sam. His tail thumped twice in the dirt.

'It's all right, Bucky,' Maggie said. 'It's Sam.' Her voice shook.

The dog eyes stayed on Sam all the while.

'Have you forgot me that quick, dog?'

Jane tugged at Maggie and sat her upright in the dirt. Then together they got her to her feet. 'Mr Taylor, is this your Maggie O'Rourke?' She still had Maggie by the arm and looked a bit put out.

He nodded, and when his voice would allow, said, 'It is.'

Maggie gripped Jane's hand. 'I'm so sorry for the deception, Jane. That other man, he's chasing me, and I had to—'

Jane let go of Maggie's arm and held up her hand. 'Excuse me,' she said, and folded her arms over her chest. Her mouth set and her head down, she walked way.

Maggie watched with a look of despair as Jane headed back to the village. Then her flashing blue eyes, now bleak, looked back at him. 'Sam, I'm so glad you're here. I've done something … I did something. I thought I'd—'

'What other man?' Sam demanded.

Her heart skipped a beat as she gazed over his face. The dark golden whiskers shaded his chin and darkened the hollows of his cheeks. The hazel eyes she'd remembered as merry and warm were stern. He was no longer lean and rangy like he had been when she'd left; he was more filled out, muscle had bulked his frame. She had to look away.

Well, that only lasted a moment—she had to look back at him. The familiar tufts of hair on his chest poked through the open neck of his shirt, like they always used to do, and right now she wanted to slide her fingers … But he seemed different, now. Distant. He looked different, too, not just the physical, but she couldn't—

'What other man?' he repeated, clipped, terse.

If he wasn't *at least* going to be friendly … *Don't be daft, Maggie O'Rourke.* There could be only one reason why he was here—it was to find her. News must have reached home that she'd gone missing.

'Mairead?' he prompted loudly.

Sounding like he was the boss. Oh, that annoyed her. She glared and said, all matter-of-fact, 'A man by the name of Robert Boyd.'

She brushed herself down and glanced around. Boyd was nowhere in sight, but that didn't mean anything. If Sam was just going to sit on that horse of his—the beautiful softie, Pie, she remembered—and act as if he'd only seen her yesterday, she would have to get on with things herself.

Adjusting her hat and brushing more dirt off her dress, she said, 'I really have to get out of sight.'

Rattled by his aloof stare, Maggie turned towards the *Jolly Miller* and, as best she could in the soft sand of the bank, marched towards the boat. She couldn't hear anything behind her, so didn't know if Sam was following or not. Bucky kept close to her side. As she got nearer the *Jolly Miller*, she saw a man waving at her, saying something. He stepped off the gangway.

'What did you say?' she asked. 'I'm afraid my hearing is not so good.'

'I said, are you all right, miss?' He spoke louder. 'We was unloadin' and seen you before, runnin' up that way with Miz Jane, and then that big bloke who was on here with his horse tore off after ye.'

Maggie's heart was thudding so hard that her head hurt. 'I'm all right, but I need passage downriver,' she said, her mouth dry. 'If only to the first stop. I can pay.'

Before he'd even answered, she walked right by him and stepped on to the gangway, her hand reaching for her little purse snug under her dress. She took the last steps onto the deck and Bucky leapt on board with her.

Out of the corner of her eye, she saw that Sam, still on Pie, was at the gangway. Her racing pulse sped up. He dismounted, seemed to be in no hurry.

'I have to talk to you, Maggie,' he called, throwing the reins over Pie's neck. 'Get off the boat.'

The steam engine rumbled to life, and its low chug throbbed underfoot. The man who'd been unloading freight raised his voice at her. 'Ah, the cap'n might not want you on—'

A terrified shriek sounded from further up on the bank. Maggie turned, and saw Jane running across the powdery dirt. She had her skirt in both hands, her hat was missing, and her unbound hair streaked out behind her.

In pursuit and on foot, Robert Boyd came lumbering after Jane with surprising speed, yelling at her to stop. His horse trailed along behind. One of the Kelly gang boys sprinted towards it and grabbed up the reins. The other boys war-whooped at Boyd, hurling sticks and pebbles at him. A stone clocked him high on the shoulder. He turned and roared at the gang, waving a fist, but ran on. The boys followed, the whoops fading as they hung back at a safe distance.

Maggie's mouth dropped open. *'Jane!'*

She flew back down the gangway, Bucky with her, past the captain—who looked as if he was preparing to say a few stern words—coming up onto the muddy edge of the water. Splashing onto dry land, she struggled to gain traction but fell to all fours, her bag dropping from her shoulder into the wet sand.

'Christ, I know that man.' Sam swung onto Pie and charged past her. Bucky let go with ear-splitting barks and followed.

More dirt, stones and twigs flew into her face. *Oh my God, what have I led everyone into?* She stared up as Sam disappeared. Searching the top of the bank, she couldn't see anyone. Not Boyd, not Jane nor the Kelly gang … Couldn't hear anything clearly. Perhaps only Bucky's excited woofs fading into the air.

She clambered to her feet, clutching the dampened bag across her chest, and staggered up the slight incline. She saw that some of the working men had begun to run towards the ruckus, throwing down tools as they went. Someone grabbed Boyd's horse from the Kelly gang lad and threw the reins over the branch of a tree. The lad shot off on foot after his mates, and the men followed.

Then nothing.

Maggie spun about. The *Jolly Miller* had chugged from the landing and was a few yards into the river when a screaming Jane burst from the scrub further on. She lifted her skirt, ran for the water and plunged straight in. Wading out, she screeched to the men on the boat. She ploughed further into the water and sank as if the river had gulped her, then floundered up, swinging her arms until her wet clothes began to drag her under.

The steamer picked up speed. The men on board were shouting and pointing in her direction.

Maggie stared, stuck fast. She saw Jane bob under the water and up again, gasping for air, then gurgle before she sank. *The river, the river had her …*

Shocked, stumbling, Maggie ran, not believing what she was seeing, and lurched along the bank. The steamer was close to Jane, but not gaining quickly enough. Men were shouting over the side, waving their arms. One was preparing to jump in, but others had a hold of him, clearly aware of the hidden dangers of this river. A man could lose his own life if he was snagged under water. They were still too far away to help, they had to get closer.

Maggie ploughed towards the water's edge. She saw the yowling Kelly gang swarm out of the scrub, only to turn and hurl more sticks and stones as they ran. Boyd crashed out of the bush, arms waving as he fended off the missiles aimed at him. He bolted straight for his horse, heaved himself into the saddle, wheeled about and took off downriver.

The men from the boat were still shouting encouragement, still too far off to help.

'Jane!' Maggie, horrified, rushed into the shallows, her own skirt heavy in the water, and knew she couldn't go further. Jane's thrashing was weaker, her screams reduced to sputtered gasps each time she came up for air.

Suddenly, a curly coated bundle, travelling at the speed of light, leapt high in the air, paws working, and plunged into the water, landing full belly-whack. Bucky paddled out to Jane.

Sam had hauled up at the shoreline and slid off Pie. He waded in after the dog, whose nose was out of the water, his eyes keenly on his prize.

Maggie doubled over, breathless, staring at the dog. *Bucky, Bucky, Bucky, get Jane …*

Jane thrashed up but dropped under again.

Bucky, valiant, determined to get this large duck back to land, circled around the floating dress, and dived beneath the water. He nosed a flailing Jane to the surface, and his head tucked under her arm. Her sodden dress hampered him a little, but he made good progress, bumping her back to the surface when she slipped, shepherding her back to land.

The boat swung towards the bank, stayed idle, the men on deck watching, shouting.

Sam waded further in. 'Come on, Bucky. Good laddie,' he encouraged. 'Come on, boy, keep coming.'

Bucky worked hard. Sam reached out for the drenched woman and grabbed her from the paddling dog before the sand underfoot gave way. He fell, righted himself and scrabbling back, he hauled Jane with him, dragging her onto the bank. She spat water, gagged and coughed as she sucked in air. The dog splashed in the shallows beside Sam, came to nudge Jane and sat, staring at her and then up at Sam.

'Good lad, Bucky. Good lad,' Sam said, his voice rough as he ruffled the top of the grinning dog's sodden head.

Men from the sawmill had sprinted into the shallows to help. Sam got out of the way as they carried Jane up to where village women were rushing to meet them. Someone waved the boat off with a yell, 'She's all right, she's all right.' It answered with a blast of its whistle and took a graceful turn to the middle of the river. The men on board waved back. 'Good dog, that curly,' someone shouted from on board.

Bucky had gone back into the water, done a few paddles, then clambered out and bounded straight to Maggie, so very pleased with himself. She was about to throw her arms around the dog when, in a violent full-body shudder, he shook off an almighty amount of water, drenching her.

Laughing and crying, she sank in the puddles he'd made, in the dirt too dry to make mud. Bucky sat with her, his tongue lolling, his sopping rump on her hip. Exhausted, she dropped an arm around him as he snuggled closer. Maggie saw Sam's booted feet and looked up.

'Nothing's ever quiet around you, is it, Maggie O'Rourke?'

Thirty

Myra Boyd was angry. As soon as the post office opened, she elbowed her way inside and pushed ahead of other customers.

Startled, Angus stared at her. 'What is it, Myra? Can you wait until—'

'Where is Robert?' she demanded, leaning as far over the counter as she could. Her voice was low, her mouth pinched.

Angus leaned in as well. 'No idea,' he growled between his teeth. 'He didn't open the store yesterday afternoon. Why don't you know where he is?' Angus looked over her shoulder and nodded apologetically at the few people lined up behind her, before looking back at her. 'Would you please let me deal with these customers?'

'If I find you have covered up for more of his philandering—'

'Myra.' Angus flattened a hand on the counter with a loud slap. 'This is not the time, and I haven't done any such thing.' He glowered. 'I will come to your house when I finish up here, about midday. Now, please go.'

Glaring at him before she turned and swished away, she decided that he was not telling the truth, once again. Of course he must know where his brother had gone—they were thick as thieves despite fighting all the time, and likely, one was as bad as the other.

Marching back to her house, and thankful the two children had gone to school—without too much protest today—Myra went straight to her sewing box. The flask felt a little light. Then she remembered that she'd had more than her usual couple of sips yesterday. Nevertheless, she pulled the cork and drank straight from the bottle. Satisfied for the moment, she re-corked it, set it down, and waited for the warmth to permeate. There was no money in the house, she knew, so to purchase more of the illicit drink, she'd have to exchange another of the baubles she had stored under the bed.

At least those women, the previous owners of the baubles, had come to some use for her. Every cloud, silver lining, she thought. About to put the flask back in its hiding place, she told herself she could do with just another wee nip. So the cork came out again, and she took another swig. *Much better.* But of course, now there was less than half left, she might as well just finish it off, which she did. She decided she needed to visit Mrs McMinn to re-stock; a good idea to do so before Angus visited.

Midmorning, Angus greeted the unhappy looking man who marched into the post office. 'G'day, Mr Cutler. How's things with you down at the wharf?' He swept dust off the counter as he spoke and straightened up his stamp blocks and ink pads.

'Good as can be expected, Mr Boyd. But I haven't come here to hand over me ledgers just yet.'

Cutler deemed himself to be a wharf master of sorts and kept records of boats and passengers coming and going in his shack there. The record keeping of produce and the like was the role of the postmaster. In any case, Cutler dutifully brought all his paperwork to the post office every month.

Angus looked over Cutler's shoulder, pleased that there were no other customers. It seemed Mr Cutler wanted to say a few words, for some reason. 'So what is it I can do for you, then?' He laced his hands and rested them on the counter, an empty smile stuck on his face.

Cutler's bushy eyebrows furrowed. 'That brother of yours—'

The smile remained but Angus's eye twitched.

'—borrowed me horse to go off after some fella looking to camp on the Lyrup road. He never brought me horse back and I want it, so I'd like to have a word with Robert.'

Angus didn't shift his gaze, but his smile reduced to one of concern. *I'd like a word with the great idiot, too.* 'I haven't seen him, Mr Cutler. You don't think he'd have stolen—'

'I'm not thinkin' that. Yet. But he's known for his shiftiness, your brother.'

Angus felt the blood warm his face. *Bloody old git.* 'Didn't he say when he'd be back?'

As he hadn't yet spoken to Myra again, he had no clue what Robert had decided to do. The fact that the shop had been unattended meant that whatever stock he could have sold was clearly still sitting there—no money was coming in. He should never have made provision to partner Robert in the shop. It had never worked, and lately Robert was displaying even more erratic behaviour than usual.

Cutler heaved in a breath. 'He said he wanted to take a quick ride to try and find this fella, and if he wasn't back before dark last night, he'd be back at sun-up today.' He pointed at the wall clock, the time nearly eleven-thirty. 'Then someone told me he'd turned up back at the wharf and got on the *Jolly Miller* with me horse. I want me horse back. Robert's late and I'm feelin' nervous.'

Another customer opened the door and headed inside, removing his hat. He wasn't wearing a coat and he had his sleeves rolled to the elbows. Around one leg of his trousers, he had a clip, the sort a bicycle rider would wear. Angus only vaguely recognised him. Holding an envelope, the man stood a little back behind Barnaby Cutler, and seemed content to wait his turn. Angus assumed he'd only want a stamp, so he greeted the man with a nod before returning his attention to Mr Cutler.

'Yes, I see. He's clearly late,' Angus said, his face, he was sure, the picture of conciliation. 'Tell you what, I'll check with his wife immediately after my boss Mr McKenzie comes in to relieve me—only in a half-hour's time. I'll answer directly to you at the wharf with your horse's whereabouts. How would that be?'

Cutler grunted. 'Best as can be, I expect. Hope you bring me the right answer,' he said, and still grumbling, he turned, nodded at the man behind him and left.

Angus schooled his features as he moved and replaced the already straightened stationery items on his benchtop. He brushed off his waistcoat and put on his smile for the next customer. 'Morning,' he said.

The man stepped up to the counter. 'Morning, Mr Boyd. We haven't met. My name is Mr Reiners.' He placed the envelope on the counter.

Angus noted it had no address on it. 'Mr Reiners, how can I help you today?'

The gentleman, slightly built, medium height and with forearms that were spotted with freckles, smoothed a hand over his sandy-coloured hair and cleared his throat. 'It might not be a happy introduction, Mr Boyd. I should start by saying—' he twisted to check the door, '—that I have been dabbling in photography, hereabouts. And I'm very keen on it, I might add, and I have a vision to make a career of it.'

Chrissakes. Was he about to try selling me some postcards of our back-of-beyond little town?

'Wonderful to have a productive interest, Mr Reiners.' Angus glanced at the clock. Mr McKenzie would be here in fifteen minutes, still in time for the handover before Angus could leave at noon.

'Yes. However, in some circumstances, I feel the need to destroy the pictures once developed.' He laid a hand over the envelope. 'Others I feel I need to keep, or to sell, or to use otherwise.'

Ah. There it is. 'Thank you, but I'm not authorised to purchase—'

'I have in the envelope something that I thought I'd ruined—much to my chagrin—in my haste to record a disturbing incident. I thought I'd developed everything from a couple of weeks ago at Olivewood, and that somehow, because of my nerves at the time, I'd inadvertently spoiled these particular shots.'

Dabbles in photography. A couple of weeks ago. Olivewood. Feigning disinterest despite his sudden, rapid heartbeat, Angus said, 'A lapse of concentration, perhaps?'

The man ignored him. 'But here they are. I want to show these photographs to you. And I want you to know I still have the negative film.'

Angus reddened then frowned. 'For what purpose?' He grabbed at the envelope. 'I should see them.'

Mr Reiners pulled it back. 'Before you do—' and once again he checked behind him, '—you need to understand that I am not a blackmailer,' he said and lifted his hand from the envelope.

Angus felt a twist in his gut. He pulled the envelope towards him, lifted the unsealed flap and slid out four photographs, proofs in sepia. He stared at the first one. There was a man—no doubt his stupid bloody brother—with a woman over his shoulder, and in mid-stride, he was heading for the olive grove. There looked to be a little movement in the picture. Angus didn't know anything of photography, but the blurring indicated Robert had indeed been running. The next picture, also with a little blur, was of another young woman running with a rod towards where Robert had thrown his captive to the ground. The third picture was of the O'Rourke woman with the rod, held over her head, appearing to be about to strike Robert, whose bulbous, bare backside was in the air.

Angus didn't look at Mr Reiners. He closed his eyes and rubbed his chin. When he looked again, the last photograph showed the women standing, one with the rod still in her hand, over Robert's body at their feet. He was on his face in the dirt.

Angus flicked the photographs back to Reiners. 'It looks a terrible incident, indeed. Who are these people?'

Again, Mr Reiners seemed to ignore him. 'Our only mounted constable is stationed at Overland Corner, as you would be aware. I've no idea when he will return here.'

Angus waited a beat. 'It looks to me by these pictures, as if there's a young woman who needs to go to gaol for a grievous assault.'

'Do you think so? I think not. It looks to me as if there's a man who needs to go to gaol for a grievous assault, Mr Boyd.'

'From what's in these photographs?' Angus said with derision, but his heart still pounded.

'There have been a couple, or more, disappearances of young women in this town. This man's actions, captured here, might explain why—the women might have disappeared because he has done something terrible and has something to hide.'

Angus swallowed. *Adeline.* Still. He tapped the pictures. 'They're not proof of anything.'

Mr Reiners continued. 'I had no evidence to show until I'd found the film. Luckily it was intact and I was able to develop it. On the strength of it, I think it would be very prudent of you to remove your brother from the town.'

The main door opened, and Mr McKenzie walked in, smoothing his great moustache, a contrast to the thinning pale brown hair on his head. He waved at Angus and went to the side of the bench to gain entrance behind the counter. He disappeared into the back room, removing his coat as he went.

'Or what?' Angus asked through his teeth.

'Or I'll simply go to the trooper with my proofs before he comes here. I was going to head off for a few days anyway, riding my bicycle to Waikerie and taking photographs along the way. It would be no great detour to go to Overland Corner.'

Angus glared at him. 'And you're not a blackmailer?'

'As long as your brother leaves and never comes back this way, I have no need to hand these photographs over.' Mr Reiners's gaze held. 'Why would I drag innocent young women into this?'

'Bah,' Angus scoffed, and looked down at the pictures. He kept his voice down. 'They tell nothin' to nobody. They're useless.'

'They tell—they *show* a man doing gravest harm to a woman, and that she is being defended by another. I, for one, am totally sickened by him.'

'It don't look like defence to me,' Angus said. 'It looks like attempted murder. She's standing *behind* him with that iron bar.'

'An iron bar, is it? Not just a rod, or a stick as it looks in the photograph, Mr Boyd? You were there, I believe. As was I.'

Angus began to feel the heat under his collar. 'And even if you did go to the trooper, who's gonna prosecute my brother on these?' He tapped the pictures again. 'Besides, no one else could tell who they are.'

Mr Reiners was calm and spoke with purpose. 'That might be so, Mr Boyd, but you and I well know who they are.'

Angus leaned forwards, a curl on his lip. 'How is it you're so trustworthy, and won't hand over the photographs any time you feel like it?'

Mr Reiners pressed on. 'And, we all know that both those women are now missing.' He slid the pictures back to Angus.

'Out of town for Mr Robert Boyd, or new copies of these go to the constable at Overland Corner and he can sort it out,' he said and placed his hat on his head and walked out.

Angus bunched his fists on the counter, hung his head, and barely held his temper. *Bloody busy-body.* But Reiners had the means to undo Robert, and Angus, because they'd all been at Olivewood on that day.

He heard the back door open and close. Mr McKenzie walked over, clapped him on the back. 'Not having a good day, Mr Boyd?'

Angus sucked in a deep breath. *Could the day get any worse?*

He headed around the back of his brother's house. If he was lucky, Myra might offer him some lunch, but in case she wouldn't, he had a thick slice of bread and jam in a paper bag.

Parking his bicycle against the timber outhouse, Angus grabbed the bag and walked through the yard.

He peered into the cookhouse, but it was empty. The laundry tubs hadn't been used this morning—no hot water in the boiler—so he assumed his sister-in-law was inside the main house.

'Myra,' he called at the open back door. 'It's me, Angus. Where are you?' He stepped inside and spotted her slumped over the dinner table. He rushed over. 'Myra?'

The sweet smell of sherry met him as she lifted her head and tried to focus bleary eyes. On a breathy smile, she said, 'Hello, Angus,' and managed to sit up by herself.

He stood back. He'd never really seen Myra smile before and that came as a shock to him as much as the fact that she'd clearly had a drink. A big drink at that. 'What are you doing, drunk at this hour?'

She lifted a hand in a dismissive wave. 'What hour?' She frowned. 'Are the children home?'

'No.' Angus didn't think his niece and nephew would be home any time soon; it was only the middle of the day. 'You'd better pull yourself together. Where have you got the grog from? Has Robert got a stash of it?'

'Robert? No,' she scoffed. 'The way he spends money on his loose women we're lucky to have money for food.' She folded her arms on the table and her head lolled.

Robert and his loose women was one thing. Angus supplied most of the family's money for food. If the store had traded poorly for the month, his wages topped up the family's grocery shop, and the children's needs at school. Now he wondered if somehow, Myra had managed to squirrel funds away from Robert and buy herself a little tipple or two. Or more, by the look of things. 'Where do you get the money to buy grog, Myra?'

Her bleary eyes shifted. 'Robert.'

Angus knew that was a lie. 'So where do you buy the grog—not from that despicable trader, Rowley, I hope.'

Rowley was a low scoundrel, plying his grog up and down the river. Some said it was a killer grog. The sooner the local Renmark district got their community hotel up and running, the better. Not that Myra would be allowed to drink in it. Hotels were no places for women.

'Not Rowley,' she said, disgusted at the mention of the name. 'Mrs McMinn. She's got a good drop. Fills me flask,' she said and waved towards her sewing basket. The flask was dropped on top of her needlework, a piece that never seemed to come to an end. It was always in her sewing box.

Angus was astounded. 'Mrs McMinn runs the brothel.'

'Really truly, Angus,' Myra said, mocking him. 'I just like her sherry.' Her head bobbed down onto her folded arms.

Angus couldn't believe it of Myra. This straitlaced, sour-faced woman who married his brother was really doing business with a brothel madam. Beggared belief. Was beyond his comprehension at this point. He stared at her. A drunk for a sister-in-law …

'Where's the money come from to buy the grog, Myra?' he asked again.

Her head came up and as she stared at him, she looked evasive, owlish. 'I sell a few things.' She waved at the sewing basket.

He never knew she sold anything out of that sewing basket. He went to it and rummaged beneath the same old piece that had been there, unfinished, forever. There was nothing under it. 'What do you sell?'

'Sold 'em all.'

'Sold all what?'

Myra clamped her mouth shut, then said, 'Thirsty.' She went to stand but couldn't manage it.

Angus filled a cup from a pitcher of water on the bench and slid it across the table to her. 'How often does this happen?'

'Havin' a drink? Each time I find out he's been chasin' someone.' She slumped, seemed tired all of a sudden. Took a slurp of water. 'Thought you must've known who this time. Is why I came to the post office.'

'Yes, thanks for that.'

'Why you annoyed? Robert's gone off God knows where, and I got no clue who she is this time.' Again, there was that shifty look about her. 'I always find them, Angus.'

He brushed that aside; he couldn't care less about Myra's detective work. 'Mr Cutler from the wharf is thinking that maybe Robert's stolen his horse. I wouldn't be worrying about whether my brother goes off with some woman, that's not an offence,' Angus said. 'But he could go to gaol for stealing a horse.'

'Should be an offence,' she said, her lip curling.

'Then the gaols would be overflowing, Myra.' He scratched his head. 'Now tell me, if you have money hidden that could best be put to paying the bills and easing the strain on my wages—'

'I don't have any money.'

'You spent it all?'

'No money,' she insisted, and her head dropped to the table.

He checked her. Out to it. Angus decided that it was best if he left. He'd make a quick run to the store and see if she had raided the till. There was never much in it, a few shillings and pence to make some small exchanges. All the rest of the cash was put to paying for stock—they'd been refused credit—and paying for food on the table.

As he got on his bicycle, a thought struck him. He remembered those trinkets he'd found under his brother's bed when he'd gone looking for a spare pair of boots.

Heading back inside, and past Myra asleep at the table, he went straight to their bedroom. Dropping to his knees by the bed, he reached under and located that loose floorboard. He felt for the box, pulled it out, and poked about in it. Sure enough the broach he'd seen before was gone. The earrings were still in place, as well as something else he hadn't seen there before but knew. He picked it up. An ornate hatpin, about six inches long, and with a carved ivory handle. Its needle was the length of a small blade and was sturdy and strong.

His hand shook. This had been passed down to Adeline from her grandmother.

Thirty-one

Ard was galloping down the driveway, heading to Echuca and the doctor. Eleanor silently prayed that Dr Eakins was in attendance at his rooms, and not out on house calls, or other emergencies.

She'd wait for him to arrive, nothing more, she could do for Lorcan now. Linley would need her more. She headed to Ard's cottage.

Inside, Eleanor helped Linley off the floor, and had her kneel against the edge of the bed. 'Rest there a minute, and keep your breaths coming in little puffs.'

'It's Toby, he's grizzly,' Linley said between pants.

'I'll look in on him.'

Eleanor crossed to the toddler's room and rocked the cradle. Toby was a few months short of two years old and was a bonny child, curious and playful. Today she hoped the tiny dash of brandy would lull him. If they were lucky, the cries of a woman giving birth wouldn't disturb him. His mouth was open and his eyes were fluttering at his dream.

Linley's groan reached her from the room across the hall. Eleanor crept out.

In the hallway, she glanced through the open front door. CeeCee, Linley's aunty, was giving her horse a gee-up as it pulled the little bobbing cart down the driveway. Ard would have given her news of Linley's labour as he rode past and now CeeCee was hurrying, poor woman. CeeCee had been attacked early last year and had been left with a long recovery, but she was now able to get off the cart by herself, so Eleanor didn't need to wait for her.

By the time she got to the bedroom door, Linley was hunched over the bed, her chemise damp with sweat. She turned her head and gave Eleanor a wan smile. 'No one told me about this part,' she sobbed between short puffs of breath. Linley was not Toby's birth mother.

Eleanor took a deep breath and pushed aside all other thoughts. 'No one would, dear girl.' She moved quickly across the room. Kneeling, lifting Linley's chemise and peering between her legs, she said, patting Linley's back, 'It won't be long now, my lovely.'

Eleanor's hands were clammy as she watched Dr Eakins rewind the bandages over the splint. The worry of what she'd found—infection on Lorcan's leg—weighed heavily on her. It could mean amputation, and though the leg might have to go, it was by no means a sure thing that her husband would survive afterwards. She almost couldn't bear to hear what the doctor was saying.

'Perhaps a spider bit him in the tree. Not too poisonous, if it was. Doesn't look like it's doing too much harm.'

'What?' she asked, not trusting she'd heard correctly.

'It's not his broken bone that's infected, my dear. It's this.' He pointed to a red lump just under Lorcan's knee, now uncovered by the bandages being wound a little lower on his leg. 'I'm not really sure what it is, it might even just be a splinter deeply lodged. Might have been what caused him to take that almighty leap out of the tree. Most annoying, and could still prove nasty, but we'll pack a drawing ointment on it. You're to change it every few hours and apply with heat. We'll see what the next few days brings.'

Dr Eakins bent to peer over the red and angry site. He prodded it and a little liquid popped to the surface. He pressed gently as more oozed out and he wiped it away. Opening a tin of ointment, he dipped a finger and slathered a thick spread over the bite, and using a clean swathe of bandage, he wrapped the knee. He slapped the tin on the table beside their bed.

'Then we must work out why the man refuses to wake up.' He leaned to Lorcan's ear. 'Time to get up, old bean,' he said kindly. 'You've a new grandchild about to appear.'

Eleanor was still taking in what he'd said to her. *Not his broken bone that's infected.* She stared at Lorc, his face composed, although pale. After she'd sponged him down on the doctor's request, his fever had lowered.

'Still, best we try to let him come out of it by himself. Seems he might have slipped into a coma, after all. Only time will tell. Come get me any time, my dear.' He stood up, snapping his bag closed. 'And now I'll go to the other house to see if Miss CeeCee has coaxed that baby out.'

Shaking with a relief that hadn't fully taken hold, Eleanor wiped her damp hands on her dress. She took one last look at her sleeping husband, not wanting to leave him, and gave thanks that he might still come back to her. After hesitating for a time, she followed the doctor out, her heart much lighter.

Tramping across the bare patch of dirt between the two occupied houses, Eleanor glanced at the third, unfinished house a little further on. Sam had been working on it when he'd left to search for Maggie. Her heart ached anew. She knew the lad still hankered for her daughter, despite what he'd said the day he left. He was building the house with hope that she'd come home, to him.

Her beautiful, headstrong, opinionated daughter was no match for the unflappable Sam. Whatever had happened between them, Eleanor was sure it was Maggie's fault. Lorc had always assumed it was Sam's fault. Of course they'd sided with Maggie, but the lad was a good man and they'd agreed—if Maggie ever found her way back to him, and he to her, he'd make a fine son-in-law. They'd left them to their own devices, but so far, to their knowledge, nothing had happened. Then Mrs Chaffey's letter had arrived telling them Maggie was missing.

Eleanor just hoped that Sam would find Maggie, and that she'd come home to them. That they both would.

As they neared Ard's cottage, a loud squall, a newborn's, reached their ears.

'Well, it appears Miss CeeCee is very good at coaxing,' the doctor said and marched ahead of Eleanor into the house.

She took a moment outside to sag against the timber wall, squeezing her eyes shut and giving thanks for the sound of a strong, healthy baby.

Thirty-two

Bucky had decided to take himself out for another swim, but there were no big ducks to retrieve this time.

Watching him, Maggie stood in the sun, drying out her clothes that were bespattered with dirt and dog slobber. Her dress was filthy. Her bag was scuffed and damp, and there didn't seem to be an end to the mud, dust and the twigs she brushed from it.

Vera had come down earlier to let her know that Jane was all right, despite being terrified by 'that horrible man', and that no physical harm had come to her. She'd just been given a great fright and she was resting. Jane would share Vera's hut, taking refuge just in case, while Vera's husband would sleep at night in Jane's hut.

No mention was made of Maggie being offered any refuge. So she'd waited at the riverbank, in full view of the working men, so that if 'that horrible man' were to reappear, she could run for help. She didn't think he would; he'd be lucky to leave alive if he did. He must be mad to chase her all the way here and then try to attack another woman in broad daylight.

Sam and a couple of others had headed out in the direction Boyd had taken and were yet to return. What they'd do with him if they caught up with him, she didn't know. Before he'd left,

Sam had stood by Pie and taken his rifle from the saddle, checked that the gun was ready. He'd pocketed bullets. Maggie hoped he wouldn't have to use it and, if this new Sam was anything like the old, he wouldn't use it unless he absolutely had to. He'd put animals out of their misery. He'd hunted when necessary. As far as she knew, he'd never fired in anger.

But what did she know? *Bah—he wouldn't have changed those sorts of things, you silly woman.* But this new Sam was cool and distant. Not the Sam she remembered. The Sam who was hearty and open and warm, and loved to love her. Loved to love her all over. She reddened. No one could see that her face bloomed, bright with colour from within, and not from too much sunshine. Besides, no one could see for the dirt. She took off her hat and shook it out. Put it back on, tied it.

Well, what did she expect from Sam? She'd sent back his first letters, and that had been two years ago. Clearly, he'd just given up. Maybe—*maybe* he was married. She hadn't thought of that. A dull thud hit her stomach. *No, no.* Her mother would have written to say so. Truth to tell, there was very little news of Sam in Eleanor's letters, only one or two mentions of him, as he worked with Ard.

The Sam she remembered was a man who embraced her wholeheartedly when he could get his hands on her—which was any time they'd found themselves alone. He was so strong, so careful with that strength—not that she wasn't a strong girl—but his sinewy arms were powerful and he barely knew how strong he was. He'd lugged cartwheels, for goodness sakes. And she couldn't resist such a big heart as his, so earthy, and alive, warm, vibrant with laughter and jokes. A sharp, droll sense of humour. Lusty. And Sam wasn't frightened of who he was. He wasn't frightened of who she was.

And he'd sung to her.

What had possessed her to throw a tantrum and run for the hills? Well, for Renmark. She'd run to where her parents were. Anywhere but near Sam. And maybe, *maybe* there was a big dollop of immaturity on her part. She felt herself redden again. Tantrum was right, covering up for her flippant neglect of caution and modesty.

Modesty? Would he now think of her as a fallen woman because she had matched him so heartily?

She sighed, wondered if he still sang. Or did he now only sing when he got drunk? Did he even still get drunk? *Of course he would.*

Still in the water, Bucky barked. He paddled harder back to shore and, still barking, he landed and then shook himself wildly again. He took off into the bush at a run. Maggie, fearful Boyd might have returned, crouched, ready to run as well.

Emerging from the bush further along the bank, with a gleeful Bucky bouncing alongside, ears flapping, came Sam on Pie.

Sam shook his head. 'No sign of him.' He checked the rifle was snug in its sling on the saddle then dismounted. 'He was a bloke who spoke to me at the Renmark wharf. Said he wanted to buy Pie.' He shook his head in disbelief. 'He said that he'd find me again, even after I'd told him the horse wasn't for sale. I reckon he followed me here.' He glanced at Maggie, who stood there, twisting the handle of her bag. He hadn't seen her this nervous before. 'How is Mrs Thompson?' he asked.

'Badly shaken, but all right.'

He nodded. 'That's good.' He looked over his shoulder at the few men on horses who rode back into the village. 'They don't want you here, Maggie.' He glanced back at her. Bedraggled, she looked like something the plough had turned over. Bits of sticks in her hair, smudges of dried mud on her face and her dress. He looked down at his hands, not wanting to stare. His mouth twitched. It was not the time to laugh.

'What did you say?' she asked, eyes wide.

He glanced at her, set his mouth. 'I said, they don't want you here.'

But her face immediately shut down and she bit her lip. 'My hearing,' she said, catching his eye. 'The blast of the boiler. My hearing hasn't returned to normal.'

Jesus. How had he forgotten what that might have been like for her? The urge, the *need* to grab her and hold her tight was strong. He bunched his hands. *Better get used to resisting, Sam Taylor. Get her home and get the hell out of the way.*

'Sorry,' he said. 'Shouldn't have forgotten that.' He looked up. The sun was on its way into late afternoon. 'Ah, we need to figure out what we're going to do. Too risky with that bloke on the loose to set off for home now.' *Home.* He needed to tell her about Lorcan. 'Before anything,' he started, and she moved into his line of sight, trying to hear him better, he assumed. He gripped Pie's reins. Bucky sat at his feet, his waggling tail creating havoc in the dust, kicking up a little storm over them. Sam pointed ahead, past the landing. 'Let's walk over there.'

'What is it? Something at home?' she asked, walking side on, watching his mouth move.

'Your pa broke his leg.'

She reached out and gripped his forearm, a shocked breath following, and her face crumpled.

Sam leaned a bit closer so she could hear. 'When I left, he was out to it. It happened a few days before your ma got the letter from Mrs Chaffey saying that you'd disappeared.'

'Is he …?'

Sam could only shrug as her hand heated his skin. 'Ard couldn't come with your pa laid up, and his baby is coming real soon, maybe even born by now. Miss Linley was just about to—you know.' Then deliberately, he looked down at her hand on his arm and she snatched it away. *That's how it should be; that's how it'll stay.*

Leading Pie, and with Bucky following cheerfully barking at blowflies, they walked in silence until they reached a slight bend in the river, a little distance from where the men worked the sawmill.

'I can camp here the night, but we need to find you somewhere,' he said. He tied Pie's reins to a low branch reaching out over the sand, its bare wood long dead. Was sturdy enough because Pie wouldn't try going anywhere. Sam started undoing the girth then slipped the saddle off. 'We'll start back first thing in the morning.'

'You said they don't want me here. I'll camp with you.'

He eyed her. 'You won't.'

'Sleeping in the open doesn't bother me. I don't think they'll help me with a place to stay.'

He swept the blanket from Pie's back and tossed it over the saddle. 'I'll ask someone myself to take you in for the night. You will not be sleeping here.' Sam didn't need to look at her to feel the anger coming off her in waves. *Too bad, Miss Maggie.* 'Wait here.' That's when he did look at her, to see if she got the message. 'Wait here,' he repeated, making sure she'd heard. She had, but she seemed nervous again. Sam relented. 'He won't come here now,' he said. 'And I'll only be a few minutes then I'm back for—' He broke off and looked over her shoulder.

Maggie had turned to see what he was staring at. A paddle-steamer was pulling in to the landing. He knew it, and not only for its name emblazoned on the wheelhouse.

The *Sweet Georgie*, Dane MacHenry's sleek, shallow-draught steamer, glided to where the *Jolly Miller* had tied up, and a black-haired man on deck threw a mooring rope onto the landing.

Sam squinted at the boat in the late afternoon sun. 'Maybe I won't have to go to the village folk after all.'

Maggie watched as Sam greeted the captain of this fine-looking steamer, the *Sweet Georgie*. He'd said that it belonged to her cousin, Dane MacHenry, and that he'd met Dane at O'Rourke's Run. Maggie had never met him or his wife Georgina.

She shaded her eyes from the sun. There were shoulders clapped, handshakes, and then the long gaze from Dane as he sought her out. He lifted a hand in greeting then, with Sam, wrestled the gangway over the side and strode off the boat to where she stood.

As they neared, Maggie saw the strong family resemblance. Dane could be her brother's twin, they were so alike. The dark hair, the blue eyes and the set of their jaw. Ard was heavier built. Dane was taller. When he got closer, his gaze was familiar—the same as Ard's when he studied something.

'Delighted to meet you, cousin Maggie,' he said and stepped forward to kiss her cheek.

'And you, Dane.' She attempted to dust herself off. 'I must apologise for my appearance.'

'Not at all.' He was searching her face. 'I believe you've had quite the adventure.' He turned to Sam and clapped him on the shoulder again. 'You must tell me all. We won't be sailing through the night, I'm not a fan of it, so perhaps we can catch up on news over a meal and some wine.' He looked from one to the other. 'Head off in the morning for Renmark,' he said. 'I would be pleased to have you stay the night on board. There are cabins, and both of you are welcome.'

That would suit Maggie perfectly well, if she could get past thinking about the boat's boiler. It might also mean she'd be able to have a proper wash.

'Sounds good to me. Especially for Miss O'Rourke here,' Sam said, indicating with a tilt of his head. 'Hopefully you have a tub on board. Might have to sluice her down before she settles into a good night's sleep.'

Dane chewed the inside of his cheek.

Maggie thought the steam coming up from her neck might be visible. She kept her eyes on her cousin. 'Thank you. A good bed, and to have a good sleep would be just the thing.' She hesitated. 'I don't mean to sound churlish or even naïve, but the … boiler? I was on Mr Finn's boat, nearly right to the end.' She closed her eyes a moment. 'I saw one of the men, I couldn't tell who, he was all burned … He slipped into the water to drown.'

Dane pressed her shoulder. 'A mercy for him then.' He drew in a deep breath. 'But an horrific experience, for you. My dear cousin, we can never be sure of anything, but I can say that the *Sweet Georgie*'s boiler is many years younger than the *Goodnight*'s was, and is many journeys shy of the old lady's record. I feel sure that we'll be safe on board.'

Maggie gave a smile. 'I would be happy to help prepare an evening meal.'

'Wonderful. My man on board, Joe, is an old farrier, new to the boats these last years when he's not looking after my horses, and he hasn't taken to cooking. I'm only a passable cook.'

Maggie glanced at the boat. 'Your wife is not with you?'

'She decided to take the children to my mother's in Swan Hill when we got news that the *Goodnight* had blown up. She knew Mr Finn, you see. Learning of his death was very tough for her too.' He took a deep breath. 'For all of us. We've just come back from the site. Nothing to see, we just paid our respects.' He indicated the boat with a wave of his arm. 'Shall we?'

Maggie stepped beside him to walk to the *Sweet Georgie*. Bucky bounded alongside, bumping her and then Sam in turn.

'I hope you are somewhat recovered, Maggie,' Dane said.

'As well as can be. My hearing is still not so good at the moment.'

'It might never repair.'

She nodded, had thought of that possibility. There was naught to do but bear it. She had her life; partial hearing loss could be lived with. Now she thought only of getting on board the boat and leaving this place, never to return.

'I see you have one of these curlies.' Dane pointed at Bucky. 'Been meaning to acquire one for myself.' He reached down and attempted to scratch Bucky's ear. The dog gave a short gruff growl and danced away to the other side of Maggie. 'Ah. A boy who looks after his mistress.'

At the gangway, Dane allowed Maggie to go ahead of him.

Sam said, 'I'll come back for dinner. I'll take the dog and my horse and bunk down on the bank for the night.'

Maggie stepped onto the deck of the *Sweet Georgie*. 'I'm sure Bucky will make up his own mind,' she said.

'I'm sure he will,' Sam agreed politely, glancing at the tangle of twigs that dropped out of her hair.

Oh dear, I think I must look a sight. There was a comb somewhere in her bag, but when she peered inside for it, she felt dismay. *Everything looks a sight.*

'Which cabin would you like me to have?' she asked Dane.

He pointed across to the other side. 'Around that way. I wasn't expecting passengers, but there's one we keep close to prepared just in case.'

Sam stood on the bank side of the gangway. He looked down at the dog. 'Come on, Bucky. We'll go back to Pie, wash up some, and return for dinner.'

Bucky seemed to consider that but then bounded up the gangway to sniff around near where Maggie stood, and plopped at her feet.

'Good boy, Bucky,' Maggie said.

When she looked at Sam, his usually placid features were disturbed by a frown.

Maggie thrust up from sleep, wide awake in the dark space, her mind still on the swirling smoke of her dream. *Where am I?* She relaxed and dropped back to the thin pillow. She was on Dane's boat.

The evening's meal had been simple. Fresh damper, a chunk of corned beef with fried onions. There was a pot of jam on board—fig, Dane had told her—so some simple biscuits of flour, water and sugar, baked with a spread of jam, had done for sweets. Maggie was too tired to be more creative.

Over dinner, she told them all that had happened at Olivewood on that awful day, and her reasons for running. Dane and Joe had interjected here and there, questioning this and that. Sam had remained stoic, unreadable, and concentrated on his meal.

Aches and pains in her back and legs had begun sometime after dinner. She was overtired, and her body cried out for the right sort of sleep. Would she ever be able to sleep that sort of sleep again?

Now, in bed, Maggie wriggled trying to relieve the restlessness in her legs, but no position seemed to work. Bathing last night using just a deep basin of hot water did not go far to easing her muscles and bones. A deep bath would have to wait.

She'd refreshed the water more than once, had washed her hair and sponged as much dirt as she could from her dress. Both would dry overnight. Her underwear had to be washed properly and so after retiring for the night, she'd stripped down to nothing but the bedsheet wrapped around her, to scrub at her chemise and drawers. They hung on a rope strung near the open window and hopefully would dry quickly. Her hat and pinafore had also been soundly washed and set out to dry. At least she felt some way towards looking more civilised than she had earlier. She remembered Sam's comment about needing to be sluiced.

She touched the little purse still around her neck. If she had a chance to go to the village in the morning, she'd offer the folk there some recompense for their trouble. It was the least she could do with what little she had.

A light breeze drifted in. She'd opened a window earlier, hoping the mosquitoes wouldn't be too annoying at this time of year. There were a few buzzing pests around, but on the whole she'd been comfortable.

She peered outside to study the sky. It hosted a glaring three-quarter moon and a clear night sprinkled with clouds of bright stars. Maggie rested her chin on her arm against the sill. She was homeward bound. Safe on her cousin's boat, she knew it wouldn't be long before she was in her mother's arms. She'd help at the Run, a place she'd not lived yet, and she'd nurse her father back to health if—please God—he was still alive. Perhaps she'd find paid work in due course. Maybe she'd venture back into South Australia. After all, women there would be voting soon. She had no idea when women in Victoria would be allowed to vote.

Perhaps she'd win Sam back, and they'd come to South Australia together, although she hadn't yet asked him if he was married. Surely he would have said, or would have mentioned a wife as men do—oh-so-casually throw the words 'my wife says this' or 'my wife did that' into the conversation as if they thought their virtue needed protection from danger in the form of a single woman.

Maggie peered into the night to where Sam slept. A low glow of campfire marked the spot. She imagined him awake. Was he thinking of those two particularly wonderful times they'd spent together, when his callused hands had slid along her skin and tingles had followed, trailing breathtaking delight? Or when he'd brushed her breasts with his knuckles, until his hand slid over her belly and between her legs, stroking and teasing. Or when she gripped his wrist, begging him to stop, to keep going, to stop …

The secret part between her legs throbbed for his hand now, but the want of it only made her cry. Time and again she had touched herself there for pleasure, but tonight she was tired, and sad. It only made her feel lonely.

She fell back on the bed, unsettled. She'd missed her chance with Sam. She knew it from the way he acted towards her. He was no longer interested.

Best thing she could do was to just get on with it.

Sam awoke, his hands still behind his head. Groaning, he brought his arms down to his side, shaking them to get the blood flowing. *Jesus. Pins and needles.* Nothing had disturbed his sleep and now his arms ached, and his hands stung as the blood clamoured painfully to his fingers.

Pie snorted behind him, and the groaning and scuffing told him the horse had lain down for a time in the night and was now getting onto his feet. A moment later, he heard a blast of urine in a long stream soaking the hard ground.

'Good morning to you, too,' Sam said, and checked the sky to the east. Still only a faint glow. Sun up was a few minutes away, but the noises of the village awakening could be heard. All on deck at seven thirty, one of the lads had said. *Like a bloody army regiment.*

Clambering out from under the thin blanket, he stretched and flexed his fingers. He needed to take a piss as well. Afterwards, he led Pie to the water for a drink and brought him back again to forage until Sam could grab his feedbag.

While he waited for the village to stir, he kicked dirt over the campfire and stared at the boat, wondering if Maggie had slept well. She hadn't looked at him when she said goodnight, and he'd caught Dane eyeing him as she left. When the door had clicked shut, leaving them on their own in the tight galley, Dane only inclined his head. 'All I'll say is that the women in this family, either born to it or married into it, are pretty damn strong in their opinions, and in their choices.'

Sam knew what he meant, and to what he referred. 'Well, Maggie made her choice and it wasn't me.'

Dane brows had shot up. 'It was someone else?'

'No. Well, I dunno. What I do know is that it was an idea she chose. No marriage, no kids, and she was going to go work for a living and make her fortune. Be independent, vote and all that.'

'Ah yes,' Dane replied. 'The modern woman.'

'Yeah,' Sam agreed and no more was said for a moment. Then he cleared his throat and took a gamble. 'I remember when we last met, you were interested in Pie, as a stud animal.'

'I'm still interested.'

'Well, after I get Maggie back home, I might take you up on that. Could stay for a while on your place, help get things going.'

Dane nodded, had seemed to like the idea. 'I still need to build stables, a few yards. There are only workman's quarters at Jacaranda now. We're not at full tilt yet.'

'If there's work to do, I can help,' Sam told him.

'What about Lorc, and Ard? Won't they need your help?'

Sam had shrugged, only thinking to get away from O'Rourke's Run as quick as he could after he'd got Maggie back there. 'For a while they will, until the old man's back on his feet. I reckon what you're all talking about—combining your enterprises—there might be work for me on both your places.'

'True enough,' Dane said. 'We can keep the *Sweet Georgie* running between the two properties. I'm keeping a few sheep on Jacaranda, getting rid of the freight boats, and then there's growing demand for Walers, good horses for the military. Seems there are rumbles that good stocks of Walers with the right attributes might be needed in the not-too-distant future.'

Sam had heard it too, here and there. The world was unstable, and it seemed that deep economic depression was everywhere. He'd heard old men say that war was usually the next step to help reset the balance.

Dane had continued. 'Lorcan and Ard have got good land for fruit and vegetables and they can irrigate direct off the river. So we'll all eat. But the bankers are still bastards, and so is the drought. We'll need all the help we can get.'

They'd decided to talk more on it once Lorcan's situation became known. Much could change if a broken leg killed a man.

Now, as dawn's golden light glowed over the river, Sam was bowled off his haunches and knocked flat on his back by a hefty Bucky, who landed on his chest and breathed dog all over him. 'Good morning to you too, you turncoat.'

Bucky gave him a lick from chin to forehead. Sam pulled a face and shoved him off. He stood up, slapping off the dirt, and caught sight of Maggie emerging from her cabin.

His heart thundered, his breath jagged. Shit, while he was sleeping, she'd crept back under his skin. *Fooling yourself, lad. As if she ever left.* He drew in warm early morning air and breathed again. *Shit.* When the time came there'd be nothing to do about it but run. Get away from being around her all day and seeing her at night at the family dinners. Knowing that when he'd wake every morning she would be no more than a hundred yards away, across a dirt block and sleeping in her ma and pa's house, it would be too much.

Maybe his time working for Dane was closer than Sam had thought. Maybe he'd go back home to his parents in Bendigo. Maybe he'd fly to the moon if he thought that he'd be free of thoughts of her. His Maggie. His girl.

Let her go. Keep your distance. Let her go.

Jesus, he still had to see her for days on end until they got back to Echuca. Couldn't get out of that. Couldn't leave her to her own devices, smart and tough as she was. He looked over at her again. Rubbed his face hard as if clearing away the sleep fog.

It was time to start another day.

Thirty-three

Maggie had agreed to be back on the boat within half an hour so the *Sweet Georgie* could get underway on time. She'd told Dane that she had to see Jane, the woman who'd jumped in the river to escape Robert Boyd.

Sam had already tied Pie on the boat. He said he'd go with her. When she'd begun to protest, he'd held up his hands and said that he'd only escort her there and back because he didn't want any surprises from a madman leaping out of the bush.

Bucky had not waited behind at the boat, either. He trotted along between them.

'Nice new dress, Miss Maggie,' Sam said walking beside her. 'But sorta looks like Bucky slept on it overnight.'

She swatted at flies. 'Oh, and you know a lot about dresses and dogs.'

Sam held up his hands. 'Not me. Did you sleep well?'

'I did,' she lied, short and curt. She wasn't about to tell him anything of her restless night. Her stomach tingled. She lengthened her stride.

'That's good,' he said, mildly. He picked up a pebble and threw it. 'Go fetch, Bucky.' Bucky didn't think so. Instead he raced off in the other direction, towards the houses. 'Might not have the right touch,' Sam said, staring after him.

At the house, Vera answered her knock. 'Miss Lorkin.'

Maggie ducked her head. 'My name's Maggie O'Rourke, Mrs Olsen. I'm sorry—I'll explain, but now I just want to see how Jane is. I'll be leaving on my cousin's boat this morning.'

Vera glanced at Sam who tipped his hat, stood back and leaned against the hitching rail. 'I'm just escorting Miss Maggie,' he said. 'Please give my regards to Mrs Thompson.'

Maggie stepped inside leaving Vera in the doorway. Jane was sitting at the little table, cradling a pannikin.

'Morning, Jane,' Maggie said, and took a chair across from her, not waiting for nerves to send her running back out the door. Jane still might not take kindly to her.

'Morning.'

'I hope you're feeling better. I'm so sorry that man chased you.'

Jane nodded, accepting. 'I thought if I ran into the river, he wouldn't follow.'

'You were right. That was clever. He didn't.'

'It wasn't clever. A little boy lost his life by drowning there not that long ago. I feel quite stupid that I went there deliberately.' She sighed. 'They didn't catch him?'

'No,' Maggie said, and at Jane's consternation, added, 'He won't come back here.' She glanced at Vera who stood against the doorjamb with her arms across her chest, her pinafore dusty with flour. There was a dark frown on her face. 'He wouldn't dare.'

Jane looked at Maggie, bleary eyed. 'Will you be all right?'

Maggie's bones ached. Her eyes felt scratchy with lack of sleep and tears not shed. Her chest felt heavy with something she couldn't name. 'Yes,' she said.

'Then I wish you well. That Mr Taylor seems a nice man.'

'Uh, he, uh sends his regards,' was all Maggie could manage, knowing Sam was just outside the door, probably able to hear everything.

Remembering that she'd planned to make a payment as recompense to the village, she thought she might as well hand the money over now to Vera, and she could pass it on to the committee. Maggie reached under her chemise for her purse, looked at Jane and paused. A better idea came to her.

She withdrew the purse and loosening the drawstrings, brought out three coins. 'I thought to give this to the chairman here, for the village, as payment for my stay. Instead, I'd rather that you have it, Jane, to get you downriver on the next boat. To start your journey, to help set yourself up, like we talked about.' Maggie knew her words were coming too fast, so she stopped.

Jane looked at the coins laid out in front of her. She lifted her eyes to Maggie.

'A gift, from me to you. I have family waiting for me. I'll have work, I'll be safe, I'll have a roof over my head without having to look for it—or fight for it.' Maggie glanced at Vera, who sighed, raising her eyes to the ceiling. Shifting on her seat, she was a little uncomfortable under Jane's stare. 'It's not me who needs to go before a court to state my case for divorce.' She heard Vera suck in a breath. 'I don't need to find security, I already have it.' She touched the coins. 'I worked hard for this money, to do with it as I please. It's mine to keep, to spend, or to give away.'

Maggie pushed the coins across the table. She'd kept one pound six and six for herself. That was only sensible. She'd proven she could earn and save, so she could do it again. It was all part of paying her way. 'I'd rather you have it.'

Still Jane said nothing. Her gaze flicked from Maggie to the money on the table.

Maggie tried again. 'To thank you for looking after me. I'm sorry I wasn't truthful. I thought only to protect myself. I didn't want anyone to know where I was, or who I was. I thought I'd killed Robert Boyd with an iron rod, in Renmark—he was the man who chased you. I'd bashed him on the head. I thought that the police would come for me, and I'd be hanged, even though I was defending a friend. As it turns out, Boyd wasn't chasing me, it seems he might have been chasing Mr Taylor, for his horse.'

'Ironic,' Jane said. She looked to Vera, who only lifted a shoulder. Then Jane flattened her hand over the three one-pound coins and slid them towards herself. 'Thank you.' She looked up briefly.

In the moment's silence, Maggie clasped her hands. 'Where will you go?'

Jane breathed deeply. 'You thought Murray Bridge might be a good place. I might try my luck there.' She glanced at Maggie again and gave her a wan smile. 'Goodbye, Ellie.' She laughed at herself. 'Maggie.'

Maggie reached over and tentatively squeezed her hand but withdrew quickly when Jane didn't respond. 'Goodbye and good luck. Thank you too, Mrs Olsen. Please pass along my thanks to the others. And to the Kelly gang. I thought they were especially brave.'

'The buggers,' Vera said, a mock frown on her face.

Maggie stood up. 'When the time comes, no matter where you are or what you're doing, make sure you vote in the coming election. I don't know if I'll be in South Australia to do so myself. It's important that you do,' she said. 'To uphold your rights, now you have them. You will, won't you?'

'I will vote,' Jane said, and looked at Vera who nodded. 'Having a voice, a say in how things are to be done, will help improve our lot, won't it?' Her eyes had lit up and she looked as if she had some hope again.

'It will. It has to. I have to go now,' Maggie said.

Jane only nodded at her, still with her hand closed over the coins. Vera patted Maggie's shoulder as she passed. 'Goodbye, dear.'

Outside, Bucky was waiting for Maggie with a large leather boot in his mouth, his golden-yellow eyes gleaming. She ruffled his head, ignored his gift and marched past Sam. Casting him a quick glance, she caught the thunderous look on his face.

'What's the matter?' She blinked in the sunshine.

'You said that the bloke who chased Miss Jane—' he took in a deep breath, 'was the same bloke you clobbered in Renmark. Why didn't you tell me that before now?'

His fierce glare was anything but his usual laconic gaze. It made her nervous. She had no answer for him. Instead she said, 'He'd … made a nuisance of himself at Olivewood, where I was working.'

She lengthened her stride as she headed for the landing. Bucky trotted beside her, boot in mouth.

Sam kept up with her. 'Mrs Chaffey told me that he'd grabbed a woman, and that something … not delicate, or …' He couldn't seem to find the right words.

Maggie felt her colour rising. 'He'd come to the house. He'd known there was hardly anyone about, and he … made advances towards me, and Nara sort of coaxed him away from me. He grabbed her—' Maggie swallowed, '—attacked her and I rushed him with an iron rod. Hit him so hard I thought I'd killed him.'

Sam was in step with her and leaned across. She heard him clearly say, 'I saw him at Renmark—the scum. He had the worst-looking black eyes I've ever seen, all the way down to here,' Sam said, his teeth bared as he tapped his cheek bones, 'and snot dribbling, bruises all over his head and neck. Mrs Chaffey had said he looked like a racc—' He floundered for the word.

'Raccoon,' Maggie supplied. 'Like our possum.'

Sam made a fist and shook it in front of him. 'I should've figured out it was him,' he said, his voice a rasp. 'If I'd have known then—'

'What?' Maggie asked. 'If you'd have known then … what?' She stopped.

'I'da killed him myself.' He didn't look at her, just strode past her heading for the boat, his head down.

Maggie tried to keep up. Bucky bounced along, boot and all. 'You would not have, Sam Taylor.'

He rounded on her, those hazel eyes now flashing glints of fire, the dark golden eyebrows low. 'I know what I woulda done.'

'Good timing.' Dane met them at the gangway and waved them on board. 'We're all ready. Joe's got her fired up and—'

'I'm coming on board to get Pie,' Sam said abruptly, and pushed ahead of Maggie. 'I'll ride back to Renmark.' Pie was tied at the stern with his head in a nosebag.

'What did you say?' Maggie asked, running to catch up.

'Wait.' Dane blocked Sam from coming on board. 'Why?'

'That bloody mongrel not only chased down a woman here and forced her into the river,' Sam said, stabbing a finger at the water, 'he was the one who attacked Maggie and her friend back in Renmark. He's not gonna get away with that.' He tried to dodge around Dane. 'I'm going after him.'

Dane stood his ground, arms now folded. 'If he's gone bush, he's already way ahead of you, and you've got no way of knowing which way he's gone.' His blue eyes, the match for her brother's, darkened. 'Your job is to get my cousin home. After that, you can do what you like.'

Sam drew in a deep breath, stepped back and opened an arm towards Maggie, indicating that she should go on board ahead of him. Bucky dropped the boot on the sandy dirt and shot up the gangway in front of her, nimbly sidestepping Dane.

Maggie looked back as Sam boarded. He was not happy, that was clear. He marched over to Pie, shoved his hands in his pockets and paced. Dane followed on board and pulled in the gangway as the boat got underway, a blast of its throaty whistle shrill in the still air.

Thirty-four

Angus put the 'closed' sign in the post office window. Too bad if anyone grumbled. No customers had been along for half an hour, and all telegrams for the day had been sent and logged. He would plead illness if anyone complained.

His nerves were almost shot, anyway. Each time the door opened he'd expected to see his gormless brother swagger inside. Best thing Angus could do was to get back to Myra and see how she was coping with those two kids of hers. No doubt her hangover would be unpleasant—if she wasn't still drunk.

If Robert had come back and was home, Angus would have it out with him. It was one thing for the madman to go rollicking off into the bush on someone else's horse—Angus didn't need horse theft added to the list of crimes he believed were mounting; he'd tear shreds off his volatile brother for that—but the nastiest of it would be fronting Robert about Adeline's hatpin.

Angus had taken it from the tin under Robert and Myra's bed and had secured it on the inside of his waistcoat. It made him feel close to Adeline. All day, it had seemed to hum against him while he'd worked. Now his heart pounded as if he was constantly on alert, constantly in a state of agitation.

Adeline, Adeline, where are you? What's he done to you?

Angus would get to the bottom of it, but even if he couldn't get it out of his brother, he'd leave him to Mr Reiners and the mercy of the damning photographs. Robert could rot in gaol.

He headed outside, got on his bike and rode off to Robert's house. As he cycled, he turned his thoughts to the things he might now have to take over. He wondered if the rent on Robert's house was paid up—he'd always left that to Robert to attend; the man had to take some responsibility, but if he hadn't … Dear God, would he have to share his place with Myra and the children? Horrible thought. Well, if he had to, there'd be some stern rules. He wouldn't put up with any spoiled brat behaviour if they wanted to have a reasonable life.

One had to be pragmatic; what to do with the shop? It would be best to close it, especially if Robert was in gaol. He'd have to sell the stock to pay off the niggling debts. There was another solution—fire. A right-roaring, raging fire. Always a terror in the bush. Always feared in the towns and the cities. Always a threat. Angus had thought of it before, but could never bring himself to do it. If he did things carefully, no one would suspect. The store had insurance, and a pay-out usually fixed the problem of debt. He glanced left and right on the dusty street as if people might have heard his thoughts, or seen them written on his face.

The bicycle bounced and threatened to toss him. If he didn't watch it, he'd drop into a hole on the road. *Don't be putting wind up your own tail, man. Concentrate. First things first.*

Robert's house came into view, a small cottage sitting in the middle of a row of three. As usual, Angus rode around the back and leaned his bicycle against the outhouse. Nothing appeared to have changed since he'd been here earlier in the day.

He couldn't hear any noise. *Where are the youngsters?* School was out; they should be home—they had chores to do. As he approached the back door, he felt the hairs lift on his arms, and a shiver gripped his scalp.

He could see Myra's booted feet, her body prone on the floor. He could hear a guttural sobbing.

Thirty-five

It was early the next morning, but Maggie knew Sam would already be in the wheelhouse with Dane. Perhaps there wouldn't be a moment to catch him on his own today either. It had certainly been impossible yesterday after they'd left Lyrup, going upriver for Renmark. It was almost as if he'd deliberately kept out of her way. Hard to do on a boat this size, but he'd managed it.

The *Sweet Georgie* wasn't a big steamer; it was sleek and elegant, and by all accounts had been quite the vessel a couple of years back, mostly for passengers. Dane had bought it after he'd purchased his company that included the other two boats, the *Lady Mitchell* and the *Lady Goodnight*. Now the boat was a little less elegant—it was used more for freight than for passengers these days, but it was still a very fine vessel.

Last evening, Joe had caught a sizeable Murray cod. While they'd waited for a snagging boat to clear a great old gum tree that had fallen into the water, Dane decided to tie up for the evening. The *Sweet Georgie* pulled into the bank close by.

Maggie cooked the catch for their supper, roasting potatoes and carrots to accompany it. She felt useful; she had a purpose. Oh yes, woman's work, some would scoff, but she knew she could make a living with it.

With a little of the rum on board, she'd soaked a supply of raisins she'd found in the pantry cupboard and made a bread and butter pudding using day-old damper. Sam hadn't looked at her throughout the meal except to add his thanks, but she could see her efforts had been appreciated, and by Dane in particular.

'My wife doesn't enjoy cooking overly much. Perhaps you would offer some advice?' he'd said as he spooned a dollop of pudding into his mouth.

Maggie had laughed at that. 'I wouldn't dare. I'm sure Georgina has many other attributes that compensate.'

'But a man could starve,' he'd said good-naturedly.

'It doesn't look to me as if you've starved so far,' she'd replied. 'I'd say she is busy with other things.'

He'd acknowledged that with a grunt. 'Our twins, and our toddler,' he said. 'And another on the way, whose arrival will occur in a few months. Georgie is also a fine horsewoman, keenly interested in the idea of our stud farm, and her correspondence with the Victorian Women's Suffrage Society takes up a good deal of whatever time she can put to it.'

'Well, she has her hands full,' Maggie said. 'Perhaps I could come and stay awhile, help out after I've got home and seen to my own family.' She'd wondered then why Dane had glanced at Sam who'd gazed studiously at his hands.

Conversation turned back to the events of the last weeks. Dane told them that he grieved for his men. His sorrow at the deaths of Mr Finn and Mr Bentley had been plain; a terrible blow. While losing the *Goodnight* in such circumstances had been a shock, he said it was forced attrition; river trade was down, he couldn't economically justify three vessels any longer, and no one was buying boats. He was clearly saddened, but stoic.

Now, sure enough, when she turned and looked up, there was Sam in the wheelhouse with her cousin. Dane waved at her, Sam only nodded and blandly looked away, as if something in the distance had caught his attention. She couldn't hear any subsequent conversation properly, but the tone of the banter and the bursts of laughter told her all she needed to know. The discussion would not include her and nor, for that matter, would it be about her.

Staring out over the river, the rhythmic paddle wheels slapping the water were dull sounds in her ears. Nothing seemed amiss, awry. The beat of the engine was steady, yet she couldn't relax.

She turned her thoughts to home. Home was where her parents were, and her brother. Home was wherever they were. Home was a refuge, that was true, but now that the overwhelming events of recent weeks were behind her, it was time to get on. Her plans to settle into a quiet domestic life on O'Rourke's Run now seemed wistful. She *must* be soft in the head. She would have better thoughts. Yes, yes, recuperation wasn't a bad thing, nor was helping at home, but she had things to do. There was a world to conquer.

But—Sam Taylor. Where would he fit? She'd never wanted anyone else in her whole life. It was just that if she was with Sam, she wouldn't be able to escape the thing she was most afraid of. No one could save her from that.

Sam had to chuck Pie's shit over the side. Thing about taking a horse on a paddle-steamer—a man needed to think about tidying up the poor fella's business. He'd left the wheelhouse and grabbed a shovel, one from the engine room, and gone to shunt the manure into the river. Bucky thought it was a fine game and was all for launching into the water after it, but Sam grabbed him by the scruff.

'Sam.'

Startled—she'd crept up on him, dammit—he dropped Bucky who sat smartly at Maggie's feet. 'Yes?' He must have yelled because she winced.

'Dane tells me we're due in Renmark midafternoon today.'

'Yes. Good.' They would be taking on freight that Dane's company had contracted to take to Swan Hill, and Sam would, of course, lend a hand. Then they'd be off again and would tie up for the evening somewhere upriver. Bloody leisurely trip back home, it seemed. He didn't know how he could keep up the pretence of ignoring Maggie for much longer.

She glanced back towards the wheelhouse. Sam knew Dane couldn't be seen, so that meant Dane couldn't see them. Joe was aft, repairing the mooring rope, head bent to his task. Sam watched Maggie run a hand down Pie's flank, and the horse whinnied at her.

She turned to him. In her other hand she held an envelope. 'Are you married, Sam?'

He nearly fell over. 'What?' he barked. ''Course not. I'm free as a bird.'

She nodded. 'You stopped writing,' she said, this new Maggie, this Maggie whose voice was subdued.

Sam held his temper, rubbed his chin hard, felt his scratchy four-day-old whiskers roughen his fingers. When he was sure his voice would be even, not forced or terse, or wouldn't break, he replied, 'I wrote enough.'

Maggie stared, eyes wide. 'Is that right?'

'You sent my letters back,' Sam ground out.

'You gave up in a hurry,' she shot back.

'Did I? *Jesus.*' He heard the fury in his voice. 'Who says it was in a hurry?'

Maggie blinked at that. When a man stops writing after two letters, it's stopped in a hurry. A woman gets the message—he hasn't persisted, he isn't interested. Not even dependable, patient and unflappable Sam would tell her it meant otherwise. He was no longer interested.

He was no longer unflappable either, it seemed. This Sam erupting with anger was not the Sam she remembered. Usually, there would only be a wry few words, deprecating or witty. Not this time.

I wrote enough. Clearly, the finality in his tone proved he was done with her. And she would not beg.

'Well?' he demanded.

She looked him fair in the face then. He stared. Glared, more like it. Those eyes of his, dark under a frown and flecked with hints of autumn and glints of fire, took her breath away.

Her hand crunched the envelope she held, uncertain. What difference would her words in the letter make now? But still, she thrust the crinkled envelope at him. It quivered in her hand.

He looked at it. 'What is that?'

'My letter to you. It explains how I feel.'

'After two years?' He snatched it. Lifted the unsealed flap and pulled out the pages.

She watched his face as he looked at one page, then turned it over. *He's not even reading it.* Her heart thumped.

He looked at another page, shaking his head, disdain a grimace on his mouth. Anger rolled off him in waves, buffeting the air between them. 'What the hell could you even mean by this?' He shoved the pages back into the envelope, pushed it into her hands and stalked off.

Maggie bent her head to the crumpled, pulpy pages in her hand, to check what she'd written, to try and understand what could have so offended him. Standing in shock, her heart crushed, her mouth dropped open in disbelief. The pages were awash with faded blue ink that had bled indiscriminately, making blotches and swirls. They'd been dampened, got wet somehow. She couldn't think when … Had she not had her bag clutched to her side the whole time? Had she not made sure she had it through thick and thin these past weeks? Yes, yes, she had, so when …?

Only the other day, at Lyrup. The day Sam had galloped off chasing Robert Boyd. She'd slipped and fallen into wet sand. *Dammit, dammit, dammit.*

She looked at the letter again, at the meaningless, whimsical shapes on it. Murray River water had dissolved every word on the pages. She shoved it in her pinny pocket.

'Sam, wait,' she cried. 'Wait.' She tried to keep her voice down as she hurried over the deck after him.

'What?'

'I'd started it much earlier, and I kept finding so much more to say, I couldn't finish it.'

'I got the message without it, don't worry.'

'Perhaps I'd been wrong to run away to Renmark—'

He made a noise, unimpressed.

'—but I couldn't be stifled by what I saw all around me. Women, only good for home and … babies.'

Impatient, he rolled his eyes, let out a snort. 'Good thing then that we stopped doin' what we were doin'.'

'I know. I was afraid, and even what I felt for you wasn't enough to stop that fear. It was easier to stay away.' She rubbed her face, wiped perspiration from her neck.

His mouth twisted but he didn't look at her. 'And all that was in this letter, was it?'

'That, and more, and I still haven't finished it.'

'Taking your time, eh? Sounds to me like you were hedgin' your bets, Maggie.'

'That's not it,' she hissed, wronged and feeling heat bloom in her chest. 'That wasn't it. You know I'd said as much to you the last time we—'

'And now—what do you say now?' His hand tapped on his thigh.

Do not beg. She floundered for a moment, trying to get it right. 'I'm still afraid of it, Sam. It's been a long time, I know, and—'

'Aye. Too long,' he cut in. 'So I understand. Time for it to be over, letter or not. You're afraid of it. You're so afraid you couldn't even post that.' He pointed at the letter in her pocket. 'I'm not second best, Maggie. I'm not waiting anymore. Stay afraid, just don't pester me again.' He stomped off.

She couldn't shout at him, the others would hear. They probably already heard. She gritted her teeth.

Damn you, Sam Taylor. Thick as a lump of wood.

Thirty-six

Angus rushed into the house. 'Myra.' He dropped to his knees by her side, astounded at the amount of blood on the floor. It was coming from her head, her scalp sliced high over one eye. He looked up at Robert, who sat hunched in a chair at the table, his face in his hands.

'What have you done?' Angus seethed. Then he noticed the disarray in the room, as if someone had been looking for something. Someone in a hurry.

His brother mumbled a few words and his hands came away from his face. The fiery bloodshot whites of his eyes were stark against the dark stains of his sagging, puffy skin beneath. 'I'm in trouble.'

Bewildered, Angus dropped his ear to Myra's chest. 'She's alive, she's alive. You can stop your blubbering. Why did you do it?'

'Not her. Not Myra. I didn't do that. She fell, the flask broke. Piece of glass.' Robert pointed at a bloody shard under the table. He wiped spittle from his chin. 'Other day, I went to Lyrup.'

'You what?' Angus had Myra's head in his hands, trying to see how bad the cut was. He grabbed a thin towel from the discarded laundry nearby. 'Where will I find bandages, Robert?'

'I don't know, I don't know.' Robert rocked in the chair.

Angus feared he'd collapse it. 'Stop the wailing, Robert,' he flared, still holding Myra's head. 'Get a hold of yourself.'

The chair stopped moving, but Robert dropped his head into his hands again.

'Where are your children?'

'Ran off.'

Frustrated with him, Angus reached over and thumped him in the leg. 'Ran off where—for help?' He looked down. God forbid he'd have to put stitches in her head.

'Dunno. Dunno. They came home when we were … havin' words.'

'You did do it. You pushed her, didn't you?'

Robert shook his head. 'She's drunk. She fell.'

The bleeding wouldn't stop. *Jesus, now what*? His knees were paining him, so Angus struggled up on his haunches. 'Let's get her into her bed.'

He didn't move.

'Come *on*, you great lug,' Angus raged, and punched his brother's leg again.

Robert's chair scraped back as he stood up.

'What happened in here?' Angus demanded. 'The place is a shambles.' He kept the towel pressed on Myra's forehead.

'I was lookin' for where she'd been stashing her coins. She's been getting grog, Angus.'

He rolled his eyes. 'Married to you, any bloody wonder,' he muttered.

'Gettin' grog when we've got *no* money. You know what she said? You know what she *said*?'

'I'm not deaf and I don't care what she said.' Angus struggled to his feet. 'You get her legs.' *Better a husband at that end*. He got his hands under her armpits. 'Lift,' he ordered, and clumsily they got her from under the table and down the hallway to the bedroom.

Heaved onto the messed-up bed, Myra's scalp ran with more blood, the towel next to useless. Angus pulled open a dresser drawer and found one of Robert's shirts. He ripped off the sleeves.

'That's my only good shirt.'

'You won't be needin' it. Now what the hell happened?' Angus wound the sleeves around Myra's head with the towel packed against the cut, and tucked in the end.

'I took Cutler's horse to go after a fella who had a good-looking stallion I wanted and—'

'I said we couldn't afford a horse.' Angus looked at him, incredulous.

Robert erupted. 'And I told yer, a man my size can't go around on a bicycle,' he shouted. 'I had that woman to hunt down, the one that clobbered me.' He paced. 'So I was gonna follow the fella on Cutler's nag and get the horse, when before I left, Myra said stock was due in at the wharf and I had to get it first for the store. Bugger that,' he stormed, warming to his story. 'There was a boat in, just about to go for Lyrup, so I got on board—'

'And paid how?'

Uneasy, Robert turned away, pacing a little more in the small room. He didn't once glance at his wife. 'Traded hats, belts.'

Angus set his mouth. 'You bloody great fool.'

Robert's eyes twitched. 'Then I get to Lyrup, and bugger me, I see the girl, the one who hit me. I took off after her.'

Angus jumped to his feet, took two strides and grabbed his brother's collar. 'Did you get her, did you hurt her?' He bared his teeth right under Robert's nose.

'She disappeared.' He stared wide-eyed at Angus. 'Truth. I lost her.'

Angus shoved him away. He glanced at Myra. Still out to it. He took a deep breath. 'So, what's this thing you've done that'll bring trouble?'

Robert licked his lips. 'She was with another piece … and so I rounded up that one.'

Angus spun back. 'And?'

A hesitation. 'And nothin'.'

'Liar,' Angus blasted. He remembered Mr Reiners's photographs. Then a thought uncurled. If the O'Rourke woman was alive …

'Swear,' Robert said. 'She took off like a bloody rabbit, straight into the scrub.'

Angus squinted. 'And then?

'Whole village of blokes came after me when she ran. I bolted. But now they'll have me for … somethin'. I dunno what.'

Angus thrust a finger at Myra. 'They'll have you for being a danger to women—'

'Ballocks. She's me wife.'

'And the way you keep makin' a right pest of yourself, you *will* get done for rape.' Fury pumped through his veins. His mind worked. He felt the hum of Adeline's ivory hatpin close to his heart. 'There's some proof of what you do, and I have that proof.'

'Whaddya talkin' about—proof?'

'That fella that takes photographs. He gave me four. And you don't look good, not what you're doin' in 'em.'

'They attacked *me*.'

'Look at yourself, you bloody great lummox. They ain't none of them fallin' all over themselves for you.'

'Bah, you don't know anythin'.' Robert checked to see that Myra was still unconscious. He turned back to Angus, and as if imparting a secret, he said, 'They all want it—the uppity O'Rourke piece. The other woman. That Adeline of yours—'

Angus launched. A red mist, a fury dropped over him and frenzied, he took Robert crashing to the floor. Arms flailing in the air, Robert landed hard on his back, his legs akimbo under his brother's full body assault. They grappled, knocking the bed sideways. Angus growled, his hands twisting Robert's collar. He wanted to punch that absurd arrogance out of his brother's fat, ridiculous, buffoon head. 'Where is she?' he yelled into the puffed-up, mottled face, his knuckles pushing down on Robert's windpipe. '*Where is Adeline?*'

Robert gripped his brother's straining wrists. 'Get off me,' he rasped. 'I dunno where she is. I told ye, I got no idea. She ran off with that other bloke.'

Rage drove Angus. He squeezed harder. 'I'll kill you here and now, brother.' He rammed his fists harder on Robert's neck and saw the moment his brother truly understood that he might be killed. 'Adeline. Did you *ever* touch her?'

Robert's words forced their way out. 'No. *No.* I never did.' Bug-eyed, fearful, he stopped struggling. 'She left town,' he wheezed. 'Ask Myra.'

Angus shoved again, his hands still in Robert's collar. 'Why are there those bits of jewellery under your bed?'

Robert blinked, bewildered. 'What?' Then his frown cleared. 'I told ye. Myra must have put them there.'

About to bang Robert's head on the floorboards, it struck him. *Myra.* Angus thrust Robert away and, on his hands and knees, scrambled under the bed, reaching for the hidey-hole.

He'd take the trinkets, force Myra to tell him where she'd got them, force her to tell him how she'd come to have Adeline's hatpin. And Robert would be reeled in, threatened with the photographs.

Adeline. Angus would get to the bottom of it. He twisted awkwardly under the bed and felt the prick of the hatpin against his chest—Myra's weight on top of the bed left less room to move underneath. He tried to relax, to turn slowly.

He heard Robert coughing and spitting as he sat up. Felt his hard kick land on his legs. Heard him curse as he got to his feet and stumbled out. Heard his footsteps heavy on the floorboards going through the house and out the back door. Then nothing. He'd gone, God only knows where.

Fingers picked at the loose board under Myra's bed. Angus managed to flick it up but found the hole empty. He looked up, saw that the handkerchief was gone from the springs. What could that mean? Had Myra traded the last of the baubles? Had she gone and got more grog with the money and really got herself cockeyed?

Angus had nothing now but the photographs—no lady's gewgaws, the pretty bits and pieces to pawn for extra cash.

Those photographs. He could blackmail the O'Rourke woman. Say they were proof that she had attacked Robert. At least one of them showed her about to belt him on the head.

He slithered out from underneath and peered over the edge of the bed at Myra. He couldn't ask her anything now, she was still unconscious. The bleeding above her eye had slowed, though a dribble ran under the bandage and down her cheek. She looked as if she was all right. Sounded all right; a soft snore had started.

He hauled himself up and looked around once again. Practicalities first. The fire. Fitted his plan perfectly. He checked Myra again. He'd leave now and get back to her—soon as he could—to shake the damn truth out of her.

Then he'd set up the high-and-mighty Maggie O'Rourke.

Where was Marcia, that snippety niece of his? No matter. The girl could come home and find her mother ill, and then would have to look after her, would have to learn quickly, like it or not. Youngsters, all for fun and no care. What was the world coming to if they had to rely on this generation of children? Still, they had to learn the harsh realities of life somehow. They would if he had anything to do with it.

He left the house after skirting the puddles of blood and the drying splotches in the back room. Marcia would have a big job cleaning, too. No clue where her brother Gregory might be, but his guess was they'd be together. Gregory was a bit of a sniveller, and when he wasn't a bully in the yard, he'd hang on Marcia's pinafore straps.

Robert was nowhere to be seen. Angus grabbed his bicycle by the handlebars, adjusted his trouser clip, hopped on and rode into the town. He would go to the store but first things first: he needed to be seen about the town so he headed for the post office to collect his pay.

Robert slunk down behind the counter of the store. He crawled around to the middle of the floor to hide under a table covered in swags. That crabby old bastard Cutler was banging on the window. What the hell did he want? He'd given the horse back, had taken it back last night when he'd got into town. All right, he hadn't brushed him down, or fed 'n watered him, but still. The old boy could bugger off.

He snuck a look. Cutler had his nose pressed against the glass of the door, peering in. Robert knew he hadn't been seen. Cutler thumped again, waited, growled and left.

Good thing he'd got out of sight quick enough when he first snuck into the store, heading for the till. Pretty sure he'd seen that young fella, the one with the good horse, come up from the wharf. What did that mean—anything? *Was he looking for me?* Had the O'Rourke tart told him everything?

Shit. Robert's head had started to hurt again. Not the thumping murderous pain when the blow had been new—he'd strangle that Irisher chit when he got hold of her—but a dull throb that didn't seem to let up. His nose was dripping again, too. When the hell was he gonna heal? Each time he'd stared into the mirror attempting to shave, his reflection still looked like some God-awful monster back from the dead. These black eyes just seemed to keep getting blacker.

Hadn't done him any good earlier trying to talk to Myra after he'd got home. The woman had been as drunk as a lord. And those two kids of his had been scurrying about, nicking he didn't know what. He'd chased the kids out, sick of their cheek and their laziness. If Myra was still in her cups when he got back, they could both bloody well go without supper. Well, so would he. He couldn't cook to save himself.

A wave of fatigue rolled through him. His mind seemed to wobble, and his thoughts weren't coming at him straight. Confused and tired. Too tired. Sleep. He needed sleep. Holding his head, he curled into a ball under the table.

Thirty-seven

Eleanor stared down at the three-day-old serene baby girl sleeping in her arms.

'No wonder you're taking a minute to have a quiet kip. It was an ordeal for you as well, we know,' she whispered, and pressed her lips to the little forehead.

Already the O'Rourke stamp was on her—a mop of black hair. Eleanor turned this way and that as she rocked. The sunshine caught at the right moment and there was perhaps a tinge of russet in the babe's hair, as if Linley's auburn colour had crept in. She wondered if this little girl would have freckles like Linley too.

She smiled as Ard hovered by her chair.

'Ordeal for her father,' Ard said. He loosened the top button on his shirt and flapped it to cool off.

Eleanor let Ard take his daughter and stood up. 'Yes, dear, you did a lot of the hard work,' she said. She squared her shoulders. 'Come get me if you need me. I'll get back to your father and his ordeal.'

Her son held the baby in one arm, the swaddled bundle tiny against him. There was something about an adult male, brawny, with large hands and gnarled knuckles, holding a bundle as delicate as a newborn, that always seemed to gladden her heart.

'Dr Eakins says Pa looks like he might be coming out of his sleep,' Ard said.

'The signs are there. His eyes are twitching, sometimes they open and look around. A smile, I think, once or twice. There has been a few mumbled bits and pieces. His good leg is moving. Seems it's akin to swimming up from the deep. A body has to take it slow.' She squeezed his fingers. 'Go look after your family.'

'There was nothing in the post again today,' he said.

Eleanor nodded and lifted her shoulders in a shrug. 'Maybe Sam's not had time to write.' Where could her girl be?

Lorcan might wake soon. What would she tell him? She'd thought about not mentioning anything at all at first, but eventually she'd have to say something. Even if he did recover, he'd be in no state to go off looking for her himself, but she wouldn't be able to hide her worry from him. He knew her back to front. The leg was still a danger. She had to be sure he wouldn't be so impulsive to try and go after Maggie himself, but she'd put nothing past her husband.

Ard bent to his mother's cheek and kissed it. 'Sam will find her.'

Eleanor turned bleak eyes to her son. 'He's been so good to us. We didn't mean to do him wrong these last years.'

'You didn't. This thing was between him and my hard-headed sister, whatever it was. She's as much to blame as Sam. Not you.'

'I … we took her side.'

'You're supposed to.'

Eleanor smiled at him, patted his cheek. Her heart was heavy, but she walked back to her house with her head high. Keeping her chin up, her eyes on the treetops, always helped to bring on a better mood. She'd check under the bandage on Lorc's leg and refresh the poultice. She hoped to see that the inflammation was reduced around the insect bite.

She didn't know what to expect if it wasn't.

Thirty-eight

The *Sweet Georgie* had glided to her mooring at the Renmark wharf, arriving midafternoon. The moment they'd docked, the three men set to unloading the freight. They made short work of it, before turning to the cargo Barnaby Cutler had earmarked for them to carry to Mildura and onto Swan Hill.

Dry heat, cloudless, and nary a breeze. Another autumn day on the river, waiting for rain. Sweating, his shirt stuck to his back, Sam snatched off his hat and ruffled his hair. There hadn't been that much to load up; Dane was only going as far as Swan Hill on this run. Besides, other boats had been ahead of the *Sweet Georgie* and had won the contracts for freight to go to Echuca. Dane hadn't minded; horse studs and timbers for building his new yards had been more on his mind.

Sam dropped his hat back on and checked Pie, who stood patiently tied to a post on the stern deck. He figured it would be quicker if he walked on foot up to the town. Any chance he could take, he'd try to see if he could spot Robert Boyd. There was no trooper about in these parts, Dane had told him. That didn't matter. He'd take care of Boyd.

Dane hadn't been too keen. 'I'm on a tight schedule, mate. Be back within the hour.'

'I will,' Sam had said, tying down crates of dried fruit destined for Mildura. He knew that once the freight was loaded they had some time before the logging cart arrived and then they'd take on a supply of wood for the engine. 'If he's not come back here to Renmark, I'll know soon enough.'

'And if he has come back?'

'He'll wished he hadn't.' Sam finished with the crates and straightened up. He eyed the rifle sitting with Pie's saddle on the deck near the horse's feet. He wouldn't need that. He whipped off his hat again, dragged a forearm over his forehead and saw Maggie watching him from the wheelhouse deck.

He turned away. 'I'll be back directly,' he said to Dane. Bucky stared up at him. 'Come on.' The dog leapt off the gangway and galloped up the rise to the top of the bank, turning around to watch Sam coming.

'Go see Barney Cutler first,' Dane called. 'He knows everything about everything.'

Sam well remembered the old boy and headed up to the wharf master's shack but the place was locked up. Cutler was nowhere to be seen. He stood for a moment, looking around. A big red-haired fella having a quiet smoke with another bloke caught his eye. 'Bert,' he called.

'Mr Taylor.' Bert lumbered over. 'What news? Did you—'

'I did. And she's on that boat there, the *Sweet Georgie*.' Sam turned and pointed. Maggie was on the lower deck, hands on hips, talking to Dane.

'That is great news.' Bert lifted his hat high in the air and waved it at her. 'Ahoy, miss.'

Sam grabbed Bert's arm. 'Don't let everyone know about her just yet. Boyd found her too, down Lyrup. Got away, and until I know he's not come back here—'

'He has, Mr Taylor, an' he looked a right sorry state.' Bert frowned, thumping his hat back on. 'He brung Barney's horse back and dumped it at the shack there. Poor beast looked half-starved, and near drank the water trough dry. When Barney found him, he stormed into town lookin' for Boyd.'

'Looking for him where?'

Bert waved an arm towards the township. 'He's got a small store in the street, and his brother works at the post office, a stone's throw away. They won't be a havin' a good day if Barney kicks up a ruckus.'

'Right, thanks.' Sam looked at Bert. 'Let Miss Lucy know that Maggie's safe, and that I'll be takin' her home to Echuca. Tell Mrs Chaffey for me, too. Maggie will write to her, but for now …'

'I will, Mr Taylor.'

'Name's Sam.' They shook hands.

'When you headin' off?'

'Soon as I've had a look around.' Sam checked for Bucky, saw him sniffing about near a horse and cart.

Bert shoved his hands in his pockets. 'Don't waste much time on Boyd. Town's done with him. Mr Watson from the farm over yonder from Olivewood has told a few people what he saw that day Miss Maggie run off. I heard the photographer fella was there too, and has a story to tell. If Boyd's not run out of the place this time, I dunno what.' Bert gazed down at the *Sweet Georgie*. 'You reckon you'll be back this way?'

Sam took another look down the hill at Maggie. *Anywhere but near her.* She was still in animated conversation with her cousin. 'Yeah, mate, reckon I might be. I could end up anywhere.'

'Dane, I can get to Olivewood on my own.' Maggie was trying her best to get him to agree to letting her off the boat. 'It's not like I don't know my way around.'

Dane shook his head. He'd wound a spare rope into a coil and dropped it onto the deck. 'You won't be able to get back in time.'

She frowned. 'You let Sam go.'

'Sam's not going to Olivewood,' Dane said mildly.

'You could wait for me. I wouldn't be long past—'

'Tight schedule.' He turned away, picked up another rope and began to run the length of it through his hands.

'But Sam—'

'Sam has got my time limit. And I know he'll be back by it.'

Oh, now she knew what was going on. She glared. 'He's said that I'm not to get off the boat, hasn't he?'

'Nope.'

Maggie tried again. 'I'll run as fast as I can to Olivewood.'

Dane turned back to her. 'You've got good sense, Maggie. And deciding to run to Olivewood now, when we don't know where Boyd is, is not good sense.' He dropped his chin. 'Sam has come a long way to find you. He shouldn't have to go look for you again.'

Sputtering, Maggie said, 'He wouldn't have to come look for me.'

'He would. You know it.'

Ready to defend herself, she stared at her cousin. 'I am grateful for—'

'Then you'll make the right decision and not leave the boat.' He threw the rope on top of the other, perhaps a little harder than before, and folded his arms. 'Especially now because I'm going to the post office to send a telegram to your parents, advising that we have you. Don't make me gallop over the countryside after you, making me out to be a liar.'

This was like arguing with Ard, who was just as stubborn. Maggie sighed heavily. Dane was right. It was more than a mile's walk to Olivewood. She'd have no real time to speak with

Mrs Chaffey—if she was even there—before having to turn around and come straight back.

But just a chance to wave at Nara would have been good. If *she* was even there.

Maggie watched as Dane strode over the gangway onto the landing on his way to the township. She looked past him a little way, saw that Bucky was well ahead, exploring at a run. At the same time, she saw Bert Hicks standing with Sam give her a wave.

Sam had better *not* be over his time limit.

Thirty-nine

Angus let himself into the post office through the back door. 'Just collecting my pay,' he called over to Mr McKenzie who was on shift by himself today.

Mr McKenzie waved and returned to serving his customer, a dark-haired man who wanted a telegram sent. Angus thought he recognised him, maybe a riverboat man. *Not important*. He headed for his pigeonhole and grabbed his pay envelope.

The dark-haired man was stating the delivery address for Mr MacKenzie. 'O'Rourke's Run, Echuca.' That caught Angus's attention. He well knew it was the O'Rourke girl's family home. He listened for the content of the telegram. The man paid and left.

Mr McKenzie, smoothing his moustache for the next customer, put the telegram into a tray on the bench behind him, so it could be logged and sent in due course.

Catching Angus's eye, Mr MacKenzie held out his hand. 'Cash that for you, Mr Boyd?'

Angus handed over the cheque, took the cash, thanked the boss. He nodded a greeting at the new customer and when they were both occupied, he swiped the handwritten page of the telegram and read, *Taylor successful. Maggie safe. Echuca in five days. MacHenry.*

Heading out the back door, he tore the paper to shreds and let them blow in the breeze. *You might be safe, Maggie O'Rourke but no good news will get to your family. I'm a vindictive little bastard with a long memory.*

He was calm as he rode for the store as planned. Robert, where the hell would he be now? Probably got himself up at Rowley's grog tent. Robert couldn't be trusted to do much anyway, the great daft bugger.

As he pedalled, Angus wondered why he had little feeling, if any, for what he was about to do. The place wouldn't be much loss. In fact, things might start to look up if they didn't have it around their necks. It'd force Robert to find a job, which of course, he couldn't. No one would employ him even if there was work. It seemed that Robert was the only one who didn't know it. Better yet, maybe his brother and the family would leave town. Much better idea. That way, Angus'd be in the best financial position he'd ever been.

He scooted the bicycle around behind the store and leaned it up against the back wall. They hadn't enclosed a yard; most of their merchandise was small stuff, and was kept inside the building. The store wasn't crammed any longer—lack of credit had put an end to buying much. Angus supposed it wasn't a bad thing. It was all paid for, this lot, and if it burned, so what? He couldn't remember if stock was even covered by insurance. Didn't matter. Any which way, debts would be cleared by the pay-out.

Twisting his key in the lock, he let himself in and headed for the retail counter. He found the tub of discarded candles, their wicks just holding on to puddles of firm wax. Another chore Robert's kids hadn't been put to yet—to save the wax and remake another candle from the scraps. He selected one with a short wick with barely any wax, good enough for his purpose. A book of matches was in there too.

Robert kept old newspapers that had come from other towns. Angus ducked behind the long bench and there they were. This would be easier than he thought.

Standing in the shadowy space, he checked his plan again. Nah, no regrets. The place was a tinder box anyhow. He crumpled up sheets of the newspaper and nestled the candle into it, gouging out a scrape to expose the rest of the wick. He lit a match and, holding it a moment, he thought about how much time he'd have to get to the back door and lock it. He studied the wick briefly. Plenty of time. He put the flame to it and it caught and burned sturdily. It was going to work.

Swiftly, silently, at the back of the store, he stepped outside and turned the key, locking up. He waited a few moments. The faintest waft of smoke reached his nostrils. Good.

It would be best to have folk see him somewhere public now. He'd go via the wharf. He could be checking on freight they were expecting. Perhaps Robert hadn't collected the last lot Myra had told him to pick up. He'd ask around. The more people who saw him out and about while the store burned, the better.

And just maybe, *maybe* he'd see if that O'Rourke chit was around. He grabbed the bicycle and rode off.

Forty

Sam saw Barney Cutler trudging back towards the wharf. 'Mr Cutler.' He ran to meet him.

The bushy eyebrows rose as he focused on Sam. 'Yes?'

'I called in the other day asking about the *Lady Goodnight*.'

'Ah yeah, I remember, young fella. Do for ye?'

Sam fell in alongside Cutler as they headed for the hut. 'Heard that Robert Boyd was back in town after being out a night or two.'

Cutler rounded on him. 'Three nights, the bastard, and nearly killed me horse. I just been lookin' for him. He ain't at his store. I know where he lives, but I don't wanna upset his missus, the poor woman, when I have to say a few words.' He kept walking until he got to the hut. 'The man's a bloody waste o' time.'

Sam stopped at the door. 'If he's not at the store, I might go see if his brother knows where he is. Post office, right? Where is it?'

Cutler waved a hand. 'Down the town. Sign says post and telegraph office, and it's got a striped iron verandah roof. Can't miss it.'

Sam glanced back towards the boat. Wondered how long he'd have. 'Is it far? I have to leave on the boat for Mildura.'

'Young fella like you, not far. Nary a minute or two.' Cutler opened the door, nodded as he went inside. He turned and closed the door.

Big help, Barney. Sam stood for a moment and gazed around. Which direction? He'd have to ask someone else. He'd just started off when he heard the door behind him open almost as soon as it'd been closed.

'I just seen him as I closed the door,' Barney said, pointing 'That's him there on that *by*-cycle. That's the brother, Angus Boyd.'

On the boat, Maggie spotted a man she recognised riding a bicycle and heading in the direction of the wharf. She shrank back against the cabin. She didn't want to be seen by slimy Angus Boyd.

Peering out, she saw Sam speaking to that Mr Cutler. Then he pointed, and Sam turned his head to watch as Angus glided down the gentle incline heading for the wharf. Sam called out to Angus, who slowed, his feet skidding on the ground. He stepped off, the bicycle by his side. Words were traded. Sam's hands bunched to fists. Then Angus thrust the bicycle away, and it dropped to the ground. His arms flew in the air. Sam stabbed a finger at him, and Maggie could see their angry faces, could hear the shouts, but couldn't make out what was being said.

Dane clambered down from the wheelhouse. He'd sent the telegram to her parents—she was relieved at that—and had returned earlier from the post office, much pleased to see his cousin still on board. Now he stopped on the deck beside her. Joe stepped onto the gangway, trying to get a better look.

'What is it?' Maggie asked. 'What's going on? I can't hear properly.'

'Looks like Sam's holding his own. That's not what's worrying me. You see it, Joe?'

'Big smoke coming from the town, boss.'

A billowing column of smoke rolled in the air. Men on the wharf leapt upright, shouting alarm. They downed tools and threw freight to the ground. Horses' reins were tied tight to the rails, the carts braked and wheels hurriedly chocked. The men ran to grab buckets and tore up the incline heading for the town.

'Don't follow them, Sam,' Dane muttered as he watched.

Maggie could hear that, and then heard his dismay when Sam shoved Angus Boyd out of the way and bolted after the other men. 'Dammit. Come on, Joe. More hands, the quicker the fire's out—' Dane stopped abruptly. 'Maggie, look after the boat. Get a rod from the engine room and stop anyone coming on board. Better yet, do you know how to use a rifle, a Martini-Henry?'

Worried now, she nodded. 'Out of practice but—'

'It's in the wheelhouse, on the wall. Bullets boxed in a compartment underneath. Any trouble, just fire a round or two into the air. Don't kill anyone, you hear me?' Dane pulled his hat a little lower. 'Where's that dog when you need him, eh? He wouldn't let anyone on board.'

Then he and Joe sprinted up the hill, ignoring Angus. She should have told Dane who the man on the bicycle was. She thought it odd that Angus Boyd had silently watched them as they ran past him, making no attempt to go back to the town. He just stood there, observing. Then turned his gaze and saw her.

She took off for the wheelhouse.

Forty-one

Maggie raced up the steps, her skirt and pinafore hitched, her boots clanging on the iron slats. She swung into the wheelhouse, yanked the rifle out of its brackets, and scrabbled around in the compartment for a bullet. Cracking the gun lever down, she slid the cartridge into the chamber and snapped the lever back, then grabbed another couple of bullets and dropped them into her pinny pocket. It looked like Angus Boyd hadn't got the guts to step onto the gangway. Not yet anyway.

Her hands shook. Her legs shook. Her jaw shook. Sweet Lord, did she have to aim a gun at someone—and shoot it? She'd only ever shot at rabbits for practice with her pa and her brother. Her father had taught her how to use a gun for her own safety—snakes in the house, or foxes around the chicken coop. Not for shooting people.

She should run for it. Blast what Dane had said about not leaving the boat—if Angus Boyd came on board after her, she'd have nowhere to hide. She couldn't jump overboard—she'd have to run.

His bicycle discarded partway down the dusty path to the wharf, Angus Boyd was a few yards from the landing. He looked back over his shoulder.

She swallowed. No one was coming, that was clear. Then he turned and took a step or two, squinting up at the wheelhouse, and stopped. He couldn't see her, but his voice rose up. 'You stay right there on that boat. My brother's none too happy with you, missy.' Angus's voice had a quiver in it. 'You tried to kill him. We got photographic proof.'

She dashed to the open window of the wheelhouse. 'You get *the hell* away from this boat,' she shouted, and dashed back hiding again. 'I did no such thing and you know it. He attacks defenceless women,' she yelled. She was desperate to see where he was, at the same time she didn't want to see.

'You never looked defenceless to me,' he called. 'Put the gun down. Got something to discuss with you. I'm coming on board.'

She rushed back to the window in time to see him step onto the gangway. 'Oh no, you're not,' she cried, and aimed the gun at him.

He stood stock still. 'Have you loaded it, dear Miss Maggie?' he asked, the derisive sneer unmistakeable.

I'm not the fool here, you toad. The gun felt light in Maggie's hands.

'I only want to talk business with you.' A whine crept into his voice. 'I need you to pay me a little something for keeping those photographs to myself.' He took a step.

Maggie pointed the rifle skywards and fired. *Oh my God, my ears.* Pain filled her head. Fingers shaking madly, she reloaded and fired again.

The heat coming out of the building was intense. Sam handed bucket after bucket of water up the line with the other men. Next to him, Bert worked as hard as any, head and shoulders above the others. Throwing buckets full of water at this inferno seemed too little too late.

Fire roared inside the building, tearing down everything in its path. The windows blew out, and fresh surges of flame and heat burst onto the street.

Then a shout came from behind. 'No more water, fellas. The cart's empty, horse trough's empty. Bastard's too far gone now to try stop it, anyhow. Pull back. Let her go.'

The line broke up as men fell back from the front of the building. The flames inside raged on, and trusses and wall timbers crashed to the ground. Fire flew, licking high and low, and smoke curled out of the broken windows, swirling over the roof and above the flames that poked through. The roar of the inferno was fierce, and then as quick as it stormed, it died. The brick façade at the front was scorched, mortar had already crumbled away, and heat pulsed off it. A loud crack or two, and a last tumble of damaged timber, then the silence was eerie.

The house next door had been saved but smoke had filled the place, sending the occupants coughing and gagging into the street.

Standing back with the other men in safety on the opposite side of the street, Sam wiped smoke-filled tears as they streamed from his eyes. Hot soot stung his hands and his scalp. Bert slapped himself down, grinning over at him as he stomped on stray embers. Sam bent over, hands on his knees and tried to take clean air into his lungs. He hoped to Christ nothing else would go up in flames. They were too far from the wharf for boats to catch fire, but the danger of runaway flames was ever present, always on people's minds, and they had an empty water cart.

'Young fella, young fella,' Mr Cutler rasped, hobbling up to him, waving his hand urgently. He got to Sam, gripped his forearm and went down on his knees in the dirt, gasping for breath. 'Hurry. Get to ye boat. There were gunshots.' The old fella was breathing hard. He must have run up from the hut.

Dane and Joe swung in by Cutler's side. Dane grabbed him before he toppled off his knees. He looked at Sam. 'I told Maggie to shoot off a couple of rounds if she got in trouble. I've got the old man. Go.'

Joe slapped Sam's shoulder hard. 'I'll be right behind ye, lad.'

Sam took off. *Maggie and a gun. Jesus.*

Forty-two

Angus had bolted off the gangway at the shots and raced to grab his bicycle. His boot caught a jutting rock in the road and down he went, hard, sprawling. Staggering to his feet, clutching at a sharp pain in his side, he bungled trying to pull the contraption upright. He saw a man appear at the top of the incline and panicking, he tripped, fell heavily again. *The pain. Shit. Must have snapped a rib* … Scrambling up, he hopped and hobbled with the bicycle, partly lifting it, partly dragging it, along the river's edge.

Short of breath, pain tight in his chest, Angus couldn't ride; he could barely walk upright. He dropped the bicycle by a neighbour's fence and staggered on to Robert's house, closer to the wharf than his. He could sit down there. No one would find him.

Lurching inside, his niece … Whatshername—God, his head was foggy—was standing over a seated Myra and dabbing a cool rag over her mother's head.

'Uncle Angus,' she cried as he pitched to the floor.

He rolled onto his back, a hand over the pain in his chest.

Myra cautiously got out of the chair, and leaned over him. 'What is it? What's the matter?'

His breath wouldn't come. 'Store is burned,' he wheezed, his gaze on Myra.

'What?' Myra snapped. 'Marcia, what did he say?'

The girl got on her knees and put her ear near Angus's mouth. 'He says the store is burned.'

'Oh, my God. Oh no, not that.' Shock was wide on her face.

Angus mumbled some more.

'What's he saying now?' Myra screeched. Blood started to drip from her forehead again. 'It can't have burned down.'

'It's all right, it's insured.'

Myra's face purpled. 'It's not insured,' she exploded. 'I spent that money getting rid of Robert's floozies,' she seethed.

Marcia only looked frightened. She bent to Angus when beckoned. He muttered, 'My chest.'

The girl peeled open his jacket. Gasping at the blood-soaked waistcoat, she snatched her hand away. Then gingerly she unbuttoned the waistcoat.

'There's something sticking into his chest,' she said, horrified.

'What?' Myra demanded, squinting.

Marcia stared at it. 'It's stuck right in.' She got up, backing away from Angus, then stared at her mother. 'Ma, what do we do?'

'Run, find help for Angus. Run, go now.' Marcia bolted and Myra cried after her, 'But I fear he might die before help comes.' Then she eased down to kneel beside him. 'You have your Adeline's hatpin,' she breathed close to his ear. 'Now, where did you find that?'

Angus could hear her strangely singsong voice clearly, even though she seemed to be fading before his eyes. Her hand was on his chest and he could feel a pressure, and deeper pain. 'Adeline,' he thought he said, his voice a murmur, an echo in his ears.

'She's dead, Angus,' Myra whispered. 'And you must have found her hatpin under my bed. That won't do. And somehow it's been knocked between your ribs. I bet it's nicked your heart just a wee bit. That won't do, either. Need to fix that.'

Myra's hand was over the handle of the hatpin. But she didn't pull it, she pushed. Angus stared up at her, tried to take hold of it. Too slippery. His fingers too fumbling. Sharp pain. Agony.

Adeline's hatpin … my heart.

Forty-three

Sam had ignored Angus Boyd, sped down onto the landing, thudded over the gangway and leapt onto the boat. He must have taken the steps up the ladder two and three at a time, for in hardly a breath he burst into the wheelhouse. 'Don't shoot,' he cried, eyes wide, hands thrust in the air.

'Oh, very funny, Sam Taylor.' Maggie turned and propped the rifle against the wall. Her whole body was shaking, and her ears rang in protest of the gunshots. She put a hand on the wall to steady herself.

Joe crowded in behind him, pushing into the small space. Then Dane shouldered his way over. 'You all right, Maggie?'

She nodded, glanced at all three men to show how brave she was, how calm, collected and—

'You don't look all right.'

'It's not often I threaten someone with a gun.' She looked at Sam but couldn't read his face. She looked away. *Hot. Shaky. For goodness sake, Mairead.*

Dane gripped her shoulder. 'He's gone, limping off in a big hurry as if you had shot him. What did he want?'

Her mouth had dried. 'He said he had something to talk about, some photographs someone had of me attacking his brother.'

Sam tensed. 'I'll go after him.'

'Not you,' Dane ordered. 'Joe and I will go find him and we'll have a quiet talk. But not you.' He glanced at Maggie. 'Wait for us. Don't leave the boat.' He said to Sam, 'On deck, now.'

Maggie felt her legs wobble and she groped for the bench seat on the side wall. She sat a moment, then slumped, and let the fright and the confusion engulf her. Her mind went blank. She closed her eyes. *All I want is Sam.*

On the deck, Sam insisted, 'I'll go. So far his bloody brother has got away with attacking her, and now there's talk of blackmail. I want those photographs myself.'

Dane shook his head. 'If I go see what this fella wanted and why, he'll still be alive afterwards. Then I'll find the photographer. You're to stay on the boat, security for my cousin. We'll be back as soon as possible, then we need to be gone.' Dane stared hard at Sam, then lowered his tone. 'I trust you to do the right thing.' He turned to Joe. 'Let's go.'

Sam watched them head off. *What the hell was the right thing where Maggie O'Rourke was concerned?* He stared up at the wheelhouse. She was there, dammit, and he was on the boat, alone with her.

He should've insisted on going after Angus Boyd. Even if the man beat his brains out, it would be easier than resisting Maggie O'Rourke. He had to resist. He cast about for something useful to do instead of standing around like a lump of lard. Have a wash, maybe. He looked across at Pie. He hadn't spooked with all the shenanigans. And he'd left another pile of horseshit. A wash could wait. He'd grab the shovel and do away with it, and keep the dog from leaping into …

Where the hell was the damn dog?

Maggie made her way slowly down the iron steps, unsure her feet could be trusted. She crept onto the deck and looked across the river. The town was on the other side of the boat, so she was glad she couldn't see anything of what might have been going on. She just wanted to get to her cabin and throw caution to the wind. Stupid. Dangerous, but he was what she needed. Sam. *No, no. Be sensible.*

That might have been a possibility except at that moment Sam tried to step around her on his way to the forward deck.

A startling voice clanged in her head. *Now, or never again, Maggie.* She heard herself breathe his name. 'Sam.'

He stopped. Grime was at his collar and she could smell smoke and sweat. A courteous smile appeared on his soot-stained face.

She knew it wasn't a real smile. He was being polite. *How horrible.* She didn't want polite. Not now.

She rubbed her forehead. 'Sam,' she said again, and felt her heart rate notching faster. She wanted those arms that were smudged with ash and dust around her, those hands on her. *This was no time to be a lady.* He did care for her, she could tell, even though he tried to hide it behind the polite smile.

He tilted his head, looked over towards his horse and back again, hands now in his pockets. 'Yes, Maggie?' Impatient.

'I need you, Sam.' She gripped his shirt in both hands.

He cupped her face, and kissed her, hard and urgent, his bristly whiskers scratchy. She didn't care. Pressed against the cabin's wall, the bulge of his penis between her legs sent a wave of *giddy* through her.

Her Sam, her Sam. How could she ever have run from this?

His chin slid to her neck, rasped her nape. His hands spanned her waist, slid up to her breasts, edging her closer to her cabin door. His teeth tugged open the thin ribbon on her chemise and the heat of sunshine fell on her skin. His mouth took hers as he reached around and loosened her pinafore, his warm hand sliding back under her chemise to claim a bare nipple. He tweaked it with demanding fingers, and rushes of need spiralled to her belly.

This this this.

He wrenched open the cabin door, swung her inside, and pulled it shut. Knocked his hat and it hit the floor. Grabbing her under her backside, he lifted. Her dress hoicked to her thighs and wrapping her naked legs around him, she squirmed, lush and loose, and pleasure streaked from where his rigid arousal hardened on her. He dropped her down on the narrow bed, and with her dress and pinny bunched, her legs open, she rucked her knickers aside. His breath was ragged. Urgent, wild, he flicked open his flies, and filled her with a thrust so deep and hot, she cried out.

Delicious shock. She rocked with him, fingers dug into his shoulders to hang on, and wave after wave of sleek teasing pleasure rolled through her. It bloomed—an exquisite burst, and she bucked. He tensed and groaned. Thrust one last time, and then buried his face in her shoulder.

Moments passed. He was still collapsed on her when she thought she heard him hum a tune close to her ear.

He moved, brought her hand between them, pressed it over her mound and cupped it. 'I couldn't stop,' he said, his voice a whisper. 'Not even to take off my boots.'

She smiled, was breathless. 'Neither could I.'

He pressed her hand again. 'Now, you.'

'I am already happy.'

'I missed it?'

'Hmm.' Her eyes were closed, enjoying the feel of him still inside. 'It's truly wonderful, that thing we discovered.'

There was silence for a time, restful, calm.

'Maggie-mine.' His voice thrummed, changed. He moved. 'I have to go. The boys will be back.' He kissed her once, and slipped out of her. 'Don't worry, I won't bother you again.'

Her heart flipped. 'Bother me? What?' She rose on her elbows. '*We* did this. Not just you,' she said, and heard the retort in her voice.

He drew down her dress to cover her bare legs, stood up and rebuttoned his flies. His mouth was set in a line.

'Look, don't think that I won't be there if you need me, just because we slipped up again,' he said, an edge to his voice. 'I'll marry you if we've made … if you become … I'll marry you. We'd get along. We're old friends. But I know how you feel about marryin', and all that.' He tossed a hand in the air. 'It's my fault, this thing. I only came to deliver you safely home.' He glared at her, eyes creased under a frown. 'I've got along just fine, you know? And all of that before, back home? Well, I've put it behind me, you don't have to worry. This isn't right anymore.'

'What?' she cried again. It was some speech. She could hear his words clearly, but could not comprehend why this man was saying what he was saying.

Sam flung out of her cabin, felt groggy. Shit, broad daylight, with Maggie, like *that*, and not a haystack in sight. Shit. His brains weren't even *hiding* in his trousers, he kept them there on a permanent basis.

Jesus. But Chrissakes, it was the best. Thank Christ I didn't fall asleep on her.

He rubbed his face hard. Felt the grit and checked the palm of his hand. Soot. Christ, it'd be all over her. Her face, her neck. Her breasts, her soft, full breasts with dark nipples and … He felt his cock rise and he shoved it down. It could stay half-hearted, the bastard.

Shit. *Shit.*

He spun around. Get washed up, get rid of the soot, and scrub away the scent of her, don't leave a reminder. But the reminder wasn't just her scent.

Jesus, man, you couldn't resist, could ye, no matter what, could ye? Some man, Taylor, some big man you are.

Not that he wouldn't marry her, but that he went *there*—again. Just dropped his pants and away he went. He ran a hand over his head to swipe off his hat.

Shit! Where was his hat?

Her cabin door swung open. His hat came spinning out and whooshed over the side into the river. The cabin door slammed.

His cue to jump in the river. If he stayed close to the boat he'd be fine. He shucked shirt, pants, socks, boots. Keeping a hold of the boat with one hand, he eased his way into the river, grabbed the filthy clothes off the deck and swished them in the water. He grabbed his hat before it drifted off and swished it too, then flung everything back on board. Soot and grime floated away on water already muddied by boats that had been here earlier.

Sam roughly washed his face. Slapped water under his armpits, scrubbed at his groin. Traitor, he snarled at his limp penis. His penis had nothing more to add.

Shit.

Maggie sat up on her bed. Bunk. It was little more than a bunk, meant for short journeys. Certainly not for the journey she'd just been on, though she hadn't minded. Now that her confusion had lifted, and if she wasn't so angry, she might have laughed aloud. It had been heady and breathtaking and wonderful, that journey with Sam. And he'd ruined it. *Again*.

Unhappy, she went to pour from the pitcher of water, and spied his hat on the floor. Snatching it up, she thrust open the door and tossed it out. *Very satisfying*. She slammed the door.

He'd just left in such haste. What did that mean?

She set about washing away the aftermath of their lovemaking. Should she call the thing they'd just done lovemaking? She didn't know. Whatever it was, it was the way they did things, even after two years apart. It was them—hale and hearty and without fear.

She bathed herself as thoroughly as possible. Of course she cared if her lack of caution resulted in the unthinkable, but it didn't *feel* as if anything would happen. *How foolish, Maggie*. Just because neither of their other times had resulted in a child didn't mean she should tempt fate. *Or tempt Sam*. For that's what she'd done. And deliberately. Despite herself, a bloom of heat burned her cheeks. Her stomach had the flutters.

Perhaps he just did what any man would do when faced with a woman who was all wanton and demanding. Perhaps that's why he sounded so half-hearted about marrying. *He'd said before not to pester him again. He said that he'd put it all behind him*. Then he'd left the cabin so abruptly, it had been almost embarrassing. Had he not felt every single thing she'd felt? Perhaps not. Did he think it wasn't proper? *This isn't right anymore, he'd said*.

Well, of course it wasn't proper—for *other* people. But for her and Sam, it was them. That's how she always thought of it. If only he didn't want the drudgery of family life. Perhaps … *Can you think of something other than* perhaps, *Maggie?* Now she felt truly embarrassed. She'd thrown herself at him and it was possible he'd just taken what she'd offered, nothing more.

Well, what did she expect? She couldn't understand herself. Terrified of having children yet deliberately throwing herself at a man. Well, Sam. Not just any man.

For the first time, things looked more than bleak. The future was a wide unfriendly landscape before her, not one filled with hope. Her heart rattled. No job. No prospects of a job to fulfil her grand plan. The only money she had was one pound six and six in her little purse. No Sam … *Maggie O'Rourke, you selfish woman.*

Her family at Echuca, probably desperate to see her, was waiting to have her back with open arms. She had failed dreams and her life was in tatters but they'd help her back on her feet, fill up her well of strength again. They wouldn't care that she had rags on her back. They wouldn't care that she'd messed things up, or that she had nothing but an adventure to tell, or that her only friends were two people who'd disappeared into the bush, and a floppy-eared dog with a long curly … *Bucky. Where is Bucky?*

Forty-four

Sam, fully clothed, was drying off nicely in the midafternoon sun. He was sprawled on the deck with the opposite bank of the river in his sights.

Maggie had come out of her cabin and stayed on the other side of the boat, pacing a little, and scanning the riverbank. She hadn't spoken to him and he hadn't been inclined to say anything more to her either.

When Dane and Joe arrived back—seemed they'd only been gone an hour or so—Sam sat up, expectantly. 'Any news of the bastard?'

'Some. Let me catch my breath.' Dane leaned over, hands on his knees. 'Looks like you've already had a good dunking. That's what I need to do.'

Joe snatched off his hat and boots. 'I'm going in while you're talkin' about it.' He slipped over the side of the boat, and splashed around, slapping off the soot and grime.

'Got nasty up there with that store that burned,' Dane said, and settled on the floor of the deck alongside Sam. 'Found a body.'

'Jesus. Who?'

'The men said it was Robert Boyd. A whole heap of canvas or something had fallen over him, protected the body from much of the fire so there was something of him left to recognise. Not much, but enough, apparently.' He shook his head, wiped a hand under his nose. 'No one saw him fighting the fire, so they reckoned he was already inside. Maybe he started the fire, got trapped. Bad business.'

'Bad business, for sure,' Sam said. So Robert Boyd was out of the picture.

Dane continued. 'They figured to let his wife know, and his brother. So we got old Barney Cutler to take us to her place first, and there on the floor was the brother, Angus, dead. Robert's wife, Myra was kneeling over him, her hand still on the hatpin she'd shoved into his chest.'

'A hatpin?'

'Hard to believe, eh? Not a dainty one though, damn near the size of a small stiletto. So out it all pours from the wife. Seems Robert had been a philanderer these past few years, and a rough one at that. Myra, rather than keep at him and copping a couple of blows for her trouble, took it upon herself to have a chat to his so-called lady friends, to get them to leave town. Mind you, from what I gather, most were only too happy to get away. They gave Myra their valuables—jewellery—as payment for her silence about *their* reputation, *their* indiscretion with her husband, and then she makes them leave town.'

Sam barked a laugh. 'Some piece of work.'

'Seems so.' Dane scratched his ear. 'But, this last time, the woman, Adeline someone, was stepping out with Angus. Myra's learned that Robert's accosted her at some point … This is where is gets really nasty.' He thought a moment. 'Middle of the day and no one about, Myra finds Adeline out the back of the boarding house. Adeline's refused to hand anything over to Myra, and threatens to go to the police about them. Told Myra that she would see Robert go to gaol. There's a struggle, and Myra grabs Adeline's hatpin and stabs her with it. So Barney sent a couple of the boys over there today. They found her body at the bottom of the long-drop in the outhouse, covered in quicklime, and all else. The stench was well covered up.'

Sam blew out a long breath. 'No mean feat for a woman, throwing a dead body down a hole.'

'One of the town lads has ridden to Overland Corner to bring back the constable,' Dane said. 'We had that photographer fella take pictures of the bodies. Gruesome.'

Sam looked up. 'Photographer?'

'I asked him about the pictures he had. He said he'll destroy them all, the plates as well. I believe him; it was Boyd he was hoping to get rid of. Now with both brothers gone, no need for those pictures. He'll do what he said he'd do.'

'Shit. So Myra was a blackmailer, as well as a murderer,' Sam said.

'And not a smart one, either. When she goes to the gallows, there's no one to take her kids. They'll be sent to an institution.'

'Christ, what could ever be so bad to drive a woman to that?'

Maggie stepped into view. Dane looked up and studied her face a moment, turned and said pointedly to Sam, 'Can never tell what drives a woman sometimes.' He looked back at Maggie.

Sam looked at her too. *Shit*. Her chin was red, so was her neck, plain as day. She'd washed off the black soot, but his whiskers must have left their mark. He got to his feet. 'Maggie.' His voice softened. She looked worried, and about to say something.

Dane stood up. 'Cousin,' he said, frowning at her before beginning to pull off his boots. 'Just so you know, both Boyd men are dead.' As she started to speak, he said, 'Let me wash off first, then I'll tell you all about it while we get underway. We've got an hour, maybe two, of good daylight before we need to tie up for the night. Have to make up time.' He glanced at Sam and said under his breath, 'Hope you both made the right decision, though I am hardly one to judge.' He lowered to the deck again, slipped into the river and dropped below the surface a moment, then came up and floated a while.

Maggie spun to Sam. 'Did I hear that right—both Boyd men dead?'

He nodded. 'That's what Dane said. A relief, I would think.'

'Relief, yes.' Her voice shook.

'So now, I'm taking you back home.' He shoved his hands in his pockets.

'I'm glad it was you who came for me, Sam.'

He took a deep breath. 'I came because there was no one else.'

Joe coughed loudly as he hauled himself up out of the water, clambered to his feet and then took himself across the deck. He removed his shirt, out of Maggie's sight, and wrung it out.

Dane swam closer and ducked under once more.

Maggie tried again. 'I know that you—'

'You don't know anything,' Sam snapped. 'So don't start, not here, not now,' he said, glaring at her. 'That's final.'

'Final, be damned,' she hurled back at him.

Joe was hovering, so Sam held up his hands at Maggie, knew he had to back off. He'd surrender, for the moment. Anger streaked colour over her face before she turned away and leaned over the side. As Dane surfaced she called to him. 'We can't go until Bucky comes back.'

He swept back his hair and spat water. 'We're not waiting for a dog.'

Maggie looked towards the township. 'I think he'll have gone back to Olivewood,' she said, as if she hadn't heard Dane. Sam heard the crack in her voice.

Dane dunked his head, came up shaking it. He rubbed his clothes vigorously under water, then dragged himself back on deck. 'If he comes in the next ten minutes, we'll take him. If not, we go without him.' He stood up, glancing at Maggie, and changed his tone when he saw her face. 'Maybe Sam can come back for him soon, or maybe I'll pick him up on another run.'

Maggie turned away.

'Bucky's a dog. He's a good dog, and dogs find their own way,' Dane said. 'We're leaving as soon as Joe's got the boat fired up. I have the last of my contracts to fulfil and I have to be on time. Grab the gangway, Joe.'

Maggie rushed over. 'No, Joe. Wait.'

'I'm sorry, Miss Maggie.' Joe was on the landing, taking the mooring rope from the tie-up post. He threw it onto the boat, dragged the gangway on board and began to wind the rope. 'We'll be a few wee minutes before the boat can get herself upriver,' he said kindly. 'Ye never know, the beastie might show up yet. They're attracted by shenanigans, a lot of shoutin' and such. But he might not'a liked the fire, and he's steered clear awhile. He'll be right.'

Standing behind her, Sam scanned the bank. No sign of the dog. He watched Maggie. It wouldn't be beyond the woman he knew to leap off the boat and wade to the shore, go scrambling up the bank and head towards Olivewood.

But she didn't. She paced a little and didn't lift her eyes to acknowledge him. So be it. It would make things easier. He hoped. He didn't believe it for one second.

Joe passed by, and Sam heard him go below deck. Not long after, he heard the thud of logs being thrown into the boiler, heard the pistons react, slowly at first, beating time.

Watching the bank, Maggie's hands balled into fists and she rubbed them together while she waited. She looked anxious. He'd never seen Maggie like this, and it irked him. It had been a big day today and the missing dog was the last straw, he reckoned. She was fond of the dog, that was obvious. Sam was fond of Bucky too, and if the truth be known, it was Bucky who led him to Maggie. But if the curly coated bugger was off on some adventure, he'd have to stay behind.

Maggie paced to the back of the boat and returned. 'I should have thought to grab him,' she said without looking at him.

'It was a while back, more than a couple of hours. Too much excitement. You weren't to know.'

The boat chugged but didn't move forwards or backwards.

'He's got his own mind, that dog,' she said, still staring up the incline.

The boat shifted again, and Sam felt it begin to pull away from the landing. He heard Maggie's intake of breath and a soft cry that followed. Her eyes were still on the sandy bank.

The pistons beat faster time. The *Sweet Georgie*'s whistle blasted, a hollow sound that echoed over the river. From the bank, the few men who'd returned from the fire hooted and waved goodbye. Sam saw Bert, who lifted his hat and shouted, 'Goodbye, Miss Maggie' though Sam wasn't sure she'd heard him. She did see him though, and lifted her arm in a distracted wave.

The boat backed out into the wide expanse of water. As it chugged into forward gear, the paddles slapped on the water and it gained a little speed. For a hundred yards or so, it followed the curve of the bank then glided out into the middle.

Sam looked over his shoulder. The Renmark wharf looked like it was slowly receding, almost as if into part of another life. If he went to work for Dane, there might be a few more river runs in it, and maybe down this way. He leaned on the wall under the wheelhouse, watching Maggie clasp and unclasp her hands until finally she let them drop.

She hung her head. The dog hadn't come.

Forty-five

Long, slanting rays of sunshine and the afternoon was drawing to dusk. There was maybe an hour in it. Sam knew Dane wanted to keep going, but he wouldn't steam at night—lesson learned from Cap'n Strike. Sam looked back across their wake, and the Renmark wharf couldn't be seen.

Maggie hadn't left the deck. She'd pulled around an empty crate and propped it against the line of disused cabins, had sat down and not moved.

Sam kept up a steady flow of cut logs for Joe to feed into the boiler. Finished with that for a while, he stood in the wheelhouse with Dane, making small talk. With little else to do, he'd gone back down to the deck and found her there.

'How far away would we be from Renmark already?' she asked, looking over the water.

'Not sure. Not far, maybe only a few miles.'

She nodded. 'I should have tried harder to see Mrs Chaffey.'

'Could always write to her.'

Maggie sighed. 'I was going to go on downriver, to Murray Bridge, you know.'

'What's there?'

She lifted a shoulder. 'I don't know. That was part of the adventure.'

'Downriver a-ways is said to be a bit wild and—'

'Don't lecture me,' she said softly.

Sam gave a short laugh. 'Wouldn't dream of it.'

Dane leaned out of the wheelhouse above. 'Dog,' he shouted and pointed to the riverbank.

Maggie leapt to her feet. 'Bucky,' she cried, part laugh, part sob, and joyful to Sam's ears.

The galloping dog bounded along the water's edge, leaping and dodging rocks and low bushes in his way, speeding along with the boat. And then two people appeared, running behind the dog, waving, calling out.

Maggie couldn't make out the words, but she knew well enough who they were. 'Nara and Wadgie from Olivewood,' she breathed, turning to Sam. Then she waved her hands above her head. 'Nara,' she yelled.

Nara ran, her skirt clutched in one hand, and waving with the other. The man yelled something at Bucky, and looked to be urging him on.

'Wadgie,' Maggie yelled and waved some more. The man's arm rose in a wave.

Then Bucky took a leap into the water.

Maggie shrieked. 'Dane,' she cried, jumping up and down, throwing her arm towards the dog.

'I see him,' Dane yelled and turned the boat towards him.

Bucky paddled out, strong and determined. Maggie slid to her knees at the edge of the boat. 'Come on, Bucky,' she urged, her worried gaze on him. 'Come on, boy.'

Joe came up on deck, wiping his hands on a rag. 'Ah, the wee beastie, Miss Maggie,' he said, laughing.

'My wee beastie,' she said, hiccupping and sobbing. 'Bucky,' she called and waving an arm, beckoned the dog. 'Come on, boy. Come on.'

Sam knelt beside her. 'Come on, laddie,' he beckoned the dog and as Bucky got close enough, he reached down and grabbed the scruff of his neck. Joe dropped to the deck and clamped a hand on the dog's rump and together they hauled him on board.

Bucky thrust out of their hold and, legs scrambling for purchase, he aimed straight for Maggie. Bowling her over, he sat on her, all four limbs akimbo. She was laughing and crying under a forty-pound sodden dog, and grabbed him by the neck and shook him, equally delighted to see him.

Sam's chest filled with a sharp breath, and his heart lifted. This was *his* Maggie. *This* was the Maggie he knew and loved.

The dog gave a huge shudder and water sprayed in heavy drops all over her. She squealed and shoved him off, laughing, gleeful. Then Bucky stepped over her, padded towards Pie and plopped on the deck close by. Joe, chuckling, went back below deck.

Sam got off his knees as the boat glided back towards the middle of the river. He looked up at Dane, who grinned at him. Maggie had stood up, dripping and was waving to the people on the bank.

'Thank you, my friends, thank you,' she yelled, still laughing and crying. They yelled something back. 'What are they saying, Sam?'

'That they're going back. Nara still has a job.'

Then they were gone, retreating to the cover of the scrub. Maggie stood there a moment, then turned to look at him, happiness still on her face. 'Maybe Bucky found them on the way to Olivewood.'

'Maybe.' He couldn't help smiling at her. This was the Maggie he knew, alive with delight in all things good. This Maggie was the heart and the soul of his life, strong and determined to make her own way.

Maybe he'd risk it, just once more. Maybe. But not until after they were home.

Forty-six

Eleanor stood at the foot of Lorc's bed, Ard was beside her, the baby nestled in the crook of his arm.

'I told Pa all about her, told him I'd bring Toby directly when he wakes up from his sleep. He makes a racket, that brother of hers, his teeth still trying to come through. He might wake the dead with all the yellin' he does.'

Eleanor took the sleeping infant from her son. 'Go see to Linley and Toby, and your daughter and I will sit here a while with old Grandpa until she needs a feed.'

'I'll come back for her,' Ard said and kissed his mother, ran a big finger over his daughter's head and left.

Eleanor settled in the chair close to Lorc's bed. She reached over and placed the baby close to her husband's head, so that she perched near his shoulder. Asleep, she only made snuffling noises. The little head turned towards her grandfather's ear, and she murmured and squeaked a little.

Eleanor sighed. She'd been repeating herself for days, hoping something would bring him round.

She tried again. 'Four days old now, our little bairn, and still no name. Never heard of in our day, was it, Lorc? The wee babes had names as soon as they popped out.'

She held his hand on the bed, whispered a few words in Gaelic. 'Ard, after Ardal the warrior. High valour, it means. He has that in spades, our lad.' Then a little sadness crept into her voice and she patted his hand. 'And the wee laddie we lost all those years ago. Ruairí, he was.' He was never forgotten, her stillborn, and grief bloomed for a moment. 'I never knew I'd risk losing my heart and soul again like I did, like we did, after him.' She brightened. 'And then along came your little tempest, Mairead. Not really like a pearl as her name means, but she's our pearl, isn't she?'

Eleanor stopped then. Her chest filled with a ball of emotion that threatened to bob right into her throat. She held her breath tight and waited until the tears backed down. She let it go slowly, carefully, and the solid pain inside eased.

'And our pearl has a right lad in that Sam, hasn't she? Though she probably doesn't know it. Or,' she said, and laughed, 'is denying it.' She stroked the big hand, tracing the bent bones of his fingers that had been broken over the years. 'Samuel. When I asked, Mrs Epstein in the town said it means "asked of God". Can't imagine that of Sam, can you? Asked of God—he'd joke around too much.' She bent her head. *But I hope he's been sent by God and finds our daughter.*

She rubbed the tiny baby's back. 'And this wee one. Wonder why they haven't given her a name, yet, Lorc? Linley's fine, she's up and about. She's already doing some chores again. Surely they've had time to decide on a name.' Running a finger gently over the infant's hair, she smiled. 'Almost the exact same look as our girl, Lorc. The black, black head of hair, the sweet face. I wonder if she'll have a sweet temper, or will she be like your little tempest?'

The baby mewled again.

Lorcan made a sound in his throat, clearing it, swallowing. 'And where is my little tempest?' he asked, his voice croaky. One eye opened and closed again.

Eleanor thought her heart would stop. Relief flooded her eyes. She edged forwards, holding the baby firmly with one hand. She gripped her husband's hand with her other and told a lie. 'Oh, she's not far away, Lorc. She's comin',' she said, hoping the wobble in her voice wouldn't be noticed. 'And she'll be a right little tempest if you're not awake when she arrives.'

He grunted as if that would indeed be so. He mumbled something else and drifted away again. His hand in hers relaxed. The doctor had said it would be a slow surfacing if he was going to come 'round, and that these sorts of signs might be the start of it.

Eleanor sat, staring at his face. His lined, whiskery face, now pale after being out of the sun for weeks. The face of a man she'd loved for more years than anything else. She hoped the thought of Maggie being close by would help. But they'd heard nothing from Sam. Conflicting emotions tore through her. Her daughter was still missing; her husband was coming out of his coma. She wouldn't risk telling him that Maggie was lost and hadn't been found, but risked his grief if he woke and Maggie wasn't safely back at home.

The baby girl made noises, her little mouth working. Lorc tilted his head towards her a little, as if to hear. Eleanor pushed down her fear. 'I'll take the wee one back to her mother for a feed before she starts up her squallin' and brings down the house. I'll be right back, my darlin',' she said and patted his arm.

Gathering up the baby, she took another look at her husband. She knew Linley had just made some bread. It would be warm and fragrant. She'd grab a pot of apricot jam to bring back with it. Food always worked on Lorcan O'Rourke.

Forty-seven

Three full days from Renmark and the Mildura wharf came into view. 'We're late,' Dane said as he swung the wheel. 'Naught to be done about it but I think we'll be met kindly by the merchants,' he said to Maggie. 'Ranald Finn and Johnny Bentley had many friends on the river. So did the *Goodnight*.'

Apart from docking at Wentworth for more freight, they'd only made one other stop to barter for an extra load of wood to see them through. At times, the snaggers had held them up, but Dane had said naught to do about that either; they were essential on the river, dragging fallen trees out of the water, clearing the way.

Joe had fished. 'Murray cod, miss,' he'd shout and show her a big fish. Maggie had cooked Murray cod after Murray cod. So much of it that she was heartily sick of it. The men of course had wolfed it down with every meal. There were hardly any leftovers for Bucky so she cooked up a concoction of scraps—fish guts and the remainder of the corned beef, too chewy to eat. He also had the pleasure of oatmeal biscuits when there wasn't a lot else left for him. He didn't seem to mind at all.

Sam had kept his distance. When he wasn't working with Joe below or with Dane in the wheelhouse, he fished and fished.

Bucky would sit with him patiently, watching any movement in the water, waiting for the next big catch.

When Maggie wasn't in the galley, she took to her cabin, sitting with a crate in the doorway, propping it open so she could gaze out over the river. She loved this river, loved its winding, tight bends in places, loved its broad reach in others, and the straggly gums that towered over it in long stretches. Loved the peace of the river as they steamed along. Here, she sat and sometimes dozed. She could forget that men had died around her. Forget that her hearing still wasn't the best. Forget that her wayward thinking and her *urges* had embarrassed her. Forget that she'd once had dreams to make her own way in the world.

She couldn't just let those dreams disappear completely. When her head was clearer, she would refine those dreams and forge ahead again. She only needed to rest up, and stop being so hard on herself. Her pa had often told her that. 'Ye can't find perfection, Maggie, me darlin'. It doesn't exist,' he'd say. She had no doubt he would be all right. It took more than a broken bone to finish him off and though that thinking was more wishful than not, she knew she'd somehow feel it if he was gone. She believed she'd feel her mother's anguish if her father lost his life.

Anguish. Going over what had been said between her and Sam only made the hollow inside her feel deeper. That he kept away from her was sensible, reasonable in the current circumstances. *Yes, yes, it was, but it's just awful being angry, and it makes my heart ache.* She did feel a finality to it though, and that made things worse. It was as if he was determined to keep things at arm's length, and she was powerless to do anything about it.

How would they get along when Dane put them onto Mr Strike's boat at Swan Hill, to take them back to Echuca? *Goodness. I'm not sure how I feel about that.* Breathless for a start, and not happily.

Dane said there would be a little time for her to meet his wife Georgina, and the three children, before she and Sam—and Pie and Bucky—would need to leave on the *Lady Mitchell.* At least Maggie had that to look forward to. It might help take her mind off Sam Taylor before they left for home.

She had no clue what 'home' in Echuca would look like, except that home was always where her parents and her brother were. She'd be happy to meet Linley again after all these years, and there would be their new baby, who must have arrived by now. Oh, she so hoped that had gone all right. She couldn't bear it if something happened to Ard and Linley's baby. Or to Linley. Toby would be there too, of course. *And Sam.* When had Sam not been there? He and Ard had been friends forever. She blew out a breath. It would be hard. Harder than hard.

The boat slowed. She heard Joe shouting at someone on the Mildura wharf to catch the mooring rope. Dane glided his vessel alongside the landing and let the engine idle. Once again, it would be a short stop. This time, a little freight would be picked up for his own use on Jacaranda.

Maggie watched Sam walk Pie off the boat, mount and ride away. Was he just exercising the horse? He hadn't said otherwise … Her heart missed a beat—had he gone for good without saying anything to her? No, no, he'd promised to return her to Echuca.

Joe had gone to the store with a list of provisions for the next three days or so to Swan Hill. Dane had disembarked to check in and out again with the wharf master, and to load his own freight that waited on the dock. Bucky, ordered to stay on board, had looked desperate to get off the boat and run. For once, he did as he was told. It was very strange to be alone on the boat. A creeping agitation unnerved Maggie and fear fluttered in her gut.

Nothing to worry about. The boat's engine was closed down. It was quiet. She placed a hand on her stomach and took a couple of deep breaths. Deliberately, she gazed out over the river, then found somewhere to sit in the shade of the deck and waited. *Nothing to worry about. Nothing.*

By the time Sam returned she was in her more usual spirits. She huffed. He was very good at not being distracted by her when it suited him, it seemed. Dismounting, he led Pie aboard, made a fuss of Bucky, then took the horse to his station and unsaddled him—without so much as a glance. When Joe appeared wheeling a barrow of goods from the store, Sam helped him unload, and took the stock to the little galley while Joe returned the barrow.

'Our vittles, Miss Maggie,' Sam said cheerily, and dumped a bag of flour under the bench. He didn't look at her as he brought in the rest of the stuff. She couldn't care less what it was, she'd get to it later.

Then on board came a hind of beef over his shoulder. 'I'll hang this out of you-know-who's way.' He manhandled it lengthways to two hooks that hung in the shaded deck area and covered it with hessian bags, well out of Bucky's reach.

'Sam, I—'

'I'm looking forward to dinner tonight.' He pointed at the carcass. 'And breakfast tomorrow. Freshest eggs in that lot in the galley,' he said, a jaunty grin on his face. 'I'm back to work.' Then he was gone, not waiting for a reaction from her.

She huffed a little more. Fidgeted as she stood staring at the provisions. Her chin puckered. That would not do. *Bloody man.* She planted hands on her hips, set her jaw, then got to sorting the stores in the galley.

No more than an hour or so later, Joe, back on board and after stacking wood with Sam, had fired up the engine. Dane took the wheel, and the *Sweet Georgie* edged away from Mildura. They were bound for a place to tie up for the night before they went on to Swan Hill.

Bucky sat all afternoon under the beef hanging high above him.

Maggie's appetite seemed to be on the wane, but nothing seemed to stop Sam's, or the appetites of the other men. At Joe's request, dinner was a pack of fresh sausages—not Sam's beef—fried crispy on the outside and firm on the inside, with a dozen eggs sizzling in the fat, and mashed potato served as a side. Gravy made with meat juices and flour was doused over three of the four plates.

Maggie was serving, but Sam had helped himself before she could smack anything onto his plate. For herself she only had an egg and a little potato. Today, not even cooking had managed to keep her mood up for long. Besides, this type of cooking wasn't exactly what she'd had in mind for her grand plan. *Oh, pfft.* That plan seemed to be receding into the dim past again. How would she ever manage it? Frustrated and annoyed, she glowered at the men, who didn't notice. Too cramped in the galley for everyone to eat there, they were all on the deck.

'Well, lads and lady,' Dane said, as he stood up and stretched. 'We're not far off Mallee Cliffs, so we'll make an early start tomorrow, first light. I'm off to my bunk. Thank you for dinner, Cousin Maggie.'

'Same for me,' Joe said. 'Will be an early start. Goodnight all.'

Maggie started. 'Joe, are we going to be all right?'

'Don't you worry, miss,' Joe said. 'The *Sweet Georgie* is resting, her engine's safe.' He nodded to her, and to Sam.

'I swear to God,' Maggie said as they left the deck. 'I don't ever want to be on another paddle-steamer after this.'

Sam had also got to his feet. 'Not long to go now and you won't have to.' It was the first direct thing he'd said to her all day. Her heart missed a beat when he turned to go. He stopped. 'Cap'n

Finn was a good man to get you onto land. He must have had a feeling that it wouldn't be safe.'

Maggie looked openly at him. His hazel eyes held compassion, concern. That meant there must be just a little hope. She nodded. 'And Mr Bentley too.' She shuddered, remembering the sound of that awful blast. 'And you're sure there's nothing wrong with—'

'Not me, but Dane thinks all is fine, and Joe. I trust that.'

Bucky had begun cleaning up their discarded plates and she bent to take them out of his reach. The sun was down, and the lingering light had set a hazy golden glow along the water. The darkening silhouette of trees on the bank signalled night was coming in fast.

Hands in his pockets, Sam said, 'If you're worried, I could sit for a while.'

Yes—please do. No. Yes. But it wouldn't be any good. Not here on the boat, not with Dane and Joe on board.

'No,' she said finally. 'Thank you. If no one else is worried, I shouldn't be.'

Carrying a stack of plates, she headed for the galley. Bucky followed. As Sam wandered past, she heard him say a quiet, 'Goodnight'. She knew he had rolled out his swag near where Pie was tied. Bucky would sleep near Sam too.

Water boiling in the kettle would do for washing up and Maggie made haste to finish the job. Safety next, and she tamped down the fire in the small oven. Checking no food had been left for the canine crew member to snaffle, she took one look around before she put out the candle and headed for her bed.

All she had to do now was get to her cabin where she would spend another bewildering night.

Sam patted Pie on the rump, talked to him and hummed a tune. He heard Bucky clump to the deck near where he'd rolled his swag. He talked to the dog as well, low murmurs of nonsense chat, his voice friendly. By the time he'd shucked his boots, Bucky was on his swag, so he shunted him a little to the side and settled down beside him.

Maggie. Two more days and two more nights and then he'd be able to deliver her to the arms of her family. He'd planned what he'd do, what he'd say. He'd get off the boat at O'Rourke's, and Mr Strike would steam on to Echuca. Sam would check to see that Ard was fine, that his pa was fine—he hoped he would be—and check the new baby and all. Maybe he'd sleep the night in his half-finished house. Then next morning he'd pack up what little else he had, take Pie and go wait at the landing until Mr Strike returned on his way downriver to Jacaranda.

Ard would understand. He knew what it felt like to hanker after a woman he couldn't have. Though Ard eventually did get his Linley. Sam laughed to himself recalling that it was with the help of a cauliflower. But Miss Linley was very different to Miss Maggie.

Best thing a man could do was to shut his eyes and let sleep come. The tune he'd hummed earlier, about the colour of his true love's hair, seemed to float in his head as he drifted off. The last thing he remembered was the dog snoring.

Forty-eight

Up until now, Maggie had been blissfully unaware of the possible dangers of the trip upriver from Mildura. Only twenty miles or so out of Swan Hill, a good thirty-five hours from Mildura, Maggie was in the wheelhouse when Dane yelled, 'Next bend, Joe. Bitch and Pups.' He turned to her. 'Bit of a tough one, this section, Maggie. Might be wise to get to the deck and hang on.'

'Bitch and Pups, did you say?'

He nodded. 'A couple of narrow bends, rocks, snags in low water. Clay islands in the way, one big one and a few little ones.' He rubbed his face. 'I think we'll be fine, but don't want to sit here on this side waiting for good flows. Nobody downriver mentioned it being bad. We've got good water here so far, there might be no trouble. But if there is, could be rocky rapids, and snags everywhere.'

He leaned out over the deck and called, 'Joe, I'm slowing her up. Sam, need you on the bow. We'll hug the Victorian side of the river but look out for rocks, and clay bars.' He turned back to Maggie. 'Once the drought worsens, this next bit will be impassable,' Dane said. Then he sounded as if he was talking more to himself than to her. 'We might be lucky now, it seems all right.'

Her breath caught in her throat as she felt the engine slow. 'What if the boat gets stuck?'

He glanced at her. 'Don't worry. If anything, it'll be a slow juggle as we ease her over any tight bits. We're a shallow-draught boat. The *Sweet Georgie* only needs a couple of feet of water.'

'But if—'

'Maggie.' He turned and looked at her, locked her gaze. 'The boat will not blow up. Now, best you get down those steps before we have to do any of the juggling I mentioned.'

Gripping the side rail, Maggie took the steps to the deck. Sam was already at the bow, holding a straining Bucky by the scruff.

'Let me take Bucky,' she said and sidled closer, worried that at any time there could be an almighty bump on the riverbed.

'Get his rope. If it gets bad, we'll have to tie him somewhere.'

Bad. Maggie's heart thumped. Casting around, she found the short length of rope they used as a dog lead and handed it to Sam, who fashioned a loop and slid it over the dog's neck.

'Might be a good time to find somewhere safe for you and the animals.' Sam handed her the lead, undid Pie's reins and walked him to the bottom of the wheelhouse, securing him in the walkway underneath. 'Come in here and stay with Pie.'

The hairs on Maggie's arms stood on end. She lagged behind Bucky, who tugged her along following Sam. *The water is so calm, how could there be any problem?* She looked at the bank and could tell by the erosion that the water level had fallen in the last few yards. She took a glance up at Dane in the wheelhouse, but he too was concentrating. Then she ducked into the walkway with the dog.

Sam brushed past as he gave her the reins. 'I have to be look-out for Dane.' His jaw was set, his frown dark.

'We'll be all right in here,' she said, quickly sucking in a breath as his shoulder bumped hers.

'You will,' he agreed. He tipped his head up to look at the sky, adjusted his hat and strode back to the bow.

The *Sweet Georgie* was creeping around the bend. Joe had come up from the engine room and was shading his eyes with a sooty forearm.

'There it is,' Dane shouted.

Maggie peered out and wasn't sure what she was looking for. Bucky lurched on the rope, his eye on Sam.

Joe called, 'Looks all right from here closer to the bank. Bloody great snag in the middle, though.'

'I see it,' Dane called and the boat slowed even more. 'There's white water eddies, maybe over the rocks.'

The *Sweet Georgie* kept close to the right side of the river, inching along in what looked to Maggie to be deep enough water, but the men could see what she couldn't. Oh, she loved the river, that was sure, but she wasn't so sure she loved being on it any longer.

Sam had leaned well out over the bow. He yelled, 'Snags on the left side.'

The boat edged closer to the opposite bank.

Pie shuffled, whinnied. Bucky jumped on his front paws and barked. Maggie had to hold him back, wincing at the noise in the walkway.

'Boss, careful—we got maybe a hand's span on her right side,' Joe shouted. 'Big old snag.'

'Rocks on the left side,' Sam bellowed.

'How far under?'

'Maybe just deep enough.'

The *Sweet Georgie* slowed to a chug only, sat on top of the water, only the beat of her heart, the engine, making a ripple on top of the river.

We won't be stuck here, will we? Maggie looked at Joe who was waving a hand up high, signalling Dane in the wheelhouse. The boat adjusted nary an inch. Crept forwards an inch. The engine powered down. Joe said something to Sam, then jogged to the back of the boat.

Next thing, Sam lowered himself over the side. Maggie let go a small cry, and Bucky lurched again, but she held on tight. She could hear more shouts from Joe. It seemed he was in the water, too. The boat moved again, silent on the water. *How?* More shouts from Joe and the boat stopped.

Maggie leaned out to check the bow. Sam was still in the water, but there was no sign of him. *Oh dear God.* Joe shouted again from the back of the boat, but there was no answering shout from Sam. *Sam.* No movement from the boat. *Sam!*

'Any rapids, Sam?' Dane called. 'Can't see at this angle.'

Nothing from Sam. Joe waited a moment, then shouted from the back of the boat for him. Still nothing.

Maggie stared around her in the walkway. There was a narrow storeroom and the door on it had a sturdy handle. It'd hold Pie's reins and if the horse didn't spook, he'd be all right. Even if he did spook, Maggie had no hope of holding him, but to tie him there would be best if she was going to check on Sam. She fumbled Pie's reins and tied him tight. But the dog was a different story.

She felt the nose of the boat edge away from where Sam had called out the rocks.

Dane shouted, 'Joe, you right?'

'All good here, boss.'

Maggie stole out of the walkway, the dog tugging her. She growled at him and he slowed down. The boat edged back again.

Sam burst out of the water, a hand on the deck. Bucky barked in fright and skidded to the edge. Maggie fell to her backside as he dragged closer to the rail at the bow.

Sam clung to the side. 'We're clear of the rocks,' he called over the top of Bucky who was barking in his face.

Dane leaned out of the wheelhouse. 'You got traction, Joe?'

'Some.' And the boat nudged forwards.

'Anything else, Sam?' Dane shouted.

'Reckon that's the worst this side,' Sam answered. Then eyed Maggie on her knees trying to get up off the deck. ''Cept for a woman angling for a swim,' he said.

'What are you doing?' she said to him between clenched teeth.

'Sam,' Dane bellowed out of the wheelhouse. 'You back on board?'

The *Sweet Georgie* slipped forwards. Sam clambered on deck, sodden, stepped over Maggie and headed for the back of the boat. 'Am now. Goin' to the other side.'

Maggie felt Bucky's rope bite into her hand as the dog hurled himself after Sam. She slipped in the puddles Sam left, fell again, but wasn't about to let go. The burn of rope seared her palm as she grabbed it with both hands, jagging her flesh. She gave him an almighty tug. 'Bucky,' she snapped. The dog stopped dead as Sam disappeared over the side.

'Maggie,' Dane yelled. '*Maggie*.'

'I'm here,' she said struggling to stand, the dog's rope wrapped around one of her wrists.

'Get to the bow. Tell me what you see.'

She took a last frantic glance at the stern but couldn't see either Sam or Joe. She dragged Bucky with her. 'Dammit, dog,' she cried at him. 'Come *on*.'

She scrambled her way to the bow, dog in tow, and felt the shift in the boat. It seemed to have freed itself. Crawling to the edge, she peered over. 'There are rocks below, but it looks like some way down. Can you get over a foot or so to the right?' The *Sweet Georgie* moved. 'Good. That's good,' she called.

And then they were moving. Maggie didn't wait. She crawled as fast as she could, her hand still wrapped in Bucky's rope, until she could scramble to her feet and get to the back of the boat.

'Sam. Joe,' she yelled. Bucky barked.

'You see them?' Dane shouted.

Maggie couldn't even speak. She couldn't see them. Not on the bank, not in the water, not in the gentle wake as the *Sweet Georgie* broke free of the Bitch and her Pups. Her heart hammered against her ribs and made her cry aloud.

The dog barked again and dragged her back from the edge. Then she heard the belly laughs and the sputtering echo through the walkway. The two men had clambered aboard and had flopped onto their backs, arms flung wide, dragging in deep breaths. Bucky barked over one then the other.

Joe laughed. 'Miss Maggie, we did it. We beat that Bitch.' His grin was beaming. 'I don't reckon I want to see her again for a while.'

Maggie sank to her knees beside Sam, relief welling in her eyes. He just smiled at her, took her outstretched hand, and closed his eyes.

'And there they are.' Maggie heard the elation in Dane's voice when he spotted his young family standing on the Swan Hill landing. The *Sweet Georgie* glided in.

He might have recovered from the Bitch and Pups; she wasn't sure she had, even though it had been a couple of hours or more. She hadn't even bothered trying to explain to Sam what she'd felt at the time. She'd rather have cracked him on the head. And Joe too if it came down to it. She pressed her hands together, trying to soothe the skin burned from Bucky's rope. It still stung but at least with some salve and a bandage, it had eased a little.

On the landing, a dark-haired woman, plump with child, stood trying to calm three children. The boys—clear to see they were the twins—jumped up and down waving and yelling, though Maggie couldn't hear what, and a little girl was twirling and waving.

Dane let the whistle blast and the children jumped with glee. The woman waved. She would be Georgina.

Family. Maggie swallowed unexpected emotion as her throat tightened. Oh, she was so looking forward to seeing her mother and father. She stared at the children. Then stared at his wife and hoped that they would be friends. Swan Hill was not that far from Echuca; Georgina didn't look to be much older than Maggie—and they would have something in common if they did become friends. By all accounts, according to Dane, his wife was something of a suffragist.

Maggie frowned. So, how can Georgina be a wife and a mother and still work towards a voice for women in a world governed by men? Why did she choose to do both? Could anyone *do* both?

Dane was out of the wheelhouse as soon as the engine slowed. The boat idled. He leapt down the stairs to the deck and landed as Joe whirled the mooring rope over his head. It sailing over a post and as he pulled it in, the boat sidled to the landing. Dane flew past him and, in two bounds it seemed, had gathered up his wife and lifted her off the ground, whirled her around, his delighted shout reaching Maggie's ears. He stopped, carefully put Georgina back on her feet and then kissed her hard. Her hands came up to hold his face, and at that tenderness, that happiness to see her man home, Maggie thought she'd burst into tears.

The children danced around them. Dane scooped up the dark-haired twin boys and squeezed them in a fierce hug, spinning with them. When he put them back on the ground, he went down on one knee in front of the little girl and spread his arms wide. She threw herself into him, her chubby little arms wrapping around his neck.

Maggie did burst into tears.

Joe had dropped the gangway and approached them, his hat off, a big grin on his face. Georgina put a hand on his arm and he clapped his own over it before the young boys ploughed into him. He ruffled their heads as they gripped his legs. He reached over and tapped the little girl's nose as she hung over her father's shoulder.

The lump in Maggie's throat had only grown bigger and she was gulping in air between sobs. *No. No. No.* She mopped her eyes with the edge of her pinny. She knew that her nose would be red and huge, and there would be no hiding it. Well, that didn't matter. This was family.

With tears dried and her nose wiped, she knew that it was time she went down to meet the rest of her cousins, and slowly made her way to the deck.

There, staring at the family on the landing, Sam had Bucky by the lead in one hand and Pie's reins in the other. Bucky strained to go, but Sam was not distracted by him. He was looking past the scene on the deck. 'There's his horse,' he said.

Maggie followed his gaze. Alongside a patient horse harnessed to a cart, tied to the branch of a tree, stood a beautiful black and glossy stallion, tossing his head and stamping his feet, garnering attention. It was Joe who loped up and rubbed his muzzle.

'That is MacNamara,' Sam breathed. 'I'd forgotten how magnificent he is.' Pie had nickered after spying the other horses, and danced a little on the deck. 'I'll go say hello to Mrs MacHenry and then take Pie for a run. Mr Strike's due in soon, I'm told. I'll be back directly.' He handed her Bucky's rope and led Pie over the gangway.

Bucky forgot the rope and shot to his feet, dragging Maggie off the boat and onto the landing after Sam. She groaned as her hands protested. Sam spoke to Georgina, hat in hand, then swooped on the young lads, war-whooping as he chased them around the landing. Pie stood waiting, stoic as usual. Amid the excited yells, Sam managed to step into the stirrup and mount. He waved and took off. 'I won't be long,' he shouted.

Maggie stared at her cousins, and her breath caught as she witnessed an unguarded intimate moment. With his young daughter still draped over his shoulder, Dane had taken up his wife's left hand and had pressed a kiss over her wedding rings, his dark gaze on her. When he released her, Maggie saw a plain band of gold gleam. The other ring was set with an exquisite large yellow stone and it twinkled on her finger. Georgina touched his face for a lingering moment, and smiled, a sigh escaping.

Maggie's heart hammered. *Yes, yes, I know,* she answered it. *This is what I want to feel in my life.*

They turned to her and Dane said, 'Georgina, this is my cousin, Mairead O'Rourke. Maggie, this is my wife, Georgina MacHenry.' He took Bucky's rope.

'I am so happy to meet you, Maggie.' Georgina embraced her as closely as she could, then laughed at herself and gave her rounded belly a gentle tap. Maggie felt her face bloom and tears threaten again, but they held off. It startled Georgina. 'Oh, have you been through an awful time?' she asked Maggie, then looked at her bandaged hands. 'You have.'

Dane stepped in. 'Maggie was on Mr Finn's boat, my love. He put her ashore just before it blew up.'

'Oh, my dear girl.' Georgina reached over to squeeze Maggie's arm. 'So sad. Mr Finn was such a lovely man. I am glad you are well despite it all.'

'Pa,' the little girl yelled in Dane's ear. 'Who is the lady?'

Dane moved his head a little, relieving his ear. 'I do beg your pardon, Miss MacHenry. Maggie, may I present my daughter, Miss Layla MacHenry. Layla, this is Maggie, your cousin.'

Layla held out her hand and Maggie shook it. 'I am pleased to meet you, Miss Layla.'

'I'm three.'

The blue eyes of the little girl were a mark of Maggie's own family. Her gaze roved over Layla's face, so recognisable even though they had only just met.

'And these two ruffians,' Dane said as the boys charged around his legs, 'are Tom and Will.'

The lads were replicas of Dane, and in that strange yet familiar way, of her father, and her brother. Maggie remembered vaguely why Dane didn't carry the O'Rourke name, something about a stepfather before Liam came to claim his long-lost family, but she seemed to have forgotten the detail. The boys were polite in their greeting but almost too hasty as the dog grabbed their attention. 'Is he ours, Pa? Can we have him?'

Bucky sat, lavished with pats and scratches. He looked up at Maggie as if to tell her he'd just found heaven. His round golden eyes had all but glazed over. She wanted to laugh but tears still threatened. *What on earth is the matter with me?*

'Dane, Mr Strike is due in any time now,' Georgina said. 'Let's go sit in the cart while we wait for his boat, and for Sam. I have cake, and a flask of tea.' She gave him a look as if she expected he would be pleased to hear that.

'Cake,' Dane said, a mock cry in his voice. 'Finally, I have a wife who cooks.'

She laughed. 'Don't be silly. Your mother sent it along.'

The boys had taken off, and Bucky was keen to go, too. Dane gently put his daughter on her feet and tugged at Bucky. 'Come on, lad,' he said to the dog. 'We have to have some cake.'

Georgina took Layla's hand and said over her shoulder, 'Come along, Maggie. We can sit in the cart and wait in the shade.'

They clambered onto the cart and Georgina doled out thick slices of lardy cake, which Maggie had to admire. Juicy pieces of fruit heavily dotted the cake, and it was spiced just right.

'I hadn't realised how hungry I was,' Maggie said. 'Feeding the men, I've not had much of an appetite till now,' she told Georgina, and took a bite. Sweet and chewy, the flavours flooded her mouth.

'You must tell me everything.' She deposited Layla between them, the little girl happily entranced by her cake.

'Goodness, where to start?' Maggie asked after swallowing. 'There seems so much.'

Georgina peppered her with questions as Dane herded his boys out of the way to play. Maggie started off about her job at Renmark, and the irrigation system there. How the Chaffey brothers had employed her parents, and her, and after they'd left, how she stayed on … And then Robert Boyd … And after that, Sam— *Sam*. 'And yes, Sam, well, he is a good friend of my brother.'

Georgina seemed surprised. 'Not your beau? When he visited us with Ard the first time after the family had got together, I got the impression—' She stopped.

Maggie shook her head. Her voice had stuck in her throat.

'And how are your parents?' Georgina asked hurriedly.

Maggie was about to tell her about Eleanor and Lorcan, when the breezy whistle of a riverboat gliding in interrupted her.

'There never seems enough time these days for me to catch up with everything, Maggie,' Georgina cried, exasperated. 'But you must visit us. I am told the men of the family have hatched a plan to make our two enterprises one entity. We'll be starting a horse stud as well. I am most interested in that, and in all the plans. It's so exciting, despite the terrible economic times. Are you interested?'

'I am. But I'm also very much interested in starting my own enterprise.'

'Oh, wonderful. We women should be earning our own money and making our way in the world. I love working for our business, certainly now that the awful morning sickness has subsided. Even better, I have a wage too. I just can't have my own account at the bank, which is most inconvenient, and decidedly ludicrous.'

'You work in the business, for wages? Even though you're a mother, even all through your—'

'Of course, Maggie. No one would dare stop me.' Georgina laughed. 'By the look on your face I'd say you haven't considered that.'

'Uh, no.' Her thoughts began to leap.

'But you must. You must keep working, in some capacity, even once you have children.' Georgina looked at her. 'Oh. What's the matter? Are you all right?'

'Weren't you ever afraid? Aren't you afraid now?'

'Good heavens. What of?'

'Of having babies,' Maggie blurted, then mortified, glanced around to see if anyone had heard her.

'Ah.' Georgina patted Maggie's hands. 'I admit, once I found out I was having twins, I was petrified, but I was assured I was healthy enough to feed two. The hardest part after the most debilitating morning sickness—all day, I might add—was the birth itself. And Layla wasn't easy either, and yet here I am going for another.'

'My nephew Toby's mother died just after he was born.' Maggie couldn't keep the shake from her voice.

'Maggie,' Georgina said firmly, 'I'm told by Eleanor that the poor woman had been beaten up all her married life, all her pregnancy. And was most probably half-starved, as well. Toby is lucky Linley and Ard have him, and he's so hale and hearty.'

'Now Linley is soon to have a baby, and I worry that something might happen to her. My brother would be devastated.' She clasped her hands. Breathless, all her fears seemed to rush to the surface. 'We all would be.'

Georgina tapped her own belly. 'We are built for bringing babies into the world. And nature has her own way with each one of us. We are strong enough to bear it.'

Maggie shredded the rest of her cake. 'I know my ma had a baby born dead, even though I'm not supposed to know about it.'

'Well, that can happen, of course.'

'I know she still grieves. Sometimes I would catch a look on her face when she'd see a newborn. It's so hard.' Maggie's words poured out. 'And even though Linley's own mother died in a terrible way, she works with women who have lost children, or have children they can't afford to keep. Some are removed from them. I don't know how she does it, how people endure any of it.' She rubbed her forehead. 'It seems all too much.'

Surprised, Georgina said, 'But it doesn't happen to everyone.'

'I could die, too.'

Georgina caught her eye. 'Maggie, are you with child?'

'No,' she answered swiftly. 'No, I'm not.' She wasn't completely sure, but as it was nearly time for her monthly courses and twinges deep in her belly were making themselves known, she presumed not. 'But I'm terrified to marry and have babies. Well, mostly terrified about having the babies.'

Georgina sat back. 'Hmm. A problem when one gets married. There are ways to prevent it, but often not successful.' She squeezed Maggie's hands. 'You should talk to your mother.'

'She wouldn't understand.' Maggie hung her head. 'She always wanted more children. Only got two. Or three, but it was the one between Ard and me who died.'

'She'd understand. You might be surprised.' Georgina looked off into the distance for a moment. 'I barely remember my own mother, and my stepfather Rupert is almost a memory. He writes from England, but I doubt I'll see him again. I don't have other family here except Dane's mother Jemimah—you'd like her. His half-sister, Elspeth—I'm still trying to get along with her. And there's Liam, your father's brother, a fine father and grandfather. You have all your lovely O'Rourkes around you. Go to them. They'll know what's right.' She patted Maggie's hand. 'But keep working. I still do.'

'I want to, but if being by myself is the only way I can earn—'

'It's not. You've heard of Miss Goldstein?'

'Yes, of course.' Maggie knew of Vida Goldstein and her work for suffrage, and for women's and children's rights.

'She has decided to remain a spinster, believing that she can't work in her chosen field and be a wife and mother. She might well be right—for her.' Georgina gazed over at her twin boys. 'When I was having these two, I decided that I'd find a way to work that suited me as well as allowing me to be a mother. I've found that way. I'm as much a part of our business as Dane is.' Georgina glanced back at Maggie. 'And I also learned that I didn't want to live without him.'

Sam galloped back and drew Pie up a little distance from the cart. He dismounted, threw the reins, and ran down to the landing. The *Lady Mitchell* glided into the wharf area and inched her way ahead of the *Sweet Georgie*. Joe was back on board, and Dane's boat was edging her way backwards as the *Lady M* settled herself in.

'Oh, what a boat,' Maggie cried, happy to be distracted.

'She certainly was in her time,' Georgina said. She turned to Maggie. 'Write to me. I think we'll have a lot to talk about. We must arrange to visit each other. There will be so much to learn about what's ahead for all of us.' She helped herself from the cart. 'You have a fine friend in Sam Taylor. I've met him a few times now.' She smiled. 'We think very highly of him,' she said.

'Yes, he is a fine friend to all of us, I know,' Maggie said. 'He came to look for me these last weeks because my father and my brother couldn't. I'm very grateful.'

Dane had come to assist Georgina as she climbed down, but she hadn't needed it. 'Ah, Sam. Fine fella, indeed,' he said and gazed at Maggie, a small smile twitching.

Dane was teasing her. She felt lucky he hadn't torn strips off both her and Sam, for he'd certainly seemed to know what had transpired between them. She was thankful he'd remained silent on it but felt blood rush to her face again.

Georgina seemed to mull over that as she looked at Sam. He'd snatched up the *Lady M*'s mooring rope and was securing it around a post. 'The best sort of man to have, I think, a fine friend.' She leaned in and whispered, 'And it's very clear you also have his heart.' She smiled again and spoke up. 'We'd better get you back on board with your dog. Now, it won't be long until this baby comes, and I'd welcome family help with my rowdy crew, once Linley and Eleanor can spare you. Sam will be working here with us too, apparently, so you and Ard will have another good reason to visit.'

For an instant, Maggie didn't hear much else after that—she thought perhaps her deafness might have finally taken over, or was it that the whole world around her had just suspended?

I learned I didn't want to live without him.

Sam would not be in Echuca working with her family after all.

Forty-nine

Captain Ned Strike had told Maggie that there was no need for her to cook on his boat. He had a cook, and she wasn't it; she was a passenger. He wasn't a man to have light conversation either, it seemed, and so she didn't feel the need to converse at all.

When she had tentatively asked him about the boiler, Mr Strike had all but growled at her. Of course the subject of Mr Finn's and Mr Bentley's deaths was raw, but had they all forgotten that she'd been on the boat too?

Sitting under shade on the deck in the late afternoon, Maggie watched the animals. Bucky had been divested of his rope and seemed much happier. He and Pie stood staring into the water for hours on end until Bucky tired of that and flopped on his side to sleep.

Sam kept out of her way, engaging with the captain, or with any of the three other men who worked on the *Lady Mitchell*. He put his back to whatever was asked of him. *He* wasn't thought of as a passenger.

Maggie learned that the boat had been part of a great river company before the economic downturn came and the railways had crawled through the colony. Its previous owner had met a dire end—on Jacaranda, Dane's property, no less—but from there the conversation had gone on in hushed tones, too low for her poor hearing to pick up. No matter, if Sam ever spoke to her again, *really* spoke to her, not just to shove things in her direction—'Here, take this plate' or 'Mind your step'—she'd find out all about it.

She'd missed so much by being away in Renmark. Family in the MacHenrys, the place at Echuca, and there'd be a new niece or a nephew waiting at home, all being well. Her heart tripped at the thought of home, even though she had never lived there. What *had* she been doing for two years?

She touched her little purse. One pound six and six. That's what she'd been doing, earning enough to save a measly one pound six and six. Well, four pounds six and six if she counted what she'd given to Jane. Maggie stared out over the water as the *Lady M* sailed on—at three miles per hour, Mr Strike had yelled to someone earlier—and wondered about Jane. Wondered where she was, and what she might have decided to do.

A creep of envy wormed its way in. She stopped it. Once back home and understanding the nature of this new entity the men of the family were planning, she felt sure there would be a place for her. Oh yes, she'd keep up her cooking skills. Perhaps she'd enrol and study at a gastronomic college, to expand her abilities as she'd intended. Oh, that would be another fight, even if she could afford it. Women were not allowed to be head chefs.

She heard the engine change, felt the swing of the vessel as it turned towards the bank. *This will be where we'll tie up for the night.*

Tomorrow would see her home. She had yet to hear from Sam that he wouldn't be working there with her family. It seemed best to clear it up before they arrived, but as usual, he avoided her. *Oh, why was all this so hard?*

After dinner, a simple meal of eggs on dry bread, Maggie had been asked to wait on board while the men went ashore and lit a campfire.

Typical. Left behind. She should just plain defy the captain and go ashore. She sighed, knew full well she'd be uncomfortable. And a woman going against the captain's orders would really upset things. It wasn't that she was nervous at all on the boat. Much. All alone. But she wasn't far away, and if something from the engine even slightly gurgled she'd be off like a shot and running on water to the bank.

Her one grateful thought was that Sam had said, 'It's more than safe on this boat too, Maggie,' before he'd nodded and walked past her to the gangway and onto dry land.

While she knew that Mr Strike allowed no grog, the hilarity that sounded from the riverbank hadn't seemed to need any. Bucky had also been relegated to stay on board; he couldn't be trusted not to run off into the night chasing a kangaroo or a wallaby, or anything else. So he stayed on deck with her, the rope around his neck again and firmly in her still-bandaged hands. He had slumped to the deck with his head on his front paws. Exactly how she felt.

This was the very thing she had tried to explain to Sam—to anyone, really: this treatment, this excluding her because she was a woman, or this patronising behaviour that was supposed to make her feel safe and protected, only made her feel useless and without a voice of her own. She detested it. It was why she longed for the chance to do something differently, to be someone who made a difference. She had to get Sam to see that. Had to make sure he knew that he was enough for her, but that she was worthy of her own place in his life, and not just as a kitchen wench and a nursery-maid. Surely he could see that.

She took a breath. Babies. Somehow she'd try to get around that, to explain her terror of it. There had to be a solution.

She didn't want to live her life without him—not now, not ever. She wanted Sam. Wanted him in her life, being her love and her lover. Wanted to feel that rush of heat every day when he looked at her, or touched her with those big hands, roughened and callused by long days working in the sun. Wanted his song in her heart.

There was only one thing to do.

After the fire on the bank had been completely doused with water and the men were back on board, candles were lit. By the time Sam got to stretch out on his swag, Mr Strike had come to get Maggie and escort her to her cabin. It seemed he had taken it upon himself to ensure she would come to no harm in the night.

She closed the cabin door as he left and waited until she heard his footsteps retreat. She waited a little longer, not trusting her ears. A door clanged shut above. She slipped out, and in the dim light, found Pie's silhouette.

'Sam,' she whispered hoarsely. She crept forwards. 'Sam.' Pie whinnied. Sam would be close by. 'I need to know something.' She stood still to listen.

'What?' she heard off to her left.

'Are you not going to be staying at our place for long when we get back?' She bobbed down, groped on the deck floor to find a place to kneel without accidentally sitting on him, or on the dog who she knew was also close by.

'Why do you need to know that now?' he grumbled.

In the silence, she strained her ears, hoping she hadn't missed whatever else he might have said. 'Sam?'

'It's none of your concern, Maggie.'

As her eyes adjusted, she could see he was sprawled on top of the swag, his hands behind his head. 'It's just that Georgina said you'd be there working with them, but I assumed you'd be working in Echuca with Ard.' *Has he heard me?* 'Sam.'

He gave an exasperated sound and that was all.

She tried again. 'I mean, I don't want what has happened between you and me to mean—'

'Go back to bed, Maggie.'

'—nothing. I want—'

'Go *away*, Maggie.' He turned on his side and there was silence.

'But I really want to—'

'Not now, and *not here*.' Sam flew upright and took her by the arms. He was very clear. 'We're on the deck of a boat with four other men on board, for Chrissakes, don't argue now. Go back to bed.' He gave her a little shake—very restrained, she thought, given the anger in his voice—and dropped his hands. Snatching the thin blanket over him, he threw himself down, and turned away.

'Dammit, dammit, *dammit*,' she sniped into the silence.

A beat later he murmured, 'Go away, Maggie.'

Bucky snuffled, chucked his nose under her arm as if to say, *off you go*.

It hadn't been a pleasant night's sleep. When she arose in the morning, her eyes scratchy, her mood sombre, the *Lady Mitchell* was already under way. Maggie hadn't heard a thing, so must have slept heavily in the last few hours. Echuca would be met by dusk, she'd been told, so O'Rourke's landing would be a little earlier than that.

The bright golden sun sent its rays through the trees lining the bank, and that meant a brand new day had begun.

Fifty

Sam knew this bend in the river, a slight curve that seemed to take them on a long stretch. Then it would ease, and there'd be a few twists testing the *Lady M*'s agility as she steamed along. Echuca wharf was not far ahead, perhaps an hour, but O'Rourke's landing would come up first.

He felt her speed drop back. Mr Strike knew where he was. Sam craned his neck to catch a glimpse of the hardy old boy at the wheel. The cap'n lifted a forefinger. Sam nodded, lifted his forefinger in return, and turned back.

He watched Maggie as she sat on the deck, facing away from him, the dog by her side. She wouldn't know where she was. She'd never visited here. When her parents first bought the place with her uncle, Maggie had opted to stay in Renmark, carving out that wonderful life for herself. He wasn't laughing at her; he admired her, even still. But it seemed that the dream she'd had then might have been shaken from her now. It was a very subdued Maggie who was returning to the family fold.

She turned in her seat and caught him looking at her. Suddenly his guts hollowed and a thud hit him inside his chest. If he took off back to Swan Hill, which he'd fully intended to do, these would be the last few days he'd see her for a long, long time. He'd get over her while he was in Swan Hill. He'd work as hard as he ever had. Burn the grief out of him under the midday sun. Toil from dawn 'til dusk and fall, sober or drunk, into his cot and sleep the sleep of the dead. He'd do anything not to feel the thing he was feeling now.

He snorted. He hadn't done such a good job of that these last years. He turned his face away in case she saw the look for what it was.

Then Mr Strike leaned out of the wheelhouse and shouted around the stem of the pipe between his teeth, 'O'Rourke's landing, laddie.'

Maggie shot to her feet. The dog danced around her, barking until she shushed him.

Sam could just see the heavy posts and the sturdy beams of the landing jutting out into a river ravaged by drought and low flows. He and Ard had built it nearly two years ago. He remembered that Lorc had come down to inspect when they'd told him they were done. Mr O had tested the posts, knelt to check bolts and joins, wandered on the deck, stamping his foot on the boards here and there. He'd clapped Ard on the shoulder. 'It'll do fine.' Then he'd nodded approval to Sam and said, 'Good job, lad, well done. Ye're an asset to us.' Sam had felt accepted finally, and he was happy that his life would be here with Maggie's family. Waiting for Maggie.

He looked across the river at the sparse, thin saplings, scraggly and struggling in the pale riverbank dirt, and at the huge fallen limbs of long-dead gums that scattered it. Looked up to the tops of the trees that towered over the bank, ageless in his lifetime. He liked it here, liked what he'd achieved here. Loved it. This was home.

He glanced at Maggie, who stood staring ahead at the landing, one hand on Bucky, the other pressed over her heart.

She was his home.

One more time. He'd think about it one more time.

Fifty-one

Mr Strike had sounded the whistle. 'But there's no one here, lad. They're not expectin' ye. What's that all about? Thought you said there'd been a telegram sent. Go up with the young lass and surprise the missus by bringin' her home.' He headed back to the wheelhouse. 'I'm tyin' up at Echuca wharf, will be back here just after dawn tomorrow.'

Sam had Pie on the landing and had Bucky on his rope as Maggie rushed over the gangway, her bag slung across her chest.

'Which way is it?' she cried and ran past him onto the powdery patch of dirt, looking left and right.

The *Lady Mitchell* reversed then glided upriver towards Echuca.

'Go a little to your right,' Sam said over his shoulder, as he waved off the boat. 'You'll be on a track. Your ma and pa's house is the second one, maybe four hundred yards along.'

She ran. Bucky wanted to run with her, tugging on the rope, and twisting and leaping in the air. Sam worried that Ard might up and shoot him, seeing a strange, loose big dog galumphing all over the property, and likely to bowl over his sister at any time. So he kept a tight hold of him. He swung up onto Pie and with the dog trotting alongside, happy to be moving, Sam rode to where he knew Eleanor would be with Lorcan.

Maggie was up ahead and now she was yelling. 'Ma, Pa.' She ran on, stumbled a time or two, but kept running.

Stupid git he was, Sam felt his eyes water as he watched her.

'Ma!' she shouted. Her hat flew off, and her plaited black hair fell in a long tail to below her waist, swinging and bouncing on her back as she bolted over the track.

Ard bounded out of his own house. 'Jesus, Maggie,' he shouted and grabbed her up in his arms and swung her around. 'Maggie, Maggie,' he cried and pressed his face into her shoulder. She pushed him away, dropped back to her feet, and rubbed his cheeks with both hands, glee on her face. Then she pointed at Sam riding in on Pie and ran on towards her parents' house.

'Pa's asleep and Ma's in the cookhouse,' he called after her, and he sprinted to meet Sam. 'You did it, laddie, you did it,' he boomed and reached up, grabbing him by the shirt, hauling him down.

Sam crashed to the ground only to be lifted into a bear hug. 'Don't start, O'Rourke. Next you'll be snivellin'. I got enough on me plate.' The dog gave a yelp. 'It's all right, Bucky-lad.'

'Who's this?' Ard asked as he wiped his eyes and pointed at the dog who stared dolefully after a disappearing Maggie.

'This is our hero, laddie,' Sam said. 'He's the one who found her. Bucky, meet Ard.'

Ard dropped to one knee. 'Good lad, Bucky,' he said, sniffing loudly, and ruffled the dog's ears.

Bucky nodded, distracted; he had a mistress he was losing sight of.

'Let's go see your ma,' Sam said.

The two friends walked, hugging each other, punching each other's shoulders until they got to Eleanor's house. Pie trailed behind them, the dog tried to drag them.

'And your pa?' Sam asked on the verandah.

'They say he's slowly coming out of it. No infection in the leg that we can see.' Ard sized him up. 'It's good to have you back, but we were waiting for a telegram.'

Sam was surprised 'Dane sent one from Renmark, last week. Said we'd be back around about now.'

'Never got it.'

Maggie thudded into the house, dived into the first room only to see it was the parlour, sparsely furnished with pieces that were all new to her. She resolved to explore later. She threw herself into the hall and across to the next room.

'Pa,' she breathed, rushing to the bed. *Is he even alive?* She slid to her knees, wiped her sweaty, hot hands on the bedcover and then stroked his face. His skin was cool. 'Pa, I'm home.' Tears squeezed. She held the sob in her throat, gulped it down. 'Pa, I'm home, I'm home,' her voice a jagged whisper.

He didn't move. He was breathing, she could see that now, but he was out to it. Then he frowned a little, nothing else.

Glancing about, she took in the chair close by, a light quilt draped over it, one she recognised from long ago. That'd be where her mother would sit, watching, waiting. Maggie looked at the medicine bottles on the little bedside table, and gasped at the laudanum.

'Pa, wake up.' There was a frown again, and he moved his head, as if he was trying to hear her better. She pressed her lips to his forehead, and whispered in his ear. 'I love you, Pa. But if you're not talking to me, I'm going to find Ma.' She kissed him again and got to her feet. Ard had said Ma was in the cookhouse.

She shot out of the house and ran across the yard. Sam and Ard were idling their way towards the house.

The cookhouse was stuffy and the task of filling the kettle seemed too much. Eleanor leaned over the chair, gripping the back of it.

Anguish sat in her bones, weighing her down. It was another day she'd have to suffer not knowing what had happened to her daughter—they'd all have to suffer it. Another day she'd watch to see if her husband would fully wake, and she'd dread to have to tell him that Maggie had disappeared.

She wouldn't give up hope. Never ever would. She hung her head and a long breath escaped.

A thud of footsteps then a beloved voice coming from the yard cut through the pain. 'Ma, I'm home.'

The room tilted. *Maggie.* Shock drew a shriek from her. She reached out—there she was, their beautiful, wild and laughing blue-eyed tempest, large as life and dusty and sun-browned, and alive—*alive, alive*—and *home.* As Maggie hurtled through the doorway towards her, the ceiling wavered, the walls moved.

Maggie caught her and they slid to the floor. 'Ma,' she yelped.

Silent, Eleanor's throat seized as her voice stuck there. With Maggie gripped tight in her arms, the room stopped wobbling.

Maggie rocked and rocked her on the floor. 'Ma, it's all right, it's all right.'

Ard pitched into the cookhouse, Sam on his heels. 'What happened?'

'She's all right, she's all right,' Maggie said, a sob in her voice. 'Ma, take some air. Take some deep breaths. Ard, help me get her up.'

He shot to her, and with Sam, lifted her out of Maggie's arms and propped her in the chair. Eleanor waved the boys away, grateful. Her breath eased in and out. She held her hand out to Maggie who'd scooted to kneel by her side.

Eleanor stroked her daughter's head, tears streaming. 'I was thinkin' I was about to spend another day without me girl come back, and here she is.' Then she held out her hand to Sam. Her voice cracked. 'Good lad, Sam Taylor. You're a good lad.'

Fifty-two

'It's me, Pa. It's Mairead,' Maggie said, clasping Lorc's big hand in hers. 'Come on, look what Ma's got for you.' With her other hand she held up a plate loaded with fresh bread and dollops of hot apricot jam. 'You know you cannot resist this.'

Sitting next to her by the bed, Bucky was watching her every move.

Eleanor was asleep on a small cot on the other side of the room. Ard had moved it in on Maggie's say-so the night before. 'Why didn't I think of that?' he was saying. He leaned on the window ledge watching his wife and baby outside, returning to their house for the baby's next feed.

'You might have had a bit on your mind, brother,' Maggie said, passing the plate back and forth under her father's nose.

'No thanks to you, Mairead.'

'And are you going to let us in on the name of our new wee one?' Maggie asked.

'We didn't want to name her until we knew you were safe. If you were dead in a ditch somewhere, we were going to call her after you.'

'And now I'm not dead in a ditch?' Maggie stopped waving the plate. Her father was being his stubborn self. Bucky sat to attention.

'Amy, we think.'

'Amy O'Rourke,' Maggie said, rolling the name around on her tongue. 'I like it.'

'Well, that's a load off my mind.'

'Why won't Pa wake up?' She picked a nice thick slice of Linley's fresh bread and dragged it through the fragrant jam, about to take a bite.

Lorcan opened an eye. 'You take any more o' me jam, girl, and I'll more than wake up,' he croaked.

'Pa,' Maggie breathed, the slice of bread held in the air. 'Are you wakin' up?'

He gave a faint shake of his head. 'Not yet,' he said, heaved a sigh and settled back against the pillow into sleep.

'Pa?'

'Leave him, Maggie,' Ard said. 'This has been going on for days. I think he'll be fine. Now it's Ma to worry about.'

Maggie glanced at her mother. 'I'll look after her. We'll be right to work the place even with Pa off his feet, won't we, now that Sam is going?'

'We will.' Ard frowned at her.

Maggie prickled under her brother's gaze. 'Don't look at me like that. I can't stop him going.'

'You never said what went bad between you two.'

Maggie stared a moment. 'We … can't agree on things.'

'What things? Like you running off?'

More prickles. 'I didn't run off. I went with Ma and Pa, to work. I had a good job.'

The plate of bread and jam dropped to Lorcan's chest. Bucky peered up at it and she waved him off.

'What happened with Sam?' Ard pressed.

Maggie, annoyed, said, 'What's it to you?'

'I don't want my sister causing more trouble with my best mate again.'

'Oh, for God's sake—*I'm* causing trouble. He thought he had to marry me.' When Ard's eyes widened, she snapped, 'He didn't—I wasn't ready to be married.'

She got up and took two steps to check on her sleeping mother. Satisfied, she spun back. 'As a child, and growing up, I was as free as you were. Well, mostly. But if I got married, I could see I'd be trapped like all other wives, expected to pop out baby after baby, tired all my life, and never living it.'

'That's not what happened to Ma,' Ard said, his voice low. 'It's not what's happening to Linley.' He glared at her.

'It's what Sam wanted. Wants. I'm scared of it.' But she thought of Georgina then, and what she'd said.

'Of what?' Ard shook his head. 'You ever had a grown-up talk with him?'

She flamed, and imagined her face would be beet red.

'Look at that,' he said and pointed at her face. 'No, you haven't. Fierce Maggie O'Rourke is still running away.'

'Leave it, Ard.' She went back to sit by Lorcan. 'Sam came and got me when I was in trouble, and for that, I'm grateful. But that's it.' That was one great big *lie lie lie* but she wasn't going to let her brother know that, either.

'We're all grateful,' Ard growled. 'And we've told him. Have you? You haven't stepped foot near him.'

Maggie's mouth dropped open. 'Of course I've told him.'

Suddenly she couldn't remember. She tried to think. Had she told Sam? She must have. She *must* have. Bucky nudged her knee and absently, she rested a hand on his head.

'Thing is, I know my sister. I bet you haven't even thought to say thanks, too busy being independent and know-it-all. Fat lot of good that did you in the end.'

Maggie sucked in a breath. 'If that man in Renmark hadn't grabbed my friend, I would still be earning my own way. And in Bendigo, I didn't need anyone to—'

'You just plain ran away, Maggie O'Rourke.'

Thunder pounded in her veins. 'There was nothing in Bendigo for me, especially when Ma and Pa moved, so I had to go.' She heard her voice rising and was desperate to keep it low.

'You just plain ran away from Sam.'

'No need for you to goad—you'd know all about running away, wouldn't you? Look what happened to you and Linley.'

'Leave us out of it.'

'I didn't see that Sam was so keen to get me back,' she hissed. 'He didn't press his case any harder.'

'You sent back his letters, I've seen them,' Ard barked. 'How much did you think he'd take?'

Maggie tossed a hand in the air. 'What are *you* so mad about? He stopped writing soon enough. I was still angry, and yes, scared, but then he *stopped* writing. I thought he might have met somebody else, but he never said, never told me that. None of you ever wrote to tell me either.'

'Not our business.'

'So why is it your business now?' She stared him down. 'I did write again, a number of times after sending the first two back. Just … ordinary letters, keeping up contact. I wanted to send something more, and I did write it, I even handed it to him, but it had got wet, and …' She looked at her brother, remembering Sam's face at the time. 'He just stopped after two letters,' Maggie ground out and then felt her chin pucker. *No, no, no.*

'Two? There's a stack of returned mail in his hut. I've seen it,' Ard insisted, incredulous. 'Must be over twenty letters, all marked *Return to Sender.* What is wrong with you?'

Stunned Maggie sat down by her father's bed. 'What?'

Ard flung his hand in the air, pointing. 'And who the hell do you think he's building that house over there for—his horse?'

'He never said he was building a house for us. He never even made out he was interested anymore.' *Well, except for the wondrous—*

'Such a joy it is to hear my two children gettin' along so well and back under the same roof again,' Eleanor said from across the room as she struggled up. 'Such a joy.'

Fifty-three

Maggie stood at the doorway to her parent's room when Sam said his goodbyes to them. When she stepped aside to let him go past, she said, 'You must know how grateful I am that you came and got me. I'm not sure I thanked you, Sam.'

He stopped then, and for a moment the old Sam was there with that twinkle in his eye. 'Oh, I think you did, Maggie.' He ducked his head a moment. 'I'll be off,' he said, the twinkle gone.

'Ard said you wrote many letters. He's seen them. All returned.'

He paused. 'Nothing for you to worry about any longer.'

'I'm scared, Sam, you know it,' she whispered hoarsely. 'I've said so.'

He seemed to be waiting, as if expecting more, but when she offered nothing else, he drew a breath and said, 'Well, I can't help you with that, Maggie.'

Struck dumb, she stood at the door of her parent's house and watched him walk away.

The afternoon sunlight was fading. They'd kicked dirt over the small campfire outside Sam's hut, no need for it anymore.

Sam snorted. 'I woulda built a house for me horse if I thought it'd make him happy.' He stuffed a drawstring cloth bag with a shirt, a pair of trousers and socks.

Ard clapped him on the back. 'Sorry, mate. My sister riles me sometimes. I've interfered.'

'No matter.' He looked around the hut. Nothing much more to pack. Still, he felt bad. 'I'm letting you down, Ard. I'd give it another shot, if I thought it'd work. It's killin' me. It's prob'ly best I just leave quick. See what happens.'

'She's hard work, my sister.'

'Seems I don't understand things. I'm not good with words.'

'Don't reckon she is either, though she's always got plenty to say. Bet there's many good words there.' Ard pointed at the bundle of letters in Sam's hand.

'Ah. I forgot to burn these.' Sam tossed them to Ard. 'Drop them on the fire when you next stoke it up, mate. I don't need to carry 'em.' He took a big breath. 'Maggie's back safe and sound, that's all that matters.'

'There's no need to go to the town wharf to pick up the *Lady M*—You know Mr Strike will come right by here tomorrow. Camp here one last night.'

'I need to go, let off a bit of steam.'

'I'll come with you.'

Sam shook his head. 'Better you don't.'

'Be a first.'

'You're needed here, you're a pa. 'Sides, I reckon you lost the taste for a big drink a while back.'

He looked out the door across to his—the manager's—house, knowing there was only a little left for Ard to do. Sam didn't feel bad about that. He lifted his chin in its direction.

'House will be right handsome when it's done,' he said and hoisted the bag across his shoulders. 'Time I was gone.'

He grabbed his hat and strode outside, lifting the bag over Pie's back, and strapped it on. He threw himself into the saddle. 'Reckon we'll see each other sometime soon. Have to help these boys get their new enterprise up and runnin'.'

Ard had his hand on Pie's bridle. 'Aye. And Maggie?'

Sam felt as if a heavy weight was sitting on his chest. 'She knows I'm goin'.'

'Have a drink on it, overnight. I always thought you'd make a fine brother-in-law. I mean it. You're bad enough on your own around here—Maggie on her own will be hell. If nothing else, for my sake, mate, think about it one more time.'

Sam laughed a little at the droll plea. 'One more time? I finally figured it out. She's heard it from me a thousand times already, so no more chasing. She's only got to say the word. She's only got to say the one thing that will make me stay. And she won't.' He pulled on the reins. 'I'll see you.'

Ard let go. 'See you, mate.'

Sam rode off without looking back.

Sam had been a speck down the track, riding out of her sight, when Maggie turned back inside. There was a finality to it, something she had never experienced before, not even when she was in Renmark, when she believed he'd finished with her and just hadn't bothered to say. Not even after they'd been together on the boat and he'd left her in such a state.

But this. This was final. Where were the tears? They wouldn't come; instead it felt as if they were behind a dam wall and couldn't get through. She pressed her fingers to her forehead, the pain in her head a tight band, and rested against the wall in the hallway. She knew that if the dam broke, and if she wailed like a two-year-old, her poor mother would come to her. That wouldn't do.

She had enough to worry about with Pa. Maggie wouldn't go to Linley either. She also had enough on her hands—a brand new baby, and a toddler with a mouthful of new teeth bursting forth, making life hell.

She checked that Eleanor was still sleeping, that Lorcan was as comfortable as they could make him. Satisfied, she slipped out of the house and headed for Sam's hut.

Was it wrong that she just wanted to stand inside the place where he had lived all the time she'd been away? *No.* She told herself no, of course she did. She didn't want to be wrong. That was the whole problem, wasn't it? Wanting her own way, making no room for anyone else being right as well.

Hesitating, she opened the door to Sam's hut. A thin mattress was still atop the slim cot. Rumpled bedclothes looked as if he'd only just climbed out of them. She sat on the bed and flattened her hand on what was a pillow, a small cushion, the cover of which she recognised as something her mother had stitched. Maggie snatched it up, breathed in the scent of him, the soap he'd maybe used last night, and then dropped it as if scorched. *Sam.* Now she felt guilty being in here.

The floor was still earthen. Not so unusual for huts, and he'd have checked for snakes each night before he went to bed. There was a little table in the room, and a cut-off piece of tree trunk serving as a chair. On the table was a nib pen and a pot of ink.

She spun around slowly. This had been where he'd lived for two years. There weren't any real trappings to it; the only other thing in sight was a stack of old fruit boxes that might have been where he kept his spare clothes or his shaving tools or some such things.

She turned, walked out, and stood for a moment. There was a well-used campfire just over there. A blackened billy was sitting in the ashes. Enamel-chipped pannikins lay in the dust nearby, and two other logs sat upright, cut for seating. He and Ard would've sat out here many times, she was sure.

The light was going. Knowing only a little time was left in the day, Maggie headed for the unfinished house. It would be similar in style to the other houses on the place—a front door, one or two rooms either side of the hallway, a back door. Perhaps a lean-to verandah until he could finish it with a proper one. The cookhouse, and outside of that, a laundry area where the copper boiler would sit.

Inside, the timber smelled new. In the first room there was a box of nails and a hammer. The window was still shuttered, so no glass panel yet. She walked out of that room into the other. Clearly he had meant this to be the parlour room. There was glass already in this room's window, and in a frame, with hinges and a latch. He would have spent good money on that. There were two chairs, sturdily built, and a table fashioned the same way. On it, he'd thrown a shirt, discarded perhaps when he'd knelt to place bricks into the fireplace he'd built in. Above it, a mantle—simple, functional and highly polished.

She ran her fingers over the glossy finish. She could feel it. This was a house meant for her.

'It's quite lovely, isn't it?'

Maggie spun. 'Linley.'

Her sister-in-law leaned in the doorway, her swaddled baby girl in her arms. Her freckled face, framed by her glorious auburn hair, looked tired.

'We watched him fell the trees, mill the timber, cut the lengths, turn the wood.' She jiggled the baby a little. 'We teased him about you. And then we sat with him when your letters kept being returned.'

'I didn't know he'd written so many.' Maggie heard the catch in her voice. 'I never received them to send them back. Not that I think I would have by then.'

Linley shook her head. 'Here. Hold your niece.' She put Amy into Maggie's arms before she could protest, and kissed her cheek. 'I'm so glad we didn't have to name her Mairead had you been dead in a ditch.' She smiled.

Maggie sobbed a laugh. 'Me, too.' She rocked the sleeping baby, bent her head to the exquisite scent of this newborn, and closed her eyes. Amy's little head was warm against her cheek. 'I've been fearful.'

'You?'

'She looks so well. Are you well? Not ailing? I haven't had a real chance to talk to you.'

Linley squeezed her arm. 'We are well, both of us. Fearful of what?'

'Of this. Terrified,' Maggie said and rocked Amy. 'Did you always want children?'

'I did.' Linley scooped a hank of loose hair back behind her ear. 'And there was a time when I thought I never would have. I was more frightened of that. Your brother was the only man for me and he seemed to be a bit tardy.'

Ard had worried that he had nothing to offer Linley, and so he'd gone to Renmark to work with his parents. Then he learned that Linley was fostering his son borne to Mary, a woman with whom he'd dallied, who'd died at the hands of the violent man she'd married.

'You still work with CeeCee and James?' Maggie asked of Linley's aunt and her husband. They'd married not long ago.

'I don't do as much now as I used to, but yes, I still find work and houses for women who've been in unhappy circumstances.'

'I could help.' Maggie looked down at the tiny face, and the mop of black hair very much a mark of the O'Rourkes.

'We'd be grateful, at least until this other family business gets underway. I imagine you'll be needed there.'

Maggie rocked the baby as she wandered the empty room. 'I thought I didn't want children. And now I can't work out whether I was only afraid and that just clouded everything.'

'Well, all the things that you know can go wrong when you're with child do cross your mind, that's certain. And I'd already seen enough of it working with CeeCee to make my nerves scream.' Linley crinkled her nose. 'And your brains seem to fly out the door at times too, over the nine months. But I survived. You would make a fine mother, so you needn't be afraid of that.'

'I never thought past what could go wrong having them.'

'You take it as it comes, Maggie.'

'And Sam was never ... He just seemed like an eternal boy.'

'They all are. Sam is good, and he loves you.'

Maggie needed more. 'But aren't you tied in one place, and dependent?'

'I don't feel tied and I'm not dependent,' Linley emphasised. 'I'm building a life with my husband, who is a good man, and he knows I need worthwhile interests that are mine, and not just within the confines of our family home. I was brought up like it.' She nodded at her daughter. 'This one is dependent for now, but I'll teach her to stand on her own two feet like I was taught. She's the fourth generation of strong women. My grandmother Nell—I hardly knew her—worked as a laundress on the Ballarat goldfields. My mother Eliza I don't remember at all. She was killed by her husband defending me when I was tiny. I wasn't much older than Amy is now. And my aunt who took me in ... CeeCee is the strongest person I know.' Linley reached for the baby who'd begun to wake. 'Now, time for her feed.'

Reluctantly, Maggie handed Amy over. 'I don't want to let her go,' she said. 'It's that beautiful scent, that new baby smell.'

Linley smiled. 'It's irresistible, isn't it? I remember how it made me feel when I first held Toby, even though he wasn't mine.' She turned to go. 'It's worth it, Maggie. All the happy, all the sad.' She looked around the bare room again. 'If it's only fear, don't let it win. Sam built this house with a lot of love in his hands and in his heart.'

Maggie cooked a simple dinner that night for her and her mother—fresh eggs, and some sausage that Ard had brought back from the butchers the day before. Ard and Linley would try to have an early night; the wakeful, unhappy Toby was keeping all hours, along with Amy. There was a pot of broth slowly bubbling for her pa.

Eleanor kept a hold of her daughter's hand whenever one was available. She insisted on hearing about all of Maggie's recent adventures, and whenever her free hand went to her heart, Maggie would stop relating the tale. But her mother wasn't afflicted with a heart problem. When the doctor had visited last, he'd said it was most likely just nerves, caused by being so anxious.

'And so what are we to do with ye? You've such fine ideas, looking for a grand position.' Eleanor leaned back in her chair as she released Maggie. 'But there's not so much work around, even for such an enterprising young woman like you.'

Maggie looked up. 'I've been going back and forth over everything, driving myself mad. I've been thinking of other things to do, around here. Georgina and Linley both seem to think the new business would be interesting. Maybe it would need a bookkeeper, a ledgers person. I could learn that. I know Linley is still helping her aunt in the women's refuge. I could help with that, too.'

'You would certainly be busy.'

'I would need to be paid something so I can look after myself.'

'The new business would look after all of us. I don't know there'd be a wage in it, not at first anyway, but ye'd want for nothing, and these times are hard. They're going to get harder.' Her mother's tone was soft. 'Maybe the sort of independence you're thinking of right now is not as important as your bein' fed and watered with a sure roof over your head, and in the safety of your own family. Look at it that way—start off on solid ground.'

Maggie knew she'd caused enough worry to her family these last few weeks, and that Eleanor was right—these were trying times. 'I'll always want to be independent, Ma.'

'I know.'

'But I'll stay, at least until the depression is over. I know it's best.'

'That would ease my poor heart, Maggie-girl. I'm still just astounded at what you went through,' Eleanor said. 'We were right to have Sam go look for you. He loves ye, you know. He always has.'

Maggie's chest swelled, and her resolve not to cry was threatened. 'I know.'

Eleanor sighed, and patted her daughter's hands. 'You think it's best to let him go again?' She tried to catch Maggie's eye.

Maggie pinned her lip between her teeth and her face scrunched, then everything rushed out. 'Too late. He's already gone. I never told him all the things I wanted to tell him. I started, I told him I was scared and he said he couldn't help me with that, and then he went.'

The smile Eleanor gave her nearly brought her to tears. 'Aye, he can't help with that. He needs you to tell him you're goin' to be brave. You love him, don't you?' She stroked Maggie's cheek. 'You trust him to stand by your side, no matter what?'

'Yes,' Maggie cried, and pressed her hands over her mother's hand, warm and soothing as it cupped her face. She held it close, rocked against it, closed her eyes as tears spilled. She would always remember Eleanor in that moment and the sudden rolling wave of love that enveloped her.

'It's never too late to tell him that, me darlin'.'

Ard appeared in the doorway. He held up a bundle of letters. Some were a little charred around the edges and wisps of smoke slipped into the air.

'Just so you don't die wondering about him, Maggie,' he said.

Fifty-four

Maggie was up well before dawn. She'd slept fitfully, kept jerking awake, then would doze, only to jerk awake again. Bucky, who was sleeping in her room until Ard could build a night-time pen for him, had nudged her worriedly each time she'd bolted upright.

When she finally got up, she felt like she'd been knocked on the head by a brick. She washed, put on one of her mother's old dresses, and brushed and tied her hair.

She reached for the stack of Sam's letters that Ard had brought to her. They'd been by her side through the night. Some of what she'd read had made her laugh—Sam having to pull Ard out of the newly dug, though empty, long-drop after he'd toppled in, or both of them having to look after Toby while they worked and had hung him from a tree using Lorc's braces. And some had made her cry—that he missed her, and didn't understand why she wouldn't reply to his letters.

She wondered why they'd never spoken to each other about hopes and dreams. She'd had her own ideas, Sam had assumed they were the same as his.

She hurried, even though she knew Mr Strike wouldn't be back before first light. Maggie would have to be there and wait for the boat to approach. Then she'd wave it down, make Captain Strike stop. She'd go on board and drag Sam off if she had to.

She hoped she *wouldn't* have to drag him. She wouldn't waste time thinking about that now. With the letters under her arm, she dashed into the cookhouse. No time to boil the kettle for tea. She just grabbed up a piece of yesterday's bread and jam and ate most of it as she stood there, sharing the last chunk with Bucky.

Then, as dawn's rays crept over the dark line of the retreating night, she marched onto the track, past Ard's house, past Sam's lean-to, and finally down the path that led past his new house. She took a deep breath. If she was nothing in her life, she was an optimist. If he refused her, she *would* think of something else.

The sun was a great golden orb now, and streaks of wispy cloud floated across it. Maggie stood on the landing, and while the dog wandered around, she turned, ready, and faced the direction the boat would appear.

The day was as still and calm as any autumn day could be. Not a ripple on the water, no flies buzzing. No sound of engines puffing, that she could hear anyway.

How long would Mr Strike be? Pacing back and forth, the dog pacing with her, the minutes plodded by. The sun rose higher. *Of course.* The air grew warmer. *Of course.* She hadn't brought a hat, but if Mr Strike was on time, she wouldn't be out in the sun for long. She shaded her eyes and looked upriver.

Nothing.

She looked at Bucky. He was only interested in a line of ants trailing from one side of the landing to the other. No indication he'd heard anything at all. He stamped a foot on the ants.

Her hands were damp. They were all but healed from the rope burn. She wiped one, then the other, switching the bundle of letters as she did so. All those letters, and she hadn't received any of them. It could only have been one person's handwriting that scrawled *Return to Sender* on each of them—that awful Angus Boyd. Maggie shuddered. She really must write to Mrs Chaffey to explain herself, to apologise, and properly inform her about what had happened. She'd write to Nara, too.

A noise. *What's that?* She looked at Bucky. The dog stared back at her then swung his head upriver towards Echuca, and his tail began to wag.

The boat was on its way. The *Lady Mitchell* appeared, serene and graceful, gliding over the water. So nervous, Maggie was having trouble keeping still.

As soon as she figured the man in the wheelhouse would be able see her, she started to wave. Waved madly when it looked like the boat wasn't going to stop, so she waved again, both hands this time. As it came closer, she could see two men at the wheel. Mr Strike and … not Sam.

Then closer still and she could hear the pistons working, the paddle wheels gently slapping on the water, but couldn't hear or see any signs of the boat slowing down. For the first time, she felt afraid that her plan might fail. The steamer was so close she could see the pipe in Mr Strike's mouth. He lifted one finger off the wheel at her and reached up to pull a lever. The boat's whistle blasted her ears and she covered them before the noise of it pierced her fragile eardrums. Her brains rattled. At the same time, Bucky let out the wildest barks she had ever heard, dancing round 'n round on the landing.

The boat wasn't going to stop. Maggie stared at it, stared hard at any individual on board that she could see, most of whom waved at her as they glided by. Dumbfounded, all she could think of was that Sam had kept himself out of sight. Even hidden his horse, for God's sake. *How ridiculous was that?*

Bucky was going mad behind her. She spun around. There, mounted on Pie and watching her with intense interest, was Sam Taylor.

He leaned over the saddle, reins loose in his hands. 'Morning, Maggie-mine. Waiting for freight or something?'

'Sam.' His name was a breath on her voice. Her eyes smarted with tears that still wouldn't come. Her throat had a lump in it.

He looked pointedly at the bundle of letters in her hand. 'I'll have a word with your brother when I see him.' Then he nodded in the direction of the steamer that left a frothy wake behind. 'You missed the boat.'

She held up the bundle and ignored his quip. 'I wanted you to see that, except for the two I did send back, it's not my handwriting on the envelopes. I didn't receive them to return them. And, I did send a few letters afterwards.'

Unflappable Sam shook his head. 'Never got 'em.'

'It must have been Angus Boyd at the post office tampered with our mail.'

'And why would he have done that?'

'Perhaps he thought you were a problem. To him. He'd asked me to walk out with him. I didn't want that.'

He tilted his head, considering that. 'All right.'

'*You* missed the boat,' she said into the silence. 'Ard said you'd gone to town.'

'Hmm.' He nodded. 'Changed my mind. I camped out, just over there,' he said pointing over his shoulder. 'Wanted some peace and quiet. No singing, no drinking.'

'Why are you here now, then?' she asked.

He lifted a shoulder as if his reason was nothing noteworthy. 'What are you doing here, on the landing?'

'I had to stop you leaving.' She waved the letters. She might as well, her hand was shaking anyway.

'You could have just thrown them back on the fire. I don't need them.' His hazel gaze was still on her as he leaned over the saddle.

She shook her head. 'I had to stop you leaving.'

'You said.'

She sniffed, held her head up high. 'I think I should marry you, after all.'

He waited a beat. Long enough for a bloom of heat to creep up her neck, along her jaw and over her cheeks. She felt it scorch her scalp.

'Hmm.' He tilted his head, considering again. 'All that drudgery and bein' enslaved to the laundry tubs and the fifty babies? I don't think so, Maggie O'Rourke.'

Still holding her head high, she said, 'We will make it so that we each have our own interests while we are married. And we'll … raise the family, the children who might come, together.'

'Will we?'

'Yes. That's fair, I think. And I will support you in what you want to do, and you will support me in what I want to do. Like Ard and Linley. Or like Dane and Georgina. Or our parents.'

'Hmm. That is fair.'

'Within reason,' she said.

But he still hadn't moved a muscle.

When he did, it was only to sit up straight and stretch. 'I'm not negotiating the finer details now. I just want to know that I've got a woman who wants to be with me. Me, Sam Taylor.' He tapped his chest. '*That's* why I'm here, to tell you one more time. One *last* time. I want a woman who wants to be with me,' he repeated. 'For who I am.'

She nodded. 'I'm her.'

'Are you?'

'I am.' She nodded again. 'I am that woman.'

He slid off Pie, let the reins dangle over the horse's neck. 'I sing when I'm drunk. I build things, and I'm a smithy, by my father's trade. I know my a-b-c, thanks to my ma making sure I went to school.' He took a breath. 'I want you. I want kids. Most of all,

I want you to be *you*, whatever that is. That's all there ever was for me. Nothing else.'

He was standing so close, Maggie had to look up a bit. 'You sing when you're sober, too.'

'When I'm happy.' He brushed loose hair out of her eyes. 'For a job, I want to breed horses.' He looked down at Bucky wedging between them. 'Maybe dogs, too. I want to finish building the house I started. For you, for us, Maggie. We can make our life something to look forward to each day. Not drudgery, not stifling.'

'I know we can do it.'

'I love you more than—' He held up her hand that held his letters. 'More than words could say in a million letters. And I have done for all of my life.'

'I know …' Her voice broke and she stopped.

'And when babies come?' he asked, still holding her hand.

'Everyone loves babies,' she burst.

He waited.

She swallowed. 'I'm scared about babies, Sam. But I don't want to be without you, I'm more scared of that. I love you, and I'll love them, too. Of course I will.'

He considered again. 'Well, we'll have to make getting babies far more interesting, then. Do a bit more of that wondrous business.'

She sobbed a laugh. Stepped into him.

Bucky ducked out of the way and ran off back down the track.

Sam wrapped his arms around her. She felt the heat of him, smelled the sweat of the day before. Then his whiskers were scratchy on her cheek, and his chin lightly slid down her throat.

She pressed his chest and leaned away. Gripping his arms, she held on. 'Don't let me go again, Sam Taylor.'

'I don't believe I ever will, Maggie O'Rourke.'

Acknowledgements

Thank you, dear readers—it's all about you! Big and hearty thanks to my beta reader, Susan Parslow for the red-pen edits. Grateful thanks to Heather Everingham, historian Renmark-Paringa, for answering email after email of mine, ensuring I had invaluable, correct information that gave me a lively picture of the Renmark township in the mid-1890s. Any mistakes within are mine. To the proud volunteers keeping the history alive at Olivewood, the Chaffey's nineteenth century home. To Barry and Maureen Wright, Burra, for their River Murray knowledge, their book *River Murray Charts* and their kind replies to my emails seeking information. Again, any mistakes are mine. Thanks also to Captain Toby Henson, Swan Hill, and to Ronald and Margaret Baker's book, *Murray River Pilot*. To Chris and Andrew 'Brownie' Brown of Ocean Grove—in June 2018 they visited Kangaroo Island alerting me to the Murray River Retriever, and to the Facebook group, I Own A Murray River Retriever. I hope I've done this wonderful breed of dog justice in my Bucky. The real Bucky's story c1931 can be found on my website www.darryfraser.com. As always, to Fiona for traipsing the countryside on research trips with me, and to Tony for holding their fort while we're away.

To the Harlequin Mira team at HarperCollins Australia, and to Jo Mackay, my publisher, my editors in-house Laurie Ormond and Chrysoula Aiello, and editors Dianne Blacklock and Libby Turner for once again making this journey back in time live and breathe. With the magic performed by Christine Armstrong, Maggie O'Rourke lives on the cover, and thanks to Sarana Behan, my brand manager. We couldn't do without our book retailers and our libraries. To my local booksellers, Big Quince Print, Kingscote Gift Shop, and Kingscote Newsagency—thank you. To the library staff and the community of Kangaroo Island. To friends who look after this authorly cave-dweller, and to family who've been on this journey with me the whole time. Lastly to the wonder dog, Hamish—life in the cave would be so different without him.

★ ★ ★

To Elder Uncle Barney Lindsey (with permission), Ngarrindjeri man, Gerard, South Australia, for his help on an earlier draft of the manuscript. To Tamara Hunyadi, Office of Deans: External Relations and Strategic Projects Portfolio - Chancellery and Council, University of South Australia for putting me in touch with Mr Lindsey.

Turn over for a sneak peek.

THE LAST
Truehart

by

DARRY FRASER

Available December 2020

One

1865
Alice and Leo

Deep inside beyond the heart is a place where truth can't be denied.

Alice knew it as she hunched over the heavy weight in her chest, her hand on her belly as if protecting the life within. Hollow, her breath short, she swivelled to stare left and then right along the busy wharf, over the top hats, the caps and the bonnets. There were many onlookers here at the Victorian port where the *Shenandoah* had been berthed for so many eventful weeks. Some were in finery, some in rags, some so wrapped up in their own affections—they all streamed by with their inane chatter and their ridiculous fawning over the dark and gleaming American ship. The awe was too much for Alice and certainly misplaced.

This afternoon she was to have been married to a man who had gleaming chestnut hair, a sunny smile and a twinkle in his eye, and yet now she stood alone watching and waiting. *No, no—he said he'd come back. He will come back. He will.*

But Alice knew the truth. That he wouldn't. That he'd gone.

At first, grappling reality, she slapped her hands over her ears to shut out the noise so she—sensible Alice Truehart—could gather her galloping thoughts. Not a sign of him. Not on the ship, not on the wharf, not in any of the row boats that pitched and swayed on the busy waves in the American clipper's wake.

Leo had gone.

The Confederates' CSS *Shenandoah* (which had no place in her home port, for goodness sake) glided out from its sturdy mooring into Hobson's Bay, sailing on greater Port Phillip Bay, past the rotting prison hulks and onto the heads, proud and majestic on her journey. A fierce huntress carrying her greedy hunters, she steamed away, sleek and sly, from the Victorian colony's bustling shores.

Something on the water in the ship's long wake caught Alice's eye. A bird? White, calm and bobbing on the low laps, enjoying the sunshine, it was odd, out of place. It sat on the gentle, sooty foam and the speckled froth of the ship's wake. But it wasn't a gull. It was a white cabbage tree hat, Leo's hat, its raven's feather still tucked tightly in place.

Her heart clenched, her body shook. He'd gone. He was on that ship.

She shouldn't have told him about the baby coming—she knew it, she'd seen something in his eyes—even so, how could he *do* it? How *could* he?

'I don't like it one bit, Leo Smith. Not one bit.' She'd shaken her head at her fiancé. It was not long after first light, and she'd stood back on the wharf and stared up. Moored at the Williamstown dock was an American ship of war. Astounding; *the effrontery of its Captain Waddell.* 'Why did we come here to visit again, and especially this early?' She squinted against the morning glare. 'These Yankees shouldn't even have their ships in our docks. We're a neutral colony.'

'Keep your voice down, Alice.' Leo had darted a look over his shoulder, as if checking to see if anyone heard her. 'They're not Yankees. They're Confederates on this ship, they're from the South.' He pulled his cabbage tree hat low over his forehead, tucking the raven's feather deeper into the band. He swiped at his dark curly hair as it spilled over his collar.

'Ahoy, mate,' someone had yelled in a terrible, flat accent. Laughter erupted. 'You got yeself a purty little golden-haired beauty. Looks mighty fine in her gown. We don't see that blue colour on our ladies' dresses much anymore.' Three sailors chuckled, leaned over the rail high above and doffed grey caps. 'Mornin', ma'am.'

'Huh,' Alice bridled but dropped her voice when she saw a couple more heads look over the side at her. 'They're called Belligerents, Leo. It means they're slavers. Going on board that thing is against the law in the colonies.' He was awestruck by the ship and nothing she said would change that. It made her nervous.

'What do you know?' Leo scoffed. 'The law didn't bother when thousands of folk came to gawk and gander inside her the other day. And I wanted another look without all the crowds.' His gaze roved over the hull. 'She's a wonder, a real beauty. Iron-rigged, beautiful teak planks. Seventeen knots under full sail, they say. What adventures would there be, eh?'

He always did have his head in the clouds, always off dreaming. She could never be sure it was *only* dreaming—now he seemed to be making something romantic out of this horrible ship.

It was hot; there'd been no breeze across the water—the great ship had blocked it. And if there had been, it would have carried the stench of sewage—from the ship as well as from land—and the briny, ripe odour of fish guts as the ship dropped its garbage.

Alice had frowned. 'She's sat here in all her snooty glory for nigh on three weeks being repaired. Everyone decent has got their innards in a knot over it yet you sound quite taken with this *boat* that acts as a privateer.' She'd noted with some satisfaction that Leo winced a little at her words. 'You *did* read that scathing article in *The Age* the day after she arrived?'

Leo's eyes lit up. 'I bet she's as fast as they say. I know she'll sail today.'

Alice had stopped in her tracks. 'How do you know that?'

'When we came to look, when she first arrived—'

'And you had to spend a shilling for that harbour trip out with a boatman.' So annoying. They were meant to be saving, not spending.

'Yes, yes, but after that, when we both went on board. You were with the other ladies, and I heard a few of the sailors say that men from here had enlisted already,'—if only there wasn't that gleam in his eyes—'but had to hide below, said it was on the quiet.' He looked up at the gun turrets, his gaze fervent.

'I know,' she'd whispered furiously. 'Because the governor wanted the police to arrest them. Enlisting locals is *against the law.*'

'The cap'n said it'd be an act of war if all them police and such went traipsing around on his ship. So, it didn't happen but the poor fella was ordered to leave the harbour, wasn't he?'

'Poor fella indeed. The captain's braggartly threat of war was called out,' she said, astounded at just how starstruck Leo had become.

'The Yankee consul fella didn't like it either that a Dixie ship was taking repairs here.' Leo went on, not seeming to have heard her. 'So we were gonna lose her anyway.'

Leo sounded so unhappy about it. Jiggling the tiny bag of coins that dangled from her wrist, she adjusted her bonnet and tidied wisps of hair back to her neat bun. The palms of her hands had been damp with perspiration.

The ship's timbers had creaked amiably, the vessel rocking gently in the water by the pier—no sly threat at all—why, just a benign presence in Victoria's calm waters. She was smug, reeked of self-importance as if in this colonial port she deemed herself of higher worth than her hosts. *Indeed, some of her officers undoubtedly thought they were above the rest of us. Silly Dilly Ashworth had got herself in a right fix with one of those so-called gentlemen.* Alice had squared her shoulders, uncomfortable at her swift judgement. She shouldn't cast aspersions on Silly Dilly. Alice found herself 'in a right fix' but after telling Leo, at least he agreed and they were to be married this afternoon. Elopement, it was, although they weren't running away. Both were well old enough to marry without consent, and neither had felt it necessary to post any banns. She'd patted her pocket feeling the blank marriage licence deep within, happy that she'd kept nudging Leo's acceptance of the nuptials.

Leo had shifted his stare and waved at a man high up, who leaned over the side and whistled appreciatively. 'Hey there, Leo.'

Startled by the familiarity, Alice rounded on her fiancé. He shrugged first and then grinned at her in that devilish way, making the deep twist in his left brow more pronounced. It was scarred thanks to a chunk of timber that had speared it after flying off his axe. Then he'd tapped his nose. 'And now, me darlin' *golden-haired beauty,*' he said, teasing her, 'with the doleful brown eyes a man can never forget, I'm just goin' on board for another look.'

I should have known then.

'Don't think yourself a Confederate pirate, Leo. No one's allowed—'

'Don't nag, Alice. I'll be right back. Then we'll go down to the registry, become mister and missus to give our comin' baby a good name, just like you decided.' He'd smacked a kiss on her cheek and more laughter had erupted from above. 'What a great day.'

Alice's belly had fluttered with nerves, as well as with the little heartbeat she knew was pulsing strongly within her. She grabbed hold of Leo's arm and squeezed it. 'Better not go. They could be hostile after all, despite our weak-kneed attempts to be gracious to them. They say the captain is a very strong-minded man. Don't—don't go, Leo.' She heard it in her voice, the pleading.

He pried her hand from his arm, impatient as he frowned, glancing this way and that. Was he worried someone would see?

'Yeah, but none of them government bods have taken him on yet,' he said, 'they're too busy keepin' their noses out of it. And look around. Half the older folk here prob'ly came out in chains on the convict ships. No love lost for England.'

'Oh, not that old whining again, Leo,' she said, exasperated. 'Your pa and ma did just fine on the goldfields after they were transported. I didn't hear them complaining too much after arriving here.'

'But we don't all love Queen and country. Bad enough her picture's lookin' at me all bleedin' day at the bank.' Then he waffled on, something about Dixie boys are more our types, and Cap'n Waddell was a champion for playing the governor right well. Alice had enough of this hero worship, it was all just noise she wanted to block out. Then he cleared his throat, his eyes furtive. 'Every man on the street knows it.'

'Leo, that's fanciful,' Alice chided, and tried to reason with him again. 'Did you miss that it's said Waddell is a pirate? That the newspapers say this ship's a man-o'-war. Look at those big guns over there. If someone really did upset him, he could blow a hole in Melbourne from here.'

'I *am* looking at those big guns.' He'd peered at the gun turret. 'I can't wait to get a closer look before they sail. Word has it that the cap'n is goin' to take her into the open sea and go to war on Union ships in the Pacific.' Leo angled upwards at sailors who were staring back at him. One man impatiently beckoned him on board. 'He's goin' to cripple their merchant whaling fleet.'

'You don't even know where the Pacific is, Leo,' she hissed. 'Besides with your two left feet, you'd fall down the ladder and drown in the bilge water before they set sail.' Not that she had any idea about bilge water.

He'd ignored her, muttering something about sailing the seas, and gazed along the length of the ship.

Alice had clutched both his arms, not caring who thought what of her. 'Don't you dare consider—'

'Just wishful thinking, my sensible Alice.' His damaged right hand clamped on hers and flicked it away. His two remaining fingers and thumb were painfully strong despite the hand missing its ring finger and little finger at the knuckles—the result of another clumsy accident with a rabbit trap when he was a child.

Then his next words had chilled her.

'But I'm goin' on board now to have another look. They'll be sailing by eight so it's now or never.' His bravado thinned for a moment. 'Don't wait, though. I'll come get you from your place.'

'No, Leo.'

He'd pulled away and moved through the early morning throng that hovered around where the gangway had already been withdrawn. Waving at someone high above, he lifted his hat to reveal his shiny, dark head of hair. Then he'd disappeared towards the bow and in the crowd. She lost sight of him.

I should have known then. I should have known.

As if to mock her, a groan from the ship had rolled around her ears. She stepped back, watching where she was going, then faced the ship and looked up once more, one hand on her hat, the other on her belly. She stared at the three massive masts, the sails furled tight on each one. The Confederate flag flew, its white background stark against the red square in one corner, and the huge blue X in the middle of it dotted with white stars.

'As if you'd know anything about sailing a ship such as this, Leo Smith.'

Despite Leo telling her to go home, Alice had waited for him. She'd waited and waited. Paced alongside the length of the ship—nearly eighty yards long, it was said—and back again. And waited some more. But when the sun rose higher overhead, and no one looking remotely like Leo Smith had been back on the dock, pushing his way through the crowd, deep inside she'd known. When she'd heard the chug of steam engines rumble and throb, heard the slap and flap of huge swathes of sailcloth unfurling and billowing up the masts, she'd known.

At the shouts of the men on board, and the thump of running feet on the deck, Alice stepped back further. She stared up, calling out, but her voice had been lost. She couldn't catch anyone's attention on board, and passers-by in the crowd jostled her, giving her strange looks. Tears had come and gone. Anger surged and died. She could not afford to be frantic. She'd tried to still the wild beating of her heart; she was sure she felt the scampering, worried little trill that followed it.

The tugboat and accompanying yachts bobbed in the bay as the *Shenandoah* had slid out of the canal on this warm and moody February morning. Straggling well-wishers still on the wharf waved at the sailors who yelled and laughed and hooted.

Now, the glossy raider finally slipped out of her sight, futility swamped her. Bewildered, numb, she stood rigid as shadows lengthened on the wharf.

He's really gone. She finally, utterly believed it. Resigned, unable to do anything about it, sensible Alice Truehart put her hand in her pocket, closed her fingers around the paper there. No more tears, she knew what she had to do.

It was time to put her *what-if-this-happens* plan into action.

It wasn't a difficult task and Alice had a fine penmanship. She was back in her room at her parents' modest home in Williamstown, sat at her writing table, her ink pot and nib pen ready.

Daughter of a local doctor, Henry Truehart and his wife, her mother Ellen, Alice had had a good education as far as it went. She could read and write well, and her father had often said that she'd learned to think for herself.

So it was with great care, a cool head and hand, and with precision that Alice wrote on the official certificate: *Feb 18th 1865, Williamstown, Leo Thomas Smith, bachelor, Williamstown* and *Alice Jane Truehart, spinster, Williamstown*. She took a steadying breath and continued. I, *Wm B Cooper* (she thought) being a *Wesleyan Minister* (she hoped) do hereby certify that I have this day at *Williamstown* celebrated the Marriage between *Leo Thomas Smith* and *Alice Jane Truehart* after Notice and Declaration duly made and published, as by law required (and with written consent of *The Guardians of the Bride*) dated this *Eighteenth* day of *February* 1865. Signature of Minister, Registrar-General, or other Officer *William B Cooper* (she couldn't really remember his name—they rarely went to church—and scribbled something barely legible). There was a small column preceding the first date and place but unsure if it needed anything written there, she left it blank. Checking the rest of the paper, she realised she didn't have to sign anything, nor did Leo. Satisfied, she thought it excellent work.

Damn you, Leo Smith. It was bad for a lady to use an expletive, but no one could hear her.

Damn me. *I should've known he couldn't keep his word. I should never have let him talk me into laying with him. Serve myself right.*

She sat back, careful not to let new traitor-tears drip off her chin and on to the paper. Straightening her shoulders, she sniffed, wiped a hand over her face and squinted at her handiwork. Once the ink dried, it would be a perfect foil if anyone dared question her marital status. Alice was reasonably sure no one she'd ever meet would even ask to see such a thing.

Taking a deep steadying breath, she rested her elbow on the little desk, and pressed a fist to her mouth. She stared at the small valise opened on her bed, and the pathetic trifling pile of folded smalls, day dresses and chemises in it. A pair of boots and a pair of house shoes were at the foot of the bed waiting to be packed into a drawstring bag and put on top of her clothes before she'd fasten the case closed. Her coat, hat and gloves were on the chair, ready. She'd been about to be married.

Her parents, attending a concert in Melbourne, had travelled early and wouldn't be back until tomorrow. The plan had been to leave them her already written note of her elopement. She'd hardly been able to contain her excitement—or the trepidation. She was twenty-two, well over twelve years old, the legal age for a girl to be married with her father's consent. Barbaric to be married at that age—she agreed with her mother. Marriageable age for a man was fourteen, but Leo at twenty-five was evidently still not mature enough for it. He'd needed to be mature enough for it; she'd missed her monthly courses twice now, and he had known it.

Damn you, Leo.

Both sets of parents had fully expected Alice and Leo to marry. But in her present condition and with Leo now nowhere in sight, she had to present herself as a married person. So she'd become an abandoned married woman.

All very well to fool a stranger, but she wouldn't be able to fool her parents right away. She bit her lip, decided to leave as planned and go to Geelong—where she and Leo were to spend their so-called honeymoon. Her family holidays were always there.

Before she was born, her parents had often visited Geelong, and they'd loved it, had made friends there over the years. They swore they'd move there where her father would open a practice, one day. The Truehearts were well respected in Williamstown—her father, born here, was a fine physician—but their hearts lay in Geelong.

Leo had said he couldn't afford a honeymoon on his own wage at the bank. Alice, about to be married, had given up her job in the local tearoom, so they'd have had to live on one wage. Alice knew Leo was uneasy about it but entertained the idea that he'd grow into his responsibility. She'd been almost sure he would. Well, she hoped he would. *Fool.*

She idly wondered if his parents knew he'd intended to 'travel' at some point, and not marry her after all. *Oh, surely not.* Alice didn't like his parents—his mother was mean, his father sly—but perhaps instead of being so hasty, she should go to visit them. Was Leo hiding from her and cowering at his parents' place? If so, she would confront him there.

She huffed. There would be no point in doing that. No, she wouldn't go squalling on their doorstep, crying foul, to then become the pity of the town. And if he wasn't there, if he truly had gone on that boat as she suspected he had, how could she tell his parents …? *Oh, damn* me *for being a coward.*

Then there were her few friends to confront. Oh heavens, they'd be scandalised. Or titillated and there'd be laughs all round. Perhaps they'd scorn her. She was never really sure what to expect with them.

No, she *had* to be 'married'.

'Oh, damn you, Leo Smith,' she muttered darkly. 'Damn you.'

Her stomach fluttered again and she swooped her arm over her belly. This little child coming—would he or she be in her image? Golden hair and brown eyes, a calm person, a reader of long books, a serious child, responsible. Perhaps a little taller than she was, but not if the child was a girl. A boy might become taller than she was, be more Leo's height, and take after him with his dark looks … *Damn you, Leo!*

She picked up the licence paper, waved it in the air to make sure it was fully dry. Then pressed it on the blotter—a double-check that it wouldn't smudge—and slipped it into the envelope she'd had ready. As she held it, she knew that it was now her most prized possession; that and the photograph they'd taken weeks ago. She tucked the licence into the suitcase, sliding it alongside the stiff card of the photo.

She propped the other envelope she'd prepared onto her pillow. Its contents she knew by heart. '*Dearest Mama and Pa, Leo and I married today and have gone away to live. I will write when we are settled. You are not to worry, you know that we are well grown up and can look after ourselves. I do promise I will write. Your loving daughter, Alice.*'

Standing still a moment she glared at the suitcase. What on earth did she think she'd do in Geelong, with child, alone? Without a husband or a family? She caught the swirling thoughts and concentrated.

This was not the way to do things now.

Her parents loved her and wanted the best for her. They'd understand. They'd understand how—and why—she'd wanted to protect herself. They were not like other parents who would cast aside their wayward daughters or lock them up in misery, forever untouchable. Not her Mama and Pa. But it did make her a little nervy again, having to tell them, to confess the truth—well, perhaps not all of it—but she would be brave and be almost honest. She'd *almost* been married after all.

She reached into the case and removed the envelope containing the licence then put it on top of her bureau. The accompanying daguerreotype she slid into a drawer, with the image down. She would face it another day.

Her heart thudded as she thought about the date she'd put on the licence—today's date, and wondered if she should change it, backdate it for the sake of her parents. But an attempt to alter it now would look fumbled, and wrong. *No.* She'd done the best she could do with that, and she hoped she'd never have to use it in the distant future. It would be the only lie she'd tell; that she was Mrs Leo Smith, albeit abandoned.

Taking the letter from her pillow she tore it into shreds and threw the remains into the fireplace. Then, from the valise, she lifted out the folded clothes and set them back into the drawers, and her dresses she hung in her small wardrobe.

Much better idea.

Alice checked her hair in the bureau's mirror. Still tidy, still gleaming dark golden in its demure bun despite the warm, insistent breeze that had followed her as she'd scurried home. She settled her hat, tied it under her chin. She jiggled the little bag—their eloping money—and slipped it once again onto her wrist, and took another deep breath. Giving her face one last swipe to dry any residual tears, she walked down the short hallway to the front door, left her home and headed for the police station.

There was a missing person to report. She was, after all, still sensible Alice Truehart.

Two

1898

Ellen's reedy voice whispered in the wind, '*You'd make your mother proud, Stella. She was a strong girl, like you.*' Stella Truehart-Smith stood at her mother's grave, the damp umbrella open by her side. Six years ago, Alice had been buried in the Geelong cemetery; she'd lost her short, fierce battle with cancer of the womb.

Glancing at the larger gravesite next to her mother's, the plot in which Grandmama Ellen and grandpa Doctor Henry Truehart (her Pa Henny), were both now interred, her chest was taut and her throat seemed to close a moment. Her most treasured people were here, side by side.

Reluctantly, with the barest nod to custom, Stella's gaze swept to the furthest corner where Lowry Hayward lay. (He couldn't besmirch any of them from there.) He'd been her husband for a short awful time after a whirlwind courtship and could stay in an unmarked grave forever; unmarked because of a lack of finances, she'd insisted. Truth was, now he was dead, she hadn't wanted to mark his grave at all. Ever.

She'd learned, from the constables during their many visits after he'd disappeared, that at some point in his short but vigorous thieving career in Geelong he'd upset the wrong man; it was said that he'd had a run-in with a dangerous 'push', a street gang. The leader of which, a violent thug named Rawlins, had wanted two men dead: Lowry, and a friend of his—whose name she'd forgotten if she ever knew it.

Lowry courted her so determinedly and swept her into marriage with great charm. They were heady, rushed days filled with a promise she thought had bypassed her. Even though she considered herself a smart, clear-thinking woman, she'd soon let down any guard she had and became dazed by his romantic onslaught. All she'd been worried about then was that he'd die from an appendix attack, the agony of which had plagued him from time to time.

Once the ring was on her finger, it hadn't taken long for his true colours to spew out. Abuse and painful blows had landed on her, strange women with painted faces reeking of cheap perfume would hammer on her door. Shock accompanied her horror that thugs were coming after him, calling at all hours with shouts and threats. And then somehow, he'd gone and got himself gruesomely murdered. Pity his reputation hadn't been killed off as well.

'I won't continue to bear his name one day longer,' she'd told her grandmother as they sat in the parlour. Ellen's good Meissen tea service was in use—a rare occurrence—to mark the solemnity of the occasion. 'Hayward just spells trouble. Even mention of it brings on the nightmares. I will hyphenate your name and my maiden name.' Stella took up her handkerchief and blew her nose. (It seemed even relief, not only grief, brought on tears.)

Ellen had liked the idea. 'Smith is such a common name, it seems that every second person is a Smith.' She'd winked. 'Now, Truehart is a name to be proud of. You always wanted to be a Truehart,' she'd then said with feeling. In the past she'd uttered it softly; Alice would've frowned darkly if ever she heard Ellen or Pa Henny say it.

Funny what you remember.

Stella had said, 'I'll be known as Mrs Truehart-Smith from now on.'

'You could be just Truehart now,' Ellen suggested. 'I can't see why not since your mother's gone. You can do what you want, forget about the gossipers.'

Stella had faltered. Smith had been her mother's married name. Her mother, Alice, and her parents had moved to Geelong from Williamstown before Stella was born, so Pa Henny could open another medical practice.

Better not drop 'Smith' altogether, after all; she'd been born to it, albeit *such a common name*. She'd declared that gossip would not deter her one—

'Mrs Hayward?'

Stella spun from her mother's gravestone, instantly wary. There was a man, but thankfully he didn't look like the tall person she thought she'd seen lurking near her house the other day. She calmed herself, blinked hard to clear the threatening tears, and shook the dripping umbrella before closing it. He stood straight. He'd taken his hat off, and his dark hair, barely damp after the recent downpour, featured a streak of white from the widow's peak at his forehead. The man's eyes were intense and alight with interest.

Her heart leapt. She hoped that in her surprise her eyes hadn't lit up nor that she'd inadvertently offered a smile. But there was something about him, something in that instant that charged her pulse—

How could that be? She didn't know him, had never met him. Sense flooded in, and with it came a fierce blush, the likes of which had cursed her all her life.

He'd addressed her by her married name—he knew her or thought he did. She hadn't used that name for some time. All the same, why would anyone be here at the cemetery on a day such as this, asking after her? The thought started a shake.

'Mrs Hayward,' he repeated. 'I'm sorry to have startled you.'

His candid stare unsettled her still. Taking a moment more to steady herself, she inclined her head at the stranger. 'It's not a name by which I call myself these days. Who might you be?' she clipped. A sliver of fear scuttled down her spine. Might he be one of Lowry's shady acquaintances come after some perceived gain from her? The police had warned of it.

He indicated the headstones. 'I don't wish to intrude if you're still paying your respects. I would make an appointment—'

'Conversations with my mother and my grandparents can be made at any time, Mr …?'

'I am Bendigo Barrett, ma'am.' He bowed slightly.

When he offered no more, she shook her umbrella, careful that no drops of rain splashed either of them. 'Bendigo?'

'Exactly named for the town in which I was born,' he pre-empted, clearly used to the query his name prompted. 'Such was the imagination of my parents. I'm only glad I wasn't born later, I might have been called Sandhurst.' He smiled a little.

Stella knew the town name changed to Sandhurst, and following a plebiscite recently had reverted to Bendigo. She smiled politely in return but wasn't yet prepared to share humour with the stranger. 'I haven't made your acquaintance before, have I? I would remember such a name.' *And your face.*

'No, Mrs Hayward—I beg your pardon. How do you prefer to be addressed?'

'I now call myself Mrs Truehart-Smith.'

He shook water from his hat and put it on his head. 'Ah. You have taken your family names,' he said and nodded towards the graves.

How did he know they were family names? She stared at him.

A light patter of rain began again. Mr Barrett stood to one side as she shook the umbrella. 'Perhaps we could move to the rotunda, it affords some cover from the weather,' he said.

'I see no reason to do any such thing.' *This is all disconcerting.* 'You've made no prior appointment with me, and I have no idea why you've sought me out at the cemetery, of all places. If you'll excuse me, I'll be on my way.' With a lift of the brolly, she stalked past him, clutching her skirt in one hand and dodging the puddles as she headed for her buggy.

'You have no driver?' he called after her.

'I have no need of a driver. I drive myself. And my horse is perfectly capable of taking instruction.' Did she just hear him stifle a laugh?

'So you'll not hear me out?' he called out again.

'If you know anyone in the district I might know, please have them introduce us. They might drop their card in my post box requesting afternoon tea at the Mack's Hotel on Corio.'

She heard him step along the path behind her, the gravel crunching under his boots as rain began to plop heavy drops and then fall in a rush from the dense clouds. At that, she turned, fully aware she hadn't been mannerly, and thinking that perhaps she should at least offer the shelter of her umbrella. Beckoning him, he caught up and ducked underneath with her, removing his hat to shake it. 'You have a buggy nearby?' she asked.

'No.'

As they neared her small two-seater, she said hesitantly, 'I could take you to your lodgings. This weather looks to be set in.'

'I appreciate the gesture but not necessary.'

He just stood there, drenched from earlier, and staring at her with a small smile as if he couldn't be happier being sodden. *Perhaps he's one of these poor afflicted people who just go about grinning at strangers all day long.* She placed her foot onto the buggy's step and hauled herself up. Settled in the seat, she thrust the umbrella at him. 'Do take this, then.'

He accepted it with a gracious nod, and opened it over his head. 'My thanks.'

Gathering up the reins and feeling strange, quite peculiar in fact—her heart pounding, her hands shaking—wanting to flee, she said loudly over the pelting rain, 'Good day, Mr Barrett.'

'Mrs Truehart-Smith, did your mother leave you any papers, any family business?' His hazel gaze was earnest now. Gone was the smile and a slight frown puckered an otherwise smooth forehead.

Stopped cold by the question, Stella glared. 'What sort of papers?'

He raised his voice over the downpour. 'Anything about your father?'

'I know nothing about my father,' she snapped. She thrust off the buggy's brake. Flustered, aware she hadn't answered his question, she said, 'Excuse me.' She cracked the reins and her horse startled forward.

He stepped back. 'I have information about him.'

Her horse was leading away. Impatient, she pulled him up. 'What information could you possibly have? This is most'—she waved skywards—'inconvenient.' The heavens had well and truly opened.

He dipped his head as heavy rain smacked the umbrella. 'It is inconvenient. But as you suggest, I'll have a card delivered to your post box and will await summons to Mack's Hotel.' Bendigo

Barrett doffed his hat. 'Good day.' Then he turned on his heels and squelched off in the opposite direction.

Well might he squelch, she decided and flicked the reins again. *Await summons.* The cheek. He was mocking her and it gave her pause. She frowned as she drove. Who of her friends would know such a man? And what information could a stranger possibly have about her father, a man about whom she knew little? He'd absconded to parts unknown, disappeared on the day he married her mother.

Stella never knew any more than that—as far as she was aware, Alice hadn't received a word from him in thirty-three years. He was most probably dead, anyway. She hardly thought any longer about what type of man he'd been. No point—he'd *absconded.* She could wonder all she liked, there'd be no answers. But Pa Henny had said that he'd liked 'the lad'. He said that Stella had Leo's looks—the same chestnut brown hair, the dark eyes and an olive complexion—due to some marauding Spaniard no doubt, Henny had winked—and a big, ready smile matching Leo's happy personality. When she was happy, Henny conceded. Stella had liked his description of Leo, but when she'd ask Henny for more information, he'd just shaken his head. 'We'll never know more, my little Truehart.'

You were my champion, Pa Henny. How I miss you. Stella's chest expanded as the memories came flooding in: his soothing voice close to her ear after she'd had a fall, or his solemn face as he listened to her relate a bad day at school or following a nasty comment in the street. 'Bear up now, Stella,' he'd whisper. 'You're our last Truehart.' She would stand taller under his encouragement, her bottom lip still thrust out, tears unshed. She'd loved hearing she was a Truehart but knew never to say anything about that in front of her mother. Alice had said over and over that she herself had married a Smith, and therefore her daughter Stella was a Smith.

I know whose name I'd rather have.

Grandmama Ellen would put a finger to her lips whenever Alice was in earshot of the conversation. What little more there was to learn about Stella's father had come from Ellen: a woman with a delight for the humour in life, and a sense of *que sera, sera.* Over the years, *what will be, will be* had been the old lady's answer to Stella's many questions.

Stella's mother Alice would simply scoff at the merest mention of the man who was her absent husband. She'd fob Stella off with a wave of her hand, her face grim and say, 'Not worth bothering about, dear child.'

The rain continued to pelt. Stella drove on, careful not to flick the reins incessantly. Inflicting her frustration on Clod, her horse, would not do—a buggy accident and an injured horse would mess things up completely—she had no extra funds to cope with a disaster. Not to mention the heartache that losing the faithful old horse would cause. Since Ellen had passed away two months ago, the house and the horse and cart had come to Stella but with only a little cash. Most of the family's hard-earned savings had all gone to Alice's medical care, such as it was, and what with the banks on a downturn, and Lowry, her husband—

Oh, for heaven's sake. I have an income, slight as it is. I have the house, and it's paid for. I just need to be careful.

Stella had often wondered if she should look for a cheaper house, in a cheaper area, sell up so she could realise some cash. As always, though, she came back to the fact that her friends lived here, and that as a widow now without extended family, she was on her own—more in need of friends than ever.

The other side of that, of course, was as a widow, she'd begun to feel as if her two married female friends were wary of her. Stella hadn't been invited to tea by either of the women lately. Despite herself, she gave a little laugh. Real friends would have known her better. Truly, their husbands were among the least attractive men she knew. Their habits, their condescension … she was unimpressed. Perhaps the women weren't friends, after all.

Constance and Isabella Leonard, sisters, however were definitely her good friends. She was at ease with them, trusted them, enjoyed their light-hearted, teasing banter. In their company she rarely needed to be reticent or mindful, she could be herself, unguarded and have some fun. They knew of her sleeplessness, and of the nightmares that had begun to plague her and ruin what little sleep she managed.

She'd met the sisters in their father's pawnbroking shop when she'd visited one day. They'd agreed, even as strangers, that a piece she'd chosen, a simple brooch for her grandmother was a wise and delightful choice. Over time, their beaming open smiles and happy hearts had chipped away her icy diffidence borne of Alice's reserve and latterly Lowry's ill-treatment. Their kindness was unconditional; they'd even offered to go to the morgue with Stella to be there for her when she identified her husband's body. She'd spared them that horror.

They were a little younger; had a spark of life about them, open warmth and were not dulled by the drudgery of housewifely duties and all its ties. They were modern women, like she was. Her mother at least had taught her to think for herself.

Stella's only lapse of judgment, in hindsight, anyway, was Lowry Hayward. And what a lapse that was. He'd taken her for a fool—and she had been, she'd admit it. She'd allowed him to sweet-talk his way past her prickly exterior and win her over. At first straight after they married, it seemed that life would be all right. He'd treated her well, in the marital bed too at that time (she shuddered now), never lifted his voice but then it all changed. Something to do with jewellery. They fought about it and he began to stay out of an evening, would tell her he took loose women one after the other, and she'd heard rumours of his stealing. She then had to suffer his profanities, 'you dull, cold bitch,' and worse, while he'd scream at her to hand over this *jewellery* she was supposed to have had. The worst of it was the beating. It was easy to keep quiet about it for there were never marks on her face. In any case, to whom would she complain? She was married, so just got on with things as best she could. Ellen had known, though. Ellen always knew; she appeared at Stella's house each time she was most needed, a pot of arnica cream emerging from her bag to help soothe the deep bruises. Other bruises couldn't be soothed; after she'd thought Lowry dead, the nightmares had begun. Why on earth would that be? It was as if something inside her had been damaged and was screaming for attention, trying to tell her something. But what? She never remembered what the horrors were once she'd woken, only that her heart pounded, and terror filled her. How could she fix what was broken if she didn't know what it was?

Clod faltered. Rain was coming down so hard it looked like an impenetrable grey wall immediately ahead. She directed the poor horse to the side of the road. Braking, and tucking herself to the back of the buggy under its cover, she wished that she hadn't—in a fit of unaccustomed generosity—given her umbrella to the enigmatic Mr Barrett. It might have protected her boots from getting wet.

Bendigo Barrett. He'd introduced himself in a well-modulated calm voice and with a smile. She'd been instantly entranced at the sight of that angled, shaded jaw, the dramatic white streak in his hair, and the candid dark-eyed gaze. His large hands, stained perhaps by ink or the earth, had gripped his sodden hat. Caution now slowed her gleefully idiotic racing pulse and she remembered what he'd said … *information about him*. Her father.

Silently bewailing her saturated skirt, she remembered that Ellen had a box of papers and such. She'd kept 'things' she believed to be of importance to the family. Stella knew that Grandmama Ellen had long ago put Alice's 'things' into that tin box. At the time of her mother's death, Stella had not been too curious, or keen, to fossick her way through any of it. She hadn't thought to look at the box again until Ellen had passed. Even then, Stella could still not face what else might have been in there. Three of her most valuable treasures—her mother and her two grandparents—would be represented in some way, and she couldn't bring herself to look. Too painful handling mementoes or letters. Or was she simply delaying the inevitable? The grief would be overwhelming. Time and again she wondered how to release it, and not have to endure the strangling weight of it locked inside. Time and again, she shied away from letting it go. She hadn't gone near the box.

Perhaps now it was time.

The rain eased, and with it the grey wall parted like flimsy curtains revealing the way ahead. First, home and stable Clod. Inside the house, secure the back door. Take the poker at the oven for a weapon and check each room. Inspect the windows for damage. Only then, convinced of her security could she be satisfied.

Then she'd change out of her wet clothes. Boil the kettle. She would seek out Grandmama Ellen's Box of Things. She'd face whatever was in there, step into the grief, and go forward.

talk about it

Let's talk about books.

Join the conversation:

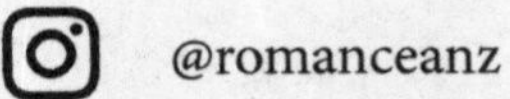

romance.com.au

If you love reading and want to know about our authors and titles, then let's talk about it.